A Duk
the Spy,
an Artist,
and a Lie

Books by Vanessa Riley

A Duke, the Lady, and a Baby

An Earl, the Girl, and a Toddler

A Duke, the Spy, an Artist, and a Lie

A Duke, the Spy, an Artist, and a Lie

Vanessa Riley

ZEBRA BOOKS
Kensington Publishing Corp.
www.kensingtonbooks.com

ZEBRA BOOKS are published by

Kensington Publishing Corp.
119 West 40th Street
New York, NY 10018

First Zebra Trade Printing: April 2022

ISBN: 978-1-4201-5227-2

ISBN: 978-1-4201-5228-9 (ebook)

10 9 8 7 6 5 4 3 2 1

Printed in the United States of America

For all those who do not fit normal,
you are seen.
Go paint the world in bright colors.

CHAPTER I

FELTON LANCE

October 18, 1814

Fade into the burnished walls of the quaint study. Give nothing away about the painting or its artist. Pretend your soul has not been quickened by seeing her brush strokes.

"The Ashbrooks have given it to me." The Duchess of Repington stood behind Felton in this front room of Finchely House, the residence of Lord and Lady Ashbrook. "Lord Gantry? Are you well?

Don't flinch, David Felton Lance.

Don't move. Live to see another day.

His body stiffened as blood pounded in his ears. If he stepped closer to the painting would the hypnotic power of the artist and her honeyed scent come through the oils and command his pulse?

His resolve to admit nothing, to shield his heart from the damning questions gnawing at his chest took control.

Yet he couldn't break his stare and face the duchess.

How could he pretend to not know the artist? If he closed his eyes, he'd see Cilia's small, gifted arms stretching, her talented hands whisking a brush about a canvas as her perfect hourglass figure tolled that time was up for them, for their marriage, for the dreams he'd begun to imagine before she abandoned him.

Her Grace tapped his shoulder. "Lord Gantry, you don't seem well at all. Should I get a doctor?"

"No." It was all he could say. He'd come to fetch the duchess in service to his friend, the Duke of Repington. To look at Her Grace would give away his hopes. The torture of wishing for a different but similar countenance to look back at him would be his undoing.

Her footfalls tapped in front of him, blocking his view of the painting, the tropical landscape of the mythical Port Royal.

"You're not well. Some men cannot handle being around a woman with child. Even a military man can become squeamish."

That wasn't it. He was a career military lieutenant with years of service in intelligence for the Department of War and the Colonies. He'd seen all manner of things and done the indescribable in service to the Crown. "No, a pregnant woman is beautiful."

The duchess's tawny brow arched. She thought him lying.

This woman didn't know the pain in his heart. Cold and calculating to some, bumbling and joyous to others, withdrawn and analytical to most—no one saw his true nature . . . well, one person did.

Then she left him.

Her Grace nudged him. "Lord Gantry?"

It was best to be silent than to volunteer information that would make him look more of a fool or say something that could shock a lady.

"I know something is wrong. Tell me now. The duke and I and even the Widow's Grace will help."

Her voice was soft, as though she knew she'd summoned Felton from a nightmare, one that had consumed him for the past ten months.

The panic, the sheer terror of his Cilia being missing, being alone somewhere in England, made his skin tight, the scars to his shoulders pained.

Balling his hands behind him, he walked to the painting and

took it off the wall. "Too many things on my mind. I think I've seen a copy of this somewhere. I . . . I should get you back to Sandlin Court."

Her Grace put a hand on his elbow. "I'm captivated by the beaches, too. The port city looks as if you can walk right into the canvas and be there. I'm mesmerized."

Mesmerized was a good way to describe what he felt.

"Sir, you do look pale, like you've seen a ghost."

"An Obeah spirit, Your Grace?" Definitely one of the past. "I haven't seen such detailed brush strokes in a long time. Look, ma'am, at the ice-blue waves curling to the land. The huts mingled with the wooden buildings with red and green shutters. It's the best of Jamaica. The legendary Port Royal with the dark clouds in the offing. That's destruction. The artist has a great imagination and a sense of irony."

She picked up the painting before he could stop her, but he grasped the edges. The duchess was in a delicate condition with her abdomen slightly beginning to show. She needed no strain.

"Yes. I see how the clouds change. It looks so true, like this was a window."

"Port Royal was joyous and then destroyed in a single day by a hurricane and an earthquake." Cecilia did have a wicked sense of humor, or was this her expression of them as a couple, happy and then ripped apart in a day? Guilt and memories and unrequited love dumped down his tightening throat. He coughed not to drown. "When did Lord Ashbrook say he purchased this?"

"I think recently. That's what Lady Ashbrook told me. It gives me hope that such talent is here in London."

Eyeing the proud woman of tawny complexion and small topaz eyes, he wondered who'd confess to recognizing the artist first.

The duchess retreated and took up her reticule and the cloth that her morning sickness might require if her jittery stomach didn't settle. "I'm ready to go, Lord Gantry."

Cradling the painting as if it were a child, like one of his daughters when they were babes, he led Her Grace to his carriage.

It was a silent drive to the duke's residence in Town. Neither he nor the duchess seemed to want full disclosure. Asking a pregnant woman about the artist's disappearance could lead to an upset in Her Grace's delicate condition that shouldn't be done. Like all the secrets he kept for the Department of War and the Colonies, he'd keep this one close while doing all he could to find his wife. It seemed Cecilia was alive and in London, painting again and perhaps ready to forgive and fight for their marriage.

CHAPTER 2

FELTON LANCE

October 20, 1811, Three Years Earlier

Felton liked all of his assignments in the West Indies—except the ones like this which could get him killed.

The heat of the day crept into the office he and his colleague had entered in the government building located in Stabroek, Demerara.

In the humid air, his long sleeves stuck to him as did his waistcoat and jacket. He needed to maintain the persona of an English gentleman coming to look at property in the colony, not that of a British operative.

Yeoman Johnson peeked through the cracked door. "We must hurry, Gantry. More people are gathering in the hall. I thought tonight's ball would keep them away."

"The information is not here." Felton eased the drawer shut. "And balls are dangerous things. Do you know how many matchmaking mamas are out there?"

"Not as dangerous as Dutch soldiers with guns. We need to leave." His friend laughed. It was quiet and merry. The transplant from Grenada loved life, justice, and his three-month-old son. "You might need to get in touch with one of those mamas, Gantry. You've been widowed now two years. You might want to think of being caught and staying home. Those two girls of yours would like that. I'm thinking of this too. We can't always be savin' the world."

The dark bronzed face lit with an internal glow when he smiled. He was wise and a good spy.

And he was right about Felton's girls.

Amelia, his precocious two-year-old, and Agatha, his pique-inducing three-year-old, would enjoy him not taking his long trips, but he was no good for them. His sister, Lady Jane, and his aunts, godsends, stepped in to help his now motherless girls.

A wife to soften him and help guide his young girls would be the best course of action.

Yet, that would play into his father's hands. The Marquess of Tramel would find him another wife and use her as a way to manipulate Felton. You'd think the man had enough time on his hands waiting for Felton's grandfather, the fourth duke of Tramel, to die.

His late Elizabeth was strong, but she fell privy to Tramel's influence and his purse, which controlled every decision, such as where Felton's family should live.

The loss of his practical, understanding wife changed everything, and he threw himself headlong into his work to assuage his guilt of leaving her alone too much during her last pregnancy.

"You've gone silent about a new wife. Gantry, did you fine something in that desk?" Johnson chuckled, a deep baritone laugh.

He shook his head. "Too many missions to remarry now. But if her face and fortune are fine, I could be tempted."

"Logical, Gantry. Always logical." Johnson leaned against the cracked door. "Perhaps when we're done, you might think of slipping into tonight's festivities. I hear Mr. Thomas is showing off his girls tonight at the subscription ball. It's the perfect place to hide until the streets clear."

"Save my boots, I'm dressed for it."

"You blend in. Nothing but white men coming to look for a

wealthy man's daughters, particularly his mixed ones. If you're not particular on the color of the money, you'll find quite a few tidy sums and lovely backsides."

His friend talked a lot of guff for a happily married man.

"The woman who'd turn my head, Johnson, has to be special. She'd need to be understanding and loyal. I don't intend to give up my work, which means long absences for the Crown. I don't want to fret about her bringing special new friends to my cold bed or her being neglectful of my daughters."

Searching another desk and coming up with nothing, Felton folded his arms. "The information was to be here. The informant who is helping the blockade runner sink our ships needs to be stopped. Good men are dying."

The perspiration that dampened his brow began to pool at his collar and run cold down Felton's heated back. Hot natured all his life, he should revel in a climate made for shedding clothes and rolling up sleeves, but Felton remained buttoned. Smallpox scars marring his arms were hard to keep secret in sweat-inducing environments.

Johnson returned to the door. "More people. Someone has told them that we'd strike tonight. We're in trouble."

Felton's neck prickled. He adjusted the ribbon pulling back his hair. "We can't stay and find out. We are too far for the Department of War and the Colonies to send help."

Holding his hand out, Johnson signaled one, two, three, four, five. That meant there were five additional men milling in the dimly lit hall close to the office they burglarized. They were compromised. They had to become invisible.

Felton closed his eyes and slowed his breath.

Calm.

Think.

Plan.

That was the mantra that had always saved his life. He just needed to get himself and Johnson out of the building and to stay hidden from the soldiers until they could get out of Demerara. "I should've brought Old Brown, the best blunderbuss pistol."

"Let's go out the window, Gantry. You have girls to go home to. I've got my family, my new son. We survive this one, I'm done."

"That will be what we discuss on the boat out of here." He looked out the window. "We're up a story. It's going to be a bit of a jump."

"Like the cliffs in Grenada, just without the water. Remember?"

That was crazy, but he and Johnson and their comrade Watson survived. "You first."

Cracking open the shutters, Felton saw two soldiers doing rounds chatting. Their words were bits of Dutch, maybe French. "I'm rusty on anything but guilders."

"Ya one to know Dutch money, my friend." Johnson's accent was thicker, as if he practiced how to blend in with the locals. He'd become invisible. Felton would stand out. It would be difficult to survive the night, but they'd always been lucky in the Caribbean.

"Johnson, the soldiers have cleared. Out the window. Hide in the brush. Get back to the docks in the morning. Since I stand out, I'll be a bumbling drunk and make enough noise for you to get away."

"A drunk is not invisible, my friend. Not your usual approach but a white man has less chance of getting shot." Johnson clasped hands with Felton.

His soulful dark eyes said all that the two men would never voice—the respect and unspoken thank-yous for saving someone's hide, stopping a bar fight, or stymying a bullet. "Good luck."

His friend climbed out the window; the athletic fellow dropped then rolled until he made it undetected into the bushes lining the road.

Before he could join Johnson, guards came around again. He

ducked down. His heart pounded, and he whipped his head from the office door to the window.

Times like this, with his chest gonging, he missed boring London and being a gentleman in the country. Johnson was right. How much longer could he do these missions with his girls needing him to stay alive?

They'd mourned too much.

He'd liked to think he'd stopped wars and disarmed attacks on the British vessels with the information he and his counterparts like Johnson purloined for the Department of War and the Colonies.

Maybe he had.

Maybe not.

Selfishly, the time away gave him the pleasure to be something different than a widower whose newborn son and wife died hours apart. He definitely escaped being a mild-mannered man with a demented father, rakish cousins, and an overly zealous sister.

How could he leave Amelia and Agatha, his beloved daughters, to that? Something needed to change.

If he lived, he'd talk with Lord Liverpool, secretary of the department. The man who recruited him from the battlefields had to be the one to let him quit.

No more noise outside the window.

No increased footfalls at the door.

His pulse slowed and he peeked again to the courtyard. The path was clear, but he stared at the leap which Johnson had made seem easy.

One foot out and then the other, he dangled from the sill for a moment then jumped for king and country.

His legs bowed.

A pain shot through him.

Since smallpox had left his limbs scarred and a little rubbery, he'd hoped they'd absorb the impact better.

Not so much.

He wriggled and hopped. Nearing his thirtieth year, he should still be nimble. Again, not so much.

He hobbled away and hoped no one noticed the window he'd left open.

Rounding the corner, he rammed into a raised gun.

Chapter 3

Felton—A Ticket to the Ball

Outside of the Demeraran government building, a soldier waved his flintlock under Felton's nose. "Halt, *wie gaat daar naartoe*?"

That was Dutch—angry, impertinent-sounding Dutch. White jacket and matching breeches with scarlet banding slung over his chest—the uniform the young man wore was very different from the one Felton donned when he was engaged in armed combat.

The soldier shoved him. The sharp smell of a cleaned barrel was lodged against Felton's nose.

"*Wie gaat daar naartoe?*"

Raising one hand slowly, Felton faked a stumble as if he were in his cups. Easy, with the pain radiating from his legs. "Oh. Sorry, old boy, I don't speak Dutch well."

"A Brit?" The soldier didn't lower the rifle. "I said, Halt, *wie gaat daar naartoe*? Halt, who goes there?"

With both arms lifted high, Felton pushed back from the gun. "Lord Gantry, the Viscount of Gantry. I'm a bit turned around."

"What are you doing behind this building?"

"He's looking for me." A sweet husky voice, a beautiful island voice, made both men turn to the vision coming closer.

Braided dark chestnut hair done up into a crown. Warm gold skin with topaz-chocolaty eyes, the young woman approached the soldier. Her blue and red floral tunic stretched with each step. "Yes, Officer, me."

Shaking his head, almost whistling, the soldier slammed the gun to his side. "Miss Cecilia. You know Mr. Thomas wouldn't want his daughter out meeting strangers."

"Georgy, I won't tell if you won't. You know I'm given to walking." The young woman's accent was light, but her silhouette was blessed with heavy curves. Very beautiful in the warm evening.

She came to Felton. "He's no stranger. He's my friend . . ."

"Lord Gantry."

"Yes, my Lord Gantry." Her slight Dutchy-island accent was intoxicating as were the green bits he now saw in her eyes. They surpassed topaz, more like polished agate stones.

"Why do these absentee Brits keep coming over here and scooping up the prettiest colored women?"

"Just lucky, I guess." Felton looped his arm with hers, leaning into her. "Miss Cecilia, I need a bit of help. I've lost my way looking for a girl like you. Would you do me the honor of escorting me to the ball?"

The lift of her brow made his palms more sweaty. He shouldn't have touched her, but he didn't seem to have another option, not with the gun being raised again.

The young lady went along with him this far, so Felton only needed a little more latitude to live. Well, that was what he'd begged with his eyes.

With her stare unchanged, he realized desperation wasn't one of her dialects.

"Sir, you don't remember your way or that we were to look at the stars before going to the ball?" Her voice was low, drawing him even closer.

"Yes, stars, Miss Cecilia. They are bright tonight." Felton feigned another stumble and towed her forward.

The more distance he could add between him and the soldier the better. Yet, if the fellow followed, it would give Johnson a better chance to escape. “Ma’am, you’re a godsend. I’ve become completely lost.”

Her smile returned, and she relaxed. “The subscription ball is in the building down the road, not the government building.”

“Yes. My head was in the clouds waiting for you. Lead the way, my dear.”

They started down the dirt road with big wood buildings and large homes dotting the side. It was an easy gait, like they’d done many walkabouts or promenades in each other’s company.

Straightening, slipping away from his buffoonish manner, Felton slowed and watched her wiggle in her beautiful tunic. “Tell me of these stars, beautiful one.”

“Sir, I see your stupor has cleared up. Miraculous.”

In addition to saving his hide, she was smart with a sense of humor.

“Lucky, miss.”

“You’re welcome,” she said in a whisper. “Well, I find walking very orienting when there’s too much noise. Balls can be disturbing if my concentration is bad.”

Very smart, to know how to restore one’s sense of calm. “Thank you, miss.” When he was sure they weren’t being pursued, Felton took a full breath. They were halfway to this ball. He’d try to gain entry wearing boots; Almack’s would never allow such.

“The soldiers enjoy giving everyone a hard time. It’s better not to poke around. Save your adventures for the daytime when their actions aren’t in the shadows. Where are you from?”

“England. It’s a very fun place.”

“That’s what I heard. My sister married and left for that island last year. She’s having so much fun, we haven’t heard from her.”

“That is a shame, ma’am, to lose touch.” He peeked over his shoulder. No one pursued, but he didn’t see Johnson. “I’m sorry. Were you truly out looking for stars?”

She stopped and pointed to the sky. “That is Cepheus. It looks like a house.”

Felton craned his neck. "I suppose it is. My imagination is not great."

"It's not with most men." She started moving again.

He watched her. She was graceful, with hips rolling as if she heard some hidden music. "Wait, miss." He caught up and took her arm again. "The infantryman didn't seem to give you a hard time."

"No, they give us *pretty colored girls* plenty of problems. But my father is one of the wealthiest men in the colony. That keeps me from having problems."

He remembered Johnson's words. "Miss Cecilia Thomas? You're the one I'm here to see."

"Yes, that's my name."

"How might I repay your kindness?"

She squinted at him with stars reflecting in her bewitching eyes. "I need an adventure that will help me escape the next few hours. When I step into that ballroom, Papa will show me off like a prized sow to every headhunter that came to town. What am I saying? You're probably one."

"I understand your lack of enthusiasm. I have aunts that try to matchmake for my sister back home."

"Then give me a fun evening. Pretend to be madly in love with me. Keep all potential suitors away. Let me have an hour or two where I'm unbothered."

Felton looked back toward the government building. More soldiers had gathered. Johnson. Did he get away?

"That doesn't sound too hard, Miss Thomas."

"You think? I can't walk the grounds and look at stars without needing to rescue a stranger. Short of a promise for adventure, a simple thank-you is sufficient."

Intelligent with an easy wit. Maybe going inside this ball wouldn't be so terrible. "Pretend, aye? Doesn't seem too hard to feign becoming enamored of one of the prettiest women I've seen."

Miss Cecilia touched his brow. "You're fevered. That happens to newcomers sometimes."

Taking her hand from his face, he put his lips to her palm, warm and smelling of honey. "Yes, very pretty."

"Thank you, I just wanted you to say it again."

He couldn't help grinning at her. "Doesn't a woman want the attention of a host of suitors? How else will she choose who to marry, unless marriage is not something you want? Sorry. I know it's impertinent, these questions. We just met."

She tugged at the formfitting skirt. "It's an honest question. My older sister, she fell in love with her husband at first sight. I paint too much, so I think my eyes have dimmed. Hasn't happened to me."

"A good sense of humor is a wonderful thing to attract love. It seems only a matter of time—"

The woman stopped and put her hands to her hips. "Oh, I don't want just any laughing fool. Nor do I wish my father to choose. He'll pick someone to better his business. I'm not the sort wanting to be sold off because I have a dowry."

Felton rubbed his hands together. "A man can use a dowry. You'll have no problems being able to choose from a crowd of men."

With a shake of her head, she started walking again.

He caught her hand. "Sorry, but I feel it's true."

"Who wants to marry because a man is broke?" She looked away like the answers to life were in the dusty road or in the halos of torchlight used to light the way. "What if they stop me from doing what I want? I have dreams too."

"You seem young, Miss Cecilia. Are you sure you know what it is that will make you happy?"

She slowed and looked again to the sky. It was magnificent, a cloudless night with so many stars out, blinking and shining. "The constellations are so clear. I'll have to remember and paint it—and you."

Looking over his shoulder, he saw more soldiers surrounding the government building. His stomach clenched but he kept his face even. They needed to get inside the ball. And Johnson better stay hidden; he had a family that needed him to live.

Miss Cecilia didn't seem to want to move. He needed to become more visible, more interesting than stars that wandered the skies and remained untouched.

"Dear lady," he said. "The lack of access to funds or unwillingness to accept the terms of the money can lead to shallow pockets. I for one think a healthy dowry can speed things along, especially a courtship full of promise. I suspect you don't like delays."

As one hand clasped her arm, she rubbed her shiny smooth elbows—not a mark or scar marring the perfection. "Waiting can be a terrible thing."

He tugged on the lapels of his dark jacket. "I'll be honest. I could use a wealthy wife. Money does come in handy."

She grinned. "You seem too honest for a man I found sneaking about."

"If it led to meeting you, then aimless searching has benefits. And if I'd known I'd meet you, I would have found you a flower, some lover's token for you to remember me by. Let us go to this ball and allow me to claim all your dances." He lifted his arm to her, and she took it.

"It does seem a short shrift, sir . . ."

"Lord Gantry, David Felton Lance, but you can call me—"

"Felton? I like that one, it's different."

Suddenly, that one of his names became his favorite. "I like how it sounds on your tongue."

Lacing his hands with hers, he lifted them close to his cheek and sniffed her palm again. His large nose was handy for something. "What is that honeyed smell?"

"Lilac. It's how I wish jacarandas smelled. Jacaranda bloom is the perfect purple, vibrant and lively."

As she pulled away, her gaze went up to the night sky. When she lowered her lashes, he wondered if she'd prayed or wished for something.

Felton forgot his mission, the happenstance with the soldiers. Nothing seemed more important than learning what she wanted. "What is it you desire most?"

She looked at him with surprise. "Not many ask. I think it has to be adventure. To see things that will nurture my art. And to be treated like a queen because of my talents, not my father's assets."

"You must have great talents for queenly attention." He stared at her pleasing figure. "And your assets look fine from here."

Her laughter was musical, caressing his ears.

Funny, bright, beautiful, Miss Cecilia had the makings of fine trouble or an adventure of a lifetime. "You will be a fine queen someday. Your king will be lucky."

The sound of a gun blast echoed.

His heart failed. Johnson! Yeoman Johnson—his friend didn't get away.

Felton closed his eyes. He'd have said a prayer, but soldiers were marching toward them.

At the steps of the banquet hall, she started to go inside, but he kept her hand. "Let's enter those doors and go beyond pretense, straight to an adventure."

"What, my lord?"

"I know this is terribly fast, and I've admitted to being intrigued by your dowry and assets, but I can take you across the sea for a fine adventure. The other side of the world can be great fun. Plenty to see and paint. Ma'am, you won't be disappointed."

"What's the cost for this adventure besides my nice dowry, et cetera? Speak fast. We're about to be interrupted by at least three soldiers."

"A kiss for the man who wants to marry you."

Her head veered from side to side. "Sure. Where is he?"

It was a spur-of-the-moment decision, but a new bride was an excellent reason to leave the service . . . and to live past tonight.

"Here."

Felton swung her around and swept Miss Cecilia into his arms. Squeezing her tight about her small waist, he kissed her. She went willingly, and they kept at it until the footsteps fell away.

Chapter 4

Cecilia Charity Lance

November 25, 1812, One Year Later

My love held an unlit torch in one hand and my father's knife in the other. The gleaming blade sparkled in the candlelight of the smallish room my husband's family had given me to use for my art.

"Cecilia, must I do this? It feels awkward." Felton's lovely voice was low and raspy from the cold he returned with from his last long trip.

"Shhhh," I said, and mirrored on my canvas the engraved gold of the knife handle and how it cast shifting reflections onto his blue-black eyes.

"The painting is taking shape, my lord. Don't mind my delay in getting this right. Waiting an additional two months for your return means that time matters not for us."

He looked down, taking his gorgeous eyes from me.

Dark and mysterious, those deep-set marvels made me wonder what he'd seen and what places he'd been this time.

Seems a wife should know these things after a year of marriage.

"Please, Lady Gantry. My arm is hurting."

I ignored his complaint and picked at the savory cheese he'd brought me. The blue veining looked as if it had been fouled but it tasted rich and intense. "What is this called, my lord?"

"You needn't be so formal, and it's Stilton cheese. I knew you would enjoy it with toasted bread."

It was good, and though I wanted to pluck a huge chunk and smack it to my lips, I refrained from the temptation. All the yeasty breads of Britain made my silhouette fluctuate from thick to thicker.

His eyes were on me again. I assumed that meant Felton liked thick.

"Discipline is what Lord Tramel would say." My father-in-law was a good mentor to me on these shores. He made the loneliness tolerable. I so missed his estate. Close to the sea, the woods of Warwick Manor were lively, with such flora and fauna. It always offered adventure. The studio the duke offered was a palace, not a lowly closet, nothing like this.

"Cecilia, may I at least lower one arm?"

"One, and for a few minutes." Holding in my chuckles, I returned my attention to my whimsical portrait. My serious compositions were hidden under cloths in piles about the room. They were for me when I was alone. I'd rather his family, the Lances and Gladstones, think me silly rather than judge my true art.

Since we'd moved to London and away from his father's estate, I let Felton's daughters see sometimes. Agatha and Amelia kept my secrets. They were good girls. They liked me, my voice, the things I offered from across the sea.

"Cecilia? Ouch. Find another punishment for me being away."

Felton did look pained and sad. "If you must take a rest, do so. Take the time to put on the toga. I'd love to see you do it."

"What?" He shook his head, then straightened his arms and lifted the torch and knife again.

Stubborn.

Fully dressed in a shirt and onyx waistcoat and not a button undone, he'd break one of his lanky arms merely to keep from being made to look ridiculous.

"Oh, put them down, Felton. And you don't have to slip into the garb of a Roman soldier tonight. I will accept your cheese sacrifice."

"Thank you. Something for the queen of our London abode." He lowered my theatric items. "Jane says you sleep in here most nights, not our bedchamber."

The small cot was comfortable, and I avoided their scrutiny of when I was or wasn't painting. "Lady Jane loves to keep track of my whereabouts." I cupped my chin and offered a thoughtful look, not something sour like I felt. "Is your sister's preoccupation a quest to hide from your aunt's matchmaking or to track the foreigner in her midst?"

His gaze darted from mine, circling about the room, the dull whitewashed walls, smallish window, the piles covered in linen sheets.

Then it returned to me, as though he'd made a turn about the ballroom and chose me as his partner. "Cilia," he said in a soft low voice, "you're exaggerating. What if we head to Bath for the week?"

"Is that a bribe? Can I count on this?" I pinched a small piece of cheese and settled it on my tongue. "You'll get one of those white notes and you'll be gone by morning. Your mistresses are too demanding."

His face became quite serious with his long nose flaring. "I'm faithful, Cecilia. Never doubt that, but my business interests require attention."

"Not much adventure in broken promises."

He shifted in his traveling boots and pumped his arm like that of a jaguarete on the prowl. The jaguarete, the largest predator in the world—well, my old world of Demerara—was a solitary beast on the prowl. Was that what I found on that road in Stabroek?

Felton snapped his fingers. "Cecilia, come back to me. I'm right here posing for you. We are good when we make the most of our time."

"That definitely sounds as if you will be leaving soon."

"Cilia. My Cilia." That purr, the way he said the endearment of my name sent a thrill over my skin. I did miss him and hated that some cheese and hearing his voice made me weak for him.

But he'd never know that.

He might give up trying to woo me.

With a flick, I uncorked my deep rouge pigment. "My lord, if you had chosen to wear the Roman toga, I'm sure I would believe your offer." I stirred the red tint into the paint on my palette and decided my canvas needed a sailor's morning sky. "Red sky in the morn . . . one should be warned. I believe that's how it goes."

"I missed your wit. Your little hums. Cecilia, may I come to you and embrace you? Then let's talk openly about our marriage."

My heart panicked.

What fault would he find? I smoothed the sleeves of my blush gown. "Complaints, my lord? I'd rather not hear those. You've only been back a few hours."

His head dipped. His shoulder-length locks, black and thick, hung free. Part of me wished he'd cut them shorter to sport a curl, but that would deprive me of the delightful image of a corsair pirate. In the mornings when he slept and a shadow had taken his chin . . . *sigh*, he was beautiful. Felton did inspire me in the mornings we awoke together.

"I should be used to our prescribed torture, Cilia. If I'm late, I'm to model for you as you paint. Then you'll talk to me."

Peering around my easel, I glared at him. "Am I wrong to be fearful of your delay? And you're more than a little tardy. Weeks overstay is more than a miscalculation."

Overstay. Overstay. Drat. I tried hard not to have my syllables hiss and expose how anxious I'd been. With no word from Felton or my baby sister, I was adrift in a house of strangers, ones who didn't want my presence at Felton's new London home, or in his life.

Half holding my breath, I made my tone as soft as possible. "Repeat your excuse this time. I want to see if it remains the same."

Felton raised his hand and hit his neck with the torch. He groaned. Hidden beneath his hair, the skin at the base of his head was so sensitive. It only had a little scarring. I think that was why he liked his hair hanging low and his collars high.

I was glad the torch wasn't lit as I had wanted. Would be a shame to burn such a pretty man, tall and thin. Pity he wasn't more reliable.

"If you want more specifics of my delay, it was in service to a friend, Cecilia. He needed me."

"Do any of these friends realize that you have obligations, a family . . . umm . . . children, a sister that needs you?"

"And what of you, Cecilia Lance? My Lady Gantry, are you telling me that you missed me too? *The husband on paper* is what you called me during our last tiff. *The skillful fortune hunter* was the nickname you gave me at Warwick. No doubt, words from my father's influence."

Lord Tramel had jokes . . . some were witty. I could see now how they could be seen as cruel or bitter with the bad blood between father and son.

Felton tapped the shaft of the knife on the bridge of his nose. "My particular favorites are your *marriage of convenience*, *partner in crime*, and your *occasional bedmate*. I must say, I do fancy the bedmate part the best."

Closing my eyes, I turned away.

Though each slight was true and mirrored our understanding of when we had schemed in that hot Demeraran ball, nothing captured how I felt now, how I longed for Felton when things were quiet and still. How his presence calmed me when things were noisy and I felt out of control.

A discernible ache fomented in my chest. How were we to grow closer if we were so often apart? "I'm shamed at my words, my lord. That's my frustration at our circumstances."

He tapped my knife along his smooth lips. "Frustrated, Cilia? You sounded quite certain of these truths."

"A thing said in anger, my lord, shouldn't be repeated."

"But you're angry now, Lady Gantry."

"How can I sustain such volatile emotions? I'm painting. You're posing. We're steady friends again. I'd say we remain a suitable match. Hapless and hopeless."

He tilted his head a little. A smile bloomed and I could imagine him with a bit more color like an emerald waistcoat with purple threading, purple like the jacarandas, the flowers we wed beneath. With his onyx waistcoat, he looked dressed to leave again.

"So, what's the next thing to take your attention? Are your preferred mistresses skin and bone, the likes of which Lady Jane thinks well of? She starves herself, you know. Barely finishes a plate."

He chuckled, that soft, silly look shadowing his eyes. "You know I like a snuggling waist and an armful of backside. I adore you as you are. You're one of the most beautiful women I've ever seen. More so when you smile."

The heat in his gaze said he'd moved past just acknowledging my presence. In his eyes, we were together, not fussing or fighting but swept away where no words were heard, just the banging of a headboard, the bating of his heavy moans, and a barrage of boom-boom hearts.

Say no, Cecilia Chari.

Make him leave.

Forget how you long for him.

Capturing my gaze, not letting go, he stepped around my makeshift table and kissed my forehead, then walked out the door.

Chapter 5

Cecilia—Painting for Pleasure

The silence of my studio disappeared.

Footfalls paced out my door.

Then a solemn knock. *Pound. Pound.*

It was probably a light rattle of the door, but sometimes I struggled with sounds. A walk would settle me, but not in cold London streets.

Knock. Knock.

"Lady Gantry, may I enter? It's been a week."

I liked that he never barged inside. Sometimes I locked the door to keep Lady Jane out, but not today.

"Answer, please. A yes or no."

"Why do you want to enter, my lord? I know how precious your time is."

"Cecilia, let me in. I want to make amends. I need to. I've been trying for days."

I set aside the brush and palette. "Have you not left already, my lord? No friend in danger?"

He knocked again. "It's been seven long, lonely days. You haven't come to dinner."

"What of breakfast? Did we not share eggs and toast?"

He tapped the door. "I meant a private meal in my chambers. Please, I've no plans to go anywhere, not anytime soon."

"The last time we shared a meal in your chambers, I didn't paint for three days. That is highly unproductive."

"But what a three days, Cilia. Please let me in." His voice sounded determined. Felton was always respectful, never making or forcing demands. He was perfect in that way, but he'd left me adrift, caught in my own stubbornness.

"I'll get the key. I must see you."

He wouldn't be deterred this evening.

"A moment." I put the landscape away in the closet where it would dry, and brought out the clownish image I'd worked on a few days ago when he posed. My Roman soldier in the woods of Stabroek—I set upon my easel and called to Felton.

With a silver tray in his hand, he came inside. "First, I'm sorry again. I'll do better. Two, you're right. I've been neglectful. Three, you're beautiful. Four, I offer chocolate sauce and blackberries."

The scent of sweetened darkness teased my nose. Hints of vanilla filled the air. Felton came near and dipped the fattest berry into the chocolate. It dripped heaven back into the bowl.

"Open wide, Cecilia."

When I did, he put the berry on my tongue. Tart and sweet, the roasted cocoa danced in my mouth.

"Aye, I think Lady Gantry likes." He fed me one after the other.

There had to be purply-black juice on my lips.

Setting down his tray, he took a napkin, patted my mouth, then he kissed off the rest of the chocolate. "There, clean and tasty."

Such a simple thing, a short touch of my lips to his, and my heart raced. Glances tangling, he had me in his arms.

His scent, the clean pines like the woods of Warwick, was what his hugs smelled of and reminded me of sheltering in his arms as we walked the grounds. I'd paint that image next week.

"I missed you so, Cecilia."

Weak, letting him nibble my neck, I began to waver. Had I forgotten, I was a strong woman. My mother's blood, her labors and sacrifice, were in me. I couldn't be reduced to wanton nothingness, to a place where his needs outweighed my own.

Pressing on his finely done-up brass buttons, I freed myself. "Felton, you just can't come here and expect—"

"Expect to be with my wife, my Cilia." His exaggerated whisper was soft, like the way he touched me.

"Only you call me this endearment. My sisters used Chari, a shortened form of my middle name."

"Like you prefer Felton, I prefer Cilia. Lovely, loving Cilia."

The way he repeated it, did he ache for me as I him? Did he wish we had more to bind us together than a contract, a dowry, and crazed impulses?

"My dearest wife—"

"Do you mean me? I'm your only living one, I think. Another household could be where you go when you leave for months."

He chuckled at my jealous words. "You're the only Lady Gantry I want." He took up my hands. "Let me confess a few things."

I held my breath.

He bit his lip and planted his bowlegs in front of me. "I travel often, too often. But I have a group of friends that I owe everything, from helping with my military commission to sorting out my affairs when my life fell apart after my first wife died. Then there's a deep commitment to support my brothers in arms and leaders of my old regiment."

"You sound indebted to many. No wonder you needed my dowry."

If he had been smiling, it would be gone now. His mouth remained a line. I could never tell if I touched his heart. "And I visited my late friend Johnson's family. I needed to see that his son's doing well. He would do that for me, if I had a son and hadn't come home."

His words tugged on my heartstrings. I'd made a joke when I

should've been listening. "That's why it's hard to despise you. Even your abandoning me is for a noble purpose."

He kissed my fingers, his lips lingering on the peaks and valleys of my knuckles. "Do you despise me, Cilia? Hope not."

Before I could protest such nonsense, he put his arms about me. Wide flat palms clung to my waist and pressed me to his chest.

Fire.

His body was always fevered. Through all his layers, the linen, the silk, and wool, he gave off an inferno of heat. My reserved husband was a lantern, a contained flame.

How I longed for the glass to shatter, and we could both be free to live and love. I thought I might love him. This was my first time ever believing in the emotion. I hated to feel it alone.

"If I say again that I'm sorry and that I missed you terribly, could that inspire forgiveness?" His whispers in my ear always made it hard to think. It was pretty impossible with Felton being near and strong and hot.

Spinning from his chest, I faced my canvas to keep his kisses from turning me to jiggly jelly, like the delightful molds he had his cook make for me.

It was a mistake to put my back to him.

Felton fast unbuttoned my smock, planting his lips to the scooped neckline of my rosy linen gown.

Always buttoned up with the thickest cravats or high shirt collars, he wasn't vulnerable to this feeling. The way he guarded his neck, I wasn't sure he had a point on his shoulder that sent him panting, or stirred visions of me and him in his bed.

My ragged heart wanted to surrender and forget every anxious moment he'd been away.

But this cycle would repeat—me feeling loved and accepted; me realizing I was too easily abandoned; me grousing between worries about him and my family back home. I needed off this boat, out of this storm of my making.

"Long ago, Felton, I craved adventure. Now I want nothing but lasting peace."

"I know this house is smaller than Warwick Manor, and London will make things seem chaotic. We'll make this a wonderful home. You and I."

He didn't understand. Not sure if he ever would. Not sure I wanted to keep trying.

Freeing myself from his embrace, I went to the table and studied my palette. The colors I'd used for my proper painting were out. None of the bright ones I used for the funny picture.

Felton wouldn't notice. Only Tramel, my father-in-law, a fellow lover of art would know.

"Cilia, I'm consistent and faithful, even when I'm called away. Is that wrong?"

"No. I'm as well, though your cousin Gladstone thinks differently. Probably Lady Jane too."

"Don't care what they think. Only what you do. Meet me halfway on this path to reconcile. Show me how to make amends. Open the door to you."

"We are good with doorways and entry." I put down my brush and faced him. "I've seen you gentle with your daughters, humored with your sister, very animated with your father, but with me always a mishmash: part cautious, part repentant, part neglectful."

His face was blank. I saw nothing to fight for other than this insane attraction to his arms, the way he kissed. Those nicely bowed legs.

Turning, I cleaned my bristles and focused on how to blend this dark palette and bring life to my Roman soldier.

"Cecilia, I'm cautious. You're an unexpected blessing. I wrestle with that and the plans I have. I want to be good to you and meet my obligations."

"What happened to the impulsive man who proposed in Demerara on a whim? Is it England? It took away my sister. Papa's solicitors say her husband is no longer answering questions. All my letters have been returned."

"I'll keep apologizing." He stuck his ring finger into the chocolate and smacked his lips. "Is it wrong when I return, hungering for my wife?"

"Ahhh. No. Bu-ut."

Licking his fingers, he slipped beside me. "You're shivering, Cecilia. The chill of London is hard to get used to. Should I have Watson bring more coal for your fireplace?"

It was cold in here.

Maybe too cold, but it was part of my efforts to not be a bother or source of amusement to his household. "I'm fine."

"I know you are, and that you're faithful. It's why I'm comforted and secure when helping my friends."

"Oh. Then it's my fault. Because you perceive me to be strong, I'm to be disregarded. I didn't know that."

"I'll do better with you and the girls. They tell me they love painting with you. Do you make them do Roman soldiers too?"

The laughter in his face was what I deserved. I hadn't shown him my true talent, just a few sketches during our wedding trip.

As confident as I thought I was in myself, my art, somehow his opinion had become too important. How could I look at a canvas and see my world, all the beauty and shades and colors, if he thought my efforts were merely cute, or worse, unbecoming his title?

The pressure of his fingers on the bib of my apron increased. He wanted me free of it. "What is this contraption? Part of the Roman garb so you'll match me?"

"It's a smock to keep paint from spoiling my gown. How are we to match when you refuse the toga? If you insist on staying, go to the other side of the table and finish posing."

Sighing, he moved there. His face held no frown but that assessing look—could he see into my soul? Could he separate what he liked from the parts he wished to overlook?

"What's the matter, Cilia? You usually forgive me by now, and we usually are quite nice to each other. This isn't you, so skittish. What's wrong?"

I pulled the letter from my pocket. "In addition to no word of my elder sister, the solicitors have no word from Papa either. I fear for my family. I feel helpless here."

"Cilia, you should've told me that right away. I could get—"

"For you to say you will do something, then forget. Why break my heart all over again?"

"Sorry." He tucked a hand to his lips. "My solicitor will make inquiries. I'll do it in the morning."

"Yours. Your family. Mine. What can anyone do? My father and Helena, they are my family. I can't lose them. I wish I'd insisted my little sister come with us and not wait. She's too young to be alone."

Felton stepped around my easel and drew me into his arms. "Everyone is well. I'll make arrangements for both your father and sister to come as soon as the blockade of the Caribbean is done. The war has made everything difficult."

Which war? The current one raging or the skirmishes about the islands which precede the next? "That could take forever. You know how long these battles last."

His warm palm caressed my cold cheek. "I want you to have faith. Then I want you to promise to tell me whatever's bothering you. Maybe we should think about us, you and me, as a family. Remember us, remember how we mesh."

"Mesh. Is that what you call it? To be waiting on you? To hope for a spare moment?"

"But we make the most of these moments."

"Is everything you're saying just to bed me?"

A smile bloomed. "Not just to be with you, but I do want you. Always have, since the moment we met."

"Do you know what it is I want?"

"Adventure. That's why we wed. It's why you want to forgive me. I'll continue to tread lightly until my wife gives me an invitation to her bed. Nothing but complete surrender will do."

"Felton?"

He beamed at me with his lips curling. "I mean that respectfully. My Lady Gantry is due all respect. And I've missed her, missed her terribly. I'm patient. Don't stay up too long. My bedchamber is always open for you." He left. The studio door shut, easy and slow, but I jittered like it had been slammed.

The man was too patient, and I was the opposite. Something needed to change.

Felton and I were either too finely matched or one of us had to buckle.

I hoped it wouldn't be me.

Chapter 6

Cecilia—Painting for Surrender

Two weeks of handpicked treats nightly fed to me by Felton had me waiting for him to show.

The foot rubs.

That was new and delightful. He tried that yesterday, and it was joyous. I hadn't painted a new landscape. The anticipation of his visit to my studio . . . my closet . . . had me too bound in knots for my art to be free.

The mockery of the Roman soldier was on display as if that was all I could do. I touched it up, adding flourishes here and there.

The vinegary smell of my oil paint filled the tiny space. If I opened the window, I'd freeze.

Looking at the door, hoping for a knock, I rubbed my neck. The tension and excitement of Felton coming wouldn't stop. Seeing him so attentive to his daughters, and to me, made me want to show him my true art.

If he saw it, perhaps he'd give me a bigger room like Tramel had done. I missed the father-in-law's visits. He came often when Felton was away. No one discussed art like him.

What if he was right about Felton never appreciating my talents?

Knock. Knock. The door rattled like cannon fire.

It gave my heart a start, then my lungs fluttered.

"May I come in, Lady Gantry?"

"Yes, my lord."

"My aunt Nelly and her Gladstone brood have left." His hands were to his back. His formal coat was gone, but his white shirt and onyx vest were buttoned up high. "You don't have to stay in here, Cecilia. You could join us. Jane's pianoforte playing is much improved."

"Has she caught someone's eye? The girls say your aunt has gathered candidates far and wide."

"Aunt Nelly has, but they must survive Tramel's interview. That usually doesn't go well."

"He's is a good judge of character. She should listen."

Felton's friendly face faded. It was only a moment, but the sourness of his feelings for his father showed. "He's a judge of something. But tonight is not about him. Tonight is about you—and this."

He lifted a silver bowl from behind his back that seemed to have frost on the side. Humming like he held a treasure, he whipped a spoon from his pocket. Then he approached crossing the magical boundary of my table. "Close your eyes."

"Felton."

"Please."

"I don't like it sometimes, what I see on my lids."

"Trust me, Cilia. And I'm right here. Not going anywhere."

Holding my breath, I did.

The disorientation started. The sound of the spoon hitting the side of the bowl was a dull gong. It vibrated through me. I clasped the table.

"Pineapple ice. Open wide."

I panted when the spoon went into my mouth. I opened my eyes quickly and re-established my balance, where I was. Then I concentrated on this thing in my mouth that was cold and fruity.

"Frozen like the rain you called snow, but this tastes good." I let the sweetness melt on my tongue.

"Cilia, I never noticed how your face glows when you try something new and like it."

My skin was flushed, but he had such a big smile on his face that I agreed. Why make him feel lesser? It was just one of those things, me and my sensitivity to temperature and noises.

"Want more?"

Eyes wide open, I nodded.

Grinning, he fed me spoon after spoon. The coldness on my tongue made it tickle, then slide down my throat.

His face changed. His cheeks reddened. It looked as if he had trouble swallowing.

"Perhaps you need some sweet ice."

He put down the bowl, bent his head and kissed me. It was light at first, then he slipped his tongue along my lips until I opened fully. The kiss went on forever.

His hands tugged the strings of my smock. It disappeared and his fingers caressed me, my curves, making my breath tumble out.

I slipped away when he fingered the buttons of my yellow gown. "My lord, you're fast tonight. We haven't bantered enough. The toga."

"You want more talk?" He clapped the spoon in the dish. "Want more?"

"More talk."

His face filled with a smile, the type that filled his entire face with strength and joy.

My fury always lessened when he looked at me like this, like I was precious to him, that he understood. What we'd found that evening in Stroebek was special.

"You, my dear, may never know the pleasure I receive by making you smile. All I want is you . . . happy, Cilia. I'll get better at saying it."

"You always say that. Then you go away. If not for Tramel, I'd be bored."

He squinted at me, the heat in his eyes lessened from flames to a stirring smolder. "My father comes to see you, here, when I'm away?"

"Yes. He knows that I miss the studio he lent me at Warwick Manor. It was very thoughtful of him to give his son's new bride a room to look out at his lands. A place with a high ceiling and many windows for the best light. He calls this a closet."

Felton's eyes glazed over, and his head turned left and right at the tiny one-window room his sister had given me for my particular use. "Yes, one needs a larger room for paintings of Roman soldiers. I've only seen the one and it's never finished."

"For art to be right, the correct amount of light is needed. But you don't like the light, do you, my lord?"

"Just enough to see you. That's all I'll ever need."

The scars on his legs and upper arms, the back of his neck bothered him. He hated me looking at them. Didn't he know he was beautiful, and the spots reminded me of a sleek jaguarete? Pity jaguaretes were solitary animals that only formed friendships when it was time to mate.

He fed me another spoonful. "Cilia, this is thoughtless. I'll get you something better than this. So many things are amiss here. But I could no longer live in my father's house. My investments—"

"The ones made right with my dowry."

"Yes." He bit his lip for a moment. "They're doing well. We can afford to be independent."

"Do you do everything to spite Tramel? Jane says that's why you married me. She thinks there's no better way to anger the old money ton than new Black money from the West Indies."

He rubbed a hand through his hair, feathering those deep black locks that covered his neck. "I wanted adventure just like you. Now I just want you."

After putting the bowl and spoon on my table, he wrapped his arms about my waist and pulled me off balance. "My sister forgets her place. She knows nothing of my heart. My lack of foresight has put seeds of war under that mobcap."

"A full rebellion, my lord."

A smile erupted. "Well, do I don the garb of a Roman senator this evening or am I Daniel in the lion's den? You do purr like a lion when you're content, Cilia."

"You say this and then nothing changes."

"Cilia, I *will* do better. Besides, it's obvious our marriage of convenience is becoming inconvenient for two headstrong individuals. One of us should consider surrender."

"That word doesn't sound very good for me."

"Then it is I who surrenders. I'm yours. I want us."

Felton kissed me, kissed me hard, then slow, then forever.

His hand whipped me up into his arms and he carried me away. In his bedchamber, in the slim light of a sole candle, I think we both surrendered. The sweet intangible fever he caused burned. Scorched by his skin, broken by want of his pleasure, I gave into missing him, needing him, and being grateful he was here.

CHAPTER 7

FELTON LANCE

May 20, 1813, One More Time

Felton slugged out of Whitehall and headed to the mews.

Angry couldn't quite describe his warring emotions. His letter to quit the Department of War and the Colonies was in his right breast pocket, the letter from his solicitors in his left, both too close to his conflicted heart.

Months of searching and waiting for news from Demerara and he'd received the worst.

How was he to tell Cecilia that her father was dead? That her sister Helena had to stay with an uncle, the blockades trapping her in Demerara. The Department of War and the Colonies would use none of their resources to rescue her if he quit. He'd be gentle and hold Cilia until her cries stop.

Then she'd sob again when he told her he had to go on another trip.

Lord Liverpool promised to make things happen to retrieve Helena if Felton took on one more mission. The man who'd recruited him from the battlefields wanted him to go after smugglers. The ones he'd chased until the ambush that killed Johnson.

It would mean leaving for months, just as his household had begun to feel like home.

Didn't he owe justice to Johnson and the man's little boy?

He visited little David last week. That brown smiling face glowed when he told him of his father's heroism. Felton had a host of stories, but nothing to offer when David asked if the bad guy was caught.

The answer was clear.

He had to do it. He'd track the clues. Then Liverpool would grant special permission for Felton to bring Helen back.

All sounded like a good plan, but he knew it would risk the happily married situation he'd enjoyed these past seven months.

One more mission.

One more chance to catch the bad guy who got away.

Taking a long breath, he puffed up his chest. How would he explain it to the girls, to Cecilia?

Tonight, they'd enjoy another private supper in his quarters.

A little sweet Madeira from a small island near Portugal would be a new experience for her. He could picture her, smiling, teasing him with her lashes half shut as he pressed a goblet to her lips.

Adventure had taken on a new meaning. The simplest things, like a pudding, made her eyes shine more like gold, so large and trusting.

This feeling he didn't think himself capable of having, that any Lance man was capable of experiencing, started to appear. He and his first wife had got along well, but his feelings for Cecilia were different, so much stronger. This marriage of convenience, which saved his life, might've become his life.

He rubbed at his skull. A logical, hardened spymaster couldn't be undone by the engaging young miss.

The contentment would pass.

All novelties did.

It was the reason he always craved missions.

On his way to the mews, he saw a familiar Berlin carriage, one with his family's crest.

His shoulders straightened as he bypassed his driver and simpler carriage, then popped inside his father's.

"Yes, Tramel," Felton said. "You needed to see me."

The old man with ash-and-silver hair had his hand clasped on his cane. "I thought you'd abandoned this foolishness. It's not befitting a marquess."

Felton opened his mouth to correct him but then realized that his father had just informed him of his grandfather's passing. "How? When?"

"Another grand tour, a Paris bordello, a month ago. Just received word."

His father liked to shock him but Grandfather was unusual, erratic, and carefree. "Suppose that means he left on his terms?"

"You come from an interesting line of men. Ones with long lives. Make the most of it. Hard to do that if you die for the War Department."

Tramel didn't look upset at the late duke's death. They were never close. They hated each other. Well, like father, like son. "Service to our country is worthwhile." Felton kept his voice even; the man sought weakness. "Since the Duke of Tramel has come to me, it couldn't be just to announce your elevation, your Grace."

"True. I want you and the family, dear Cecilia, to move back to Warwick. Especially if you're abandoning her to take on more missions."

"Lonely, Tramel? No one to torture?"

The man balled his fist, then set a shaking hand to his side.

Felton had to blink and focus on the metal of his father's ring to relax. His father already sported Grandfather's signet.

"Lady Gantry's not happy. You've given her a veritable closet to paint in. She had the best at Warwick and meadows to stretch her legs."

That was true, but she hadn't touched her paints much. Felton kept her preoccupied. She might be very well along the path to a new project, producing an heir.

She seemed to like the idea of a child bonding them together.

Still forcing his breaths to be even, not smiling ridiculously thinking of Cilia, he eased back against the onyx tufted seat. "Why are you so eager to please my wife?"

"Someone should. She has a gift very similar to your mother's. It should be nurtured."

Felton had heard his mother was a genius painter, very talented.

Cecilia's mad Roman soldier sketches were nice, but also ridiculous.

Tramel leaned forward. "Gantry, you don't think her talented?"

"My wife makes fine sketches, but you sound as if her work should be hung on the walls of a gallery or museum. She's—"

"Neglected and gifted, that's a bad mix. Why did you marry such a lovely creature if you intended to leave her for trollops?"

Trollops? "You're hardly one to discuss fidelity. And I've long since given up explaining my life to you."

His father laughed. "Doesn't sound like a denial. You're like me, like my father. A fool who doesn't know what he has until it's gone."

He threaded his hands tighter on the bronzed handle of his black cane. "Perhaps this is my fault. I never modeled marital love; you flounder with an angel."

"What do you know of love, Tramel? As I recall, Scotland's liberal laws and your coins eliminated difficulties or difficult women. I'm glad you're not Henry the Eighth."

"I know love, son. It's why I tortured myself when I lost your mother. You nearly destroyed yourself not recognizing your feelings for the late Lady Gantry until it was too late."

His father knew how to strike a mortal blow. Losing Elizabeth and never expressing his true feelings haunted Felton. She was more than a valued partner. Much more, and she died not knowing his heart.

"Oh, don't get sullen, boy. I'm here to protect the current

Lady Gantry . . . and you. Do you need assistance arranging an annulment or Scottish divorce?"

The man kept visiting Cecilia. They'd formed some sort of confidence. Felton would make it clear he deserved her trust. "I'm very happy and content with my wife. I've no need to stray."

Grimacing, Tramel nodded. He was searching for something or hoping for something. All his training kicked in.

Be calm.

Think through the options.

Plan each step to be executed.

Remaining unbothered would keep Tramel talking and lead to a confession. "You do want me happy, Papa? Happy with Cecilia."

His scowl deepened, merging with his chin. "Of course, Gantry. Of course."

"You've come down from the country, your idyllic estate. Should I set another seat for dinner?"

The old fool folded his arms across his perfectly tailored onyx jacket. The fellow might be in his early sixties, but he was strong and fit. A most interesting man of his generation. "Please don't use your tactics on me. They're tiresome."

"Then what reason brings you to find me and deliver such a warning? There has to be a reason, Tramel."

"Just a concerned father, looking after my heir and his happiness."

If Felton broke into a full laugh, the duke would quiet and Felton would fail. He didn't like failing, especially to his father. "There is something you aren't saying. I'll find out sooner or later. You know what I do for the Department of War and the Colonies?"

"You may not believe me, and the years between us have not been good. I hate that it's that way. Though he died on his own terms, I regret the last time my father and I spoke it was an argument."

Felton rolled his palm like an orchestra conductor. "And . . ."

"I want . . . to take care of your household. You've gone and made one in London. Keep it."

"You know where Liverpool is sending me, don't you?"

Tramel smoothed the handle of his cane. "Grenada. Maybe Demerara too. I have friends who talk. That's how I know you were almost killed when you met the enchanting Cecilia."

"Can your connections in governments and shadowy places tell me who killed Johnson? He was the best man. And a good father."

This time Tramel laughed, bold and haughty. "When you left the military, I thought you ran scared. The family peacemaker couldn't handle the gunfire, but—"

"Peacemaker? Not by choice. Your wives two and three needed someone to maintain the tranquility of Warwick."

The man glared at him. "I was going to say you made me proud risking life and freckled limbs for crown and country."

He popped on his hat and readied to get out, when Tramel raised his cane and blocked the door. "You lived back then, surviving smallpox, but now you seem to be searching for a bullet with your name, David Felton Lance. My namesake should be smarter." He eased his cane to the floor. "I like that you've been wily enough to stay alive, but luck can run out. Gladstone's brat son, Jeremiah, becomes my heir if you die. You've just sired girls."

"Well, they love their grandfather too." Felton sat back but stayed close to the door. "Are we done?"

"No. I hope you're smart enough to know when you should engage and when you should leave island smugglers alone."

Ahh, the shadowy places. Tramel's network had sent him a message. He reached over and jerked the man by his lapels. "Someone alerted the Demeraran council of my last operation there and killed my friend. Tramel, if you're in league with traitors, so help me—"

"No, Gantry. I'm not in league with people who'd kill good men, just bad ones."

Felton opened his mouth, then closed it. There was nothing helpful in deciphering what Tramel meant. And he didn't want to try.

"Son, I don't want you killed."

He let go of the man's jacket and plopped back down on the seat. "The smugglers I'm after not only set up an ambush, they sank the *Henry* as it left Demerara. Too many good men died."

"Don't add to the death count. You've responsibilities to your daughters, to Cecilia, and me. Don't forget that."

"Are you involved in this? Is there no depth to which you won't sink?"

"You've been warned. You've been smart. A lot smarter than I gave you credit for, but you have more to lose. I'll protect you as much as I can, but even I have limits."

The man knew more, but he'd not say. He'd dangle unsettling things in front of Felton to twist him up. No more. He slid to the door and pried it open. "You taught me how to survive alone."

"Sometimes you have to think of *we*. It's not just you anymore."

For a second, it sounded like something Cecilia said, but this was more Tramel's machinations. "Have a pleasant day, Father." He stormed out and waited for the new duke to leave.

Then Felton stalked to his carriage and his man, Watson.

"Sir, ya don't look happy." The steady man from Grenada had been a faithful advocate these past years, since he had provided Felton's team ground intelligence on the island. "Ya father give you a talkin' to?"

"Congratulate me. I'm a marquess. My father is finally the Duke of Tramel."

"Fancy. But are we still employed, my lord?"

Nodding, Felton tugged on his gray jacket. The letters in his pockets made crinkling noises. He still had two battles to engage at Mayfair. Three if you count his new elevation. "They say death comes in threes, Watson. I'm not feeling lucky right now."

His driver shrugged. "But another trip?"

Telling Cecilia about her father, then his girls that he had to go on another trip, would be hard but he had to do this for Johnson. "Yes."

"Oh boy." Watson laughed. "Just one more assignment. That's how Liverpool be getting to ya. Lady Gantry and Lady Jane will be so unhappy."

"Lady Jane and Aunt Nelly will keep things going in Town."

"And the wife, Lady Gantry?"

"I'll quit for good once I catch the informant. Who knows, maybe I can bring down the whole smuggling ring."

Watson had that look about him, almost the same as the one Cecilia offered that made Felton think he'd buttoned his buttons wrong.

"I asked about the wife, my lord."

"Lady Gantry is a strong capable woman." She'll hate Felton and he'll have to win her anew. The risk in that sounded fun, adventurous.

"Well, your special weapons will be oiled and ready. Never truly put them away, sir. Had a feelin' ya weren't done."

Felton climbed into his carriage, comforting himself that it wouldn't be a long time away.

His man stuck his head inside. "Between Tramel's visits and that of your cousin Gladstone, the London house will still be lively."

The door slammed and Felton sat back with an odd feeling in his gut. Though he welcomed his aunt's family entertaining his household, he didn't like Jeremiah Gladstone or Tramel intruding. Jane wasn't fond of their cousin either. He bragged too much about managing his father's investments in Demerara, and he stared at Cecilia too much.

Cecilia detested him.

His man would have to keep an eye on things.

One last mission would set things right for Johnson. He'd leave the service with all his missions complete. And if Felton returned feeling the same way he did about Cecilia as in his heart now, he'd admit he was in love, and hope her missing him would mean she might love him too.

CECILIA—MAKING UP IS HARD TO DO

December 3, 1813

The knocking outside my studio door made my head ache. I was more sensitive to noise now. Everything was loud. My vision swirled.

I blocked my ears, but the pounding continued.

"Cecilia, may I come in?"

"I'm busy." The painting of this landscape, Demerara's coast, was nearly complete. I just had to finish the waves of water flowing to the docks. It needed greenish-brown waves topped with white foam.

"Cecilia?" More banging. It was a gong, the way the noise rattled. "Please."

I knew that wasn't how the noises truly sounded, but my mind sometimes had problems separating true from imagined.

"Let me in, Cilia. Please." Felton asked again.

The begging was real and loud.

Just because he was back after so many months away didn't mean my bed was open to him. It didn't mean anything at all.

"I've been home a fortnight. You haven't spent a moment with me."

Didn't sound like he would stop. I took my canvas and stashed it in the closet like normal to dry. In its place I put the silly imagery I'd started with Felton as a Roman soldier. This time it had his face.

Half closing my eyes, I filled my chest with air. "You know my terms."

Silence, but no boots knocked away. I went to my easel and awaited Felton's next move.

The door jiggled. Watson stood there with his ambivalent stone-faced smile. He tucked the housekeeper's key into his pocket. "It was actually open, sir."

Then the man-of-all-work bowed to me and left.

My husband came fully inside and shut the door. A brilliant white shirt covered his chest, the sleeves rolled up only half his forearm. He was very tanned. Wherever he'd gone this time had given him plenty of sun.

Without a word, he wrenched off his boots and stockings, then stood before me in chocolate breeches and naked feet.

The pockmarks on his feet weren't so bad. Just more spots for my jaguarete.

"I've come to surrender."

"You can earn the right to speak to me if and only if you're in a toga. It's on the chair next to your wriggling toes."

The linen sheet I'd prepared, with an ivory satin ribbon stitched along the edges, was folded the same way he did his shirts, along the seams. "I had plenty of time to make it special, with you gone for seven months."

"Wait." He went back to the hall and returned with a tray of Stilton cheese, unleavened bread, and something that looked like jam.

Those blue-black eyes shimmered. He looked healthy and strong. I'd gained weight, nervous weight.

"This orangey heaven are quinces cooked down with honey. We call it marmalade. It's a sweet to go with your favorite cheese."

It did look good, and I'd skipped dinner, caught up in my latest landscape.

When he waved, the tray made my mouth water. Spittle settled on the corners of my lips. "You think I'm easy. A little food—"

He brought it near again. The salty stench of the cheese, the sweetness of the quince jam made me very hungry.

Felton set the tray on my supply table and lifted a tiny spoon of the marmalade, and a bit of cheese, on a pinch of the cracker-like bread. Then he set it to my lips. "Taste."

If I did so, he'd think I was his, set to forgive him, but how could I deny a treasure?

"This is for you and you alone. You must know you were on my mind constantly."

Wasn't sure if I heard or comprehended what he said, not with a treat dangling so close and Felton looking as if he'd gobble me up like a delicious dinner.

I took the spoon from him. "You've come to pose so I can finish my Roman soldier?"

With a nod, he skipped the sheet pile and picked up the torch and knife from the table.

As he settled into our standard centurion pose, I gobbled the contents on the spoon. Heaven, just like it smelled. The tartness and salt and honey—I might as well surrender, tell him he was forgiven and let him hand-feed me. Now I knew how Esau felt, selling his birthright for lentils.

But marmalade was better than beans.

"My dear, let's begin my penance."

"Penance? Does the Anglican religion permit such, or have you become Catholic—or turned to my hedonism, as Jane would say?"

He banged his cheek with the torch, then rubbed his face. "I'm not happy with my sister. I'll speak to her."

I leaned over the table and lit his small torch, my improvised candle and candleholder. Swoosh. It ignited, casting smoke and a bright orange glow about the room. "Use your own time to mention her. While you're here in my studio, you can be silent."

"While I was away, I pushed some people I know to find information on Helena. They have found nothing. I'm sorry."

Helena missing. All my family gone. What I thought I'd found with Felton disappeared too. He left a few weeks after telling me of the loss of my father.

Suppose he thought he'd done enough comforting.

"Cecilia, please look at me."

His face was either a puppy dog's countenance of repentance or a jaguarete waiting to strike—I couldn't tell his thoughts anymore.

Maybe I never could.

"Please, Cilia."

"I will allow some level of conversation whilst you pose with hands up and a foot up."

"A foot?"

"Yes, my lord. You can choose the right or the left."

With a shrug, he lifted his right foot.

While he balanced, I fixed another combination of the cheese and marmalade on bread. "This is very tasty. You get these when you leave, or on your return?"

He lowered a hand close to his neck and almost set his hair on fire. "I'm sorry. You weren't talking with me yesterday, so I went to visit the Duke of Repington. He is my dearest friend."

"This man you only mentioned today is your dearest friend. Interesting. And of course I wouldn't meet a dearest friend." After wiping my fingers free of crumbs, I dipped my brush into the brown paint I'd mixed for the Demerara sea. "The red sky does not hold enough dread. I think this Roman soldier should wish himself dead if there was a jaguarete in the distance. Yes, this large cat will pick his flesh clear to the bone."

With torch secure in his palm, Felton clapped about it. "Ahh. Your poetry now has a homicidal bent. I take it you missed me a great deal and the loneliness has driven you mad."

I snorted a giggle. "Jane frightens more easily."

A tentative smile spread on my foolish husband's face. "But I'm not Jane. I know you to be a gentle flower." He sighed, making his shirt buttons flutter as he wobbled. "Except in your art, I truly do not wish to meet the fate of your lone soldier."

After offering him a shrug, I continued imagining the jaguarete. "Perhaps a chase scene by disappointed villagers would be more appropriate. More people for you to help."

"Cecilia, my friend was in need. He's been injured in the war."

The jaguarete was not close enough to the Roman guard. I stippled in the hint of a second one in the jade grasses for good measure. One of them would do the deed. "Which war, Felton? The one started in 1812 that prevented my youngest sister from joining us but has allowed your cousin Gladstone to return to and from Demerara several times? Or this thing in the Peninsula that has everyone so bothered."

"The Peninsular War. The Duke of Repington was hurt in the Battle of Badajoz. He was very kind to me when my first wife died. I'm greatly indebted to him."

Part of me wanted to be snide and ask if it was boredom or neglect that took the first Lady Gantry, but their love according to Jane was deep and abiding. Her death weighed heavily, nearly destroying him.

A horrible loss was nothing to mock. "Was your lengthy visit successful?"

He frowned like it was none of my business, this new secret friend he felt compelled to visit. "It was, but my friend is different. Something is amiss and his motion is stunted by horrid back pain."

So many questions popped into my head with this moment of unexpected honesty. I covered over the second jaguarete with jade grasses. Perhaps the soldier should live.

"Cecilia, I know you're angry. I overstayed. I was out of the country for most of my trip, then in Bath with my friend. I didn't write because I didn't know how long I'd be away. The girls are mad at me too."

"They're getting older, Felton. They are pained by your leaving. You must consider their needs. Then, if you have a spare moment, you should consider what I want."

"What is that?"

"My family, which means my sister's company above all else." I held my breath before blurting the next. "And a formal parting for us."

His eyes widened, his cheeks reddened. "What?"

He'd heard me with his perfect ears, but I needed to say it again before my nerves abandoned me.

Raising my chin with my mother's pride, I sought and held his gaze. "Lord Gantry, I want a formal separation. I want you to have yours and me mine, without all the guilt. I want to be on my own."

Blinking as though I'd shoved the burning candle in his face, he shook his head. Then I waited for him to exhaust his logic and reasons before accepting what I had during all these months alone. We weren't a great adventure, we merely ate wonderful food and, upon occasion, enjoyed a bed. He and I weren't meant to be.

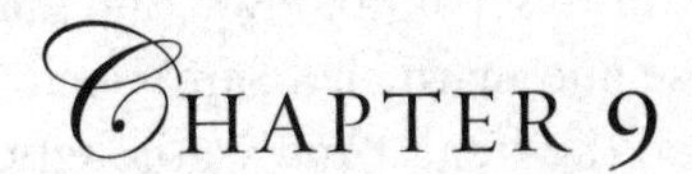

Felton—Wife, I Have a Profession

Felton paced in Cecilia's studio, back and forth, back and forth. The candle sent smoke everywhere. "No. Cecilia. You're joking."

She shook her head. "No. End us."

He dunked the candle in the bucket of water near the table. "I'll wear the toga if you will rid yourself of this notion."

"What? Wanting my sister here with me is wrong?"

He flicked the knife and it tumbled, *thwack*, and hit the table. The blade impaled itself half an inch into the wood. "Not that part. Your sister should be in London. She'll be, the minute she's found. It's the foolishness of a separation that needs to be tossed away."

"I can't keep reminding myself that this marriage is an accidental one with no expectation of closeness or accountability."

There was closeness, and now that he'd quit the Department of War and the Colonies, they'd have endless accountability.

Cecilia's agate eyes of topaz and bits of red and green looked wet, a flood of tears. "Felton, you had a life and children before you knew my name. I've nothing here but a borrowed closet for my art."

He slapped his forehead. "I forgot about getting you a better room. Cilia—"

"Since it is still merely you and me, not us, no children of our own, I think it better to separate now." She said the bitter words, then stuffed cheese and marmalade and bread into her mouth.

At least she liked the treat. "You've thought on this?"

Munching, she nodded.

"No. Cilia, I've erred. My friends needed me, but I have need of you. Give me a chance to make amends."

When her mouth cleared, she said, "Tramel agrees. He thinks nothing will change, that we're too different."

"You talked with my father about leaving me?" His face, he felt it drain of blood. How could she talk to that man about their marriage? "You betrayed my confidence?"

"You get to have an old newly discovered friend, and my father-in-law can't be my confidant. He visits me more than my husband."

Trying to maintain no expression was hard when he felt his head might explode.

"Felton, this silly posing ritual, and money, is all that binds us."

"And the duke told you to do this?" He kept his voice low. "Don't go to him . . . Cecilia. Don't . . ."

Though he felt that everything inside might break, she was sobbing.

He rounded the table. "You never cry."

"You never saw."

His throat tightened at that notion, that she hid how she felt from him. He had to make her understand. "You wouldn't cry if we were done? We're not done."

"We should be done, then you wouldn't feel guilty for how you spent your time. Every one of your noble causes would be a celebration."

"To be in your arms is a celebration." One hand went to her waist and he brought her to his chest. "Hey, hey. I'm here. I won't be going away again. I want you to pour into me. Confide in me. I'll be enough for you."

Putting her tear-soaked palm to his cheek, she shook her head. "How can that be when you don't know what I want for me?"

"I know you, Cilia. You want this marriage to be different. I can be different for you."

"You haven't so far. Five or six months of you being around, that's all I'll ever get. I can't pretend nothing matters anymore. I can't compete with everything that draws you away. My lord, let us be done."

He angled her face to his and flicked droplets from her long lashes. "Always formal when you're miffed."

"Then I shall forever call you by your title."

"Repington needed me, Cilia. The questionable deaths of my comrades in arms when they return to the peace of these shores, it's taking a toll."

"Questionable?"

He looked down for a moment. "Suicides. I had to make sure he was fine."

"Again, how can I be mad at a saint? I should set him free. Free the Lord Gantry."

"I'm no saint, for I didn't know you suffered like this. You're so strong. I'll speak to Jane about her advice. I ended her squabbles over the household budget. My frugal nature influenced her withholding the costs of your paints and canvases. You need your joyful portraiture."

"Portraits?"

He scooped a bit of the sweet marmalade and dangled it at her lips. "Yes. I imagine you teach sweet things, faces and such, to Amelia and Agatha."

She took the spoon and slurped up the sweet preserve then slammed the shiny metal onto his hand. It hit a knuckle and stung.

"Neither you nor Jane understand why I need my art. Her notions of exhibiting won't let the world see my paintings. I feel like the marquess's little secret."

Cecilia made cute Roman soldiers. He'd seen a dozen or cute but embarrassing pictures. Why should the world ever see them?

But he couldn't say that and expect to reconcile. "Cilia."

"She thinks her disdain is warranted since she you'd rather be away than with me."

It was time to tell her the truth. "It's not that I wanted to be away, I had to."

"Yes, for your friends."

"No, for the Department of War and the Colonies."

"What?"

"I work or I worked for Lord Liverpool at the Department of War and the Colonies."

"Another name I don't know has given you a job?"

"I'm not supposed to say. The Department of War and the Colonies deals in secrets and spying."

"You have a job and you're sneaky?"

"I don't think you understand the point."

"Yes, I do. You're a member of the ton. Lady Jane goes on about things one can't do, like working or exhibiting, and you have a job."

Exhibiting the Roman soldier paintings was not to be done. He'd have to hire her a tutor for lessons to improve and make something sensible that he could show the world. He stepped closer to her easel, readying to gently illustrate why London wouldn't be on fire for pictures of a silly husband holding a torch, and he gaped. He had to force his mouth closed.

Expecting something silly, he saw shocked by the divine. The grass and land looked like Demerara. He knew the spot. It was near the government building where they first met.

It looked as if he could walk right into the painting. The Roman soldier did look like him, or was it a younger version of

Tramel? The fellow looked regal and strong in the toga. Not a scar marred his limbs. "You somewhat captured my likeness. That is me?"

Her lips trembled. "It's no good. It's hard to concentrate when I'm upset."

Why did her face leak more tears? She was a waterfall, a wave of sobs poured down. "This is very good. I'm sure you'll get better with more practice. No more fretting. I'm here now."

"You have a job, you're a spy." Her red eyes grew larger. "Were you spying on my colony when we met? Oh goodness, I'm a traitor."

Her accent was heavy, and it sounded of heaven, soulful and free.

But there was no freedom in her face—just frowns, frowns that broke his heart. "It's British now, more or less. And you saved my life that night. My friend Johnson was shot by those guards. Pretending to make love to you on the steps saved me."

"Did we pretend to marry? It happens sometimes with Brits coming and going. Girls are used up, confused by you slick-talking men."

"Cilia."

"Is this fake? Have we been living in sin? Is that why you go away? Penance?"

He rubbed at his face. "This is by far the worst confession I have ever given."

"Don't spies get confessions, not give them?"

Calm. Don't react to her frustration.

Think. Think of the reward of her in his arms.

Plan. Make the movements, this dance of touching and sensations, do the negotiations.

Felton turned from her painting and put his hands to her shoulders. "I'll try this again. I'll listen to all you have to say, but know we are married, formally and legally and righteously under God."

Then he caressed her neck, working the muscles with his thumbs. "This feels tight, very tight. Ah, let me make it better."

"You're trying to distract me, my lord. It won't work this time."

That was what she said whenever they touched. Yet, like always, she leaned into him. Her mouth ripened like a lush berry.

Felton sought a tighter grip of her waist and went for the kill, a searing kiss to capture her heart.

Chapter 10

Cecilia—Marriage and Cheese

In my studio, Felton held me. His light kiss teased my mouth. He pulled back an inch and lightly blew on my bottom lip before having at me again.

His embrace tightened, growing more possessive. I didn't know how to resist. I missed him so much, but didn't I deserve more than passion?

Yes. Yes, I did.

I pressed on his gray waistcoat, then slipped to his side when he released me. "So, when is your next mission, my lord?"

"I resigned when I returned. The Department of War and the Colonies can no longer use me. Liverpool says I'm cut off."

"See. Even this Liverpool talks with you before me."

"Cecilia, I wanted all my business done, so I can be completely open."

"Were you good at it? Seems odd he let you go after a chat. Makes me wonder if that was all that occurred."

"I caught one of the informants that led to the botched . . . led to Johnson's death. The main person, the one who originally leaked the information to the council is still unknown."

Felton was still talking, but all I heard was what Jane said, that I had become a party to botching his life.

"More marmalade, Cilia?" He offered another scoop. When I opened for the cheese and jam, he kissed me.

Salt and sweet and Felton.

My pulse thudded and his scent of pine made my head light. I was getting swept away in him. That wouldn't work no matter how I craved him. I pushed free. "No."

"You're right, not here. Our bedchamber. Why do you sleep in here when I'm gone? The paint fumes can't be good for your health."

"I'm tired of maids inspecting sheets for my courses so they can gossip about the state of our affairs. They care less if I sleep in this closet."

"I'll settle things. I will—"

"Wrest command of your household from Jane?"

His eyes darted.

That was my answer. "Nothing will change. I'm not mistress of any house. I'm a guest. And if that is to remain my station, I'd rather be forgotten in Warwick Manor. Tramel has a lovely studio for me, and I can walk by the cliffs and hear the water and imagine I'm home with my family, my father and sisters. Sometimes Mama's ghost is there too. I told Tramel yesterday how I wished we hadn't moved."

"The duke has given you his sympathetic ear. When you see his other face, it'll shock you, but not me or Jane. We've seen his manipulation and cruelty."

"Manipulation, like constantly abandoning me over two years to only now admit you had a job."

"Cilia, I was a spy. I'm not supposed to tell."

Moving from Felton, I picked one of my new brushes, the good ones of horsehair. It might be better to finish out Felton's sad dark eyes.

Arms dropping to his side and then swooping behind his back, the man paced a little, like a bowlegged swan, then he handed me a handkerchief. "The duke visits quite often?"

"He's taken to his town residence."

"Parliament is not in session."

After wiping my eyes with Felton's cloth, I returned to my table and blended a deeper blue, midnight blue, to paint the jaguarete Tramel's eyes. That seemed appropriate, him stalking and waiting to protect his family. Yet, how I'd drawn it, the beast in the painting was set to eat the soldier.

"You continue to capture his attention."

"If one has two residences, each as fine as the other, why not stay at either?"

"He never cared for Town." Felton bit his lip for a moment. "I'm glad that he has interceded and has kept you company. Tramel loves his art."

"That he does. He has a painter's soul."

"You sure he has a soul? I thought it missing."

Felton bore no easy smile, not even the one he dangled to feign agreement. The bad blood between him and dear Tramel seemed silly, but his reasons must be another of those things I was never meant to know.

Head down, he came to my side, lightly massaging the crook in my neck. "The girls have been no trouble whilst I was away? They refuse to chat with me too. Do they know you want to end things?"

"I'd never tell them something like that, not without you here. Amelia is a dear. So full of curiosity. Agatha, well, she's warmer. I reminded her once more that I only wanted to be her friend. It's taken these two years for her to believe my intentions."

"You're their stepmother." He spun me to him, then set his hands to his side. "In time you'll win them as you've won me."

"That sounds depressing. How can you admit to winning when we are only in accord in bed?"

"No wonder we're arguing. We're standing."

My husband looked at me with that restless glance where I could feel his caress, his fingers undoing my laces.

My desire for him, for what we shared in the quiet of the night, hadn't left.

I hated my weakness for a man who put everything else above us and our unlikely union . . . like I had.

Guilty.

For the want of Felton, I was here without my sister, without allies, and had to invent one in Tramel.

"Cecilia, what are you thinking?"

"Fatherhood, my lord. For three months while you were gone, I thought I was with child."

His cheeks bloomed red. There was joy in his wary eyes. "Are you? Is that why you're upset?"

"Would things change if we had a child of our own?"

"Yes, I'd hand-feed you all the cheese and marmalade and chocolate you wanted. I'd rub those feet. I'd—"

"I'm not with child. And I'm not sure that I want a baby merely to secure my husband's cheese."

His palm cupped my elbow. My thin sleeves heated. He was the warmest man, with permanently fevered skin. "Now that I've returned and told you the secret that I've carried, I can begin set things right. Then if we are blessed with a babe, you 'll have no doubts in our marriage."

His arm wound about my middle and drew me to him. "What if we all go on a holiday to Bath, better than Warwick's cliffs of Ballard. The coasts are impressive."

"Another broken promise, my lord. For me? You shouldn't have."

Color warmed his cheeks, and he offered a sheepish gaze. "That's the past. I want to go, and you'll be so pretty painting in the sun. I'll watch and admire."

Part of me wanted this to be true; I'd waited more than a year for him to find time to show me this country. But it wouldn't happen. Something would steal my joy.

"Cilia, we need to begin again."

I lowered my hand onto his, not to pry it away, but to covet his heat. "Your sister said something about what a lady does in society. I don't think you watching me on a beach will be acceptable to her."

"Then we'll go it alone. When we're together, nothing else matters, Cecilia." He spread the lace of my collar and kissed the beating vein that trembled upon my neck.

Then he looked over my shoulder toward my canvas. "You painted me in a toga with two large . . . jaguars heading toward me. Good, the likeness is mine but I'm taller, my limbs—"

He put his hands to my thighs, thick and fully filling his palms. "Sizeable," he said with a laugh.

My breathing hitched as I shot to the table and stirred my spoon in the marmalade like it was a paintbrush. "I create things that I imagine or how I wish to see them. See the nice ankles beneath your tunic. I've made you manly."

Felton glanced at the floor, his flapping feet. He had scarring on his legs and a little on his arms, from smallpox. He seemed embarrassed by the marks.

"Cilia, you've never needed me to pose. You can do the portraiture without me."

With a slight nod, I offered my truth. "It's the only time that's ours. You step in here and you're under my command."

"You want to order me about? You can. I'll do just about anything so I won't be sent away."

He touched points on my shoulders that were tense and ready to explode. Why did he know my body and not my soul?

I had to break this draw and decided to talk of the duke. "Tramel will see the humor of the Roman soldier."

Felton's lips curled down. "Don't show him this, and refrain from saying his name with such enthusiasm. Sometimes I wonder if you prefer his company to mine."

"You kiss better."

Something broke in his eyes, like a mirror shattering.

I grabbed his shirt. "It's a joke."

Tapping a fist to his wide chest, his smooth lips, he released a shallow breath. "Gladstone, my cousin, said he caught you two . . . steeped in conversation the other week, before I returned."

"Talking to the duke is easy. No one is more passionate about the French masters like the Le Nain brothers or Le Brun, and unlike the Gladstones, there are no jokes of massas and plantations added to the discussion."

"What? I didn't know. I'll speak to my cousin."

"No need. Tramel solved the problem. He has worked to get the rest of your family to respect his son's Blackamoor wife."

"Cecilia, I'm going to be around now for good. I will talk to Gladstone."

"And Jane? And your aunt, your staff?" I looked up to the ceiling. "You'll be all talked out when you get to me."

Ohh. I covered my face in my palms. I hadn't meant to confess all this. "I was supposed to sound reasoned, not hurt by everything surrounding me."

Felton put his hand again on my arm. Still such fire in his touch. "I'm sorry."

"Are you? You keep leaving and I must depend on my father-in-law to right things and not his allegedly liberal son."

"What is that to mean?"

"You're caught, Felton. Stuck between what's expected in your society and doing the opposite to anger Tramel; and now you tell me you're a spy."

A new frown overtook his face. The hurt in his blue-black eyes melted a smidgeon of the hardened glaze I'd enwrapped about my fragile heart.

"Felton, you must see this is fruitless. This union is fruitless. Pray, while we are still friendly, let us end to this marriage. Jane says a church divorce or an annulment is possible."

His hands went again to my waist, and he leaned in and kissed me. His mouth was rugged, demanding in a way. Felton scooped me up, making my gaze level to his. This hold gave him better access to my bosom, the thick curve of my hips. I was solid, no wilting lily.

I liked my porridge as much as pudding. Slay me with mammee apples and custards and cheese, and now marmalade.

Drat. Now I was hungry for food and my husband.

"Cilia, Jane and Tramel need to stop meddling. You must give me one more chance. I'll do better."

His words kissed at my throat and lodged right there where his teeth raked my skin. I wanted him to leave my chambers, but I clung to his chest. My body was winning over my soul.

"Tomorrow. After Jane's recital, I'll speak to them all. I'll make changes. They'll know how I adore you. That I'm proud of your jaguars and togas or anything else you paint. Please, Cilia, may I stay? Then I will know I'm forgiven."

It wasn't like I could say no. I was hungry after all, and Felton was the most delicious, warmest thing in the world . . . when he was with me.

Closing my eyes to all the reasons why we didn't work, I clasped my palm about his neck and let him carry me away.

We gave in to this sensation, this something-like-love emotion. Nothing tasted so sweet, felt so strong or so safe. I refused to think of how long these feelings would last or when I'd starve again.

Felton—Wait. Wait, I'm in Love

December 4, 1813

It was terribly inconvenient to fall in love with your wife when her excitement for being wed had waned.

Felton stared at the doorway, looking for his dear Cecilia to float into the music room. As soon as she came, he'd take her hand and in the midst of all his family he would publicly declare his love.

Well, this plan sounded good, sounded as if it would convince everyone that Cecilia was not just his wife in name only but his life partner, a big part of his heart.

If he hadn't been so cynical and doubting of these feelings, he would have confessed before he left this last time. Then she'd not doubt his declaration now.

Before Jane's recital, Cilia was emotional in the dining room. Felton had interrupted her and his cousin Jeremiah Gladstone, steeped in conversation. Whatever the fool said, it couldn't undo two days of love and marmalade.

Cecilia and Felton were united. No one would come between them.

Yet where was she?

His wife should be here by now.

He'd stared at the doorway hoping to enjoy her movements.

Graceful, with wide hips that made flat gowns drape like she'd worn an extra petticoat, his Cilia sauntered across any threshold like violins played.

Listening to a young woman, a friend of Jane's, exhibit on the pianoforte, his hands sweated. His heart had never felt like this, full and fearful and dare he say, free.

Adjusting his cravat that seemed to tighten with each shift of his arms, he sampled a breath and closed his eyes. Thoughts of the first time he saw Cecilia floated. Her spunk and graciousness made him willingly become a fortune hunter.

Today he'd stop being afraid and just admit that he had fallen for his Cilia.

Aunt Nelly clapped her hands, bringing Felton's attention to the crowd of relatives and social visitors gathered. Her pinched nose rose. "My niece, Lady Jane Lance, will now entertain us."

The crowded room, piled with chairs and dozens of people he didn't know eating and drinking his expensive wines, seemed wasteful. He studied this room with the light. It would make a grand studio, one to rival the Tramel's at Warwick.

His sister Jane had told him when he came into possession of his own home, one separate from their father, that he'd need a music room to appear civilized.

He didn't realize that meant expensive curtains of yellow silk and a glossy mahogany pianoforte only used for Saturday teas.

Jane's taste was as expensive as Aunt Nelly's. If he'd been more present, he would've recognized the insult it was to give Cilia a *closet*, as she termed it.

It must be more humiliating knowing their present situation, leasing a house in Mayfair, wouldn't have been possible if not for the income he'd made investing her dowry. His fortune was under Tramel's control and wouldn't be liberated until the man's death.

Not one to root for such things, but he didn't exactly mind his posthumous prospects. Felton pounded his skull. His thoughts were scattered. Is that what love did, make one insane?

Jane sang. Her sweet, high-pitched voice barely covered the errant notes her fingers had jumbled. Younger by ten years, she was the baby of the Lance family, and its brightest musician. She typically was quite a tolerable one, except when trying to catch the eye of a gentleman. Their cousin Jeremiah Gladstone had brought many of his old university friends, a few wealthy shippers, and a couple of widowed peers.

Where was Gladstone now?

Cecilia said he'd been to Demerara earlier in the year. He must be involved in smuggling. Visiting Demerara—wouldn't he know the Thomas family? Maybe he had some news of Helena that would set Cecilia at ease.

Now that he'd quit the Department of War and the Colonies, could he maybe seek out Tramel's or Gladstone's contacts to get Helena out of Demerara? Felton could no longer count on any help from his former colleagues.

He searched the room, noting things like always: where people stood, who they talked with, how close they were to an exit.

Gladstone appeared to be missing. That meant he was in Felton's study smoking a cigar, away from the eye of Aunt Nelly, the man's mother.

Jane plinked the keys again, wrongly. Her notes often became showy, out of kilter, or simply flat. She had no right to criticize Cecilia. His wife's Roman soldier piece was outstanding.

Perhaps a good but gentle talk would help Jane understand that changes were to be made. Cecilia was his wife. She was mistress of this house. It was time for Felton to assert her position.

Looking again toward the door, he felt his face fall when it was another woman, not Cecilia, entering.

How did one tell their wife they'd fallen madly in love with them? A direct address? A quiet whisper over dinner? Perhaps he'd pose for her. Maybe he'd swallow his pride and go fully Roman, the sheet and all. She seemed unbothered by his scars.

Clapping.

Jane must be done.

No.

She started a new song.

He'd pounce like a jaguarete at the next opportunity to leave the room to find Cecilia.

Footsteps too heavy for a gifted dancer sounded in the hall.

His cousin Jeremiah Gladstone entered and sat beside him. With sandy-brown hair and an athletic build, the man looked sweaty and disheveled. The knot of his cravat was mangled like someone had tried to strangle him.

"Gladstone?" Felton forced his voice to lower to not upset Jane's music. "What's the matter? You look like someone threatened your life."

Jeremiah turned beet red everywhere, from his long nose to his five-finger forehead. His mouth opened then closed. Nothing came out. None of his famous excuses of why the world was against him.

Felton clasped his cousin's arm. "Are you ill, man?"

Eyes big and bulging, Jeremiah looked nervous or guilty or both.

Felton grasped the man's cravat and tugged him near. "Have you seen my wife?"

Again, his cousin's mouth opened, but no explanation uttered.

As he let go, Felton had blood on his hands. "You've been attacked."

Gladstone pulled at the cloth and exposed a small slash on his throat. "Goodness, I'm bleeding."

Felton dragged the man into the hall. "Who did this?"

"I told Tramel and Lady Gantry I wouldn't tell." Gladstone tore away. "Say nothing, cousin. It's for the best. You saw nothing."

The man fled.

It took a moment for the shock to wear away.

Felton's heart trembled, then raged. He stormed down the hall looking for Tramel. The man always brought chaos and sorrow wherever he went. This time he'd involved Cecilia.

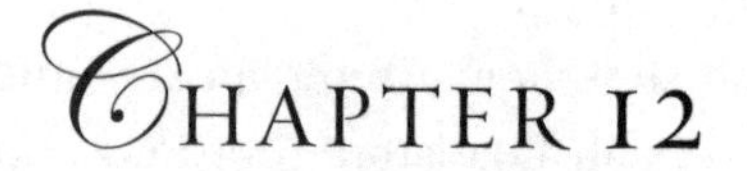

CHAPTER 12

FELTON—BAD DADDY

Noise spilled from Cecilia's little studio. He stopped at the door. She must be inside. She always hid from these Saturday gatherings. Starting to turn, he stopped. He should get Cecilia and together they'd confront Tramel. At last, she'd see that the duke was nothing but trouble.

Was Felton smirking? His insides surely must have a smile at the duke finally being exposed.

With a quick knock, he waited. "Cilia—"

"No, Papa."

Agatha?

He pushed on the door and found his eldest, the six-year-old miss standing at a small easel. Her creation looked like trees. What type, he wasn't sure.

Five-year-old Amelia waved at him. She too stood at a smaller easel. This one looked more like trees, a little more like a forest.

Between his two strawberry-blond children was a large easel, the one that held the whimsical toga painting from last night. Now it showcased something very different.

The landscape could be a mirror image of the fields of Warwick Manor. Every detail was there, the massive pastures, the rocky cliffs, the sea foaming on rocks below.

There were hints of Cecilia's talents last night in the Roman soldier picture, but this was magical. The passion and energy of the composition was undeniable. This was true genius.

"Papa, your mouth is open," Amelia said. "Didn't you say that I would catch flies?"

"Probably. Your father is known to be stupid. This art is fantastic."

Amelia grinned and did a little jig in her white gown covered in the blue smock. "See, sis, I told you he did know how good Mrs. Cecilia is."

Agatha rolled her eyes. "Lady Jane or Great Aunt don't. Neither do any of our cousins."

Felton hadn't thought her this talented, not until this moment. Shame warmed his cheeks.

"Pick your favorite, Papa." Amelia's paint-stained fingers grabbed his hand and led him to a pile covered by sheets.

Her tiny hand pulled at the largest one, but Felton whipped it off like a magician. The shroud from his eyes had been torn. He saw the truth of Cecilia's genius. Flipping from canvas to canvas, there were images of Demerara, of their boat to Jamaica, the one to Portsmouth, the seacoast of Ballard Cliffs and the Isle of Purbeck, and a few adorable ones of the girls.

Each was a masterpiece.

Why hide these?

"See, Papa, now you know her secret. Mrs. Cecilia says only true artists should see those."

"True artists? Like you and Agatha."

"And Grandpapa," his oldest said. "He comes and watches us paint sometimes. He and Lady Gantry discuss some old dead men. I mean artists."

Felton nodded even as his throat became thick. Somehow this part of his wife had been withheld. Why be silent to her husband on this matter? He spun in his low heels to his girls. "Lady Gantry is very talented."

"Grampa says she is a savant, not a servant like Aunt Jane says."

He rubbed at his jaw. "It seems the family is divided into those who love art and the brutes that don't." Felton was sure he was on the "brute" side.

"We love art, Papa." Amelia rubbed her thumbs on her tiny smock, adding yellow stains. "Mrs. Cecilia lets us paint if we don't argue."

"Her name is Lady Gantry," his oldest said. "You know Aunt Jane said to call her Lady Gantry. The other way is not proper."

With his handkerchief readied, he knelt in front of Amelia and wiped green paint from her palms. "She is my Lady Gantry."

Amelia frowned. Her poked-out lips then covered her small face. "Why can't I call her mama? She stays with us and is fun and cares for us like what mamas do."

"That's not all they do." Agatha's sharp voice boomed. "You don't remember anything. You're such a baby."

"Am not."

"Are too."

"Not."

Amelia took the handkerchief and tossed it toward her sister, but Felton caught it. "Sweetheart, you two were getting along so well."

"Agatha doesn't even like her. How can she have a say?"

"I do like her," his oldest said as she waggled her hands behind her ears. "I just don't show it like Grandfather."

"Grandpa shows he likes Mrs. Cecilia," Amelia said. "He brings her flowers and new brushes. He even stops her from crying when others say mean things."

Until last night, Cecilia had never cried in front of Felton, not even when he told her of her father's passing. What had he done to make her hide so much of herself?

The joy Felton had felt at discovering Cecilia's talent disappeared. That sick feeling returned and stewed in his gut. "Girls, have you seen Lady Gantry?"

"With Grampa." His daughters' high-pitched voices blended.

He backed from the room and knocked into Watson, his man-of-all-work. The flexible fellow caught a falling glass while balancing a bottle of port. "Sir, did you need something?"

"Yes, Watson. I'm looking for Tramel and Lady Gantry. Have you seen them?"

His man said nothing. He merely moved the bottle on the silver tray.

It would be wrong to grab Watson by the collar and jerk him off his feet, but that was exactly what he did. The tray tottered and fell, but Watson caught the bottle and Felton the glass.

"Well, your reactions are still good for a retired department man," Watson said, chuckling.

"Where are they?"

The fellow's deep bronze face glowed, but whether in a military uniform or a dark mantle, he was the same—even and cheeky. He took his time and pointed. "The smallish garden. It's beginning to snow, so take care."

Felton smoothed Watson's uniform, offered a *sorry* and took off to the patio. He launched through the door and stumbled onto the garden's stones, sliding in the fresh dust of snow.

Cecilia sobbed, wrapped in Tramel's arms. His father looked at him, offering a triumphant grin.

FELTON—WORST DADDY

Standing on his patio, Felton didn't feel the cold anymore.

Snow fluttered and stung his face, but he didn't see it.

It wasn't quite a blinding rage, but Felton thought he had achieved it, his vision becoming pitch-black as he witnessed the loving embrace between Cecilia and Tramel.

His father smoothed her back and with his eyes dead on Felton, kissed her cheek, then her brow.

When his shock cleared, he could somewhat think straight, and jumped in between them separating the two. "What's the meaning of this?"

The duke whacked with his cane. "I know you to be of small mind, Gantry, but why do you keep hurting this dove?"

"You make an advance at my wife, and you call me small-minded."

Cecilia stepped in front of Tramel, a man a little more than twice Felton's thirty years. "He did nothing. Nothing that I didn't want."

"What?" Felton shoved his hand behind his back to keep from strangling his father. "How long has this been going on?"

Her eyes were distant and sad. "What's been going on, my lord?"

"Your affair with my father."

Her face pinched as she shoved her hand in the pocket of her heavy purple redingote. "You think . . ."

She closed her eyes and bowed to the duke. "Good day, my lord." Then she bowed to Felton. "Goodbye, my lord, goodbye forever."

That didn't sound guilty or repentant. And his father's smirk drove a dagger into Felton's heart. "My cousin's bleeding. There's a stack of hidden masterpieces in your studio. You're in my father's arms. And he's in love with you. I need to know what's happening."

Not a word left her lips. Cecilia kept walking.

He caught her arm at the doorway. "Go through this entry and head to our bedchamber. Wait for me."

Head high, tugging her coat about her shivering limbs, she went inside.

Cecilia put up no fight. She was leaving too easily. Felton went in after her and caught her hand. "Your fingers are cold." He entwined his thumb about hers. "I'm sorry that I accused you of such, but you haven't denied a thing."

With a labored breath and a shrug, she pushed his fingers away. "I know what you want, Felton. What is it that I want?"

Her tone was small, very soft, but not easy. She repeated her question from last night.

He put her hand to his chest. "To be loved and cherished like any good wife."

With her teary gaze, she looked in Tramel's direction, then to the floorboards. "Goodbye."

As Felton tried to stop her, he brushed her side and felt something hard in her pocket. A knife? That sharp blade of her father's that he'd posed with—did she cut Gladstone?

"Cecilia." Felton called after her again, but she kept walking.

Tramel's blasted laughter started slow but soon raged. "Well done, Gantry."

The duke's powerful hands slapped together, slow loud pounds. "You've lost her, lost her for good, my boy. Well done."

"Tell me now what this is? Why were you trying to seduce my wife?"

The tall man sat on a bench framed by white snowdrops, winter jasmine, and dark evergreen bushes beginning to collect snow. "You had a goddess and couldn't keep her. You're a fool. Just like me."

Felton's breath steamed the cold air. "Cecilia will calm down, and I'll wear the toga and all will be fine."

"You're odd, son, but those endearing quirks won't work this time. Ashes to ashes, you've burned it all down."

"Tramel, why are you trying to destroy my marriage?"

His father stretched his arms onto the back of the bench and smiled with a know-it-all curl of his lips. "For you to be my son, you're terribly insecure."

"That's not an answer."

"Not one that you want, but it's an answer. Gantry, if you weren't my son and I was ten years younger, I'd take her from you and enjoy every minute. The lass is so trusting and kind, and you're so easily manipulated. You're the perfect kind of fool to drive her straight to my bed."

"Stop it, Tramel."

"Oh, my goodness. She does feel good in my arms, small and round. Gives me life thinking of her. Maybe I'm not so old. You think my shaking hand could feed her better cheese? Something smuggled from France."

Cecilia had told the man intimate things. If not for his training, a lifetime of being reasonable and invisible, this would push him, shove him to that knife's edge of reason.

"I'd love to love her, Gantry. You're lucky I have one foot in the grave."

"You will quiet, or I'll push you all the way into the ground and bury you underneath my flower bed."

"The spy, not-a-spy-retired spy can't figure out what has happened?"

"I'll dig the hole so deep and seal your tomb myself. No earthquake will unseal the rock I find."

The man hooked his cane on his arm, then stretched his hands to the bench. Muscular in his physique, with salt-and-pepper hair, Tramel's black eyes stared at him. "Son, you get your clever humor from me, you know. I wonder where the stupid comes from. Must be the Gladstone side through my sister. They are a bunch of cowards."

"I left every service honorably. I only took leave when Elizabeth needed me."

"Yes, the first-wife-dying excuse. Now you can't protect wife number two."

His father knew how to bait Felton. He'd taken everything, every tragedy, even Felton's surviving the smallpox that scarred him, to belittle him.

Now that Felton had achieved financial independence, the man couldn't hurt him anymore, or so he thought. He stepped closer to the bench and put up his foot near Tramel. "I'm used to your games, how you make everyone a pawn, but not Cecilia. Why can't she see who you truly are? An evil, soulless troll."

"Well, you're not one to sing my praises." The man clapped again as if he'd suffered through Jane's recital. "It's your wife's artistic soul. She sees only the best in the world unless circumstances force her to confront the way things are. The poor dear is longing for care, for someone who'll slay her dragons, who'll kill for her. I love her. I'll kill for her."

The glint in his eyes—his father knew something, but he'd never tell. She'd confided in the very beast, the devil himself, not Felton.

He kicked the bench, jostling it. "If I find out that her tears are your fault, you will pay."

"I didn't cause this, but I might be the solution. You think she'll paint me as a Roman soldier if I give her what she wants?"

It took everything in Felton—all the times that he abstained from fights, all the shots he refused to take to avenge a friend—to temper his spirit and refrain from striking Tramel.

"You've visited her so often since I moved my family from Warwick. You put this distance between Cecilia and me. I'll never forgive you for this." He pointed to the door. "Get out, don't come back, ever."

Tramel arose—tall, thick arms, powerful—and strode to the door. The sound of his cane slapping the patio stones echoed. "I'll return if Lady Gantry invites me and there's nothing you can do about it. You should've taken the time, my boy, to puzzle out your goddess instead of playing spy in the West Indies."

"Get out before I finish what Mama couldn't."

The smirk dissolved from his father's face. Felton's mother was the only one of Tramel's three wives the man actually cared about.

"Don't be like me, so consumed with being right, you let all the wrongs in the world pile up. It chokes out the light."

He unbuttoned his sleeve and prepared to slip on a Toga and do all the begging in the world to get his wife to talk to him and to confess to what was going on with his father and Gladstone. "Choking you is too good and too quick."

"You're funnier when you're not fretful. You don't realize how badly you've done. You've lost her. Now both the past and future Duke of Tramel will grow old, alone, and bitter. Ah my father's revenge."

"Tramel, you're already old. Remember that foot in the grave?"

With chuckles falling harder, his father withdrew, but his malevolent laugh lingered long after.

The old man stirred trouble. Felton wasn't going to lose a thing. He'd let Cecilia settle. When the house emptied and his children went to bed, he'd put on the toga and join Cecilia in her studio.

They'd talk. He would tell her everything, and he'd listen to everything. Any change she needed, he would do. He loved her, and she would know that tonight.

Tapping his foot on the cobblestones, he took another deep breath of the chilly air. Felton and Cecilia were always good at making up.

This time would be no different.

CHAPTER 14

FELTON—EMPTY BED

December 15, 1813

Agatha and Amelia sat on the floor of Felton's bedchamber. Dresses of cream and light yellow curled about their lean ankles as they craned their sad faces toward him.

Packing a portmanteau, he eyed his special chestnut cases with his weapons. They should be put away now that he was no longer in service to the Department of War and the Colonies, but he'd left them on his dresser.

The weapons were too refined for merely shooting pheasant at Warwick. As his friend Repington complained, one couldn't shoot guns in Mayfair without hitting a door knocker or visitor.

"Papa," Amelia said, holding tight to her stuffed doll, "why isn't Mrs. Cecilia back like you told us?"

That was a good question. *Where was she?* was a better one. And why had he waited hours before he took action?

The misplaced hope she'd return and walk through the door any moment hurt.

The false pride of thinking he was in the right stung.

"Lady Gantry had to go away. She'll be back—"

"Before Yuletide? We won't be able to exchange presents like last year." Amelia sort of whimpered her words and Felton's heart fell deeper into his chest.

Agatha's arms folded. A defiant frown filled her oval face. "She just won't get hers. And she won't bake the coconut bread either."

Last year, it had taken Felton several attempts before he located coconuts. He and Cecilia walked the markets together until they spotted them being sold in Covent Garden. Cecilia's smile had radiated as he broke open the shells and scooped out the tender flesh.

He realized too late that they both wore shells, protective armor. They were well matched, even from the beginning. If he'd recognized and not fought his feelings, they'd be together. "I'll see if the cook knows her recipe."

"Not the same." Amelia shook her head, her riotous curls escaping her chignon. "Cook won't burn it right."

Cecilia wasn't much of a cook. The flavor was there, the chewy texture too. "It was good dipped in chocolate sauce."

He stopped his woolgathering and gathered the girls. With kisses to each of their brows, he made a commitment, a solemn vow. "When Lady Gantry is done with her adventure, she'll return. Our family will be complete again."

Amelia tugged on his waistcoat. "Must you go away again, Papa?"

He tweaked her sad lips. "Yes. I need to hurry your stepmother from her visit. I think I can speed her up."

"Why would she leave without us?" Agatha broke free from his hug and plopped against the footboard. "Or even say goodbye."

Cecilia had left, in her purple coat and bonnet, almost as soon as she'd stepped back into the house. Why did he stay in the garden with Tramel when Cecilia needed him to convince her to stay?

Why didn't someone warn him that she went for a walk on a

blustery eve? His wife loved walking, but not the cold. Like Jane, he'd thought her locked away, painting. He would've started looking for her hours earlier.

No reports from the coroner of anyone found frozen around Mayfair. That was his fear: that she'd succumbed to the weather. He'd seen her get disoriented sometimes when the streets were noisy. A snowy evening was not the place for an upset woman to be.

Like a bad spy, he'd taken his eye off the mark. You'd think a beautiful woman in a purple coat out walking in winter would be easy to find.

"I'll hurry her back." He hoped his voice sounded strong, even though his gut stewed.

The little red faces of his daughters didn't look encouraged.

Felton had nothing to lift their frowns. "I'll return as soon as I can."

His daughters looked at him, then each other, then grew quieter.

He knelt near his eldest. "Lady Gantry is well."

Agatha bounced up and gripped him tightly, like he'd vanish. "How do you know, Papa? She didn't say goodbye, just like Mama didn't."

His oldest was two when Elizabeth died. Of course, she'd remember.

Felton wished he could comfort her, but a man who'd spent years tracking down people knew better. The trail was cold, cold as the white ice Cecilia called the snow.

Believing with his whole wounded heart that his wife was fine, that he hadn't lost the second woman he loved was better than the truth—his arrogance and neglect had cost him his happiness and put his Cilia at risk.

He gave each girl an extra squeeze. "You'll see. Everything will be well."

His man-of-all-work came out of the closet with shirts and began filling a portmanteau.

"My heavier coat too, Watson."

The fellow grimaced, then disappeared in the closet. The man knew Felton would begin searching on foot, street by street, as winter raged.

No longer able to maintain a smile, he turned from his children and stoked the coals in the fireplace. Cecilia was out there somewhere. He had to find her.

The poker made ash waft and cover parts of the grate. He banged the metal and tried not to strike too hard and show his frustration.

Where was she?

Why hadn't she at least sent word she was safe?

Watson came out of the closet with several waistcoats, as if this was to be a social trip. "Are these enough?"

"Put half back, sir."

"Papa, if you're to be alone"—Amelia lifted her dolly—"you can take Ellie Lance to keep you company."

He snuggled the cloth thing with shiny brown button eyes. "What's that, Miss Ellie? Address Ellie as Miss Lance." He put his ear to the doll again. "Oh, you have an older sister." He bowed. "A thousand pardons, my dear."

"Papa!" His little girl's voice was a squeak.

Again, he put the doll to his ear. "You wish to stay and take tea with Amelia. Of course. A gentleman always honors a lady's request."

He handed back Ellie to his youngest and she hugged the toy to her chest, wrapping it up in her yellow shawl.

Agatha gawked, then folded her arms. "She didn't finish the jaguarete. Lady Gantry should come back to finish it. She should be good to her word."

"We do want her back, but I think Lady Gantry had to go away to figure things out."

"Is that why you go away so often, Papa?" That soft tone of Amelia's chipped at his soul.

"I've debts to pay, obligations to men I fought with, and sometimes I can prevent people from being hurt."

"That sounds important."

He took Ellie from his daughter's small hands again. "If Ellie was away, hurt . . . you'd want me to do everything to get her and make things better."

His youngest's blue eyes looked shiny and wet. She wiped at her face. "Of course, Papa."

"Then it profits me to do so for my friends, to feed them, clothe them, help them find new purposes. Or find ways to make England safe." He noted his eldest's cross face. "Yes, the Honorable Agatha Lance, what's your objection?"

"No objection, Papa, more an admission. I don't think we made Lady Gantry feel welcome."

The little cherub looked so sad with her lips drawn to a pouty dot.

He stroked her chin. "I'm at fault, but when she returns, and she will return, I want you two to think about how we can make Lady Gantry feel happy to be with us."

"Let us go with you. We can convince her together." Agatha looked very serious. She'd thought about this.

It comforted his soul that indifferent Agatha now wanted Cecilia back, but until he knew with certainty that Cecilia would return, he'd not put his children through rejection.

Rejection was meant for Felton alone.

If he could talk to his wife, touch her, convince her of his love, they could start anew. There was a sort of energy that happened when they touched.

If he'd listened to that feeling from the beginning and not turned from it, they'd be making snow angels in the garden.

"Papa, I don't like you going. It always takes you so long to come home."

He tweaked her nose, then stood. "I'll be back for Yuletide.

And my friend Repington will help in the new year." Now that he was cut off from the Department of War and the Colonies, he needed the duke's military connections to determine if Cecilia had found a way to return to Demerara.

She was brave and foolhardy enough to try to run against the transport blockades.

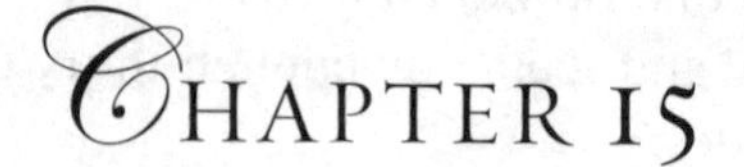

CHAPTER 15

CECILIA—A TRUE STUDIO

December 23, 1813

The room held the proper warmth. Not too hot or too cold, my studio at Warwick Manor was always perfect. The footman in the shiny silver livery adjusted the coals in the fireplace. Then he exited, leaving me alone in the vastness of the room that had gorgeous, gilded moldings on the pale sea-blue walls.

The ebony table next to my grand easel held a Wedgewood platter of delightful French cheeses—the Comté, the Gruyère, and the Beaufort. Each paired well with the fig preserves and champagne.

Tramel was the consummate host, delightful and funny. The adjacent bedchamber that I had shared with Felton when we first lived here was completely redone in flat yellow with an emerald tapestry bedspread. In the closet were gowns of bright colors, some so fancy that I couldn't bear to touch them knowing I would be up late painting.

The duke had found me on the side of the road walking away, not knowing where to go in the cold. He said he saw my purple redingote, and knew I was in trouble.

He saved my life and stopped me returning to Felton and beginning again the vicious cycle of forgiving him only for him to hurt my heart anew.

Yet, I felt guilty enjoying Tramel's company.

As if he'd heard my thoughts, the duke came in. His tailcoat of burgundy looked elegant. He didn't seem so old, and used his cane less.

"I have a note from Jane. Neither she, nor Gantry, nor the girls are coming for Christmas. I'm sorry." His voice was winsome, and he took his time easing into the gilded chair where he sat and watched me paint. "I hate disappointing you. I know you hoped he'd come."

"Didn't expect him, but I wished he would. I should run my plans by him. He says . . ."

My lips fastened.

Couldn't tell Tramel of his son's disclosure of working for the Department of War and the Colonies. Pretty sure one wasn't to say they were a spy, or a spouse of one either. "He must be furious at me. I don't blame him. Leaving without a word, I must seem heartless."

"Cecilia, you're too generous. This is my fault. My son and I don't have the closest relationship. I fear he's punishing me, which means he's punishing you."

The kindness of this man who literally saved my life seemed endless. "I fear I've added to the enmity."

"No fretting, my dear. He'll come around. You're his wife." His hand moved from his cane to under his chin. A sad, thoughtful look crossed his countenance. "Do you still wish to be married to Gantry? You've not been happy for a while, particularly since you moved from here to London."

The tone in his voice held more sadness, more than usual. I felt for him and wished I had something to say to encourage his relationship with Felton.

Yet, since I wasn't speaking to my husband, I didn't have any good counsel. "What do I do? I care for him so much, but if there's no trust. If my easier moments are here in this studio than London—"

"Lady Gantry, Cecilia, my love, you're an angel. All will be resolved, and you'll have love and the adventure you crave."

How could Tramel be so confident when I felt lost? I took down the canvas of the cliffs of Warwick. I'd finish it later. "It's good that someone has hope." I tapped my paintbrush along my easel. "I think it is time to paint your portrait."

His finger waggled. "No. That's for you young persons, so you can dress in various stylings."

A grin formed, tugging and lifting my sad lips. My special teasing of Felton in Roman costumes was something I missed. If I'd stayed, he might be donning the toga and caressing me with his repentant gaze. It almost felt like love.

Almost.

"Lord Tramel, you're young at heart. You must let me paint you."

He folded his hands and sat in a noble pose. His waistcoat was onyx in color. The revers cut into his jacket were smart as were his dark breeches. He wasn't styled like an old man. I wondered how old he was.

"I should take you in my carriage back to London immediately. I know your heart is breaking. There must be something I can do for you. Yet, I'm enjoying listening to you and watching you paint. It's a pleasure I've come to love. But you belong with your family, your close family."

An errant tear fell and ran the length of my cheek. "Only you have known what I want. Why is it the man I married doesn't? Sorry, I shouldn't speak of this but I shall burst."

"You tell me everything. I'm at your leisure."

If I closed my eyes, the way he said that, I could imagine him to be Felton.

A new feeling of disappointment shook me. The duke was more attentive than my husband. "My marriage is the saddest of all my adventures. I deserved better."

The glint in Tramel's eyes warmed me. It said he understood

and agreed. Nonetheless, I had to be careful. A broken heart could heal up wrong.

He shifted his feet and set his bronze-tipped cane to the side. "We haven't discussed the information my informants discovered. What Gladstone said in London was true. He enslaved his wife, your sister."

My face had to be a bowl of water, with the liquid spilling over. I couldn't believe the fool taunting me in my husband's house. Jeremiah Gladstone, Felton's cousin, sold Helena to a plantation. "How could he do such? And how do I save her now? The blockades which kept her from me—"

I smelled cedar and lilies when Tramel took me in his arms. His footfalls were silent. No noise to addle me.

His embrace had more strength than I imagined. And his cane, was that not on his chair?

"Let it all out, my dear. Then I will make things better. I promise."

With my head to his chest, I cried like a babe. "My sister, my freeborn sister . . . entangled by the fiend . . . dealt with so cruelly. I don't even know if she is alive."

His hand caressed the tension in my neck. Then his thumb flicked away my tears. "We must hope that she is. Once my contacts discover where she was sold and where she now resides. With all the blockades, interisland transport of slaves is high. I'll send you there via my connections. You'll save Helena and bring her here to me. I'll rebuild your family. I know that's what you want above everything."

His gazed burned, very blue-black and shimmering of fire. Like Felton, I couldn't tell what he was thinking, but I believed the duke. "How do I thank you?"

"Your friendship and smile are enough. I'll remain your friend even when my son seeks to end this marriage."

I pulled away and turned to my canvas. An unexpected sharp ache stabbed at my chest. "That would be the normal course for a wife who ran away. Thank you, for your care."

Tramel put his arms about me again. "Let's focus on your sister. We save her, then we save you."

My friend went back to his chair. This time I heard his footfalls and his sigh as he lowered into the seat. "Gantry may come to his senses. If I were him, I would fight for your love. Alas, I'm not. So, I will merely make your dreams come true. Perhaps seeing you happy at last will make amends between father and son."

Rolling my brush between my fingers, I studied Tramel, trying to decide how best to capture his spirit on my canvas. A comforting silence filled the room and I stared at the openness of Tramel's hand and the strength I imagined as he folded his fingers about the cane.

Gratitude for him should overflow into this painting. It should be my best. "Thank you, Your Grace."

His smile lit the room.

The duke cared about my heart and would help me save my sister. Nothing else mattered.

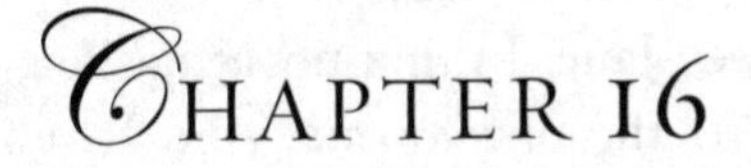

Chapter 16

Felton—Cleaning House

December 26, 1813

The Mayfair house with its candles and bits of fir branches bracketing the windows made it seem as if Felton's town residence was abuzz with Yuletide gaiety. That was the outside, which spoke nothing of the loneliness and gloom behind the glass.

Perhaps he should've taken the girls to Warwick. It was beautiful in winter with the thick woods, but the dread of Tramel's gloating and the hope that Cecilia would return for Christmas kept him in Town.

"Papa, the windows look lovely."

"They do, Amelia." He'd walked from the mews holding each daughter's hand and stopped in front of the house.

Agatha was quiet. She'd been so since he'd returned from his failed search for Cecilia in the streets of London. Finding people without the help of the Department of War and the Colonies proved more difficult. London had thousands of places to hide.

"Let's go in, girls. Perhaps Cook can make us something hot."

They walked into the house and he was surprised to see Gladstone milling about.

"There you are, Gantry." He stuck out his hand, but Felton kept his to the side.

"Girls, go on in and find your aunt."

Gladstone rolled his top hat in his palms. He was well styled today, buff breeches, bottle-green waistcoat and brown jacket.

"What brings you here today?"

"I wanted to see Jane. I think my attentions have grown upon her. She might be the one for me. And I wanted to know if it were true, that you separated from Lady Gantry."

No mention of being cut by Cecilia. Felton pulled off his gloves. "Nonsense. She's out of the country right now. As soon as she's back I'll tell her you asked about her."

When the man's eyes darted, Felton knew that his speech was not what his cousin wanted. Something more had happened the day of the recital, but Felton wouldn't tip his hand. Gladstone had information.

"Cousin, when was the last time you traveled? Your aunt didn't say."

"It was—"

"Felton, you're back." Jane sauntered down the stairs with her chin elevated as if her pale green gown had a regal train. "Mr. Gladstone, I was unable to find the book you lent me."

"Keep it and think of me." He put on his hat, waved broadly, and then almost ran out of the house.

Another time. Once Felton located Cecilia, he'd know what happened that day. Then he'd right all the wrongs. And from the feeling in his gut, he knew there to be very little that was his wife's fault.

"Are you brooding, Felton, still?" The sweet voice belonging to his sister Jane startled him. Then he remembered Jane was the only one unaffected by Cecilia's departure.

She came near with a bounce in her step. Was she possibly thinking their womanizing cousin would propose? And that Felton or Tramel would approve?

"Jane, I'm going away again."

"To Warwick? Christmastime is so love—"

"No. I'm in no mood to hear the duke's gloats."

Watson appeared out of nowhere—well, almost nowhere. A spy's assistant was always around no matter what. "Sir, I will get your bag packed. Both portmanteaus?"

"No, just one." Felton didn't need his guns. He'd accompany the Duke of Repington on a hunt across England. The man chased his ward and needed to search every shadowy place from here to Scotland. It was the perfect excuse to look for Cecilia who might venture to places about England Felton had promised to take her. She was on adventure and having access to Repington's resources might hasten locating her.

Jane clasped Felton's arm like they would go for a walk. "Why go anywhere at all?"

"I should join my wife in her present adventure."

She dragged him into the parlor with the big windows and perfect light for an artist. "May I say sorry again?"

"You may, for all the good it does."

A frown consumed her lips. She clasped her elbows. "What if we all went to Warwick for the new year? It will be a merry journey."

"Merry? It's almost a two-week journey with the children and the number of stops, not to mention the maids and nurses we'd have to tow along."

"We could be leaner. I can handle the duties of managing the girls." She grinned like she'd won a prize. Maybe there was one for perseverance. Hadn't she always wanted to run everyone's household, Tramel's and Felton's?

"Father wrote again. He says you're welcome. All can be forgiven."

"No to both lies." Hot natured, boiling in anger, he went and opened one of those perfect windows. "I'd like to go into the new year with hope, not biting my tongue or bidding him to hell."

Jane laughed a little, but her tone was tight. "Felton," she said with the proper arch of her voice. "Father can help you legally end things with Cecilia. You can be an unmarried man again."

He glared at her. "Sis, I love you dearly. It's always been you and me against the world, but we both know that the faith I had in you is misplaced. My neglect has allowed you to disrespect my wife. That pains me."

Eyes blinking like a moth blinded by a lit candle, she craned her head. "I don't know what you mean. But if I've done something, you always forgive me."

"What is it you're asking, Jane? Forgive you for alienating my wife? Forget that you made her feel less than an accepted member of my family? Ignore that I let my duties lead to my wife being forsaken and that you led the hateful efforts whilst I was away?"

She strutted in front of him, pointing her bony finger. "I meant to help. I'm the one who's been running your house while you traipse off to help every man under the sun. I gave your house stability after Elizabeth died."

He hung his head for a moment, then looked at the young woman with stars in her light blue eyes. "You've done me a great service, but I'm married to a woman who is capable of running my house. I didn't want to displace you. I thought you both could work together."

"If Cecilia was committed to running things, she would have stayed."

"Why? Why stay? When I've made it seem that you were more important than my marriage."

She swatted the air as if to dismiss his rebuke. "Are you married, Felton? It doesn't appear to be that way."

"Jane, I am. And she would be here now if I'd put her first."

"First? Above your blood children, the ones borne of my dearest friend who died giving birth to your son?"

He rubbed his forehead. "Jane, you don't think that I could love Elizabeth and our children and be in love with Cecilia?"

"You . . . you can't?" His sister's face wrinkled. "No, you two are so different." Her foot stamped, making the burgundy rug shift. "You're confused."

She seemed to grow angrier, but he stepped closer and looked into her eyes. "What differences are you thinking, Jane? She likes art, and I barely understand it."

"She's no artist. I saw the beginnings of a clown sketch of you in a toga."

He grasped his sister's hand. "Come."

Down the hall they went to Cecilia's closet. The small room had been left untouched under his orders. "Not an artist?"

After lighting sconces, Felton lifted the cloths off his wife's stack of paintings. "Look at these. Cecilia Charity Lance, my Lady Gantry, did all of these. She's the best artist I've ever seen."

The landscapes.

The scenes of castles and men swept away in battle. All the things of Roman lore, gladiators and the Colosseum.

Then the beautiful nature scenes of Warwick, the cliffs, the sea, and the meadows. "They are dated. When I'm here the setting is ideal. When I'm away and she's miserable, they become sad, even dire. But they are all beautiful."

Jane's mouth hung open. "These are wonderful. I didn't know."

"The girls knew. It was their secret. Agatha and Amelia were the only ones in this house she felt comfortable sharing her talent with. Oh, and of course, Tramel. Why is that, sister? You with your attitude and me with my neglect."

She wiped at her cheek. The painting of his sister leaning against the pianoforte in tears made Jane's eyes water. "I didn't know."

"Cecilia wasn't comfortable. I gave you the best room to badly exhibit the pianoforte, and I let her have a closet for her artistry. She deserved better than that. Allowing you to have a say in my affairs made it seem as if I was ashamed of her. So, she hid her talent. One of the biggest parts of who she is, and I made her to hide it."

Mopping her tears, Jane set down the mirror-like portrait. "Are you saying it's my fault she's gone?"

"You weren't a reason for her to stay."

Jane frowned, her expression ugly and prudish. "She should've complained or shown me."

"What would you have done differently? Nothing, I suspect."

His sister sobbed harder, but he hadn't said the worst. "I want you and the girls to go to Bath with Aunt Nelly in the new year. I made arrangements with her."

"But what of this house? Engagements in town?"

With a shake of his head, he rendered judgment. "This house wouldn't be possible without my investments of Cecilia's dowry. Doesn't seem quite right we should have use of it if the benefactress has gone."

Jane closed her wet eyes. "I thought I was doing what was best."

He put his hand to her shoulder, wilting the cap of the sleeve. "You did that for a long time, maybe too long."

"How do I fix it? I don't want you angry with me. Remember, you and I against the world."

"Jane, I have to fix this. And you need a household of your own. Aunt will help with that or you can go back to Father. Warwick has no mistress to run its accounts."

"Now I know you hate me. Neither of us can stand being there more than a week unless Lady Gantry's there. She made him civil."

Felton offered a shrug. "Then Aunt Nelly in Bath it is. Odd thing, Cecilia only confided in the devil."

"It's that woman, Felton. She's changing the duke and you, like she has voodoo or magic."

"No, Jane. Her art has healed him. That's what's wonderful about it, about her. Think of how to be better a person while you're off to Bath."

Jane's expression blanked, no smile, no frown, no more sobbing. She moved to the door. "I do hope you find her." She left.

Felton laid out the paintings, hoping to see a clue. In the deepest part of the stack were images of Warwick's pastures. Another four looked like they were of Demerara. The one he couldn't take his eyes off were of jacaranda flowers. The spot where they had wed had these flowers hanging above them.

With his pinky, he traced the delicate brush strokes. "Where are you, Cilia? Where have you run to?"

Finding her would be difficult, but if she'd found peace somewhere other than London, in the countryside or a British colony, what would make her return?

He'd have to figure out what she wanted, what she needed more than his love. He covered up the stack of paintings, vowing to his heart that he'd not lose his second chance at happiness.

Chapter 17

Cecilia—Werk-En-Rust, Demerara

May 8, 1814

With an arm underneath my head, I stared up at the Demeraran sky. The back of the dray wasn't comfortable but up in the hills we had a wonderful view of the stars.

"The big orb of orange stripes, our papa said it was Galileo Galilei's Saturn." I whispered the words aloud, as though my sister and my newborn baby nephew could hear. He slept peacefully, though his birth was almost breached.

Cupping my hands to my eyes, I stretched to see the constellations a little more and made the same wish I had when I learned of my father's death. "I want my family. I need it restored."

Then I added a second one. "I wish for revenge, too."

My sister Helena coughed.

This one rattled more than the last.

The birth of her son was so hard on her, but I managed to get Noah to breathe. With the aid of Tramel's smugglers, I found her and helped my sister escape the plantation.

The trees overhead had the purple blooms of the jacaranda.

They would amaze me in the morning as they always did, such a bright color of purple. Beautiful like my wedding day. For the first time in months, I wished Felton was beside me.

No matter how cross he was, he'd hold my hand. He'd tell me things would be well.

Nothing was good right now. I watched a moon move so high I couldn't touch it and flowers overhead whose blooms wouldn't open until morn. My sister was going to die, die of the birthing fever. The man responsible, Jeremiah Gladstone, would continue to live.

How was that fair?

When you have a chance to kill a man who deserves it, do it.

That would be my new creed. I'd had a chance in December. I pressed my father's knife to Gladstone's throat like he was a fish to fillet, but Tramel, dear Tramel, had taken the weapon from me. He started to kill him and began slicing the fiend's neck wide open, but I asked him to stop.

Why did I prevent justice? Silently sobbing I heard the breeze return the sound of my shallow breaths. My heart thumped like it would crawl free from my ribs.

A jaguarete could be in the tall grass looking at my sister and me and the baby the way I viewed Stilton cheese.

We were prey, probably smelled like it too, with all the bloodshed from the birth and the battle to escape the Elizabeth Ann Plantation.

The Gladstones owned part of that foul place.

The smugglers made it seem as if Helena's escape was a part of a rebellion. The enslaved rose up. Many were freed but more died.

"Chari, don't fidget." Helena's whisper sounded weaker.

Teasing her like I always did might help rally her strength. "You sound like Mama. Next, you'll tell me to walk across the dray with a book on my head."

The rumble in my sister chest wasn't laughter. It was that

heavy, throaty cough of the birthing fever. It wouldn't break and she'd grown more tired. *Keep breathing, sweet girl.* That's what I wanted to shout.

Those words would only leave me in prayer.

"Tell me about London, Chari. What's it like, the world across the sea?"

"Large, Helena. With big buildings. And the fashions are amazing. I'll take you shopping in warehouses with silks."

She wheezed. "Tell me of your art. Your Gantry let you keep painting?"

"Yes, I paint. Lord Tramel, he arranged for me to meet people at the theatre. I may paint for them if I choose."

"They let a woman do that?"

"My father-in-law sent word on my behalf, along with one of my paintings. That convinced them."

"That's nice, Chari. Do they call you that? Probably not. Lady Cecilia."

"No, they call me Lady Gantry. There are so many rules of address."

"Our big sis hated rules. I hope to see her soon. Mama and Papa too."

That sentiment chilled. I can't lose my last sister. Please let the fever break.

I grasped Helena's hand and pumped her fingers. "No, don't you give up. I came for you as soon as I could. My father-in-law forced your lover to confess."

"Husband. I married Jeremiah. He has my papers. But, Chari. You talk more of Tramel than Gantry. Is your husband dead?"

"No. He was quite fine, last I saw him."

She bit her lip and winced. "Chari, you married on a whim to a man you'd never seen before. Did you never learn to love him?"

That was a sticky question. "I loved him when he kissed me. He was mysterious and exciting. Then he promised me adventure."

"That's nice. True love—"

"It's not. I think I know how love dies. When the wanting and joy go away, apathy fills the empty places."

She pulled our hands to her stomach. "And now you love this Tramel."

It couldn't be that simple, but I was here with my sister in her final moments because of the duke. His men guided boats through the British blockades for me. "I think there is something bigger than love, Helena. Respect. No man since Papa has treated me so well or done so much for me, for us."

My insides felt tight. My stomach twisted. I was glad that Tramel hadn't come. I'd spent too much time with him. Nothing improper or indecent, but a soul can get use to endless kindness. Longing can be kindled when dark eyes see you as beautiful and whole.

Distance and perspective might fix my heart. When Gantry formally ended this marriage, I'd like to be friends. When I found a way to disgrace his cousin Jeremiah Gladstone, and expose the fiend for his evil, I didn't want there to be hard feelings between us—Felton and me.

"Make sure my Noah knows them. This Tramel and Lord Gantry, they are his family. They have to protect his birthright."

"You can do it. We, you and Noah and me, can get on a boat in the morning. Tramel will know what to do."

She patted my hand as if to comfort me. "You and Noah. You two. You'll do it."

Helena was dying. I didn't need to be pacified. I needed a miracle. "I left everything to go to a new world. Then I left Lord Gantry to find my place. But I have to get you to English shores, so you and Noah will be free again. Then we'll find our spot together."

Helena opened her eyes. "Chari, when you close your eyes, who do you see? Who is it that your heart wants?"

Couldn't close my eyes. Sometimes it made me dizzy, especially when everything was loud. Yet in this moment, I was afraid of who'd be painted upon my lids. "Can think of nothing but this family, ours."

Her forehead glistened. Beads of sweat hung on her lip. She was in such pain. "Chari, don't fret. You need your strength for what's to come."

It was impossible to put my sister's words into my heart, not with it breaking. I'd arrived too late to rescue her.

The growling sound returned. That jaguarete was hungry and I had no Roman soldier to protect us or to offer as a sacrifice.

"Gladstone said if I bore a boy, I'd have Gantry's heir. You go back to your husband and Noah will have such honor."

My head shook like it was a puppet on a string. "I can take care of us."

"Then go to Tramel."

Ridiculous. Before I could correct her, a bark wailed in the air. That wasn't a jaguarete.

Oh no! The dogs should've given up. The slave trackers didn't like the deep woods. They feared the Obeah ghosts hidden in the trees. Evil men should be feasted upon by the snarling beasts.

Feast.

Beastly beefsteak.

I wish I'd had a nicely charred cut of the meat, with potatoes or a piece of sweet black cake or dip of breadfruit stew with salted cod.

"Your stomach, Chari, is talking. When my friend Quamina, the church deacon, comes back, maybe he'll have something for you to eat."

"You need to eat, Helena. You need food to gain strength and to feed this little one."

Her cough raged. She fought for air until her lungs settled. "Quamina brings a wet nurse for the babe. He knows I'm not going to make it. Take her to freedom in my stead."

My palm to her forehead burned. Her skin was warmer than Felton's. "Don't give up. It's you and me. I should never have left you."

"You've always followed your heart. Never question it. Never doubt it. You're owed happiness. Close your eyes, Chari. Don't watch me go to the shadows."

But what if my heart doesn't know what's right? I rubbed my elbows and stared at my sister. "A little late for me to start listening now."

Helena covered her face with her sweat-stained sleeve. "Sleep, Chari."

Watching her suffer, struggling to breathe, if I closed my eyes, I'd be in Felton's garden taking the opportunity to kill Gladstone. I'd do it this time or allow Tramel to do so.

The newborn between us lay bundled in a tartan blanket. I'd wrapped his little bottom in mud cloth—not awful osnaburg, the fabric of the enslaved.

"Promise me, Cecilia Charity Lance, the Lady Gantry, that you will raise him with honor." My sister's eyes were open, burning, intense.

Like when we were little, I'd recite a story to keep her company until she slept. "Let me tell you about snow, Helena. It's freezing. Britain has bone-chattering cold and infernal white ice that children love to throw. How does God do that, make the rain form frozen stars? You know that people actually lie in it and wiggle and call it an angel."

"Our older sister, she would say it was Agassou's doing. Papa put away those ideas of Mama's gods when she passed. He took us to chapel every chance he got. He talked a lot about forgiveness. Remember forgiveness?"

Weaving my fingers with hers, I pulled our hands to my lap. "You get on that boat with me, Helena, I'll do what you say. I'll forgive the world."

"I'll be with you always. My Chari. Forgiveness. Your name is love, Charity. Forgiveness, it is merely another form."

My sister shuddered, then went very still.

I held Noah in my arms and began to pray to everyone—Agassou, Jove, even the church deacon Quamina, and the smugglers who helped us escape.

My sister needed healing, and I didn't care who did it.

Chapter 18

Cecilia—Escape for Freedom

The morning light filtered to me, warming the wood of the dray. I traced the outline of the purple blooms of the jacaranda above me. Pity that when they fell and were trampled, they smelled like horses' leavings.

Didn't matter.

Felton said I was so pretty the day of our wedding with my hair braided with twigs of lavender in the tightest crown. When we left on the schooner, I thought the world was ahead of us. Just didn't know we'd keep going on separate adventures.

"Little Noah, I'm going to take you on a ship across the sea. I'm going to love you and make you great."

Those words fell easily, but then doubt crowded in. I hadn't exactly been a good stepmother. I'd been a friend to Agatha and Amelia. What would make me a good mother?

Noah began to cry. His gums started to suckle.

"Oh, please. I take it back, whatever I said wrong."

Quamina, the enslaved man who helped us flee the Elizabeth Ann Plantation, came out of the bushes. He wore a white tunic and pants, looking like a holy shepherd.

Well, he was a deacon for the Anglican missionaries now coming to Demerara.

He clasped the side of the dray. "Lady Gantry, the boat's in the harbor. Your friends are waiting. My sister Enna is there now. She'll go with you. She'll be a wet nurse. She lost her babe. This will be healing for her."

The man had made preparations, and I was thankful. Noah wouldn't survive without mother's milk.

Quamina cast his eyes to my silent sister.

No words had to be said, and I couldn't say Helena would never awaken. She'd fed Noah one last time before drifting to permanent sleep.

He made the sign of the cross over the shawl covering her face, then climbed into the driver's seat. "You take your fancy papers and go. Don't return."

Picking up the reins, he headed the dray down the reddish-brown dirt road.

"You'll never be safe in the colony, Lady Gantry. Papers or not, someone who liberates a runaway slave will be hunted."

"What of you? Surely you should come."

"Lady Gantry, I'm helping the priests bring liberty here. Can't stop now."

"Then pray for me. Jeremiah Gladstone did this. I want him to pay."

"The Gladstones are absentee planters who make money from enslavement, then pretend they do not to know it's blood money. Their young men come here to do things away from the eyes of their mamas."

I fingered Papa's knife in my pocket. He meant it for protection, but I wanted to deliver vengeance. Tramel was right. "Gladstone killed my sister. He needs to die."

"Woman, find forgiveness. You can't beat the Brits at the game they've made."

The shawl I'd pulled over her slipped. She looked peaceful, like she slept.

"Mrs. Helena was the kindest of souls, ma'am. The planters know how to hurt our women. When I was a boy, they made me choose our girls for their parties. Helping you and her is redemption."

The holy deacon couldn't be guilty of things he was forced to do as a child in service of a horrid system. The paperwork she kept with her was as a marriage contract with my father's signature. Gladstone's too but he sold my sister like she was nothing. She was born free. He had no right.

If I had left Felton earlier, Helena wouldn't have been ruined by Gladstone. While our father lived, he protected us, all three daughters. When he passed, I should've been here to keep Helena safe.

Quamina pinned his gaze forward to the road. "We go." Once I'd climbed aboard the dray, he started it up a hill. The rising sun showed thatched roofs of huts on provision grounds of the plantations, a distant wooden church, then fancier houses. Demerara was a dichotomy of resources and wealth for some, and lack for so many.

I'd said goodbye to the colony before. I'd kissed the reddish-brown beach sand and waved at the evergreen palms. Silly me, a jacaranda's purple bloom had fallen on my head. The stinky scent made Felton and I laugh. How could something so pretty smell so bad?

Watching my nephew stir, I rocked him in my arms. "He needs to feed. Can't lose him, too."

"My Enna," Quamina said, "she'll do it. When you get to London, you free my sister."

"She's free now, soon as we are away from Demerara. And she'll be my sister now, part of my new family."

Everyone was safe from slavers once they stepped on English soil. That's why I had wanted to get Helena there. That would fix her and Noah's status.

Killing Gladstone would fix everything else.

Looking up, I saw Quamina's deep brown face filling with a frown. The smart man saw the anger building in me.

Felton said he could see all my emotions in my reddening cheeks.

Guess that wasn't a lie.

"You will keep going, Lady Gantry? Helena and Enna will be found missing from the Elizabeth Ann Plantation as soon as morning chores are called."

"Yes, Quamina. I promise."

The dray edged closer to the beach.

Silence, except for tiger herons' throaty chirps, made my pulse race. I kept looking for a torch or dogs chasing us, or a hungry jaguarete.

The dray hit a bump.

The babe in my arms jostled. His pink puckered lips pursed to cry.

Yet, no sound.

Noah was too weak. He needed milk.

"The sea. I see the boat. Almost there," Quamina said, whispering, as if he'd prayed.

Sunlight bounced and shimmered upon the water, the brown and white foam, I wanted to shout and clap my hands when I caught a glimpse of the smugglers boat in the distance.

Soon the trees fell away. The blinding sunrise filled my eyes.

I smelled the salt of the water, maybe a cooking crab.

Forgot how hungry I was.

"This canoe will take you out to the open waters," Quamina pointed to a sleek thing honed from a gommier tree.

"Helena, we made it. We . . ."

Forgot.

My sweet sister wasn't ever to answer. I touched her face again. The warmth hadn't yet left her.

So many regrets raged.

If I'd found her sooner.

If I hadn't gone to England without her.

If Gladstone had been a decent man.

Her death was his sin. He had to pay.

Quamina took Noah from me. "Hurry, Lady Gantry. Gladstones' managers still might catch you. They know there's a child. That's more property. Get to the big boat and don't turn back."

The smugglers. They'd get us past the blockade back to Jamaica and beyond.

I put my short leather boots on Demeraran soil. If there was more time, I'd pinch some and put it in my pocket.

No coming back to this place, ever.

All my people, the ones that mattered, were all lost to me and this babe. Then I thought about all the faces who were still enslaved that I had to leave behind. I swallowed bitterness.

"Get in the boat. Enna's waiting. She will give this little one her strength. Maybe you too. Leaving is hope."

A young woman with a deeply tanned face sat near the boat. Her hair was wrapped in black mud cloth. It was as good as black British bombazine.

"Follow the currents. Get to the big boat."

"We'll stop in Jamaica. From there, it's forty days and forty nights to Portsmouth."

Noah started crying. I rocked him faster. He hungered but I stalled. "My sister . . ."

Quamina tugged me forward. "Go. I'll bury Helena in the church field. Reverend Wray will understand."

The Anglican missionary? Didn't want to think of all these faiths in Demerara, not when mine faltered.

"Go with God," Quamina said.

No. I went with fire in my belly and heart.

I set the crying Noah on a blanket in the boat.

Enna said something in Dutch, then made motions with her hand, pointing to the sea.

"Yes. Together."

We pushed the boat until it floated.

Feet wetting the hems of our dresses, we climbed in, then she fed my hungry nephew.

I paddled and looked back at the purple blooms. Should've gotten a petal or two to press and keep forever. The bad smell had to go away eventually. Everything bad had to.

This boy would be free in Portsmouth. I wouldn't be, not when I wanted Gladstone dead.

He killed my sister.

He needed to die.

Chapter 19

Felton—Back to the Future

October 20, 1814

Two days had passed since Felton stood with the Duchess of Repington, both of them admiring Cecilia's painting.

Standing in the vestibule of the King's Theatre in the Haymarket part of London, he wanted to go to Her Grace and confess that his wife was her sister and that he needed that painting almost as much as he needed Cecilia.

It had been ten months since he last saw his wife. Ten months since she was in his arms. Ten months since he'd accused her of the unthinkable and she left him.

His heart hadn't changed, hadn't moved an inch. He was desperately in love with his wife. Hope was restored after seeing her new art. He shifted his stance and checked his pocket watch. Lord Liverpool was late.

The man promised help if he'd return to service. Felton was desperate and almost willing to go return to the Department of War and the Colonies.

Yet, he wouldn't.

Agatha and Amelia loved that he didn't journey anymore. His smaller household with just Watson and minimal staff proved to be more peaceful.

Tramel seemed more peaceful too. He'd offered again to get Felton's marriage annulled. Before seeing the painting, the idea had begun to take hold. It was very hard to stay in passionate love with someone when they'd made it obvious that they were done with you.

Then he saw Port Royal.

If he could have one last chance at loving Cilia the right way, he'd stay a monk until he won her back.

Pulling out his watch, he saw the hands had barely moved. Liverpool was never late.

Jeremiah Gladstone came toward him. The fool's conversation would be abominable. Felton tugged at his collar. He'd endure it waiting for his old employer.

The crowded vestibule would begin to feel hotter. As soon as he talked with Liverpool, he'd beg off this night at the theatre.

The hope that Cecilia was living in Covent Garden, where Lord Ashbrook bought the painting, made his heart beat faster. He'd searched the area twice, once in December when his wife first disappeared, then again in January with Repington.

Forget Liverpool.

This third time was charmed. Out the corner of his eye, Felton saw his heart, his runaway wife.

Chapter 20

Cecilia—Reunited Not Quite

The noise of the crowded vestibule of the King's Theatre normally would make my head hurt. The echo in my skull, of conversations and laughs and greetings, made me dizzy.

Nonetheless, I had something else to obsess upon: the strange sight of my estranged husband standing next to the man I wanted to kill.

Ten months had passed since I last saw Felton, when I stormed away from his Mayfair house.

We now stood in the same place and I wanted to cry.

He'd half turned. His back was to me. He must not have seen me.

I filled my lungs.

When I returned from Demerara, I didn't think I'd have to hide anymore. I was sure some mission or some woman, or both, would keep our paths from crossing.

Didn't Felton hate the theatre?

Maybe he just liked dressing for the theatre. Men wore white gloves. They covered the spots on the backs of his hands.

Tall and thin, thinner than I remembered, he chatted and laughed with his evil cousin.

He didn't like art. Why was he here?

Had he discovered me? Only Tramel knew where I was.

Stiff, still looking like a Roman soldier on patrol, he shifted his stance, his head turning to the entrance doors of the theatre. He had to be looking for me.

Was there an easy way to escape?

He chuckled again with Gladstone.

What could my enemy and my husband think funny?

Was he chuckling about his betrayal of Helena? Or maybe it was a cruel joke to make fun of my *foreignness*?

Yet, Felton, he'd never laugh about that. I don't know why they'd be together. Tramel said since the new year my husband kept away from family gatherings. I wished father and son would reconcile. That was another reason to stay away from all of them. I wouldn't be the thing that deepened the hate between them.

My stomach rumbled.

It was nerves . . . or the remembrance of the cheese and marmalade Felton fed me when we made up. My stomach needed to forget our old patterns.

I'd come for my money. That was all I was here for, and the size of the crowd meant the manager couldn't deny me.

One easy step then another, I moved backward, inching my way deeper into the crowd. My estranged husband seemed preoccupied and kept looking toward the entry.

Well-dressed in his formal black and white, he must be meeting a lover. Why else would the casual man be in a place he thought frivolous?

Probably one of his sister's smug friends who took every moment to point out my shortcomings. Actually, no, that was Lady Jane.

Only my father-in-law, the dear duke, stood up for me. I missed him. I hated giving up my only friend.

A woman in white, in a snowy cape with a gown of angel lace, stopped in front of Felton.

A knot tightened in my gut, but it eased when another man came. A short, balding fellow claimed her hand.

It was ridiculous to be jealous, when I had walked out of his life. I had to accept that someone would take my place, someone would share his bed and enjoy all his lovely heat.

Why shouldn't my jaguarete garner favor?

He'd used my dowry to grow his investments to make himself wealthy. His temperament was kind, his manners unassuming. What Englishwoman wouldn't want him?

My thoughts became bitter, but I had to remind myself I left. I chose to not contact him, to hide.

Dark hair secured with an onyx ribbon at his neck, Felton fidgeted, still looking at the door. If not a lover, what mission of his friends would bring him here?

Jeremiah Gladstone, evil Gladstone, made the circle of men laugh. If I ran fast and made it past Felton, I could take Papa's knife and strike.

My eyes stung.

Gladstone killed my sister. He needed to die.

Fingers tightening on the handle, I wanted to stalk the fiend like a jaguarete.

But Felton wasn't Tramel. He'd not let me injure *his* family. Mine was expendable.

The doors parted for the audience seating. Gladstone went inside. He'd enjoy the canvases, my landscape that extended two stories high, I'd painted for the scenery—Shakespeare's Padua along the Italian river. The money I earned would pay rent and allow me to buy provisions for his son.

This success was something an artist from Demerara should savor.

I released my fingers from curling about Papa's knife. Wouldn't even be able to collect my outstanding payment if I stormed to Gladstone and made him bleed out.

When I sought revenge, I had to make sure I couldn't get caught. Noah and Enna needed me.

Putting my knife deeper into my coat, I moved to the box office, but took a last gape at Felton. In the middle of the night, I still craved his heat like that stinky cheese.

The theatre manager came down the stairs. He waved at me and opened the door to the small closet-like room where tickets were sold.

My money must be ready. I could at least gather that.

Still, I hesitated. The way I gawked at Felton, it was obvious to my lying soul that I hadn't completely stopped caring for him.

Cecilia, get your money. Then buy your own cheese.

Head down, hood drawn tight about me, I ignored everything and made my legs move.

In a way, he'd be proud of the new, pragmatic, money-first me.

The theatre office was very small. I purposely left the door open. I'd grown to hate anything that felt tight, and my trusting of British men was small.

"Ah, Mrs. Cecilia. I told you I'd have your money in full tonight. It's a packed crowd. I thought Miss Enna would be coming for the money."

Why, so you could cheat her? "I had an appointment tonight nearby. I decided to come in her stead."

"You're looking at another theatre production?"

I was, but I couldn't say that and expect to get all my money.

Mr. Downes took out his purse and counted out twenty pounds and two shillings. "Here is your fee."

He slid the money close to my gloved hands but kept his fat thumb on the big silver pieces. "When do you think you will be able to do another?"

"I'm not sure, sir."

"You can bring the sprat, anyone you want. I won't make a fuss this time. Your artistry is worth every inconvenience. All are raving of your scenery. I suspect the ton will come for it as much as to see *The Taming of the Shrew*."

That was supposed to be a compliment? The big man rarely gave them. I nodded and slipped the money in my pocket. "I'll think about it."

I turned to leave, but the exit was blocked.

My husband was here for me after all.

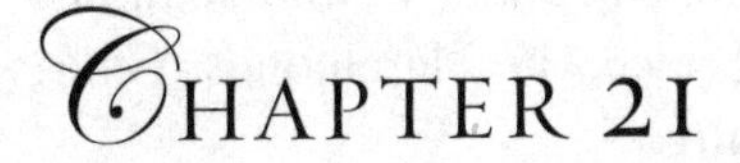

Felton—Where Have You Been?

Wound so tight he thought his veins would bust, Felton stormed into the theatre office. His wife, missing for too long now, stood a few feet away.

Her eyes were wide.

Her breath, like his, came in spurts.

The manager, an odd duck named Downes, stood up behind his desk. The oily fellow with messy hair leaned over his stomach and desk, scowling. "No one is allowed back here."

Felton wanted to hit the man. Instead, he picked a coin out of his pocket and slammed it on the table. "I need a word alone with this young woman."

The man picked up the gold piece and bit it. "Part of your entourage, Mrs. Cecilia? For a widow so absorbed in art, you have a lot of company."

The woman he'd been hunting, fretting over, half closed her eyes and clasped her elbows. "Can you allow us a moment, sir? It's less noisy in here. I need to concentrate on what he'll say."

"Your next appointment, aye? Fine." Downes pointed at Felton. "Remember my kindness. No permanently stealing my set designer. This woman is amazing if she'll fit into your schedule."

Felton grunted and put his arm on the door. "Yes, I know the difficulties of gaining any time with the *widow*."

The man looked at Cecilia, then left.

With a swing of his palm, Felton slammed the door. "You're Cecilia Charity Lance, the Marchioness Gantry. And I, your husband, am quite alive."

Her brilliant agate eyes with bits of green and topaz bloomed wide like a trapped kitten's.

Then he realized he must be frightening her. He didn't want that. He was no ogre, just a frustrated man in love with a woman he didn't understand. Lowering his hands to his sides, he tried to hold in all he felt. "Can't believe I've stumbled upon you. I came to meet Liverpool."

"Oh, you're a spy again?" She choked and patted her chest.

Felton moved closer. "Are you ill? Do I need to get a doctor?"

She coughed and sucked in a quick breath. "No. I'm not ill, but you . . . you look well, Lord Gantry."

Her tone was stiff and formal. She'd perfected diminishing her wondrous accent.

He rubbed at his neck. He'd dreamed of this moment so many times, but now words failed, all tied to his tongue with strains of anger and longing.

Swallowing it all he focused on the fact that she was in front of him. "You look more than well, Cecilia. You're beautiful as always."

Her palms slapped her hips, which made her coat highlight her fuller figure, the thick thighs and small waist he missed.

Her golden cheeks blazed. Her emotions always set her skin on fire, bursting with color. "Thank you, my lord."

Overcome by it all, a flurry of memories, their happier times, he folded his arms behind his back to keep from reaching for her.

Felton didn't trust if he'd merely embrace her or shake sense into her vivacious limbs. "Where have you been?"

"Art took me away. Mr. Downes is quite happy with my work." She jiggled the coins in her palm. "Wasn't a waste of time and no one complains if it's the proper occupation for a peer's wife."

That sounded like something Jane would say. "I should've stepped in and said something to my sister." He moved closer. "I do apologize for that. It doesn't reflect my sentiments at all, now that I know how good you are."

"So, my passion must have a qualifier to be indulged by the Lance siblings."

"I don't know, I'd have to check with my older sisters; all of them including Jane are away. Why didn't you tell me about your art? Why did you make it a secret for just you and the girls?"

"And Tramel." She started to chuckle—her nervous laugh—then bit down on her lip. "They still dream, Felton. They don't need a lot of words to believe."

Felton clasped his neck. "I want to believe now. I do believe. I had months to study your canvases. I can see them all in my head."

"You too?" Cecilia looked to the door then back to him.

"Are you wondering if I'll let you leave? I didn't stop you before, why would I stop you now?"

She drew deeper into her coat, the coat he'd bought her for her first English winter. A little worn on the elbows, she still looked like a choice blueberry.

This wasn't at all how his dreams of reuniting went. Someone would say sorry. Then the other. Then they'd pick right back up with the loving. He could taste her—her kisses, the edges of her fingers, that spot on her neck.

He tugged at his waistcoat and decided to confess . . . mostly confess. "Nothing in my heart has changed. I still want you . . . in my life. I'm still miserable without you."

"I'm sorry to be the cause of your pain, my lord. I must be going."

She brushed his sleeve, trying to rush past.

And he reacted and swept her against him. "I'm flesh and blood, not stone. I've struggled to keep myself sane with the hopes of finding you. That you were alive and well. I've missed you so."

His arms wrapped about her middle and she eased into that spot on his chest against his breastbone like she'd never left.

Her hand lowered to his. Her palm rested on his wrist, fingering his cuff and sleeve buttons.

Her posture, her spine, her will slackened to him. Her head tipped against his arm.

Quiet, except for their breathing, he held her, and she let him.

"I have another appointment, my lord. I must be going." Her voice was airy.

Everything he felt, the energy surging between them—all remained. "How did I let my dream fly away?"

"My lord—"

Turning her, he kissed her before he said anything else wrong.

Delicious and true, warm with that taste of mango and sea. God, he missed her, missed this.

For a moment, a single slip of time, she kissed him back. Then heaven ended abruptly when she pushed away.

"This is the part, Cecilia, where we forgive each other."

"Do you know what it is that I want, Felton? Have you used these ten months to figure that out? For I know, I have always known what it is, and I have it now."

Reconciliation was within his reach if he convinced her he'd changed. "An apology? An apology for everything. I'm sorry."

She fingered her reddened lip. "What is it you're sorry for?"

"For not respecting your art. For believing gossip."

"Those are nice things, but not what I need, Felton."

"Whatever you wish, I'll give it."

Cecilia shook her head. "Anything? No. Not anything. Everything has conditions. Good evening, sir."

"No. Wait. May I answer tomorrow?"

"That's a condition, my lord." Her chest rose and fell quickly. Her heartbeat had to be as heavy as his. Passion was never the problem.

It only hid them.

"My lord, I don't think it wise we continue this conversation. We've seen each other, and now if you do visit the theatre again and I see you, it won't be so awkward."

"If I'd never let go of you, if I'd chased you through the threshold immediately, even tossed you over my shoulder and carried you away, we'd still be together, Cecilia. We'd be happy this time."

"I realized, Felton, that I'm happier now, apart from you. I have a life, a peaceful one without frets or concerns. No more wondering when and if you'll be back or how things will be if you're around."

"Cecilia, you've taught me what that feels like. The separation. The anxiety. The worry. I have those concerns now too."

"Then you will know this talk is senseless. I must go. Excuse me."

"No." Cecilia needed some proof of his love, something beyond words and affection. What? He didn't know.

By Jove, how he wished he understood her. "Please, don't go. Give me another chance to answer. You deserve that. We deserve it. Tomorrow? Next week?"

She moved closer to the door. "Don't tell the girls you saw me. They won't understand why I haven't returned."

"Cecilia, I don't understand. I know you're recently returned to London. Were you in Scotland trying to divorce? When did you come up with this fake-widow scheme?"

His voice regrettably had an edge, but it was impossible to be without emotion about the woman he loved.

She winced like he'd cursed at her. He'd never done that, never would, but he couldn't be silent and accept her leaving. Cecilia married a man, not a mouse.

"Don't go through that door, Cecilia. At a door, an entryway, in Stabroek, we decided to be together. Here, you can decide again. Don't you believe I missed you?"

Palm on the threshold, she stopped and faced him. So pretty, so angry. "You want me. That's not a reason to stay."

He hooked his hands together to keep from grabbing the dream that almost slipped away. "Cecilia, my Cilia, give me one more chance to guess what it is you need."

"You don't guess about a soul you're meant to keep. You just know. That's when it's meant to be."

Smoothing her purple coat, she curtsied. "Enjoy the theatre, my lord." And walked out of his life again.

CHAPTER 22

CECILIA—MY LITTLE BOY

As soon as I was out of the theatre, I ran like Demeraran planters chased me. My heart raced and I looked for dogs.

No dogs. No chase. Just more noise of people milling in the streets.

I was in danger, danger of falling into that old rhythm, of letting my heart be fooled by sad, hungry eyes and a searing kiss. I couldn't be that young girl that married for adventure anymore. Life and death had matured me, and I had my new family, Enna and Noah.

By the time I reached Charles Street, I fumed at myself. Why did I let Felton kiss me?

This hunger for him, all these irrational feelings should be gone.

They weren't.

His kiss was like it had always been, full and all consuming. In that moment, I was safe and treasured, and beautiful—the woman he desired.

But moments never lasted.

He needed a shiny trinket, a woman like his sister. Someone who'd make menus and entertain his friends, while being frugal and unassuming in all aspects but the marriage bed.

That was not me.

It wasn't who I aspired to become.

I stopped and looked back. Felton was nowhere to be seen. This route might've worked if I'd killed Gladstone. Surely, I could hide in the crowds filling the area.

Link boys held torches and guided carriages to the nearby mews. The area would be packed. I needed to hurry and leave the streets.

Sleep would be hard when I finally crawled onto the sofa.

Helena had asked me who I saw when I closed my eyes. It changed nightly. I often saw her or Demerara and jaguaretes. Sometimes I saw a hero or nothingness.

Tonight, it might be Felton.

Yet, the fear that it wouldn't be also hurt. It ramped up my guilt. It was very clear Felton was pained at our break.

How did you make your heart stop feeling so much for a man who was wrong for you?

I slowed my footfalls and made it up the back stairs to the place I rented.

Knocking four times was our code, with a pause before the last. The way the door rattled open trembled through me.

Enna let me in and inspected my hands. "You didn't do it. You didn't kill anyone."

"Course not." Not today.

She hugged me and drew me into our room. Her thick accent sounded like Mama's voice and reminded me of her little hums she sang around the fire, roasting pheasants.

My stomach purred.

"Mrs. Chari. You no . . . you not cheated."

Her English had improved greatly. I was proud of that. "He paid in full. Mr. Downes was pleased. He'll hire me again."

Enna nodded as she took my coat. "Very good. Your *weldoener* said Downes would be good."

Weldoener? My benefactor? No. Tramel wasn't that.

Looking away from the window to the vases Enna used for fresh flowers, ugly mud-brown vases she'd bought for a penny in Covent Garden, I sighed. Here, deep in the city, they'd never hold anything wild, but day-old fare bought on the cheap.

I took my pretty purple coat from her fingers and laid it over a chair, squaring the seams like Felton taught me. "Lord Tramel has been helpful, but I think I can get commissions now on my own."

Enna went to the crib and retrieved a yawning Noah. His blue-black eyes were a match for the Lance family, but he had Helena's skin, dark gold and soft.

"You sit. Then I give 'im a bath." She made faces at the little boy.

It still didn't feel quite natural holding this little person who'd just learned to keep his head up.

"When do you think he'll start to talk? Then he could tell me what he wants. That seems a problem for boys and men."

She looked at me the way Enna always did when I said something stupid or she couldn't quite translate. She put the babe in my arms. "Women know not what they want too, Mrs. Chari. Even when it's clear."

Her words shook me. Then Noah cried until his little hand snatched my nose. Did he know I wanted to kill his father tonight?

Enna came and steadied my hands, shifting the babe to a more comfortable position, tucking Noah fully into my arms.

He looked content, cooing, with his lovely eyes following my finger. But sometimes I didn't feel very maternal.

"Your *weldoener* sent another package." She took a pot of water and heated it. "It's on the sofa."

Though it was probably brushes or French cheese, I couldn't look at the parcel. The dear duke had already given too much. If I encouraged his attentions, he would deliver what I desired: revenge. Gladstone's death. I couldn't ask that of him and be more indebted.

"Noah, what are we going to do?" My whisper made him blow spittle.

The bubbles were pretty with translucent rainbows caused by the candlelight. Unless one thought about how fragile the surfaces, how easy they were to pop, you'd think them safe.

I had a feeling with so many Lance men bumping about the theatre district, the protective bubble I bound about my family would soon be pierced.

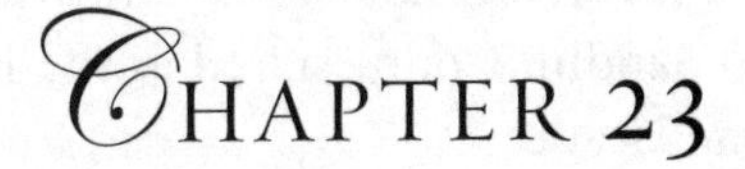

CHAPTER 23

FELTON—CONFESSION AND COCONUTS

It was a universal truth that if a wife wished to be a widow, her living husband had cheated her of the one thing that would bring her peace.

His daughters' laughter rang loud in the hall of Sandlin Court. They made no attempt to hide the joy they found visiting the Duke and Duchess of Repington. They learned everything from battlefield engagement to cannon maintenance to how to bribe a man with coconut bread—properly cooked coconut bread.

Felton did miss the overly browned caramelized bits, but he'd never say it. You don't touch another man's bread. The duke loved his just as Her Grace made it.

Patience Thomas Strathmore was Felton's sister-in-law. He wondered if she had instructions for wayward wives as much as she did for widows of her secret society, the Widow's Grace?

Cecilia, gone ten months and then two days ago she was in his embrace returning his kiss.

Warm. Vibrant. And he had to let go, again.

More singing from the hall.

A deep baritone echoed. The duke's voice was distinctive and blended with Her Grace's low harmony. Her friend Lady Ashbrook's high-pitched voice joined. Yet nothing covered Amelia's nasally mid-level tones or Agatha's loud alto.

Felton should laugh; he wanted a home like this, one filled with laughter and love. Yet, he sat and did what he always did when he came to Sandlin Court: stared at the landscape of Port Royal, Cecilia's landscape.

Months.

Months since they'd talked, since they'd last given in to the love that bound them.

How could it still be so strong after all the time wasted, all the places searched, all the moments he pretended she didn't exist, all the nights his dreams of her were so vivid?

He was nutters.

Totally mad to be unequivocally in love with Cecilia still.

The duke entered the parlor, his Pott's limb made only little clicks when he moved his injured leg. "Staring at that painting again." He shook his head. "After a successful cleaning of my battle cannon, Lionel is napping. He now says Papa and Wellington. I take such pride in that boy. Oh, the women are heading to the porch to sketch."

The duke came farther inside. His gait was slow and careful as he pushed on his cane and eased into a chair. Maybe his war injuries were hurting him today.

"Refreshment, Gantry? I'll have Mr. Gerard bring us some."

The weight of the world felt pinned to Felton's shoulders. He shrugged. "Pride cometh before the fall, Your Grace. That's how the saying goes, but no one says how it feels to fall or how much it hurts to be a fool."

"Oh. Oh." The duke squinted at him. "You're in a mood, Gantry. Can my old lieutenant use his expert marksmanship to shoot through the excuses and say what's wrong?"

"Haven't touched a gun since your drills in the countryside. Before that, not since my last mission for the Department of War and the Colonies. Maybe that's what I need, to go shooting. You have anything I can aim at, like between its eyes?"

The duke waved him to the sofa. "You're suffering, and you haven't said why. And we are in my wife's parlor again, not my office—that's another unanswered question."

Felton shifted but didn't move. "The painting's in here. Can't come to Sandlin and not see it."

The duke took his time, stood erect, then walked to the masterpiece. "It is a fine piece. The bright colors. But I don't understand your fascination with it, or my wife's."

This brought a chuckle to Felton. "You honestly haven't figured this out. Do you need the Widow's Grace to bring you clues?"

"The meddlesome Lady Shrewsbury and her women's group have left my duchess alone for now. So don't mention them, or my darling bride might revert to breeches and sneaking about even with her pregnancy in full bloom."

"Then she definitely won't want to hear what I have to say."

Deeply frowning, his friend offered Felton a sour Lionel-like look when the babe was given pap milk. "Duke, you can't be so thick as to press and make me say the truth aloud. No, make me say."

Repington tapped the arm of his chair, his nails galloping fast like a horse. "We'll be heading back to Hamlin Hall at month's end, and I will walk into the house."

"Ask me. I'm dying to tell."

The duke ignored him again and waved his hands and hummed. "Going to the country home to nest. Lionel and I will begin walking practice. I'll have to rest up so I can show the eleven-month-old what to do."

The duke had backed up the conversation so far, his words might fall off the continent. Yet, Felton couldn't contain his secrets any longer. He sat up, stared the man in his eyes. "Walking practice? At least your stepson is old enough for your schedule now. Repington, how do you continue to have the best luck? Your wife, your poor wife, Patience Amelia Thomas Strathmore, puts up with such stubborn foolishness. I wish mine did. How can sisters be so different?"

The duke's spry cheeks lost all color. It took him at least a minute before any signs of life made him stir. "How long have you known? And this is the soonest you would say?"

"Since you had me investigate Her Grace, daughter of Wilhelm Thomas."

"That was months and months ago, I had you do that to find her family. You said nothing?" The duke banged his cane. "Mr. Gerard? I know you're around. Rum and brandy, please. As much as you can carry."

The man with wild gray hair peeked inside. His dark cheeks huffed. "Now, Your Grace, are you sure? Old Jove been sending you blessings, keeping that back nice and tight so you can pace like every other man when his babe's due to arrive."

"We have time, and I'll proudly whip my wheeled chair in the traditional position, rolling back forth outside her door until the doctor says all is well. Please bring the bottles now, especially the brandy for Lord Gantry."

The butler dashed off and soon brought a tray of sweet coconut bread and the amber bottles the duke hid in his study. There was really no need for the secrecy. The duchess indulged him. Again, how could the duke be a fool and the luckiest of all men?

The door closed behind the butler.

"Let me understand this," the duke said after clearing his mouth of the chunk of coconut bread. "Your wife, the woman you married three years ago. The one who left you in December, is my wife's sister."

Felton plucked at a toasted corner of the bread. The sugary textured crisps and caramelized bits made the edges a chewy heaven. "Repeating any of this does not change the facts."

"I need a full confession. You upset your wife, allegedly my sister-in-law, so badly she left. What happened?"

The man fidgeted like he searched for a sidearm, and Felton didn't know if that was a worthy punishment for a fool loving and losing an estranged wife.

CHAPTER 24

FELTON—FRIENDLY FOOLISH ADVICE

Brushing the crumbs from his fingers, Felton prepared to voice his faults. "I was stupid. I overreacted. My cousin was bleeding. I thought she stabbed him."

"What?" The duke began tugging at the top of the rum flask like he would drink straight from the bottle. "My sister-in-law attacked someone."

Waving his hands, Felton started again. "Forget about that part. Gladstone said something that made me think Cecilia was unfaithful. She wasn't. She left before I could apologize. It's the old duke's fault for baiting me, but the actions are mine. I did this. I made Lady Gantry think she'd lost my trust."

Repington poured a third of a glass of his treasured rum. The droplets of amber shimmered in the candlelight, much like Cecilia's wondrous eyes. It merely needed to reflect the bits of greens and red-brown in the center.

"You thought Lady Gantry was unfaithful with Gladstone?"

"Worse, Repington. With my father."

The duke took a sip, then another sip, until he kissed an empty glass. "Your father, the man who has made your life difficult, the man who's cheated people of their land and property, the scoundrel with, let's say, rigid views on race—"

"Prejudice. The word is prejudice, Your Grace."

"How could you let anything this cousin say make you think my sister-in-law would cheat with the Duke of Tramel, this prejudiced duke?"

Felton looked at the large bottle of brandy which called him to drown all his sorrows, but he abstained. "Tramel. Ah . . . he liked Cecilia. He's in love with her."

The duke's gaze narrowed. "We're talking about your father. He liked your foreign . . . Blackamoor wife?"

"One could swear it was love. Their first meeting was awkward. Then he saw her paint. After that, they got on quite well. They spent lots of time together, even more when we had difficulties and when I went on missions for the Department of War and the Colonies."

"What are you saying, Gantry? Did you suspect something between them?"

"Yes. No. I know Cecilia was faithful to me now, but then. I . . . I was a jealous fool. I figured out too late that my father used her as another pawn to torment me. Cecilia and I were both pawns. I'm such a fool."

The duke loosened his cravat, then slouched in his chair. "Do you know where she is? Patience has nightmares. She often talks in her sleep about her two sisters. That painting she said looked like her sister's work, but it had been years since she last saw Miss Thomas's art. She wasn't sure."

"Covent Garden is where Cecilia is now. I've had some surveillance done. Yesterday, she was hired to do another theatre commission. Lady Gantry is pretending to be a widow."

The tapping of the duke's cane on the floor became more apparent. Felton's friend was a man of action, not one to sit around miserably staring at oil paintings.

Felton lifted his hand to Repington. "You must calm yourself before you do make your back go out. Your duchess is growing heavier with your babe. Be at ease, ready to be of comfort, not laid up in bed."

The cane stopped jittering. "So, what's the plan? How do we win your wife back?"

"We?"

"I'm woefully underutilized by the strategists at Whitehall. The women have the Widow's Grace, but since you live, that sort of disqualifies Lady Gantry from seeking their help. That leaves you and me. Don't you think there should be a countering group for men?"

"Always looking for a new battle, aye, Repington?"

"Maybe it takes a war to show the depths we'll go to protect what we love."

His words seemed to be more wisdom than bluster, but Felton didn't know what to do or how to answer Cecilia's question: What was it that she wanted most of all? He sighed and rubbed at pockmarks on his wrist. "Tell me how to regain the love of a woman who doesn't believe in me, and it's my fault?"

Skin all aglow, the Duchess of Repington waddled inside. For a brief moment, Felton saw Cecilia in Her Grace's stance; the poise, the music in her motion. If he and Cecilia had stayed together, would their family also be increasing?

Her Grace whispered something to the duke that brought a grin to his face. His palm absently brushed her stomach.

His eyes grew wide. "A kick. A strong one. Fantastic."

If Felton weren't brooding on the sofa, those two would delight in their privacy and probably sing to each other.

It was nauseatingly joyful.

Why, Jove? Why?

How did the duke, a cantankerous, obstinate fellow get so lucky and marry the more compliant, logical sister of the Thomas brood? And did Felton's good works—to help the households of his comrades in arms, and his service to his country—mean anything?

Felton had to look away from them. The likenesses of the

sisters about the nose, wide and pert at the peak, made him remember navigating kisses when his broad bridge nuzzled Cecilia's jaw.

He centered his gaze on the ironic scene of Port Royal, Jamaica—colorful and bustling with shadows of people. He'd told her of the lore on their wedding trip. Cecilia's vision of the city the day before an earthquake and a tidal wave destroyed it like Sodom and Gomorrah.

Yet, this mirrored December. One minute everything was perfect, the next broken to bits.

"Don't suppose Your Graces would consider another offer to buy the painting?"

Sadness settled into the duchess's eyes. "You love it that much? Every time you come to Sandlin, I find you staring at it. Does it remind you of something or someone, Lord Gantry? It's that way to me."

The duke lowered his head but exposed nothing. Felton wouldn't cause this pregnant woman any strain fretting about a sister who didn't want to be found.

"Lord Gantry," she repeated, "who?"

"Yes, Your Grace. Reminds me of a moment with my wife."

She smoothed the front of the bright orange madras of her tunic. With a nod to the duke, the duchess said, "It's a gift for you, for being such a good friend to my husband."

A good friend to everyone but Cecilia.

How did one recover from that? "Are you sure?"

"Yes. Take it with our blessings."

A little overcome, Felton wiped at his mouth. "Thank you. Thank you, ma'am."

Almost running, he stepped to the painting and gently lifted it from the wall. If he embraced the thing, the duchess would know something was afoot. "Thank you again, Your Graces."

The duchess put her hand on his arm. "Are you ready to go on with your life? A woman gone this long doesn't sound like she'll be coming back."

That had to be wrong.

Everything in him said it was wrong. Two days ago, Cecilia melted into his chest. Her resolve to stay away weakened for a moment. He only needed another minute of her time to convince her their love had a chance. Months and months of Hades had to be exchanged for hope. "What's your advice on winning, Your Grace?"

"Tactics will help." The duke eyed him with an authoritarian gaze, straightforward, not blinking or smiling. "Such as, agree to anything even if you disagree."

With his arm starting to rise in salute, Felton stood up straight. "Yes, Commander, you think it—"

"Two, do what it takes to maintain contact. Keep the target always in view."

"What are you talking about, Your Grace?" The duchess folded her arms.

"Nothing much but ways to win a war, a long war with many battles." The duke stretched his hand to hers.

When she grasped it, he again turned to Felton. "I repeat. Two, do what it takes to maintain contact. Push for contact. Be in the target's sphere."

The duke was talking about Felton's missing-not-missing wife. As much as he wanted to be with Cecilia, how could they be together if the woman kept running?

"Three, don't complicate things for any reason. Make peace with Tramel. He might be helpful. And remember, surrender is sweeter, but only if you've won."

Felton rubbed at his neck. Peace with Tramel. Impossible.

The duchess squinted. "Your Grace, are you telling him how to pursue his missing wife or a new one? You're going to get him in trouble."

"No trouble, my dear," the duke said, smiling at his wife. "Just a chat amongst soldiers. And, of course, advice about Tramel."

Pounding of steps sounded in the hall. Too heavy for the children's footfall, Felton braced and lifted his eyes to the man in the silver livery at the door.

The fellow bowed to the duke but stepped to Felton.

"Lord Gantry, your father, the Duke of Tramel, has sent me to ask your return."

Great, mentioning the man created a summons. Clutching the painting, Felton closed his arms about it. "Tell him I'm busy. It is impossible to comply."

The young fellow looked nervous with wide-stretched eyes. "His lordship is ill. Your father hasn't much time." The fellow bowed then backed away.

The duke and duchess of Repington stared at Felton—one with a sympathetic look, the duke's a solemn face reminding of duty and honor.

"Gantry," the duke finally said, "you remember how your grandfather died alone. You said it was such a tragedy." He pounded the chair. "I'll track the concerns we spoke of and make sure the soldier's wife is protected in his absence. That will ease your mind."

Rubbing her belly, Patience's gaze swiveled between them, "Is this woman a widow?"

"No, Your Grace," Felton said, "do not fret. The duke and I have all well in hand."

"Then with your sister away, shall we keep the girls?" The duchess clapped her hands. "Perhaps the Ashbrooks' little girl will stay too. We will be a merry party."

"Patience, we're being invaded by all these little ones, I see. I'll have to come up with a schedule for them."

She put her head on his shoulder. "But you're so good with little soldiers."

"That I am, my love." The duke chuckled. "All is well. Go, Gantry."

"No, if this is the end, the girls should say goodbye to their grandfather."

"Traveling with children might slow you down."

Yes. Yes, it would. Perhaps arriving at the last minute would make the devil admit the truth. "All will be well. Excuse me, Your Graces."

When he closed the door, he heard the duke admitting they'd found her sister.

Felton smacked his forehead. It was probably too great a secret to keep.

With the painting tucked under his arm, he headed to the patio to collect his daughters. His thoughts remained scattered and shattered and sad. When a man cared for a woman as deeply as Felton, he'd do anything, absolutely anything to have his love returned, even make a deal with the devil.

Lucky for Felton, Satan had summoned.

Chapter 25

Cecilia—A Terse, No Grovel Letter

Noah's tears made me stir from the sofa. I'd only just begun to rest my eyes when his voice rattled then wailed. The noise stunned me.

I waddled off the sofa and almost knocked one of the mud-colored vases off the table. With a shake of my head, I focused. The boy's wails startled me again. I fought to get to him.

Enna was sound asleep, but not the babe. I scooped him up and held him. He soothed and my heart started again.

"Come, Noah. Let's let Enna sleep."

I lit a candle and then dried his wet bottom. Wrapping him in a fresh napkin seemed to make him coo. "Does that make you well pleased?"

The boy burped. That must mean yes.

In the quiet of the room, I snuggled Noah on the sofa and pulled my blanket about us. "Hope you don't mind my cold hands. I guess you hated a wet bottom worse."

He didn't burp again, but the new quiet was fine with me. My new commission at the Drury Lane had my mind turning almost as much as the letter waiting for me there this morning.

Felton had discovered I worked there and left a wax-sealed note for me.

My husband had never written me anything. Though he sent word by Watson, no notes to dismiss his tardiness were given to me. No love notes either. I had nothing to dispel my worries or to soothe his precious daughters.

The rustle of the letter in my hand disquieted my soul. Noah went back to sleep on my stomach.

Prying at the wax seal, the folds of the foolscap opened.

Unfolded, it exposed Felton's script.

It was awful.

Sloppy and uneven. No one would ever call it a beautiful hand.

Not quite what I expected.

Was that why I'd never been sent the slightest missive?

Dear Cecilia,

I want one chance to tell you in person what your greatest desire is. I will visit in a few weeks.

Just one chance.

F

Succinct.

Nonthreatening.

Not very specific, with no date or time.

Definitely no promises of forever or anything.

Noah awoke again. The boy cried and waved his hands. His gaze had the wettest blue-black eyes I'd ever seen.

"You must be upset. It will be alright . . . son."

Wishing he'd garnered Helena's golden eyes, I rocked Noah, and he yawned.

Being easy wasn't a Lance family trait. That was all Helena. It might even be my mother, the way she was with Papa.

Mama loved my father, didn't she? I wondered sometimes. She was free and stayed with him many years before they married. Could she have left him if she wanted?

Or was it to her best advantage to stay? I didn't know anymore. Those definitions of love and commitment floated about me, covering my heart.

"You have faith in me, Noah, even when I'm wrongheaded?"

He smiled, but unless the long burp puckering those pouty lips was commentary on a conflicted heart, I didn't think he could read my mind.

My education and dowry made me an eligible candidate to marry a son of a British peer. This was all due to my father. Did Mama stay for us girls, her family, or for her heart? Did she love him, the man, or the good that their marriage brought?

"You reading that letter?" Enna rolled over in the bed she'd positioned by the crib. "I should've gotten up. I didn't hear him."

"No, you sleep. We're a team. We're sort of . . . we are a family, Enna."

My friend smiled and pulled the covers up to her chin. "Thank you, Mrs. Chari. It is good to have friends and good care on these shores."

Her sentiment was wonderful, but with Enna there was always a measured bit of wisdom that followed.

I shifted Noah to my other arm. "Yes, and friends should say what troubles their hearts."

The young woman nodded. "We are doing well. So much better for me here than Demerara. I wish this was enough for you. I wish you could say goodbye to revenge. I fear you find this Gladstone then never *come* home to us. I hear they'll kill a woman for killing a man, even if justified."

"I won't risk you or Noah, but I'll have revenge. My sister can't be forgotten."

"Wish some of that forgiveness my brother talked about would take root. There needs to be some other way to make things right without putting you in bondage."

There was no escaping my fate.

Helena Thomas Gladstone would be avenged.

Her lousy husband, Felton's cousin—Gladstone killed my sister. He needed to die.

One man could fix things so there would be no repercussions.

Tramel.

The duke's shadowy connections helped me get to my sister. He knew how to get revenge, but that was too big of a thing to ask from someone who had done too much for me.

"A man can change, Mrs. Chari. Killing him gives no room for that."

The tone in her voice sounded sharp, almost accusatory, but I'd not relent. "Gladstone killed my sister. He needs to pay. He needs to die."

"Mrs. Chari, your sister lives in the goodness of the babe."

That was true and blew a kiss at the boy. "I'll keep you and Noah safe."

"You're not a killer. You heal with art. That's your destiny."

Shifting Noah to my side, I put my hand over my stomach.

Art was the only thing I'd ever birth. It was my calling.

Scooting the babe deeper into the crook of my arm, I returned him to his crib. Covering him in blankets, I whispered a prayer.

The babe stared back, but I saw his yawns. Then more spittle flowed.

Running water. "Noah, you've inspired me. I know what to do at Drury Lane Theatre."

He burped again and smiled before offering his happy coo.

Knowing Helena sacrificed to bring this babe safely into the world, and then entrusted him to me raise him—it wasn't something to take lightly.

Despite Felton's attempts, I wasn't his priority. My little family of Enna and Noah was my first priority, and unless I could determine a way to have revenge and keep them safe, I'd have to forget Gladstone. Forget, not forgive.

My stomach soured thinking of relenting. I ripped up Felton's note. Being last on anyone's list was not something to consider. It was something to reject. No matter what this overture was, I refused to be a part of his new mission.

Chapter 26

Felton—The Devil's Summons

It took a week and a half to travel from London through the countryside to Warwick Manor. Agatha and Amelia were much better company than he remembered.

Except for the occasional you-not-you spat, they were pleasant. If there had been more time, he would have taken them to visit some of the local sites like Stonehenge. The friend of the duke and duchess of Repington had proved to be a good counsel and knowledgeable on little girl likes.

Sitting back on his seat, he studied the girls. The matching capes of red velvet looked wonderful. Lady Ashbrook's gift for the two was lovely.

He folded his arms and offered a smile. The fear of being inadequate in his household, with just him and the girls, lessened. By Jove, his present circle of friends had helped, and perhaps righted any wrongs that he or Jane or even Tramel had done to his little family.

He wondered if his sister would see this as a good thing. She'd been with Aunt Nelly since he sent her away. According to what his cousin told him at the King's Theatre, her mood had improved but she didn't seem to have any new suitors.

Fluttering her lacy handkerchief, Amelia rocked on the seat. "Will Aunt Jane come? We must tell her of our adventures."

"Yes, sweetheart, but don't tell her of the cannons. It may cause her to fret."

Jane should be at Warwick by now. He intended to tell her that he forgave her. Maybe making a habit of such would prepare him for all the groveling he was set to do with Cecilia once he'd seen to Tramel's affairs.

"Papa," Agatha said as she set down her sketchbook. "Is Grandfather very ill?"

He hesitated for a moment. Not saying what he felt when he felt it had been a hallmark for Felton. It cost him Cecilia. "It sounds as if he is. I'll need you two to be on your best behavior for the duke."

"Will Mrs. Cecilia come? She's good friends with Grandfather." Amelia's little face looked so sad. "I miss her. She's away much longer than you."

"I'm sure that if Lady Gantry could, she would attend him."

"That's wrong, Papa." Agatha's tone was loud and harsh. "She was good friends with you, and she left."

Everyone sat silently as the carriage rounded the final stretch of road to Warwick. The meadows to his right, the cliffs on the left would soon fill the windows like one of Cecilia's canvases. Now that he wasn't rushing, he saw the beauty. It made more sense why a place like this would inspire Cecilia.

Felton reached out and grasped each girl's hand. "I wasn't a very good friend. I'm trying to convince her to cut short her business and visit with us. If she did, do you think we could all be nice to each other?"

Shrugging, Agatha picked up her stick of charcoal and began to sketch again.

Amelia jumped onto his seat and put her lanky arms about his neck. "I will, Papa. I'll be extra good. I'll be good for both you and Aunt Jane too."

He hugged his youngest and then also drew Agatha into an embrace. "We have each other, you know. We are enough, together. No matter what."

"We are, Papa," Agatha said. "But I do hope you can convince Lady Gantry to come back. Her going off on a mission is just as bad as when you do it."

That was the rub of things. He now understood how his leaving hurt his household. Hopefully his new understanding would show when he saw Cecilia. Felton knew he'd only have one chance to show her he'd changed.

The carriage stopped on the gravel drive of Warwick Manor. Red bricks to rival the color of the girls' capes stood before him. It was impressive. Cecilia had nearly screamed with pleasure when she saw it. Nothing like this was in Demerara.

She called it an adventure to walk in Warwick's halls and in its woods.

The guilt in his gut poked then lodged like a stone. Taking Cecilia from here and installing her in London must have seemed like a punishment.

Shrugging off his disappointments, he tossed opened the door and helped the girls down. Together they went up the massive marble stairs and into the grand house.

With the exception of the gilded pattern low on the walls, the sea of gray was a sea of nothingness. It wrapped about him.

His heart rattled against his ribs. Memories from his horrid childhood returned. He could hardly breathe.

His dread returned—the dressing downs, the verbal punishments for never being good enough, being trapped here instead of schooling at Eton because his grandfather wanted no one to see the pox scars on Felton's body. Tramel said he didn't want him teased, but like the late duke, he surely didn't want the family name drawn into ridicule.

The noise of footmen in silver liveries descending the stairs shook Felton free. Watson guided them to the carriage and all the luggage.

Felton should go up and see the old man, but his feet were planted, his bowed legs locked.

The disappointments. The arguments where Felton tried to defend Lady Tramel numbers two and three repeated in his head. All ended in damnation—father and son each wishing the other to hell, grandfather mocking both.

Agatha's warm hand clasped his. Amelia helped and pulled him forward. "Do we get our old rooms, Papa?"

Jane was overhead on the landing. "Of course you do, young ladies."

His sister looked healthy, with her hair pulled high in ringlet curls. Maybe a little tan too. She ran down the corkscrew stairs to greet them.

She bent to the girls, and they leaped into her arms. "Oh, I've missed you, missed you all terribly."

Her shy glance at Felton seemed tentative, but what could he truly tell? He'd just committed to breathing.

"Girls, it's been a long drive." His tone was low and as always, he looked to his sister for help.

With a smile, she pointed. "Your rooms are prepared and there might be a gift."

She jangled a bell and maids in white aprons and mobcaps came from everywhere. "They will help you settle."

As Agatha and Amelia were shuttled upstairs, Watson and four footmen came inside with their travel trunks. In his man's hands was Cecilia's Port Royal painting, the one gifted to him from the Repingtons. He couldn't bear to part with that.

"No. Watson, leave that . . ."

Jane went to him and took the canvas. "It's lovely, Felton. Did Cecilia send this for Father?"

Hadn't she just learned of his wife's talents in December before Felton sent her to Aunt Nelly? Where was this enthusiasm coming from?

That feeling of being the last to know anything surrounded him, squeezing at his chest. He seized the painting and shoved it toward Watson. "Please, put this back in the carriage."

"Papa would be so cheered, Felton. He'd love to see new art."

New.

That was a comparison of some sort. It didn't sound like the art Cecilia made years ago when they lived here. It barely sounded like the ones from last December. "Jane, what more do you know?"

That look on her face, the shrewish drawing of her lips, the jealous lifting of her short nose—she knew more, much more. "The studio he let her use when we all lived here, he's let no one inside . . . it's full of new canvases."

Felton heard her words and added it to all the things she didn't say, like the room had been emptied of everything when he'd moved the family to London.

No longer empty.

He pushed past his sister and lunged up the stairs. Almost breaking down the studio door, he rushed inside the room that was adjacent to their old bedchamber.

No longer empty.

Paintings were hung about the room. Each was a vision, a complex narrative of color mirroring people and places.

Two were of her jaguars. The eyes, they could be Felton's or Tramel's.

Next to the balcony doors, overlooking the property, was the largest painting of the collection, almost nine feet in height. It was a portrait of his father sitting, with Felton standing behind the gilded chair.

Cecilia, no one else, could paint these. While he searched all of London, every inch of England and Scotland, his wife, she had been here, here with Tramel.

He pushed to the balcony and opened the doors wide. The fresh sea air was the only thing keeping him calm, for he was ready to tear Warwick down to its foundation.

Felton turned to the bedchamber. He gazed upon the bed, the one he and Cecilia shared, and wanted to set it on fire. Expensive gowns hung in the closet. Many seemed untouched.

Maybe she and his father weren't playing house.

Maybe she hadn't fallen in love with the mad duke.

Jane was in the studio when he powered back inside.

"Sorry, brother. I suppose it couldn't be helped. You always abandoning her, and me being so mean, she was pushed to Tramel."

He was about to agree when she laughed. "Wake up, brother. The manipulative thing from Demerara has been scheming and ingratiating herself with the duke since the moment she arrived. She's probably had you all—you, father, Gladstone."

"No, Jane."

"How does she do it? How can that foreigner snap her fingers and have you all so twisted? What is her secret?"

"A kind spirit. A genuine spirit to create. That draws us all like flies to pure honey."

Her mouth fell open. Then she covered her face in her hands. "I don't know how not to be jealous. How can I not hate her when she has everything and everyone spinning?"

"You're not an awful person, Jane. Don't be one." He lifted her chin. "There's a caring person in there somewhere. Find her. Let the girls help you find her. That's who I want in my life."

"What about Cecilia? Do you still want her if she's fallen in love with your own father?"

"Cecilia might be confused and hurting but she is loyal."

"She walked out on you. How loyal is that?"

He returned to the balcony. The breeze met his heated face. His mind went to Jamaica. The storms that delayed their voyage to England. He spent weeks merely talking with his new bride. Hours he'd never give away as they communed in a small house near the sea, one of his safe locations whenever he was in the country.

It was an adventure for two.

She doodled and he studied, intercepted correspondences. Each kept their secrets even as they began their married life. The rustling of her curly hair in his fingers, watching how the sunset hit her locks, bringing out the reds in the waves—he'd never forget.

She was happy, so pure.

Yet Cecilia never mentioned this great talent.

Or had she, and he wasn't listening to anything but her smallish waist, her well-endowed thighs.

Felton wrote to her, before he left London. He hoped she had his letter and would grant him that final audience.

But how could he ever forgive her for leaving and running away to his father?

That relearning to breathe thing—it was hard.

Jane leaned against the balcony door.

"How long did you know my wife was at Warwick?"

"About a month ago. When I couldn't take being with Aunt Nelly anymore, I came here."

"Was Cecilia here? You could've—"

"No. She'd already gone, but you can tell she'd been here for weeks."

"Well, I should ask the man who knows everything how long he secreted my wife here whilst I went mad."

"Felton, no. Calm down. Father is fragile."

"Good. I need him to break."

With his sister clinging to his coat, Felton marched to the devil's chamber to face the man who continually ruined his life.

CHAPTER 27

FELTON—THE DEVIL'S DUE

Felton reared his hand back to knock on Tramel's door, but Jane caught his fingers.

"Wait, brother. He's delicate."

He spun to her. "Too delicate to pay for purposely putting a wedge between my wife and me?"

"Lady Gantry chose to leave. She couldn't bear to stay with you, and she walked out in the storm. The duke didn't force her. Perhaps he did this to keep an eye on her."

"Cecilia is not sinister. She's been wronged."

Jane dropped his arm. "You believe as you want, but our father is truly ill."

"How can you forgive him but hold such contempt against Cecilia?" He turned back to the massive, whitewashed door of solid mahogany and pushed inside.

He paused at the empty chair by the fireplace, where he expected to find the man sitting, plotting mayhem.

The powerful man lay in bed, pale and bundled up in blankets.

The sickness was true.

Felton stepped closer, rounding to the side of the bed near a grand window. He extended his hand and waved beneath his father's large nose, a Lance trademark.

"I'm still breathing, you fool." The duke gripped his thick covers. "You haven't been elevated . . . yet."

Moving to the footboard, Felton grasped the knurl post. "You summoned, Tramel?"

Tired eyes opened, but his drawn sneer remained the same, tight and ready to toss a caustic reply. "I did want you to come earlier. I thought dying might garner your attention."

"Seems I should've come for Christmas after all."

The chuckle held power, despite the coughs. "When you see a purple snowdrop shivering on the side of the street trying to figure out how to walk to Demerara, I think it best to offer her a ride and someone to listen. I wouldn't want her to freeze to death as she would've on such a night."

"The thought of returning Cecilia to my house slipped your mind."

Tramel's palm fisted, and Felton jerked. The memories of a harsh slap across the cheek always followed such a move.

"You basically called your adoring wife a jezebel and your aged father her paramour. Seemed more like you gave me permission to see if I still had it in me."

If Felton asked the duke if he'd seduced her, it would feed the jealousy in his heart. Instead, he'd go with faith, faith that no matter how mad she was, Cecilia wouldn't betray him, and faith that if had Tramel won Cecilia, he wouldn't have let her go. "Father, it seems you and I keep losing track of the woman we love."

"If you'd come sooner, you may have been able to help. She had to go on a spy's adventure alone."

"Spying? What are you talking about?"

"Now you're curious. You didn't exactly come quickly. Took you more than a week to arrive."

"I was in no hurry and you're still alive. No loss."

The man coughed, then laughed. "She could be in trouble. Without your or my protection, she's vulnerable."

The stewing in Felton's gut became a rapid bubbling boil.

Calm.

Think.

Plan.

All of this was a little hard, knowing Cecilia had been at Warwick being daily poisoned by his father's forked tongue. "What is it you want, old man? Except for my children, you've taken everything that matters."

"Never had use for little ones, or a son whom I thought weak and sickly. And you took all that mattered to me. My dearest wife died birthing you. That can make one resentful."

"Making Cecilia hate me is how you avenge something I couldn't control?"

Tramel pulled higher onto his pillow. "My being cynical and hateful to you has been irrational. I'll admit that. But you're my legacy."

"Facing your mortality has made you reconsider your unimaginably cruel life. You've always wanted me to suffer unless I did exactly as you wish. Can't be strong and your puppet."

His father sighed. "That's the rub of it all. And Cecilia, beautiful Cecilia, has helped me see another side of things. She says we are similar. I wonder, when she closes her eyes, who does she see? Who does she hope for?"

Calm.

Plan.

Kill.

"What is it that you want, Tramel? I could go away and return when you're in the grave."

"Tell Cecilia I value the intimacy of her friendship. Tell her."

Kill.

Bury the body.

Dance on the grave.

Felton slapped the post of the footboard. "I'll try to hurry her along to attend your mourning party."

His vision was beginning to blur from pure rage. He forced his legs to turn. "Good day."

"Wait. Cecilia is at risk. I need you to help her. Bring her here."

With fingers on the brass door pull, Felton paused. "Why? So she can again be your caged painting bird?"

"No, so I can give her what she most desires."

This low whisper did as his father surely intended. It drew Felton back into the room to park at the old man's side. "What would you know of that?"

"You do still want her. I expected you'd annul your union or divorce her, with the lady being gone so long, but you didn't. You still care. Thus, you can save her from jeopardy. I can't help her this time."

This time? Felton's heart ticked faster, readying to explode and splatter red on the endless gray walls. "What danger? What desire?"

The palsy slowing the movements of the man's face made it seem as if his lips half dragged to a smile. "She still won't talk to you. Just me. There's comfort in that."

The duke never did anything without a reason. Felton merely had to offer him something to loosen his tongue. He moved to the window and marveled at the view to the cliffs. "I was delayed collecting a new piece of art. Cecilia's art."

"Art, you say?"

"Yes." He stopped tugging the curtain and again faced his father. "Lady Gantry painted a piece in June. I know she was out of the country. Was it Demerara? Was that where her adventure was?"

A snowy brow raised. "Has her technique greatly improved from what you see in the studio?"

The man didn't dispute the Demerara part. Lord Liverpool's one missive had said it was suspected. No confirmation, but it was no small task to get around the blockades.

"The painting—it's Port Royal, the moment before it was destroyed like Sodom and Gomorrah."

He smiled and seemed to hold in a cough. "Where is it?"

"In my carriage. It will return with me to Town."

"You mean to torment me too. Well done, Gantry."

"I meant it for a bribe. The painting for the truth."

"My son, my legacy. You do have the heart to be the duke. Just missing the brains."

Felton forced a swallow. "It never made sense to me why Cecilia disappeared so completely. I knew she needed help, but I assumed her late father's trust fund, or his solicitors, had provided support. The War department kept me the dark."

"Well, you know what happens when you assume. You'll always be made the fool. And Liverpool has no more use for you. One wonders what would've happened if he'd thought you were expendable on any of your missions."

Though his tone was raspy and dark, it was also steeped in the pride of knowing more than everyone. It was oddly something to admire, to be so confident in himself that all others be damned. "Tramel, I'm a fool. Warwick would be the only place I'd not look. The invitations to come here for Christmas must've tormented her."

"Finally using your brain box. And she was welcome to continue with me for as long she wanted. She stayed until she returned to Demerara. I didn't complain, not once, of buying her paint or listening to her talk. She does like cheese with or without a toga, as long as it is quiet and intimate."

If Felton vomited right now, he'd miss the man's confession. So he only gagged a little in his throat. "I'm not an ogre. I simply don't understand art. I thought it a hobby, like embroidery."

"Yes, with your plain attire, I can see you don't understand embellishment either."

"Tramel, I can learn about art if it is life to her. I'll encourage her in it."

The man clapped his hand, a slow, loud pound. "Been practicing that, my boy? You think you can convince her with your charm? You're a handsome devil, but she has only two loves; one is family, the other, art."

Felton remembered her speech about his and hers. That was part of her pain, something he'd have to unravel. He willed his brow to not show how hard his mind turned. "Did you confuse her and make her think you care?"

"I do care." Tramel closed his eyes. "If I had more time, I'd win. She's more confused now, but I do know what she wants more than anything."

That was Cecilia's question, but the man wouldn't say. With a shake of his head, Felton started to the door. "Don't need riddles, just Cecilia. She'll tell me. Now that I know where she is."

"Angered, Gantry? Angry enough to kill?"

With hands on the polished pull, he wanted to rip the door from its hinges.

This was Tramel's game. He'd goad Felton into acting the fool. He stopped playing these torments when he'd left for the military. It wasn't the time to return to bad habits. "Good day, Tramel."

"Gantry, that's what she wants. Someone to kill for her."

"Now I know you're insane. The palsy has addled you."

The duke laughed. "If you think so, son. But I told you the truth. Now reward me."

"Cecilia is the gentlest flower. She'd never kill. That's you. You haven't changed her."

"And you haven't listened to her. You closed your ears to her pain. Then you sided with her mortal enemy."

This drew Felton back in the room, back to pound the footboard. "What are you talking about?"

"The day she left. You sided with your cousin when you accused her of infidelity, then you asked her to leave to compose herself, like she was some sort of wilting violet."

"I had to get rid of you. I didn't want her to see us arguing."

"Did you wonder why she was so upset?"

"Because of you. Because I accused her—"

"She was upset because of Gladstone. Don't you know how he tortured her?"

"He hurt Cecilia? You were protecting her. He was bleeding. She—"

"She will try to kill Gladstone and will fail if you don't do it for her. You're a supreme marksman. I taught you well. Get to it. Kill Gladstone."

Felton squinted at his father. "You're serious. Why are you like this? You're going to die. Why are you lying?"

"It's my habit to antagonize you, but I'm deadly serious. Cecilia wants Gladstone dead. He deserves it. The man who does it will have her heart. I'm trying to help you and her. One of us should live to love her."

The man clutched at his chest and shook.

Felton wanted his father to suffer for every twisted thing the man ever did, but he'd not stand idle. Instead, he went and put his hands to the man's shoulders, steadying him against the pillows. Only the smallest inkling in his head wanted to smother the devil.

"Jane!" he called. "Get the goat's doctor."

With a gasp, the duke started laughing. "You're not weak, Gantry. You're my legacy. She needs you to be strong. Be me. Kill her enemy. Get our woman back."

Other than Napoleon's forces and the informant who led to Johnson's death, the only person Felton wanted to kill was the man in this bed. Felton flung his hands away like he'd touched hell's fire. "You're insane."

"Then tell her I want to see her. And that Jeremiah Gladstone will be here in two weeks to say his goodbyes. I'll find a way to do what she wants. I will also get her the Demerara information. She'll know what I mean."

"Running shadow networks while you've a foot in the grave."

"Tell her and she'll be here. She'll come back to me."

This was Tramel's master play, bits of truth wrapped in lies. "I'm leaving with the painting. Pass in peace."

Felton had given each of his girls a goodbye embrace and was halfway down the stairs, when Jane chased him. "Gantry, stop. The painting. Father's mumbling about a painting."

"Must be on my way, sister."

"But he could die, Felton."

If he said he didn't care, that would be mostly true. There was always a part of a son that wanted honor in his father's eyes. Felton shook himself of the sentiment. He was foolish, just like Tramel said. "It takes a great deal to kill a bull. There's more time."

He looked over the stair railing where his extended family would soon gather, pretending to mourn. Would Cecilia come just to kill Gladstone? What had Gladstone done to warrant death?

"Felton, please stay. I need you."

"You can run this house until I'm back. That's what you've wanted to do, control my house or the one that will be mine. And I'm retrieving Cecilia per Tramel's orders."

Jane shook her fists. "How can you both still be so devoted to a woman who left each of you?"

"Just lucky, I guess." He trotted down the final treads.

"Felton!"

"She's some kind of woman, sis. It's not a competition though. You can be too when you're not fretting about who gets applause."

He left his sister with her reddening cheeks and climbed into his carriage. Felton needed to get to Cecilia and dissuade her from murder. Tramel lied a lot, but not about Cilia.

If she indeed wanted Gladstone dead, his crime must be egregious.

He sat back against the seat holding the wonderful Port Royal painting.

Watson ducked his head in. "Sir, it will be dark soon. You sure you want to leave? Travel by the cliffs can be tricky at night."

"I have to return to Town as soon as possible."

"Very good, sir. Shall I set this painting inside Warwick?"

It would be an offer of peace to do so, but the peacekeeper needed war. This was the first step.

From the window, he could see his father's bedchamber.

It would be wrong to drive away waving the painting, for he might not see the gesture from his sickbed.

"No, Watson. It stays with me. I'm not letting go of anything that's mine. Make good time."

"Very good." His man shut the door. The carriage sped away.

Felton steadied the painting, the tropical Sodom and Gomorrah, on his knee and planned his next move.

CHAPTER 28

CECILIA—ESTRANGED TAKES TWO

November 15, 1814
London, England

Bouncing Noah in my arms, Enna and I walked through the people milling on Brydges Street. It wasn't quiet, but not crowded like in the evenings. I could manage and keep myself distracted.

"Mrs. Charity. London is different than Demerara. Where do they get so much stone? You said there were no enslaved here."

I wondered that myself sometimes. The columns of the Roman architecture that Papa loved, like the Colosseum—were not its arches and cut stone built with the labor of the enslaved from Judea?

Who built the things in London? This marble was old. Were the workers free?

The streets around us were filled with all kinds of people, but no one was in shackles. Never saw provision grounds or sick houses for the enslaved. I had to hope this place had more fair-minded people than it did Lady Janes and Gladstones.

"Mrs. Charity, you in there? You slip away sometimes."

With a shrug, I forced myself to see her and remember the hopes I had for her and Noah. They were free. No one would change that.

She nodded and dipped her head closer. "You've been distant

since visiting that king's place. More so with the letter from your husband. Hope you're thinking more of forgiveness than revenge."

Felton was in my thoughts more than I wanted to admit. I wiped Noah's face. "The king's place is a theatre, not a palace. And my art is on one of the largest canvases in the world. The audience cheers it."

Enna offered me that look Patience would give when I avoided answering questions. This lady was wonderful, but I missed my older sister and I hurt for Helena.

A cloth mopped at my cheek. Enna had leaned over the babe to dry my tears. Wrapped up in my thoughts, I was crying, a big horrible sobbing fool in the middle of the road.

"Everything changed cause I took a walk down a street in Stabroek. I should probably stick to the pavement."

"Britain is good. We need to be here until the world changes, maybe becoming more like what your eyes see."

I shifted Noah and kept his little head with curly dark hair covered in the blanket. He wasn't a fire brick like Felton, the writer of terse notes. "Sorry, I have been dull."

"No, Mrs. Charity. You've been fine. And it's fine to forgive everyone and return to your husband. I'll be good in this country."

I took her hand. "We're a package, a parcel wrapped in bright ribbon. You and Noah are my family. Family is everything. I'll not be rash. So, no fretting about when I take up revenge. You and this boy will be safe."

"You can be safe too. You're not a killer."

In my head, I was a jaguarete and I stalked Gladstone and struck him down.

But I was probably more a baby lamb or calf that mewled in the street. "How do I avenge Helena and not be caught?"

"Another way will manifest. Another way, as my brother would say, comes for the faithful."

She took Noah from my arms and held him up. "This one needs you alive. You're his mother."

"Not his mother. I couldn't even feed him. I'm terrible at the wraps for his bottom. They're a lot stinkier now that he eats mushy food. Right, Noah? Good and stinky."

"You feed him porridge. And you love on him. He's yours even if you've not birthed him."

Enna's words gnawed at something deep inside. I despaired of all the things I wasn't capable of when it came to children. No seed had firmly planted in my womb. I wasn't great at guiding Felton's two daughters. "How do I find my way if I'm to lead us? Life is easier when all I think of is paint."

With a shrug and a tug, she kept us walking. "You let the worries tear at you, and you go into that art world. It's hard to let the colors go when you've made them. The world outside of your head can be nice. You have to try to make it like you see it when you paint."

Her wisdom and friendship meant so much. It kept me grounded, like when I took walks when noises made me jittery.

"Mrs. Charity, you go and paint. You've a big commission."

"I'll be late, Enna, coming home."

"Always on the days you finish, but when are you early? Never."

"You could come watch. Drury Lane's manager agreed, like at the King's Theatre."

"No. It's near someone's naptime."

"I'm not sleepy. Oh, you meant Noah. Yes."

Enna gripped my hand. "There's a man looking at us."

"They're always looking." Blackamoor, brown, Sephardic, white—they all looked at me. Some made offers, outrageous ones.

"Not the way this one is."

Tall and thin, looking dead at me. Felton. He said he was a spy. I wished he was an assassin for hire.

"Go, Enna. I'll be alright."

She wrapped Noah up in her scarf and dashed down Brydges Street. I glanced at Felton and the party he chatted with across the street. No more running. With my head high, I walked into Drury Lane Theatre, daring him to follow.

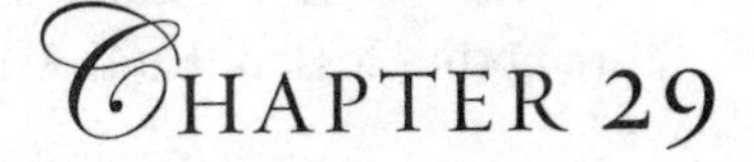

CHAPTER 29

FELTON—ENGAGING THE ART LOVERS

Felton spied Cecilia standing in front of the Drury Lane Theatre. She noticed him. He felt her gaze, and his blood raced in anticipation.

He'd returned to Town two days ago and had made Cecilia his mission—tracking her location, her employers, her food habits. Tramel was right. She still loved cheese.

"Lord Gantry," Lord Ashbrook said, "I hope that my overview about art is sufficient."

The earl and his wife had accompanied Felton to Covent Garden on a quest for a pomegranate or fruit for some sort of mash.

The two were cozy, arm in arm, another ridiculously happy couple.

"Sir, have I answered your questions about art? It's difficult to describe a lifelong passion in a few passing minutes."

"I think so. I don't know how remiss I was in this area. I want to be open to learning."

Ashbrook's face blanked. "Open? You, indeed."

"Yes, my dear," his countess said. "Lord Gantry has turned over a new leaf. Staring at your former painting for hours on end will do that."

Felton nodded but his gaze stayed on Cecilia, who didn't wait to see if he'd approach. She darted into the theatre.

"You have a great deal on your mind, Lord Gantry." Lady Ashbrook's loud voice broke through his fog and his planning of what to say to his wife. "For another lesson, Lord Ashbrook will be in town a few more days."

"My dear, the marquess knows how to contact me. You don't need to volunteer my help."

At the brisk tone, Felton glanced at the earl, who brushed at his immaculate indigo coat for imagined lint.

"Have I offended you, sir?"

"No, not particularly, Gantry."

"Then generally?"

Ashbrook sighed. "You're not comfortable in my counsel. Something I've experienced a long time, but I'll tolerate it for my wife's sake. You're her friend." The bronzed man added a smile to his sanitized words. "Decide what's your comfort. And be happy in that decision."

Though he'd never been rude to the barrister, he might not have been friendly, for Felton, like the duke, looked at the earl's involvement with the Widow's Grace as an enabler.

Could Felton's aloofness, his need to step back and observe, be looked at as similar to Jane's behavior?

Wasn't that sentiment the "alleged" liberal label Cecilia tossed at him? Felton was liberal in his notions, even if didn't show it.

The earl kissed his wife's hand. "I'm off to the Old Bailey."

"Ashbrook, wait." Felton adjusted his gloves, as though his mottled scars had been exposed. "The duke says that you host a card game. He says they are quite spirited. I'd like to know if I'm welcome."

The earl stopped. He doffed his hat and exposed waves of tight curly black hair. "Most welcome, sir. My dearest Lady Ashbrook—"

"Is there another one who is less dear?" She offered him a sweet look.

"My love, don't buy up all the pomegranates." He chuckled. "Make sure she's frugal, Gantry. Too many pomegranates can go bad before I can separate the sweet, tart arils."

Felton nodded. "I'll make sure and will send her on her way in an hour or so."

Ashbrook left, and Felton and Lady Ashbrook began walking the other direction to the open market.

"You asked to accompany me. I suspect it was not to learn how to choose a pomegranate. The season has almost passed."

"I wanted you to show me where you discovered the artist Ashbrook bought the painting from. I'm fact-finding, as you Widow's Grace operatives say."

"I'll show you as we shop."

They walked in silence, occasionally stopping at a vendor.

But the silence was too much for him. "Describe the artist in every detail."

"Not sure if it was the artist or an assistant, but she was a quiet woman. Light brown complexion. Very pretty, buxom sort of girl. Ashbrook took me with him to see if she had another of the Jamaica paintings." The countess rubbed her forehead. "I wish I remembered more. Well, memory and me are still sort of strangers."

The buxom part sounded like Cecilia. Now to know when the picture was actually bought. That would help put together her travel timeline. Before he engaged, he needed all the facts, not just crumbs—unless it was Stilton cheese.

"You're not listening, Lord Gantry."

"Sorry. The Duke of Repington and I have been looking for the duchess's sisters. I suspect she is the artist of the piece, and Lord Ashbrook purchased it in March."

"Yes. Patience wasn't sure if it was her sister's. She didn't want to hope for something to find out later she was wrong." Her lips pursed. A new sense of caution covered her wide eyes. "What have you learned about the sisters' whereabouts?"

"A few clues, but nothing I feel comfortable bringing to the duchess. Tell me what Her Grace mentioned."

"About your wife, her sister? Her Grace told me that part too."

"Yes. I didn't want to say anything unless I found her again. I don't want to cause more pain."

Lady Ashbrook's shoulders eased. "That her younger sisters are sweet girls. The middle sister, your wife Cecilia, worked the hardest to keep the family close. And an odd things about her disquiet when things were noisy."

Felton had met her, walking. Didn't Cecilia complain about the noise of balls? Was there another reason to avoid Jane's recitals?

The countess stopped again and asked a vendor to dish out green beans. "My daughter loves these. Lord Gantry, your new interest in art, your almost worship of the painting, Port Royal—has your heart moved forward? Our are you preparing to confront the past?"

Both would be the right answer. "I don't want to draw you any further into my difficulties. I only want to do the right thing, though I'm not sure what that is."

It seemed like an eternity passed before she moved them to another table. "It's hard, but there's always a light when you look for it."

A light?

Why couldn't happy talk be true? He scratched his head, attempting to smile as Lady Ashbrook purchased the last of the red pomegranates.

She grew quiet as he signaled for a jarvey, then gripped his arm. "You need to figure out what it is you can live with. Chaos wouldn't be good for any artist. This one especially, I suspected her to be with child. She needs stability and care. I hope she finds it. You too."

Lady Ashbrook picked up her skirts and dashed up into the carriage.

Felton assisted her but he was numb. The artist was pregnant? Cecilia was pregnant when she left him? Would she knowingly take such risk traveling to Demerara with a babe?

Worse. Would she deny him access to their child?

What was the more unforgivable sin? Not making her truly welcome in his family or denying him his rights?

His pulse exploded like gunfire. The friend Cecilia talked with on Brydges Street, holding the babe, was she holding Felton's son or daughter in her arms?

He turned back, heading to Brydges Street. He needed to seek an audience with his wife . . . the woman who might be the mother of his child . . . the mother hiding his child.

Chapter 30

Cecilia—Scaffold Work

With his greatcoat fluttering behind him, the lean form of my estranged husband paced to my stage.

Up on the scaffold tying off the drop, the final panel of the scenery that Drury Lane had commissioned, I watched him pace, circling like a jaguarete.

Then I laughed.

He craned his neck. "Will you come down now?"

"When I'm done."

He went to the other side of the large hanging canvas and poked at my buckets of paints, my jars of pigments. "I don't see the torch or the knife. No toga either."

"My lord, I had little notice of your arrival. I would've been more prepared."

"The note I sent to you two weeks ago, that was not sufficient to expect me?"

"Maybe for the woman waiting for you in a tiny closet. This is a large theatre. The manager needs me to finish ahead of schedule. Imagine waiting on me."

Felton looked angry and conflicted, his smile nonexistent, very different than a few hours ago when I saw him on the street.

Something upset him, more than me, his runaway bride. I wondered what had. My heart went to his girls, but something affecting them would lead him away—not to—me.

"I do require your time, ma'am, unless you are ready to fall into our old comfortable routine. That will require all of your time, for the rest of our days."

The intensity in his stance radiated. It reached to the ceiling and heated my cheeks.

Yet this solid canvas hanging between us was emblematic of us. We were never in the same place once we came to these shores, not for very long. One of us had to look over the barriers or around them to enjoy the other.

He tapped the scaffold, making it rock. "Cecilia, please come down."

There was something ironic about this private man sharing his frustration in this showy space. "I love it up here in the quiet with just my thoughts and the colors. Please return another time."

He moved to my side of the canvas, squarely to the front of the stage. "Are you done with your adventure? Tell me about it. Please, please come down and share every detail."

His voice was low at first, then grew with volume and power.

"You missed your calling, my lord. Your voice is lovely, but I've no time for you today."

"I'd like to think I was missed. I certainly missed you. Oh, come down. Your husband, David Felton Lance, wishes Cecilia Charity Thomas, his Lady Gantry, to come down."

His words echoed in the vast hall. The noise of it made it hard to think, to balance. I clutched the scaffold. "Formal perfect speech, my lord. Drury Lane was designed for such direct addresses but ones with more passion. Just tell me what you wish and be gone."

"You want more passion? Come down and I'll do my best." He ran a hand through his hair, loosening it from its cinching ribbon. "Please."

With the canvas secured by knots, I lowered it but held the

rope. "The curtain has closed. This new performance of a somewhat understanding husband is no longer required. Definitely not one who's embarrassed by his wife's antics."

"Embarrassed by you—no. Embarrassed that it took you leaving me to understand your art—yes." He stepped back and craned his head toward the canvas. "I'm in awe of the shading, the selection of the hues. The luminosity of the colors. You're a savant."

What?

Rubbing at my eyes, I looked at him again. "Are you indeed David Felton Lance? I assumed he cared not for my squiggled lines."

"I went through the canvases you left in London and at Warwick. They're amazing. They show your heart and even how it was breaking."

Warwick.

Felton knew I hid there.

He didn't sound angry or accusatory, but then my ears heard noises, rushing air.

The doors were sealed. No breeze at all cooled my skin.

This was my panic, my guilt. I eased down on my knees and hands, trying to steady myself. "Please leave, my lord. I'm working. That concept is anathema to the ton."

"Until last December, I had a profession too. I suppose we're both to be outcasts." He shed his greatcoat, a deep chocolate brown weave, and grasped the shaky scaffold. "Since the King's Theatre, I've been made more desperate. I've waited, given you time, but our business is urgent."

"Your short note didn't state a date." The ringing in my ears continued." I suppose a letter without specifics is better than none."

"Cecilia, are you alright? You sound breathless."

"Fine." Liar. I lied and clutched more tightly to my perch.

He tapped the board I'd nailed up to keep the scaffold stable. "I was a spy. Not much time to write home when I'm trying to be invisible. Cecilia, my pulse is racing. Can't you still feel us?"

"That sensation is the onset of gout or whatever ailment your Aunt Nelly complained of. You must've caught it."

He glanced up with a smile. "I miss the sound of you, your voice. Come down, or are you practicing becoming a pretty parrot, plaything for a jaguarete?"

My mobcap let a few braids fall as I eased my swirling head to my platform. "I think a jaguarete would eat a parrot. It's safer up here."

"You'd make a delicious meal, Cilia." Felton climbed on the scaffold. The whole platform shook.

Again, I gripped the side. "Stop, or we will fall."

He kept going. "We'll do it together, we both will. We'll be a pained wreck."

That didn't sound like cautious Felton, wanting to risk injury.

The platform swayed and hit my canvas.

"My art! You're going to ruin it. My lord, I wish you to back away from the stage."

"I wish you back."

He stretched out his hand. "Come to me, Cecilia. Join me here unless you're frightened of us standing together."

"I've no time to be distracted or told that my worries or fears are overblown."

His brow arched and climbed a little higher. "Overblown? Not me. Overbearing would describe a different Lance."

When he was midway up the creaking started. "Felton, you know this is not safe."

"When has anything between us been safe? We're an adventure, remember."

More pings and moans from the scaffold meant it would fall. "Not that I have such talent, but I do wonder if Michelangelo had such problems. In the midst of finishing his commission, did he suffer a spouse giving chase?"

"Not sure he had a fool to run from." He jumped down. "I won't put you at risk. Never will."

He banged on a strut. "Come down and at least let me fix this. I want you safe, so that you can finish another masterpiece."

I'd never seen him so determined to help unless he fed me. "Am I your new mission?"

Instead of answering, he took off his waistcoat, then touched the bindings and nails holding the wood braces. He wasn't leaving.

"I'll come down. Then say what you have to and leave. I must finish this commission tonight."

His head nodded. "It's the afternoon. How late will you work?"

"As long as it takes, my lord."

"That doesn't sound safe." He hung his head, his shoulders drooping.

No, no, nope. The tender part of my heart couldn't be drawn in. Staying distant from all the Lances was my only way to keep Noah safe. Felton's cousin, hateful man, would have more say in England over his son's welfare.

My descent was slow, but I ran to the one side of the drop. He remained on the other, facing the audience and orchestra pit. Cowardly, but my art would protect me from those Noah-like eyes trying to carry me away.

"Slide the papers. I'll sign to formalize our divorce. I'm ready for the end."

There was no response, just the shadow of him touching the landscape I'd painted.

"Please, sir, I'm ready."

"Cecilia, we're still married. I've no plans to change this."

"Well, the woman in the square doesn't look like the type to wait. You should hurry."

He chuckled and the drop rippled. "And here I thought I was the jealous one. Lady Ashbrook is newly married and quite happy. She's a friend. I think I'm beginning to understand much better how such friendships work between men and women, between a father and daughter-in-law."

Was that true?

Felton no longer felt threatened by Tramel?

"Your children, are they well?"

"Yes, the girls are. Amelia misses you the most. She cried every day for a month when you didn't return."

My heart broke. That was the worst thing, leaving them. They struggled so often when their father went on missions. My deepest regret was that in saving me, I lost them.

He came to the edge of the canvas. I saw half his face. He could view all of mine.

"You've been greatly missed, Cecilia. Has your adventure been what you wanted?"

"Does it matter? I'm sure Lady Jane made up for my absence. She reminded me often that I'm not the girls' mother."

"Jane hasn't been with us. For the most part, she's been away at my aunt's. I sent her away before the season. Since late March, it's been just the girls and me in Town."

That was a great number of months for Felton to be present with the girls, but I wondered if that was meant to convince me he was ready to accept domestic life. "Lady Jane missed the season. That's surprising."

"I was displeased with my sister. I asked her to leave. I did it for you."

Jane and Felton were very close, thick as thieves. I shook my head and retreated closer to my bottle of tint. "Don't do anything on my behalf."

He put his hand to the cloth, the heavy canvas of my drop. The coarse weave that bore my almost completed landscape was slightly tougher than the harsh osnaburg fabric of the rags of the enslaved. That was what Helena was given to wear. We, the free daughters of Wilhelm Thomas, were arrayed in silks and linens, never that.

Not until Gladstone.

If Felton thought he could change my mind about us or his family, he needed to take that nonsense and leave.

CECILIA—BEWILDERED AGREEMENT

"Excuse me, Lord Gantry." I picked up my bucket and went the other direction, away from him. "I need to finish tonight. A pleasure to see you. Good day."

He took the bucket from my fingers. "Is it wrong for me to just look at you?"

"Yes. I've work to do."

"And I arrived with a request from my father."

Tramel. My heart began to pound.

"Cecilia, my father wants to see you. He's most anxious. The man is dying."

"The duke?" It was all I could say for at least a moment. "He has a will of iron. You're being overdramatic."

Felton stepped closer. "He's had a type of palsy. He'll die. It's his last wish to see you. Please do not deny him."

Tramel helped me so much, to travel to Demerara, passage to secure Enna and Noah's way. Every time I needed encouragement, he gave it. I owed him everything.

My husband put his hands on my shoulders. Then drew me into an embrace. "He needs to see you. Don't let him be chased by the Obeah spirits with things unsaid or done. The hauntings of the land of shadows—"

"I don't believe in that. I was Catholic, Felton. Then I converted to Anglican to marry you. It's my older sister who believed in spirits." Maybe Helena too. "I'm not sure what I believe anymore, not when the miracle of us went so wrong."

His fingers smoothed my chin, and he tilted my head until our gazes met. "My fault, Cilia. I let the adventure die."

Felton's face was so blank I couldn't tell if he believed anything he'd uttered. "You'd say anything to get me to come."

"Yes, and the duke would, too. But you've returned to London, when you could've started your adventure anywhere, even Warwick. That has to mean something."

It did.

Being here secured Noah's freedom, ensured that I had the means to earn money, and hide from the Lances and Gladstones, or so I thought.

My silence, our silence, grew.

"Tramel needs to see you. You know the bad nature of my relationship with him. Would I come to you on his behalf if it were not dire?"

A chill swept over me.

Blood sloshed in my veins as if it looked for a way out. I tried to still my hands.

"I close my eyes, Cilia, and I see us happy. Surely we can take this trip together and see Tramel and be civil."

The word *no* should be on my tongue, but it was always hard to say that to Felton when his voice was low and his eyes glowed of fire.

Under a Jamaican moon, he swore he understood me. He was my muse, my Roman soldier. Then we were at cross-purposes in Britain, strangers at Mayfair.

"Sweetheart." Felton peered down at me; with his loosed hair he looked like a corsair pirate. The auburn locks hit at his shoulders, waving in the air scented with paint fumes.

"I'm not asking for forgiveness or even a second chance. Just for you to agree to come say goodbye to a man who thinks the world of you."

"Felton."

His hand slipped to mine. His skin felt like a coal fire. "Wouldn't dream of asking you to listen to my taking responsibility for my mistakes. Or even asking you to explain why one mistake had to end everything."

One?

It wasn't one. The large, most unforgivable mistake wasn't even his. It was mine. I didn't keep pushing for Helena to come with me to England. I left her where Gladstone could take advantage of her.

Felton released my hands and walked past. His back was an inch from me. "I'll be your assistant tonight to help you get things done. Let me open this and stir it. I think that's how I can begin."

"I haven't agreed. You don't need to do that."

"No problem. This will hurry things along."

If I stretched my finger like the hand of God in Michelangelo's painting in the Sistine Chapel, I could trace the lines of Felton's straight shoulders, the curl of his legs as he stooped.

My heart, which should be frozen like that white ice of winter, lurched. Tramel was dying and Felton was acting like the duke—sweet and attentive.

"Cecilia, all this time apart, it should've softened us. Should have made us wiser. We can work together."

A hint of sage from his cologne wafted to my nose.

The scent reminded me of the good times when I thought I was the luckiest woman, when I believed in our marriage of convenience.

Comforting lies.

I knew better now. "Felton, I'm not sure that I can afford to leave, with so many theatres in need of scenery. It's the height of the season."

"This will give you a chance to offer the girls a proper goodbye. They miss you. I told you about Amelia. Have I mentioned how Agatha waited in your studio, hoping you'd return? She wanted to show how much more improved her brushwork is."

An ugly cry built.

I loved his daughters.

"Give Tramel his last wish, then I will give you yours. I'll find a way to end our marriage."

"That's quite a bargain."

He stopped stirring and wiped his hands on his handkerchief. "A desperate man can only hold on so long."

"Felton, let me think about it." I wanted to turn but his hand caught mine. Our fingers locked and his warmth crept up my arm.

I could curl into him, flat against his white, white shirt, and the heat of his body would overcome the chill in the air.

"A simple yes or no."

"I have people who depend upon me. I can't—"

"Bring them. You know how big Warwick is. You will have your studio and bedchamber. I'll stay in another wing. If we need more rooms, I'll make them available. Just help me with the duke's last wish. Help me say goodbye a proper way, like you wish you could have with Mr. Thomas."

My father . . . Felton didn't play fair. He twisted my heart, trapping it in such a thick web . . . how could I say no?

His voice was soft and tight. It was a melody of caution, the same sparse notes that he used when mentioning his father. "If you don't do this, what chance at reconciling will I have with the duke?"

He touched my cheek, warm, searing. "I have enough regrets. He does too with his own father."

The duke told me of his regrets. He feared dying alone like

him. I understood Tramel and knew he hadn't been good to Felton. The son would always struggle if I didn't help.

"Please, Cilia."

"I've responsibilities with the life I've chosen. I'm on a new adventure, one I'm crafting. One I control."

He bit his lip. His smile was as pained as it was forced. "Let us be off to Tramel. You remember it, Cecilia. The land, the windows. I know you were happier there. You must see it one last time. One last adventure for us."

It was impossible to ignore the pain Felton tried to hide.

And Tramel had been so good to me.

Head bowed, I conceded. "I must finish this commission before I go. I'm almost done. Then I'll collect my friends. Then you, Felton, you promise to make things right between us. You will end our marriage, fixing our grand mistake."

He released my hands and bowed a little. "I intend to fix every mistake."

Turning, he trotted off the stage and moved beyond the orchestra pit. "I'll sit and watch like a spectator. I modeled, but I never watched you paint."

The man sat with hands stretched behind his head.

Climbing up the scaffold, I was mad at myself. He'd done it again, charmed me to returning to Warwick with him, and without a tasty snack.

Hungry, self-conscious, I blocked everything from my head. It was about the art, not handsome Felton, who seemed to be unbothered about spending days journeying to Warwick so I could see the duke, a man who loved me more than his son.

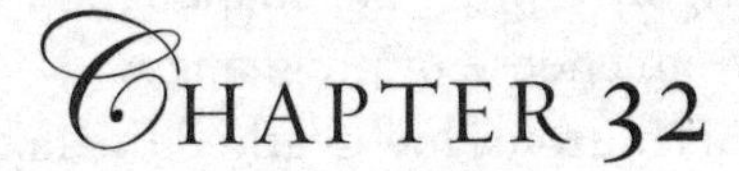

CHAPTER 32

FELTON—COMMANDING THE THEATRE

The theatre chair felt hard beneath him. Uncomfortable, angry, Felton pumped his hands by his sides. How long did he have to pretend he wasn't dying for her?

Calm.

Think.

Plan.

Well, he might look placid like a still lake, but tidal waves battered his soul. His training and all the situations he'd survived around the world hadn't been dimmed by his retirement.

Tramel wasn't here but he was still between them.

She'd agreed to return to gain a formal separation and to see the duke and the girls.

In desperation, he switched to Repington's advice. The clever fellow was right again. One, agree. Two, contact. Three, win.

Well, Cecilia would accompany Felton. Would the outcome have differed if he'd brought snacks? Would some Stilton cheese for his soon to be wife-no-more do, or had her taste changed to Tramel's illicit French treats?

He groaned, knowing it was Tramel who'd fed those lips. Who knew what smuggled delights he'd used to entice her?

He stole a glimpse of her, up again on that rickety scaffold, of her figure beneath her smock—fuller hips, thicker backside. Cilia was always a handful, wonderfully graceful, but she'd gained a little weight, making her shapelier.

Was the gain from cheese or pregnancy?

Fussing with his buttons, he breathed the faint honey scent on his fingertips—her face lotion. That smell reminded him of how she curled upon his shoulder as they slept at Warwick with the sound of the sea gentling them.

Gazing at Cecilia working at her passion, he calmed more. There was something magical, something wondrous about watching his wife lean and stretch with the poise of a dancer as she painted the larger-than-life landscape.

Beautiful.

The arch of her hand gliding and turning colors into a fence and meadows—life.

Agreeing to allow her *friends* to accompany them was the worst. How would that be romantic? The week-and-a-half trip was supposed to give them time to talk, time for him to dazzle her again.

Unless the friend was a son or daughter with her eyes.

His anger dissolved. Nothing mattered but her love. Absence and longing made him want her more.

His feelings had been frozen, put away since that December morn when he realized that he was in love with Cecilia. He should've been brave enough to say it. Why was it that a man who survived war and hundreds of dangerous engagements around the world feared admitting the truth?

"Are you bored yet, my lord?"

"Only of you being so formal, Cilia."

"You don't have to stay and watch. I said I'll go with you. I've given my word."

"Yes, but that doesn't seem to apply to vows. That 'till death do us part' the minister encouraged—I don't recall it being optional."

"Lord Gantry, I don't recall an exception for the Department of War and the Colonies either." She dropped her paintbrush. "I'm losing my concentration."

Felton rushed to the stage, picked up the fallen bristles and cleaned them with his handkerchief before climbing up. "I'm at your service, my dear. I'm glad to help. Tramel shouldn't be the only helpful one."

Grasping the handle, Cecilia caught his gaze, but her wary one made him look away. Attacking Tramel would win nothing.

It might make Felton lose everything.

"I'm glad that you went to him. Tramel kept you safe. I can't quibble with that. I merely wish that I knew how to make my wife as loyal to me as she is the duke."

"But I did go to him or leave you for him, as your sister or Gladstone would say."

He put his boot on the base of the scaffold and leaned on it. "Are you saying they are right?"

"I'm not going to convince you of anything."

"Cecilia, you truly should try to convince me of something."

"I did, but you're still here."

"That doesn't sound very generous." He released the scaffold support and it swayed. "Doesn't sound like you at all."

"Did a lot of growing up whilst I was away," she said with a laugh. "See things more as they are, not what I hope to paint."

That sounded like Tramel's influence. Ten months away did this. Couldn't love and care change her back?

She turned to her paints. "I suppose I'm done living as second place."

"You left because I was a fool, but you stayed away because you're choosing you, Cilia? Being friends with Tramel does affect a person."

"Someone other than my father-in-law needs to choose me. Don't you think?"

To regain her trust, Felton needed to become the person she turned to when she was fearful or sad or in need of a laugh. Like

Ashbrook had said, he needed to act fully committed, no longer standing back, no more doing enough to win the battle merely to lose the war.

Stepping away from the scaffold, he folded his arms and chuckled. "Words were cheap, I suppose." He clapped his hands. "Tell me how I'm to get started. Command me, Cilia. I need to do more."

She peered down at him. "Give me your opinion on my art."

Oh, no.

This could be tricky and further push her away. Too light and pithy or too syrupy in his praise, she'd never think well of him.

"Are the brush strokes too heavy, my lord? Does the scale not look right? What's your judgment?"

Back to formalities? Hand shading his eyes, he scanned the massive canvas while furtively gazing at her and the lip she bit.

He'd never noticed how sensitive she was to his opinion. Cecilia couldn't be indifferent to him. "Something about the way the light hits the clouds and spreads. It offers such perspective. Like all your paintings, in Town and at Warwick, I feel I can walk right in."

"You looked at them all?" Her voice had taken a light and airy tone. He must've said the right thing.

"Yes, I've studied them." He paddled back to the scaffold. "You never said why you made me pose as a Roman soldier and not like the one of the girls picnicking in a meadow."

"I like Rome. My father traveled there and told us of the massive stones. He always said we'd go and have an adventure."

"You never thought to go there when you left me. Your talent will only grow by seeing these things in person. I remember when . . ."

Her head dipped and she tugged off her paint-stained apron. "Other considerations take precedence. You understand competing priorities."

He did, and as he studied Cecilia's puffy cheeks, the wonderful weight gained in her bosom, Lady Ashbrook's words repeated, *the artist was with child*.

Theirs.

Not his, nor hers, but theirs—his and Cecilia's from the night he should've said he loved her.

Would Cecilia not tell him? A woman accused of infidelity by her husband wouldn't. Recovering her love wasn't all that was at stake. Saving the family they should've had was his new plan.

Felton—The Helpful Husband

Cecilia touched her face. "Do I have paint on my nose? You're staring."

"No. You're perfect. Still perfect." He tugged his hands behind his back. "What may I help do, my lady? Stir colors? Tidy rags? Take you home and feed you properly?"

"I'm working, but you can go home. This will take all night."

Maintain contact. That was Repington's second tenet. The man could give Liverpool a run. "I'll find a way to be useful. Being somewhat out of a profession has made me aimless. With the girls at Warwick, there are no demands of my time. Tonight, I can be out as long as I wish."

She shrugged and started adding more details to lines she'd drawn in the upper corner.

He relaxed his shoulders, trying hard not to look forlorn or torn or concerned.

Felton was all of those things, including mourning. Ten months apart when he could've been with her, protecting her, loving her, finding British treats to enthrall her and make her eyes sparkle—this was time they'd never get back.

He turned to jump from the stage. The notion took him back to the beginning, jumping out that government window and gratefully meeting Cecilia.

"Tell me about your party, Cilia. I want to make sure I have enough room and provisions for them. We will be a merry group."

"Just two, not much room at all. If that's too much, we can take the post."

A baby doesn't require much space. He'd loved holding Agatha the day she was born, and Amelia was most adorable at three months when she could hold her head up. The babe had slept against his lapel. "There will be enough room for two, and more."

She smiled at him, then stretched to the sky she'd made.

Lady Ashbrook missed a detail or two upon occasion. She could be wrong about the artist.

The changes in Cecilia could be the difference of ten months apart. None of them were bad. Who didn't like more woman to hold?

Maybe a babe is why she left Warwick. His father was miserable, but he'd tell Felton about a child, especially a son.

Where was this babe now?

In whose care did she leave his son or daughter?

No child of his could live in Covent Garden where so much vice occurred.

Felton had to do something with his hands. The scars on his left looked very exposed. "Your platform looks unsteady."

He moved to the base of it and poked at the limbs and struts. "Let me make this safer. A good foundation is best."

This was his truth and he'd grown in it since watching the Duke and Duchess of Repington and the Ashbrooks navigate their married lives.

Cecilia stretched to the top of the canvas to touch up a star, then bent to her paints. The scaffold rocked, and he put his weight against it. No more ignoring her safety, even if he was mesmerized by the smooth flexing and stretching of her trim arms.

The delicate motion of her hands changed the shape of the clouds, shifted the way the light reflected on the image.

"I could walk right into that meadow."

She stopped and dangled the paintbrush. Then she glanced at him.

For a moment, a second or more, she smiled, and he lost all comprehension of the wobbling.

Her half sleeves exposed her arms. His wife was a sculpture of the finest copper. She was Helen of Troy with a face that sent men to battle—a duke and his son.

Or Felton versus himself. He was at war with his soul, for all his missteps. Weeks had come and gone. Did she ache even a little for the times they had things right?

"Do you need any help, Cecilia?"

"No, Felton. I'm quite capable. This is my third commission."

Her tone sounded brusque.

He immediately raised his hands straight up. "I didn't mean you weren't capable. I merely want to help."

Even at this distance he could feel her bristling.

Was it his tone? Was there something wrong with her needing him? He decided to get her talking again. "First-rate, your landscape. The finest quality."

Her head whipped in his direction. Her hair, thick and curly, had come down from the thick braids she wore in her chignon.

"I think I must stipple more blue in the sky. What is your opinion?"

If he said yes, would that be interpreted as her art was lacking? If he said no, would she think him patronizing?

"I . . . I'm not sure. If I came closer, I could study it and be more sure of my answer."

The tip of her thin brush handle was along her soft bottom lip. "No. You stay there. But you're right about how things look different depending upon where you stand."

She turned back and added more indigo into the sky.

Felton wasn't sure if his answer passed muster, but he hadn't lost ground. Her heart was linked to her brushes. A little bit of herself went into her work. Such tension.

He thought taking a new bride to a new world would be

enough adventure for Cecilia, and that she'd make an unassuming wife. Her conversation was pleasant. She seemed grounded and thoughtful. The not so observant spy missed her passion. Art was her soul.

"Do you think about how we started, Cilia? I think people focus too much on endings and what went wrong, not enough on what was right."

"Felton, I need to get this right. Then we can leave and get to Tramel before it's too late. Unless you're here stalling. Is that what you and your cousins the Gladstones want—Tramel's death?"

"I'm not sure what they prefer. You can ask them about it. They'll all be in attendance at Warwick."

The grip on her brush tightened, and she snapped the handle in half. "Your cousin Jeremiah Gladstone will be there?"

"Yes. I'm sure he and my aunt would love to see you again too."

"More of your beloved family." Her tone was harsh. She began climbing down, and Felton braced against the shaking scaffold.

Halfway down, the bright chandelier light poured through her loose smock, illuminating the woman, the wonderful curves.

So many things to rediscover once her love was restored.

"Except for Tramel and the girls, my family hasn't been kind. Perhaps I can make a point of clearing things up with them."

"Yours. Your family." She bit her lip and turned toward the audience's chairs. "Does it matter? You're going to end us. They'll be happy."

He helped her the final distance, setting her slippers to the stage. For a moment, she was in his arms.

Thick thighs, small waist, more heft to the perfect bosom—Cecilia, with the paint smudge on her nose, was more perfect. "I won't be happy . . . knowing that I didn't at least right this wrong. My offering them grace may have given them and you a false impression. You're my Lady Gantry. You deserve your due respect."

Her hands were on his chest; the coldness of her fingers seeped through his shirt.

He tightened his arms about her. "Still always chilly. I'm almost always hot. Missed giving you my heat."

She jumped away, breathing heavily as always, every time they were close. Pulling on her coat, she headed down the steps. "I need air."

"But it's colder outside."

Those sweet lips parted, then she shook her head. "This won't take long."

Trying hard not to smile, he dipped his chin. "I'll see if I can get the scaffold tighter. It will be steady and dependable when you return."

Across the empty stage, their gazes met and tangled like time hadn't gotten away from them.

Then she left.

There was no need to give chase. Felton knew she'd be back. An incomplete work, one commissioned by the theatre, would be finished. Her love of art would allow nothing less.

Tightening the ropes, binding limb to limb, he needed a plan. Just being in the same carriage with strangers to Warwick wasn't enough privacy to air and forgive all the grievances needed to repair their marriage.

Yet, he still lacked the clues to what would heal the rift. Like his bride, time would soon run away.

Chapter 34

Cecilia—Rumbling Remorse

Walking outside into the cool evening air was an act of defiance, the need for distance from my husband and his dispassionate politeness. I'd left him and he didn't have the decency to be angry at me. Was saving face and returning with the wayward wife worth more than his feelings?

Felton wasn't invisible to me. He was a good man.

The chill in the air snaked up my arms. My purple redingote had thick sleeves, but the cold still got to me.

My personal coal pot was inside, fixing my scaffold and now resolving to defend me.

Unbelievable. Wanting to scream, I clasped my elbows and shook myself. Instead of banging my head on the stone of the theatre walls, I studied the sounds of the city. Link boy shouts—they were beginning to gather to light pitch torches and guide the carriages of night revelers.

The streets would fill with crowds, hungry for the night's entertainment and so noisy.

Clang. Bang. Shouts.

Covering my ears, I held still, or maybe I couldn't move. Closing my eyes, I calmed.

I should move back inside the theatre, but I couldn't take those steps for I was at risk the minute I saw Felton.

I still cared for my husband, cared about his opinion, cared about why he put himself at risk for a country that made him lie, cared about all the times I was angry at him and he might not've returned.

Felton could stir both my temper and that intangible thing that made me feel warm and secure and beautiful.

I was all those things to him, even when he was mad.

Months and months away should mean that I was no longer susceptible.

Yet, here I was, fearful of falling apart or back into his arms.

My eyes snapped open, for I wasn't sure what the darkness meant. Or what met me there.

That was the problem. For now, I hoped my friend the duke recovered, and prayed to the Holy Father that the rift between father and son would heal.

A bell rang in the distance.

The shouts of boys sounded louder.

Everything would be starting. The sizzle. The adventures.

This one with Felton had to end.

No settling for last place. No hiding to keep a peace that violated mine.

Me and my family, first, now, and forever. "If that means giving up my vow to kill Gladstone, I'll abandon it."

I said it aloud again. That should mean it was true.

Clasping my elbows, I started back inside. I had a commission to complete before I began practicing more lying affirmations.

When I returned, I spied Felton climbing on the scaffold.

A leg here, taut arm there, he'd straddled the thing.

Not a dresser like Tramel or the men of the ton, as they called the fashionable set here, but he looked well in his fitted chocolate breeches and cracker-crisp white shirt.

Lean and muscled he remained, but I'd eaten so many coconuts and mammee apples and hundreds of other things that shouldn't be baked with sugar, I wasn't thin.

Well, I'd never been thin, but I was always happy.

This glorious fuller-figured me—it was another thing to criticize. His family loved to poke. Felton would ignore it to keep the peace.

"Cecilia. You're back." He leapt down.

"No need for concern. I said I would be back, my lord."

"Yes. You did." His smile was broad, big enough to fill the stage. "Pleasant walk? I know you enjoy walking."

"It was, but it's getting crowded." My stomach rumbled. The noise sounded like the trumpets in the orchestra pit.

Tossing on his waistcoat, Felton whipped up his coat. "Knowing you, you haven't given a thought to nourishment. What if I go find something for you to eat?"

Why did my hungry stomach tighten at the thought of him feeding me? "Um. No, my lord. You needn't bother, but do leave and come back in the morning."

"I'm prepared to spend all night with you. I love watching."

Was Felton tormenting me on purpose?

Cruel for the handsome—

"What say you to a little cheese toast? With good crusty bread, slathered in creamy butter."

Everything in my middle churned. "No bother. The old masters suffered for their art."

Gripping my hand, he led me up the stairs. "It's my pleasure. Slowing down, taking time. Touching and tasting—I see the value in all of this now."

My cheeks felt hot, but I shouldn't fall prey to his teasing words.

After spinning me out of my coat and lining up the edges, he laid it gently on the stage. "I will take my time and look for the constellations you taught me. Remember lying awake in Jamaica? What was that twinkling planet?"

My face fevered. He purposely brought up us watching Mars blink red and white in the late night sky while we lay together in a hut in Kingston. It was romantic.

"Cilia?"

"Oh. Mars. Food. Thanks. More work to do, my lord."

"Felton. Call me that as you've always done when you're not cross. I'm your Felton, and you shall always be my Cilia. Your gentling accent is the only way to make that name, Felton sound strong and amorous. I love it, Cilia."

Only he called me that.

And I liked his middle name, so different from his ordinary first one of David.

"But . . ." Felton said, biting hard on his lip, a gust of hot air fleeing his nostrils.

Now my hand shook. "And here it comes."

"It's not very practical to do a large canvas, so much labor and it lasts for a month. Then it's torn down or replaced or heaven forbid painted over."

"It's the purview of the manager to want new and better."

"I'm a fan of old and reliable. Is that what the manager at the King's Theatre does? I suppose it's better than your talent being hidden under a sheet. Or sold for pennies in the market."

He'd said he discovered my art in my studios, but I hadn't mentioned the ones I sold. "You truly are a spy, nosing around. I'm surprised you didn't just appear."

"Retired, but I waited for an invite. I want you to trust me, like when we met." He still had my hand from helping me onto the stage. He put his thumbs to work making circles on my wrist. "Your hand still tenses in the same spots."

That feeling, that old draw started in my heart.

"And I'd love to be selfish and have every piece of your art forever."

"Like father, like son."

A tremor set in his cheek. "I can see why Tramel and I are in agreement."

He released me, and I climbed the scaffold. It didn't rock. Felton had made it sturdier. "How long will it take for us to get to Tramel?"

"A week and a half, almost two depending upon the state of

your party. I just did the trip with Amelia and Agatha. With the stops and starts, it took ten days. We won't be traveling with little ones, right?"

If Felton used his connections to learn I'd sold art in the market, he probably knew where I lived. He might even know about Enna and Noah.

Color stained his cheeks, but his smile was small and set to unreadable as he said, "I see that brow furrowing. Bring your party with us. If a second carriage is needed, I'll get one. Everyone will be cozy."

There was a time at the beginning when we met, when we left Demerara as a newly married couple, that I knew Felton's thoughts. I didn't know this look.

He buttoned his greatcoat. "I'll bring back coffee and some sort of hearty roll. Maybe a bit of cheese if I'm lucky, or the toast. That will keep you energized and help you to complete your work."

"Thank you, my lord."

He stopped at the edge of the stage. "Is it your sister who will be joining us? I look forward—"

"She's dead, Felton. I didn't get to her in time."

"Cilia, I'm so sorry."

Palm lifted and flat like a shield to bat away hollow words, I nodded. "Not as sorry as me. I let my sister down, and it's my fault. I chased adventure without her. I didn't live up to my promise."

"It was the war, Cecilia. That's not your fault."

"Like I said, I went to Demerara and returned. The war still rages."

Even at this distance I saw his coat sleeve ripple. He yanked at the door. "Illegally breaking the blockade is not something to brag about. You could've been killed."

"It was worth the risk if I'd saved Helena. She didn't die alone, but in my arms. I suppose that's something."

Felton clasped his fingers like in a prayer, but what could he do? Pray for her resurrection? Give thanks for Noah, the boy I'd never, ever let a Gladstone or a Lance control?

I touched my rumbling stomach. "A roll would be nice but save the dispassionate speech. I don't want to argue. My emotions are for my art."

"Cecilia, don't be fooled by a calm exterior. I'm mortified. I know how you loved your sister. I failed you and Helena. If I'd known she was sick—"

My glare silenced him.

She didn't die from a cold or weakness. She died bringing life into the world, the seed of a man who betrayed her. I couldn't share a word of this. Felton's family had power. They could take Noah and could even return him to enslavement. Would never risk my boy to prove a point.

Looking down, Felton rubbed at his chin then sought my eyes again. "I'm glad she wasn't alone and that you decided to return to England. You could've stayed. Coming back means you know that your place is here."

"The art brought me back."

"At least you didn't say you came back for Tramel." He went down the steps then came back up. "Why didn't you tell me? I could've done something to help."

"When? Between your visits to your dear friends or Department of War and the Colonies missions? What would you have said differently to support my family? Wait longer than May, so Helena could die alone?"

Fat braids fell from my chignon like a veil. Then I realized I was shaking. Putting my arms about myself, I bent my head. "You won't understand. Thank you for the coffee. Make sure it's hot."

"I will get piping hot coffee, because I know how you like it. I've studied what you like. It's my pleasure to do so. But I wish you'd studied me, then you'd know how I ache for you and am dying inside for everything you've endured. Don't think I didn't care. That's very wrong."

The heat and bitterness in Felton's tone was new.

I'd never heard him angered, not since the day he jumped into Tramel's face because he believed Gladstone's lies of an affair.

With a shrug I started to paint. "It's nice to care but better to have passion and choose a side. The duke did."

"Of course he would. He'll always do something self-serving or morally wrong. The laws be damned. How can you be in his sphere, Cilia, and not see the corruption? His sins will burn you."

"There's beauty in ashes. And there's something to say about a man who openly asks for forgiveness of past misdeeds and means it."

The stiffness in Felton's stance, his squinting stare blazed with fire. "You don't know him like I do. I pray you never will."

He turned, putting his back to me. "Coffee, hot coffee. It shall be yours. I'll make haste."

Powering out of the hall, his slam of the door made the wall shake, everything but the scaffold he'd shored up, which held steady.

My husband was mad, but instead of seeing my sister's death as our failing, our inability to make good on promises, he'd turned this into another gambit between him and the duke.

What would happen to all that anger when his father died?

No longer able to think of them, I stirred my paint. I had to finish this commission. Perhaps I could repay my debt to the duke by helping Felton.

That might make things easier between Felton and me, when we finally let each other go.

CHAPTER 35

FELTON—PEACEFUL COFFEE BREAK

It took everything in Felton—his training, his trademark logic, his resolve—to choose peace and remain calm. Storming down Brydges Street, he counted stars, carriages, prostitutes, and fools, he being the first member in this latter category.

How could Cecilia think him unconcerned about her sister?

How dare she place him, a man of reason, into the shoes of an unfeeling dullard.

Breathing fire, he crossed to Russell Street then journeyed to King. The prostitute counts continued to rise. Covent Garden at night was a source of endless entertainment and deadly distractions.

If he'd known Helena was ill, could he have asked Liverpool to allow him to journey to Demerara? No. An operative who quit was of little value. He'd been cut off—no intelligence, no access. He would've rejoined if it meant saving Helena.

No wonder Tramel was her hero. He'd break any rule to serve his needs.

For a moment, one solitary second, Felton envied the duke, the freedom with which he went about his life.

Head down, Felton kept alert, though he almost wanted to encounter one of the Garden's infamous pickpockets just to beat upon someone to release his rage.

Cilia, poor Cilia. It was daring and showed such heart to try to rescue her sister, but that wasn't the adventure she deserved.

The trip he'd concocted to draw them together as they ventured to Warwick looked like a failing plan. His spy tactics didn't work and the Repington's advice merely had him agreeing to separate. How was Felton to win his wife?

The longer he walked in Covent Garden the more he tried to remember why they worked. In Kingston, a week after their wedding, they were kindred spirits sheltering in a small hut waiting for a hurricane to pass. She was so nervous, so jittery at each noise. He was her rock and assured her that all would be well.

Cecilia trusted him.

In that hut, the winds banged on the green and white shutters. She seemed lost until he held her. He liked holding her.

Then he thought it silly, as a man of the world, to be so thoroughly beguiled. If he'd trusted what he felt, he'd still have her love.

The duke gave her what she wanted. Did *he* have her love?

Felton stopped mid-step.

He'd never ever wanted to be his father until this moment, the moment he could see things as Cilia did. The duke respected her art, gave it honor, and tried to save her sister.

The man was her hero. Perhaps Tramel, seeing Jane and the Gladstones alienate her, seized the opportunity. Felton's stupidity surely pushed the two together.

Yet, why would Tramel say that Jeremiah Gladstone needed to die? Why did the duke want his nephew dead to please Cecilia?

Stewing, breathing hard, even punching the air, Felton walked until King Street dead-ended at Rose. Carriages whipped past as link boys waving torches guided them toward the mews.

A shiny black barouche, with a gilded crest that resembled Repington's, whipped past.

Couldn't be.

His friend was less of a theatre patron than Felton.

No, he was at Sandlin, personally overseeing the packing of

his military maps for his family's move to the country and caring for his pregnant duchess.

Rose Street was noisy. The Lamb and Flag tavern was open for business. Cheers and jeers sounded from the patrons. Was that cooking beef and onions scenting the air? Cecilia's favorite was beefsteak.

Food. Their special language.

Her face lit when he'd brought her treats from his travels. Through the window of the loud tavern, he saw his man-of-all-work sitting at a table swilling ale. Watson might be singing.

More hidden talent amongst those closest to him.

The door of the establishment opened, and the song and fragrance of the hot food touched Felton. When he stepped inside his stomach growled almost as loudly as Cecilia's had.

Drinking tunes were boisterous. People stumbled over one another.

Watson waved him forward to his table. "You done, sir? Can we go?"

Thick, tightly curled hair parted to the side and tied back, Watson sat back with his red jacket opened. He stared at the singers in the back of the tavern. "I can get the carriage."

He didn't ask about Cecilia or if Felton had made amends to his wife. The matter-of-fact man must not think it possible.

"Lady Gantry is in the middle of finishing a commissioned painting. That's when we leave."

"Oh, the marchioness is working. I see, my lord. Modern marriages, I take it."

This didn't feel very modern. It felt very old, a mirror to his stepmothers' and the duke's fraught unions.

Oh lord, that couldn't be how Cecilia felt—trapped and angry.

Sighing like his soul would escape, Felton called to a barmaid. "I'm going to head back to the Drury Theatre with something to eat and a tankard of coffee that Lady Gantry and I will share."

Watson's thick brows went up. "Oh. Very good, sir. She's happiest when you two are together, eating."

His tone was sarcastic and grating.

Felton sighed again, his lungs shriveling as he dropped into a seat. "My wife and I are speaking to each other. That's progress."

"Modern and with progress, indeed."

Even with a little island accent, the flat pronouncement of Felton's failings was not appreciated. He'd fire the man if Watson wasn't a paragon of hard work and good sense and hadn't saved his and Johnson's backsides in Grenada.

Felton leaned forward. "She's painting, sir. You remember how focused she becomes."

"Yes. Yes, I do." Watson drank more. Foam covered his lip.

Drumming the table, Felton glared at his man. "Maybe you can suggest what's good."

"The food here is quite delicious, my lord. She'll appreciate it like the marmalade. Spared you the toga, I believe."

Did everyone know his business? "You do ridiculous things when you wish for peace."

Watson chuckled. "When you were away, Lady Gantry would paint all day without stopping. I think only you made sure she ate."

He glanced at his man's face. "You never saw to it?"

"Lady Jane had me on other tasks. Then I was to take care of the Gladstones when they visited. They were a sizable contingency with competing attentions."

"You mean they liked ignoring Lady Gantry."

"They believed their actions were sanctioned by your absences. She didn't contradict them, but Tramel did. He's probably the reason she didn't leave sooner."

"You know that my service to the Crown meant I had to be away."

"I know that, sir. But no one else." He chuckled and gulped his ale. "Ask yourself why no one else. Maybe you're pushing up this hill because you don't like to lose. I think Lady Gantry is worth more than a half-hearted effort."

That sounded like Ashbrook's notions. "I love her. I was too foolish to admit to loving her instantly. I thought myself ridiculous to love so fast, so completely."

"Sorry, Lord Gantry." Watson nodded. "As voluptuous as the beautiful Lady Gantry is, even I thought you concocted this marriage as something the Department of War and the Colonies made you do."

"Tell me about Gladstone. How did my cousin act while I was gone?"

"Like a spoiled rich man. He made some very wrong remarks to her. Tramel made him apologize."

"Why is my father the good one in this scenario? You remember—"

"He's focused on what he wants. He wants Lady Gantry."

"Why can't she see that?"

"She's here in Town, not at Warwick, the place she loves. She knows. A woman always knows."

If Cecilia knew, was that why she left the duke? Felton tapped the table again. "Tramel said she wants Gladstone dead. What have you seen to warrant that?"

Watson sat to attention. His military training certainly stirred. "Assassination, my lord?" He rubbed his hands together like an evil henchman.

"What have you seen? Liverpool let you retire to be able to watch my family while I was away in case one of the governments or rebel leagues we disrupted decided to pay a visit."

"Yes, and I was able to be with my Matilda until the end." The man's cheeky smile faded.

"Tell me, Watson, what could put the artist and the duke in league? Gladstone can have nothing on the man; Tramel would kill him. With his underworld contacts, it's possible. It sounded to me that the duke wanted to do it himself. It's personal."

"And now he wants you to kill Gladstone." Watson grinned as if he'd been given gold. "Do we break out the suitcase?"

Felton's suitcase—his case of special weapons—went into the

attic last December. "What did you see when my cousin was near Lady Gantry?"

"Antagonism. Slights. One time he was very aggressive towards her when he was drunk. Tramel sent him away."

"Tramel did that?" Felton was grossly unaware of the goings-on in his house. "Then I owe him. But is that enough to warrant killing him? Duels are illegal."

"It's the duke, my lord. Perhaps Gladstone has outlived his usefulness, or he's a threat somehow."

His bumbling cousin, a threat? Felton started to laugh. "I act invisible to observe everyone. Gladstone acts like a buffoon because he is one. That's still not a cause to die. Half of London would be gone."

Watson slurped. "Well, I'll make sure the old suitcase is ready to go."

"You can head back to the house and get things prepared. Only one person can tell me why Gladstone must die. She's painting all night."

"Order the sweet biscuits, my lord. She'll like that. And plenty of coffee for the both of you. That'll get you through."

Felton crossed his fingers. "Head out and be back at first light."

"I'll wait here till the tavern closes. You might need a way home."

"I won't, not until Lady Gantry is done. We'll leave together."

"Very good, sir." Watson started singing again.

A server finally came, and Felton ordered a feast. Whatever Gladstone did, Cecilia would say before they arrived in Warwick.

Yet if she confessed that something egregious had been done to her, something that hurt her, Gladstone would pay. The buffoon might lose his life. Felton did love Cilia enough to kill.

Chapter 36

Cecilia—Art Appreciation

Finished. The Drury Lane commission was complete. I stood on my scaffold, admiring my handiwork.

The sky had that distant feel I wanted, with hints of red. It blended in the gray to make the eye sense that something stirred, in the offing.

Stretching, Felton arose from his seat in the audience. "Cecilia, are you dizzy? Are you in need? You didn't eat much of your biscuits."

"Better than dizzy. I'm done." I lifted my arms and gave a blood curdling yell. "Done! What do you think?"

He took his time, his head turning left then right. Everything grew loud as he clapped like his hands would fall off. "You've done it. It's brilliant."

Felton's reaction startled me. He sounded like the duke with such vigor in his tone.

Tottering, I almost lost my balance. The next thing I knew, Felton's hands were on mine like he'd anticipated my going wobbly.

"You're dizzy from this accomplishment, Cecilia."

Before I could say otherwise, he'd spirited me over his shoulder and off the platform. Then he made me sit on the side of the stage. My feet literally dangled into the orchestra pit.

In my palms, he put a biscuit. It had a sugary glaze. Then he poured a mug of coffee. "It's cold now. But it should restore you."

I blinked at him feeding me treats like before.

His high-bridged nose lifted, and a smirk filled his face. "I might be overdoing it, but I missed doing things for you."

"Does that mean you'll be leaving soon?"

He frowned and I felt awful. "Sorry, Felton. I don't want to say the wrong thing."

He picked a piece of the crust from his basket and buttered it, then he lifted it to my lips. "Cilia, I just need to work harder."

His finger touched my mouth. It sent a flush to my face. My pulse rushed.

The buttery joy, he pushed across my lips. "Let me have a better look at your canvas."

Relief and disappointment swept over me as he moved away. With his back to me, I couldn't see if his countenance filled with joy or disapproval.

He was silent for a long time, too silent.

"What is it, my lord?"

"I think this is the first time I've seen you finish a piece in my presence. Sadly, you never finish the Roman soldier piece. We get distracted."

Kisses and hugs and that thing that felt like love, surrounding me when I was in his arms. It was the best and worst distraction. "My lord, that painting was silly."

"Never that. It has given me fond memories."

With his hands to his hips, he turned to me. "I hope Tramel didn't laugh too much."

"Only a little, Felton."

"This was a treat for me, Cilia, watching you move, the decisions you make about the pressure and colors you put to your brushes. It all amazes me."

"That's what Tramel said. You sound . . . just like him."

His face clouded.

I shouldn't have said that. He'd come back with coffee and

food and remained patient and encouraging throughout the night. "Sorry."

"No. Continue." He again put his back to me. "You say I sound like him when I praise your work?"

"He loves art. We would talk for hours about technique and hues."

"Is that what you did when you stayed at Warwick through March? It was quite clever. That would be the last place I'd ever look for you. I even refused his Christmas invitation. And yet, you would have been there. We could've started over sooner."

"My lord, please."

He knelt and fussed with his boot. "Is that when you went to Demerara?"

Stuffing the rest of the sweet biscuit in my mouth, I kept quiet. I didn't want Tramel's help to be another complaint from Felton. They needed healing, not more enmity.

Stretching again, he came closer and attempted to retie his cravat. "Sorry. Secrets and curiosity do get the better of me, and you're pretty clever to outwit me."

"Your pride prevents you from seeing any good in Tramel." I stuffed another biscuit to my lips. "Forgive me. Not my place to comment on your family." My words were full of crumbs.

Felton's fingers flared, spreading open then closing to a fist as he pulled his arms behind his back. "No, continue telling me of his goodness and mercy. Perhaps the wisdom will now follow me all the days of my life."

"He saved my life as I walked away, struggling in the snow. I wasn't coming back to you just to be warm. Don't take what's wrong with us out on the duke."

His mouth dropped open, then he sat at my side. Long legs dangled near my short ones, and he scooted until we were hip to hip. "It's clear that I owe my father. He did us a service. You and I can talk, even argue with one another, and no one has run."

He glanced at me, the sweet way he did when we awoke together in his chambers. "Your neck is stiff."

His index finger swirled along my throat, tracing the stiffness that led to my shoulders. "I don't want you troubled; let me stop being a pain in your neck."

The massage and kneading of the muscles along my spine began. The man knew exactly what to do and how—the right pressure, the heat of his skin to mine. "I need you to help the girls understand that this is my fault. That it's me you no longer want. They aren't the reason we are done."

"They can't think that, Felton. It wasn't."

My head dipped to his chest as his hands shredded my knots. Thumbing circles behind my ears, along my throat, he dipped his brow upon my crown. His coffee breath warmed my cold nose, and I remembered the intimacy of his touch. "They miss you, Cilia."

I missed them too. And somewhere in my icy heart, I remembered this, these quiet moments when Felton's touch meant so much.

When his hands dropped away, I longed for the sweet tension to continue. Blinking, willing away the sleep that wanted my eyes to close, I stared at my canvas. "Three weeks of work, and now this is done."

His face held the brightest smile. Was that pride beaming in his eyes?

That couldn't be.

Art wasn't practical.

My tiredness made me see things, things that could never exist.

"You need to sleep. My carriage is in a close mews. I can take you to your residence to gather your party and we can be off."

The ride to Warwick was a long one, but was it wise to sleep in a carriage and afford Felton the opportunity to interrogate Enna?

He rolled down the cuff of his white sleeves. Everything was wrinkled. He was thin but well muscled, almost deceiving in his strength. He turned to the scaffold. "I shall take this apart."

I tugged at my apron. It swallowed my thick limbs, my small frame. "It's not necessary. The theatre manager will attend to it."

"Instruct me, Lady Gantry. Like you did in our posing, tell me exactly what you'd like me to do."

To have his hands on me again was a scandalous desire. It'd not bode well for me, even if they could stave off the light pains of a headache.

He glanced at me. "Cilia, you look exhausted. Let me help."

"My paint palette is up top."

Felton climbed the scaffold and scooped up the treasured one I'd brought from home. It was made of gommier tree, like the boat we'd used to escape Demerara.

Felton lay flat on the scaffold, looking up at my canvas. "It is wondrous. Wish I could take it with me."

"Then I wouldn't be paid, my lord. Hurry down. I don't like looking up to you."

His head bobbled over the side. "That wasn't always true."

It wasn't.

On the fateful day he proposed at the doorway to the Stabroek ballroom, he mesmerized me, changing from a court jester to what the British called a rake, to a debonair fellow who commanded the room. My father couldn't deny his offer for my hand.

On our wedding trip to Kingston, he fascinated me with his knowledge of the terrain, the people, even the secrets of Jamaica. He was my adventure, until I realized I needed one of my own.

"I see you thinking down there. Are you coming up with your next masterpiece?"

Wiping at my eyes, I glimpsed at him in astonishment. "What a transformation a separation can make."

Wary blue-black eyes sought mine. "Change is good, I hear."

This was beginning to feel too cozy, too comfortable. "Once we are back from Warwick, I'll need to quickly seek out my next employ."

"Of course." He climbed down. "Let me hand you your brushes. I'm told an artist's tools are very important."

"They need to be cleaned and dried so the bristles remain sharp, the belly and heel stay nice and tight."

He handed me my fine brushes and my bucket of cleaning water. Felton stood over me as I washed them free of the colors.

"Lean against me. I'll steady you. You need to be off your feet."

Yawning, I surrendered to his strength and slumped against his leg.

Closing my eyes, I was in my studio at Warwick. The hold about me tightened. When I peered up, my friend, my rock, was shadowed. I couldn't discern who—

"Cilia, you've fallen asleep."

I startled and Felton bent down and picked me up.

The heat of him.

The smell of starch and coffee and man wrapped about me as surely as his embrace. In the silence of the theatre, I fit against him, like always. I missed his heat. Before my limbs turned to a jelly, wobbly like those desserts on fancy tables, I tried to move, but couldn't. "We are all done . . . here."

Felton's hands slipped to my sides, and he offered a gentle rub to my lower back. "Love being your assistant. Maybe that can be my next profession."

My brain was slowing, fighting the dreamy state and that hunger to be safe and supported.

"Now what do I do, Cecilia? How can I help you more?"

Felton the planner, the obligation runner, always knew what to do. The man I fell for under a Jamaican moon looked at me now, nervous and curious, drawing closer.

Then it hit me, waking me from a fog. "This is like before. You feed me. You act sweet."

"Then we make amends and end up forgiving each other." His voice was steady.

Yet mine was low. "No. Not this time."

"But, Cilia—"

"We're done. The manager will be here soon."

His face didn't change. He stepped from me and put his hands to his sides. "We should do something with the small paint samples. They all can't go to waste."

"The theatre might have need of the special blues to touch up the art during the shows. I'll make new colors when I need them. Do not trouble yourself."

He picked one jar of the translucent silver that I'd used for the clouds. "Seems a shame to let all the good go to waste."

I took my brushes and laid them in the muslin to form a tight bundle. "Sometimes starting anew, I can make the colors brighter, better than before."

"Letting things be is not something I've learned to do."

His tone held an edge even if it was a whisper. It was an omen that Felton wouldn't give up. He wouldn't let me be during the confines of our trip.

He finished packing my supplies. "The manager should hurry, Lady Gantry. We'll gather your party and head to Warwick."

I nodded, realizing that this visit to honor the duke would be one of the hardest things I'd ever done. My trust in me and my knowledge of what I wanted would be challenged mile by mile by one of the king's spies, one who'd use his wits to win.

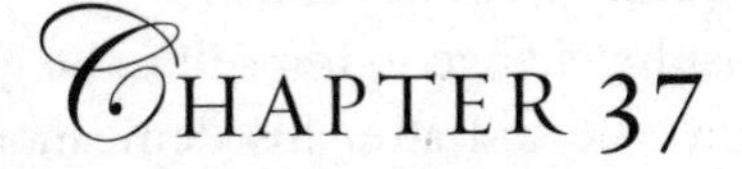

CHAPTER 37

FELTON—WORTH HER WAGES

This was all a test.

That was how Felton had to look at things as he squatted to pick up the last of Cecilia's drop cloths.

In his work for the Department of War and the Colonies, he'd become used to having to blend in and to not be noticed. Assimilation in country was his specialty. It was why Lord Liverpool, the Secretary for War and the Colonies, had Felton go on so many missions once he left his regiment.

Yet, being invisible wasn't what Cecilia needed. Like her art, she craved sparkle and flash, those types of adventures.

Glancing at her securing the pigment bottles, those tantalizing fingers slipping along the caps, he noticed she still wore the simple gold band he'd given her.

That had to mean something.

She smiled at her brushes like they told her what to paint next. Her round face, the lift of her lips—he'd missed it all far too long. When he'd offered her support, she had to feel the tension betwixt them, the attraction and pain of not tasting her mouth.

Repington advised him not to give in to these tender emotions swirling about them until it was clear she was ready to surrender and love him again.

She wasn't where Felton was.

Unless he was a canvas, he doubted she'd find any joy in him.

He stewed and stared, wanting to be handled like her dependable brushes, never far from her reach.

What else must he change in himself to be given such care?

On assignments, he did alter his demeanor—from suave, to bumbler, from priestly to militaristic, from fool to assassin. What did she need?

"Where is Mr. Smithers?" Cecilia untied, then retied her bundle. "Is it almost seven?"

He checked his pocket watch. "Almost. It's still early, my dear. What if I take you to your residence? You can gather your friends and then return here to wait. The ladies, I'm sure, won't mind."

"Ladies?"

The look on her face with her brows knitting indicated a mixed party. A man, or more so a little boy. A son could be her companion.

His throat tightened as his resolve sharpened. There wasn't anything he wouldn't do to reconcile and rebuild his family.

"Are you changing your mind, my lord? You want me to come by myself?"

"No. Of course not. The more the merrier."

The front door rattled open and in came a fast-walking man. The way he checked his watch, one would imagine that something was behind schedule.

Pulling off her smock, Cecilia laid it over her bundle. "Looks like we don't have to make any new decisions, my lord. Mr. Smithers is here."

As the man grew closer, Felton became angry. What type of man would require a woman to work all night without any apology?

The balding man was well past his prime, slouchy and disheveled. He stopped close to the stage.

"Mr. Smithers," Cecilia said, "I've finished on time as promised."

"I'd heard that you were working through the night. But I still didn't believe—"

"It was a struggle." She pulled on her purple coat. "Then the right way to finish came at last. I think it one of my best."

The man clapped his hands. "This will keep my production on schedule."

He lifted his gaze again toward the panel. "Mrs. Cecilia, well done. But, the more I look at it, it's not quite what I expected. But it'll do."

Smithers's words didn't match the greed in his bulging eyes.

Felton had hung back near the scaffold.

Invisible.

Nonetheless, he couldn't be thus and allow her to be cheated. He stalked forward. "Another masterpiece. Betta than what she done for the King's Theatre."

With his cockney accent perfected, Felton added a grunt and then tossed on his waistcoat.

Her lips wriggled, then her gaze returned to Smithers. "It's better than you hoped. Admit it, sir. The audience will see the hero's journey when they think of a dusk sky of azure and silver. It brings the peace of the countryside to London."

"For a foreigner, how can you be so sure? I suspect you haven't been anywhere but here or one of the port cities. That's where—"

Felton's loud cough filled the space, cutting off what had to be something small-minded and a slight.

Cecilia grabbed her smock and brush bundles. She suddenly looked very small, very tired. "My travel is nothing to this. Fields are fields everywhere, but these are fields leading to the Isle of Purbeck."

It was of that and more. Behind Warwick, away from the cliffs of Ballard, was a quiet meadow, one of Cecilia's favorite walks. He'd picked flowers from the distant bushes she'd mirrored. Felton noticed the white and blue petals of the sweet violets. Was this from her memories of when they all lived there, or from the early spring before she went to Demerara?

"Mr. Smithers," she said, with her accent beginning to flare. That happened when she was mad or filled with emotion. "Admit that this is more than you expected. Your patrons will be moved by it."

Felton was. It stung his insides that Smithers objected and forced her to defend her art. Something would ease in his chest if he laid the fool flat out on the stage.

"I finished the commission." Her voice rose, the words sounding proud like a command. "Compensate me."

Smithers rubbed under his chin like one of the awful villains of theatre pieces. "What if we settle for half? Then we can be done with this haggling."

"That don't sound quite right." Felton pressed forward. "In fact, I'd call you a cheat. Finished fine and ahead of schedule. And ya want to cheat." Felton raised his fists. "Outside to settle ya debt."

Smithers eyed him up and down. "Who's this man? You're a widow, Mrs. Cecilia. Thought you were decent."

Her face reddened.

"I'm the good woman's helper and part-time bill collector." He yanked at the canvas. "I take this down for ya, ma'am."

"Sirs, please stop." Panic sounded in her tone, but Felton had to carry out his threat.

"Which half do ya want for the cheap price, Smithers? Say the pieces ya gonna pay for."

Hands waving, Smithers stepped to him. "Don't do that. It will take too long to get a proper one made. She should get less. My patrons may not like what one of these people painted."

The man winked like somehow two males should be in league to cheat a woman.

A quick dip in his pocket, Felton pulled his knife and picked up the edge of the canvas. "Ya want only the bottom. Bottom it is."

"Now wait. You can't do that." Purple in the face, coughing like his lungs would explode, Smithers sobered.

"Pay her," Felton said again. "She's worth her wages."

"So loud. Too loud." She held her ears. "Men overtalking me. Smithers wants to be cheap. My hired help just wants this transaction done. Smithers, you owe me two guineas, pay me one and a half, then we're done."

"Fine." Grinning, Smithers dug into his purse and pulled out the coins. "I think this is fair. You're not giving me what I wanted. But I'm sure your muscle here will take care of anything extra you need."

Putting the jingling coins into her pocket, Cecilia nodded, clutched her brushes and smock bundles and started up the aisle, running again.

She was good with being cheated?

Growling at the fool manager, Felton threw on his greatcoat and gave chase. He followed in silence until they were on Brydges Street.

"Cecilia, order me to get all your money."

She stopped and turned to Felton. Squinting a little, she put a hand to his cheek and shook her head. "That's kind, but it's not worth the trouble."

"But you spent so much time. Your art is worthy. Let me battle."

"The theatre community is small. The Smitherses of the world will say I'm difficult. If that becomes my reputation, I won't make enough to pay rent and buy food for my household. I stuck my hand out to get what I could. For now, it's enough."

He caught her wrist and resisted the urge to kiss it—across the palm that bore stains of silver paint or along the sensitive skin between her knuckles. "Say the word, and I'll fight for you. That's what you want. That's what you always wanted, for me to fight for you, to prove how much I admire and care."

"Wanted. Not what I need now." Tears laced her lashes. "Please, Felton. I must get to my party, or has the urgency for leaving changed?"

"Cecilia, let me help. You needn't fret about the rents. I have money now. My investments have worked. I could give you anything, anything that you want."

Swiping at her face, she glimpsed at him like he was a stranger, not the man who'd fed her sweets, gotten her coffee, and stayed alert with her all night.

"No, you won't, my lord. You wouldn't know how to give me things that last."

"Lasting? Let me say what's lasting. Cecilia, I l—"

Her small hand, smelling of paint, covered his mouth. "Don't."

"What, don't say what's obvious? That I love you. That I probably fell in love the moment we met on that Demeraran street. I'm in love with you. This's lasting."

"Will you say anything to manipulate me?"

Cecilia ran up the street.

Felton had forgotten the rules of engagement. Declarations too early would doom things. "Wait. Please ignore."

She stopped. "I forgot my bucket of paint. Now Smithers has everything but my brushes."

"I'll go back and get it for you."

"No, my lord." Her voice had more of her accent. "Sometimes you can't go back."

Felton caught her hand. "You can sometimes. We're going back to Warwick. That was our home in the beginning. That's when you were happiest."

"You still don't know me." Cecilia shook her head. "Nor do you know what I want."

"Well, it's not sleep—you seem energized and emotional, Cilia."

"Sleep sounds good, my lord." Hugging tightly to her bundle, she sped away. This time down an alley.

And he gave chase.

There was no way he was going to let her go. No way at all.

Chapter 38

Cecilia—Bittersweet Surrender

Cutting though the first alley, then the second, I hastened my speed. I wasn't trying to lose Felton. I'd given him my word. I merely didn't want him to see me cry.

Yet, my tears forced me to slow. I couldn't see.

It might be the tension of working so hard and not sleeping. Or having to defend my art to a buzzard. Or breaking my vow to stop lying to myself. Felton, after all these months, loved me. I wasn't supposed to be moved by it.

The confession shouldn't, shouldn't make me wobbly.

He shouldn't be in love, not now.

Not after everything that happened.

Not after what I'd done.

At the door to my flat, I reached the pull, but Felton blocked me, and his handkerchief went into my hand.

"Cilia, I made a bargain with you, and I'll keep it. I will draft a legal separation, but my truth needed to be said. I can't keep secrets from you anymore."

Mopping my cheeks, I saw Felton, his blank face, stone chin. His ever assessing eyes seemed to frown. I saw his heart in the sea of blue-black. I'd hurt him, for he had to see I could no longer say the same to him.

"We still have our bargain, Cecilia. You and your party will come with me to Warwick. You will see Tramel. Then I'll do as you want."

Nodding, I folded his handkerchief on the seams. "Yes, to visit Tramel. Meet you in two hours on Brydges."

"Cilia." He grabbed my hand when I offered his cloth. "Let me come inside and wait. Or let me walk you to your door. I want to make sure you're safe. You don't know how I've tortured myself every day wondering about you."

"It's safe in here."

"Please."

"You trust me, Felton?"

"Well, you did leave me, before . . . but I do."

"How could I stay with all the mistrust? No one in your family wanted me there and then you thought the worst of me. I know we married for convenience, but those words said before God meant something."

He ran a hand through his hair; his locks were thick on his shoulders. Unbrushed, it looked wild in the morning light. "My cousin said something daft, and I'm a jealous fool. It wasn't rational and the attention the duke showed you made me crazed. And envious. I hated how he could make you smile when I couldn't."

"Tramel is my only friend. He helped me smile when I had nothing but sadness. He's always protected me. That's why you should know that I'll go with you. My party and I need to pack."

"Tramel says that you hate my cousin Gladstone. Did he do something to you that December? He was bleeding that day."

"Jeremiah Gladstone should've bled out, slaughtered like a pig."

He gripped me by the shoulders. "Did you cut him? Do you want him dead?"

There was no sense in explaining. I couldn't look at him as he searched for truth. Truth I couldn't offer. "Two hours, Felton."

"Cilia, let me accompany you to your door. We do so well with thresholds."

He started into the building, and I wrapped my hands about him. Face bouncing against his back, I stopped his advance.

In the hall of the boardinghouse, we stood together in the odd embrace.

My fingers skimmed the buttons of his open waistcoat, the smooth linen of his wrinkled shirt, and his fast-beating heart. "These lodgings, they're only for women. The landlord is already uncomfortable with my late hours. I don't need any trouble."

My words slurred. To my ear, my accent held tiredness and a heavy island roar. "Return for me here. That will be after ten. We'll be ready."

"I'm not letting you out of my sight, and I'll get you a safer place to live, one without a landlord that makes these kinds of threats. It will be part of our church settlement."

Since he'd know about Enna and Noah soon enough, I yielded. "Fine, but be quiet."

He didn't move and even pulled me about him like I was a blanket. "Ahh. Our first agreement of the day."

I tapped his back. "My lord, go to number seven before someone sees us."

"Lucky number seven," he said and moved down the hall with me glued against him.

When we stopped at my door, I broke free and dug into my cape for the key.

He took the heavy iron key from me and jiggled the lock.

We stepped inside the thick darkness.

"Odd. My Enna always burns a candle."

He clasped my hand. "Be careful, Cecilia. You might walk into furniture."

"I might say the same to you. It's my home, remember."

"Not your home, just a place you're staying. For I don't live here."

The sound of his jacket rustling had to be Felton searching his pockets for matches.

Within my palm, he put the wood sticks. "I trust you know where a sconce is."

"It's my home. I should, Felton."

When I tried to strike a match, icy fingers grabbed my wrist.

My bundle fell to the floor as I struggled. "Stop. Wait, my lord, that's not you."

"What the devil?" The sounds of struggle came from the right.

"Felton?"

Wham. Broken pottery sprayed my ankles. Something had crashed to the ground or had been thrown.

"Who's here? Felton? Felton, where are you?" He didn't respond.

I ripped away from whoever had me. "Gladstone?"

Swinging like a mad woman, I was determined to defeat the beast in my apartment. They'd gotten Felton too. Panicked, my heart exploded.

Matches lit.

The smell of sulfur filled the air.

Then I saw everything at once like the world slowed to a crawl.

A ring of light—women of all faces and races stood shoulder to shoulder around the room.

A man down—my husband lay at my feet with a smashed vase near his head.

A chest moving slow, but moving—Felton was alive.

Enna, my friend, my nephew's nurse, sat on the sofa but her empty hands were folded in prayer.

"Where's Noah? Enna, speak to me."

"Chari. Chari, calm down."

A treasured voice—the perfect alto pitch recalled memories of years gone by, of silly sisters running along the shore.

My face became the flooding Demerari River. I ran to the woman, coming out of the shadows. She rocked my . . . our Noah in her arms.

I hugged my family, my blood family, my sister Patience. I held her with all my strength.

CHAPTER 39

CECILIA—WE ARE FAMILY

Enna slipped from the sofa and took my nephew from Patience.

Then I gave my lost sister a bigger hug. "How are you alive? You've been gone so long."

The tall woman tucked me under her arm, and I held her about her expanding waist. "Oh, Chari, my sister. It's a long story, but Colin Jordan, the man I married, was misguided. He hid my letters that I sent to you. Only Jove knows what he did to the ones sent by him for you and Papa."

My sister was alive. Her beautiful face—brown from the sunshine and round from the miracle of a child. She and Noah and Enna were my miracles.

Patience waved her hands. "Ladies, let's put the marquess onto the sofa."

"No. He might awaken." A mousy-looking woman with reddish-brown hair came to my sister's side. "I don't think I hit him hard enough with the vase that he forgets his memories. You think he saw us and will tell?"

"Jemina, I'll take the blame. No one can be mad at a pregnant lady."

"Sister. Who are all these people? What's going on?"

"Cecilia," she said. "These are members of the Widow's Grace.

These women and I help widows across Britain to reclaim their lives."

The ladies—Roman soldiers they weren't, but in a way, with their protective stance of locked arms about my fallen Felton, each could be a jaguarete.

With one final squeeze, I let my sister go and went to my poor husband. Stooping to him, I felt the heat of his skin and the hot breath fleeing his nose. He'd be alright.

"How did you find me, Patience? And I'm not quite a widow, unless your friend intends to do more to harm Lord Gantry."

The woman, the mousy lady I saw with Felton yesterday, stepped forward. "We make exceptions for Her Grace. Your sister is one of the dearest people, and you've been missing from her heart far too long. I'm sorry for hitting your husband, but I couldn't tell it was Gantry I hit. He's a friend too and has been looking for you everywhere."

"So, he has many lady friends?"

"Cecilia, it is not like that." Patience sat on my sofa and turned her wet face to Enna, who was still making signs of the cross.

Enna rocked Noah, then fed the wiggly fellow when he started to cry.

"He and my Lionel will be the best of friends. And we will honor Helena every day."

She swiped at her leaking eyes. "Ladies, go with Jemina, our Lady Ashbrook. She'll take you all home or to Lady Shrewsbury's. Thank you all. Searching Covent Garden can be dangerous. Bless you all for helping find my sister."

"My driver will take them all back," Lady Ashbrook said. "I'll send the ladies, but I'm staying with you. The duke would be so upset if he knew your visit to my house was a mission."

All the Grace women left except my sister and the Ashbrook woman.

"He'll have to know. We have no secrets, not anymore." Patience patted her pregnant stomach. "He told me the very moment Gantry left our house, that my sister Cecilia was alive and married to his dearest friend."

Patience cooed at Noah, then frowned at me. "But it can't be much of a marriage if you've been in hiding for months."

Lady Ashbrook came closer. "A woman only runs for two reasons: to be away from an ogre or to be with another."

Both of those options weren't quite true in my case. Nor were they wholly deniable. I left because of the horrible accusations, but I ran to Tramel.

"There can be a third," I finally said after a long, guilty pause. "To find oneself is my reason."

"Was Gantry mean to you, sister? You can never trust the quiet ones. Jemina, get ready to hit him again."

"No, Patience. He's never been cruel. He's never lifted a hand to me unless it was my command to brandish a torch or Papa's knife." Like I used to, I ducked my head onto Patience's shoulder. "She called you Your Grace. Jordan was not titled. Did your husband become so?"

"My second husband is the Duke of Repington. He was one of Wellington's strategists in the Great War."

"Which one? The revolt of the Americans? The revolt in Haiti? That thing in 1812? There have been many."

"Too many, Chari, and I dread knowing the number of times my husband has risked his life for the king."

I threaded my fingers together. "How did you rid yourself of Jordan? A church divorce?"

My sister's brow raised and she had that look like she'd drunk sour wine. "Death. Jordan was killed before I bore his son. Lionel is a beautiful, healthy ten-month-old. My duke and his dearest friend, your husband, helped me figure out that Jordan was murdered."

Felton did that? That was the type of mission he did for others?

Looking down at the floor, at the snoozing man, my heart went to him. He was good at aiding others. "He helped you, my sister. I don't know what to say."

Noah cackled and made a big kissing noise as Enna rotated him against her bosom. Hungry little dear.

My sister and Enna gave life with their bosoms. I wanted to pick up my parcel of brushes and hug it. My art was all I'd birthed.

A little empty, yet full when I thought of my passions, I looked again at Felton with the bits of ugly vase near his face, and wondered what notions in him had changed.

"Chari, I know you liked Jordan."

"He made us all laugh when he came and swept you away. The house was so thick with mourning." I tugged up the blanket, exposing Noah's perfect toes. "I'm so sorry about him."

"I am too." Those eyes of Patience's looked glassy. "But because of the Widow's Grace, and Jemina, and the duke and Gantry, my life is so different. I have peace. I'm able to offer that to others."

"Your son is ten months and you're already married again. Isn't there some British rule about waiting twelve months to marry? I suppose Jordan can't complain, being dead and all."

"There's always a rule or something to stand in the way. Things just happened between the duke and me. Two stubborn people found that we could be happier together than apart."

My sister was very smart. I knew she'd phrased her words as a way to make me think differently about Felton. She must've forgotten that I was stubborn too. Both sisters were born kicking like goats, as Mama used to say.

"Your husband, Lord Gantry, found out about Papa's death."

"Did he tell you what they did to his land? How his brothers and the other landowners strangled his business because he wouldn't comply? He wouldn't work his fields with enslaved people, and they made him suffer for it. Helena told me all as she lay dying."

Patience's eyes had tears in them again. "No, he didn't say that. He spared me that truth. Enna told me about Helena. How you rescued her from her shackles and how you helped this one breathe."

Enna settled the now loudly snoring boy into her arms. "I had to tell. Too many women breaking into our lodgings to not say. I'm sorry for being disloyal, Mrs. Charity."

"Enna, all is well."

"That may be, but don't . . ." My friend turned her head toward Lady Ashbrook, who stood over Felton looking at a few of my hung pieces—paintings of Agatha and Amelia, another of Ballard Cliffs near Warwick.

"Mrs. Cecilia, only say no more. We are in mixed company."

My sister shook her head. "Jemina is my dearest friend. She's my sister. She—"

I crossed my hands to keep from pointing at the redhead. "She's not Helena. She can never replace her. No one can."

Cheeks growing dark, like roses on snow, Lady Ashbrook went to the door. "Perhaps I'll—"

"Stop, Jemina. Come here." Patience's tone was hard. "Take my palm, sister." She lifted her arm to that woman, not me.

Lady Ashbrook returned and clasped Patience's fingers and held on to them like it was a lifeline.

"This, Chari, Enna, this woman has proven herself over and over to me. Jemina saved my life when I was imprisoned. She helped me get back my son. Don't cut her, direct or otherwise."

"And Patience kept me sane when I thought I wasn't." Lady Ashbrook pulled their entwined fingers to her chest. "She's my sister too, but I'll wait in the hall if that means you two will reconcile. No more fighting with those who should love."

Enna and I surely sounded mean-spirited. "I'm sorry, Lady Ashbrook. It has been hard here. Many here have looked at my curves as if I were some sort of jezebel. Other's think I'm after their husband. I have a husband that I left. I've no need of theirs."

Looking again at him, I heard his snores. He was still unconscious.

"Or they think Enna and I should be cleaning their houses." I stooped and waved my hand at his face to see if he was faking. Felton didn't snore, from what I remembered.

He must be waking up.

Crossing my arms, I stood. "I've no problem with honest work, but Patience knows I lost interest in sweeping many moons ago."

"Yes, you weren't very good at chores. Always off in the corner painting. I hope we all will be friends, but no one, not a soul, will replace Helena. She was the sweetest girl ever. Now, tell me while my face is already swollen with tears what you know of her enslavement, as Enna said."

"My father-in-law tried to help me bring my sister from Demerara. He was willing to run the blockades. Tramel has been a good friend. Then his solicitor found out that she'd been sold into slavery by her husband, Jeremiah Gladstone. The way his mother and their entire family behave, he must not have wanted to bring back another Demeraran woman or baby to these shores."

My nervous laugh started. "One of my first theatre commissions was for a play called *Wowski*. It's about a man who sells his lover. I thought it just a twisted dark story. Something to make the beastly theatre patrons go wild, the salacious nature of it all."

I looked to the ceiling, willing my eyes not to run with tears. "Jeremiah Gladstone is the embodiment of evil. You know he laughed the day I left my husband, his cousin. He taunted me with what he'd done."

Jemina handed me an embroidered handkerchief. White and starched with a big letter A. A was alpha, the beginning. I had to own my part in all this sad stew. "I chose to marry and didn't take Helena with me. Papa thought it best that I go first and establish my household. She was so young. Another year at home wouldn't matter. Then the war set up blockades. No one could legally get to Demerara. Then Papa's death left her vulnerable."

"How did you get to her and Noah, Lady Gantry?" Lady Ashbrook looked down at my husband as she handled the other ugly vase.

"Tramel, my father-in-law, cares not for rules."

Patience glanced at me with a countenance that wasn't blank. It held questions, questions my heart wasn't prepared to answer, about rules and the duke.

CECILIA—A NEW BARGAIN

Felton began to stir.

Wasn't sure how to explain everything.

Lady Ashbrook dropped the second vase on Felton's head. "Oops."

"That has to hurt." Enna shook her head, then handed the awakening Noah to my sister. "But the vase was ugly, Mrs. Cecilia."

This time he had a cut. I dropped to my knees and fished out his handkerchief and held it to his temple. "It's a small bleed. No more. When he awakens, we'll tell the truth."

Patience's friend shrugged. "He'll live. I've had worse injuries with our missions, but we need a head start. Her Grace needs to tell Repington of our activities before anyone else."

I looked at the lady and wondered if she knew about Felton's true work or if she was just being critical. Wanting to shield him, I crowded closer to my poor Felton. "Will you all stop attacking my husband?"

Patience lulled Noah to sleep. "So, you do still consider him yours? That's good."

I picked pieces of the mud vases from his hair. "We'll get a formal separation once we return from Warwick. It is for the best."

"Is it, Chari? The man has been in agony for months. I know he loves you."

That mirrored the confession he offered when we left the theatre. It didn't change the confusion in my heart. Holding Noah, Patience stood and moved to the paintings of Agatha and Amelia, the pictures of us picnicking on the grounds of Warwick. On a clear day, one could hear the sea, even if one couldn't see it.

I missed the girls. For a moment, I let my heart grieve. If I closed my eyes, we were all there, but I couldn't drop my lids. I didn't want Patience to disappear.

"I wasn't prepared to be a wife." The words crawled across my tongue. "I thought it would be a big adventure. If I had not wed, Helena would be alive."

Patience came to me. Over sleeping Noah, she pulled my wet face to hers. "Chari, my heart breaks for Helena, but what happened to her is not your fault."

"Then it's Gladstone's. I want to take my knife, my topaz knife that Papa gave each of us, and stick it into his gullet. The scoundrel should be flayed."

"Chari, no. We have to move forward. Hate will keep you bound."

"How? This boy. That's all that remains of our sister. It's Gladstone's fault. He should pay."

Lady Ashbrook gasped. "Gladstone could gain custody if he knows about the boy. We've seen this in the Widow's Grace."

No. No, I've kept Noah safe, not to hand my boy over to that evil family. "Gladstone must never know. He'd be ruinous. I think the man should die. I think I want to try."

Patience pulled me into a tighter embrace. "No. I just got you back. You can't do anything so stupid. We're family. We're restored. Stop thinking of killing."

That was the problem. It was always in my thoughts. It was easier to think of revenge than the state of my heart. Patience's world was set, a new husband, one baby here, one to come. She could care for Noah and Enna if I was caught.

"That look. Chari, no."

Felton moved a little but didn't awaken.

"It makes no sense, Chari. Lord Gantry has been a fine friend to Repington, but if he abused you, I'll hate him forever. I will find a way to rid him from our lives."

"No. Gantry never hurt me, never lifted a hand to me. He's not that type of villain."

Noah rustled and Patience's belly jiggled. She arched her back and sort of looked at me. "What type of villain is he?"

"The type who makes you think he believes in you, that he trusts you, then in a moment of confusion, he leaves you bereft. He has no faith."

Jemina rubbed at her forehead. "Speak plainly. It's been a long night. We've checked a few wrong places before finding Enna. What exactly did Lord Gantry do?"

My eyes closed and I was again on the patio. Tramel was comforting me over Gladstone's gloating over what the fiend had done. Then Felton stepped through the door, over the threshold, and held me in such contempt.

My sister put her palm to my face. "You went silent, Chari. What did he do?"

"He thought I succumbed to his father's charms. He thought we had an affair. What type of faith is that?"

"What?" Jemina sat and slipped off the couch. "I heard he's an awful man. And hateful."

"Never. Tramel, Lord Gantry's father, is misunderstood. He's not hateful. At least not to me. Always kind—"

Patience stared at me and stole my breath. That was the same look she had when were younger and I told her I had a crush on the vicar's son.

I closed my eyes again and wanted to disappear.

Patience put her hand to my shoulder. Her eyes were kind, understanding. "It's obvious your husband made a mistake. Friendship and love can be deceiving. He must have misread kindly affection for something else. I know him to be very sorry."

"You know me, Patience. I make up my mind quickly. He had no faith in me after two years of marriage. I have none now."

"I'll support you. I only know that he's been miserable without you."

Awake and cooing, Noah reached for me and I took him from Patience. He clung to my neck and dribbled onto my coat.

Maybe I wasn't doing so badly by him. Maybe I was more maternal than I gave myself credit for.

Patience peeked over my head. "You and Enna and Noah will come with me. You'll be away from Covent Garden and be safe in residence with the duke and me. Noah and my Lionel can grow up together. I want them to be as close as brothers, like we were close. Then Gantry can visit with you in safety, in a place where you have power."

"Are you trying to take over, Patience? I mean, I haven't done so badly, sis. We're safe. We've been safe."

"You've been amazing, Mrs. Cecilia," Enna said. "But you know how you fret about us when you go to your commissions. I'm in constant prayer until you return. The activities about here are scandalous. Let's go with the rich one and the friendly white woman."

Patience put her hand on Noah's cheek. "That boy clings to you like you're his mother. But this is not the place for any of you. You went to Demerara to save Helena. I've come to save you."

The activities in Covent Garden could be bad. I had to acknowledge this. Sometimes I wore costumes to seem older or slovenly, anything else to escape men's attention. I had stayed invisible until that night at the King's Theatre.

"Patience, I don't know about permanent living arrangements. Or the future. With the coins I've earned tonight, I'll pay you to lodge Noah and Enna until I get back. I have to go with Lord Gantry to Warwick. Tramel is dying. It's his last wish to see me. I came here to get Enna and Noah to go with me."

Jemina stooped to Felton. "He's starting to stir. I think we need to decide now."

She was right. We were out of vases.

* * *

Between the broken vases and my sister, the other ladies and Noah—it would be too much to explain to the retired spy.

I ran to the door and flung it open. "Patience, take Enna and Noah. I'll make excuses to Lord Gantry. Don't want you in trouble with any duke."

She put the coins back into my palm. "You'll need this so you can catch a stagecoach and come back. We're at Sandlin Court, here in town. In two weeks, we'll be in the country at Hamlin Hall. Enna and Noah will be safe with me. When you're done, you promise to come to me. No matter what."

I fisted my fingers about the coins. "Yes. As soon as I'm done at Warwick, I'll have Lord Gantry take me to you or I'll hire a coach to do it, but no more time away from our family."

Enna started making those signs of the cross motions again.

With Noah in my friend's arms and Lady Ashbrook in tow, my sister headed to the door. Her waddle was so cute. She said, "If Gantry is the man I've come to know, he'll prove himself to you. He'll fight for love."

"This trip is to fulfill Tramel's last wishes, but I'll speed to you. I've family to come back to. Family, my family, is all I ever wanted."

Patience started to slip away. My chest felt so heavy. I didn't want to say goodbye.

Capturing her fingers, I drew them to my broken heart. "Sandlin Court is where you all are? I will talk with Lord Gantry. If I can get out of going, I will. When you find the family you've missed, one shouldn't chase ghosts."

Felton shifted, and I pushed them out the door. "What? Cecilia."

I closed the door, then rushed to his side. "Wake up, my lord."

He punched with his arms, but it took a few moments for his eyes to open. "What happened? Did someone strike me?"

Picking up the piece of the mud vases, I waved the broken curve. "These fell."

"I tripped on it, and hit my head on a brown vase?"

"Don't know. I guess you may have, walking in the darkness." I put my hand under his head and lifted it to my lap. "I'm just glad you're awake."

His puzzled look would be comical if I didn't know how heavy the ugly vases were or how they could've hurt him. "You're right. This place is not safe."

He closed his eyes and grew comfortable on my leg as though it was a pillow. "Glad I didn't trip and fall onto you. Here I'm wanting to protect you. Can't do that if I'm bumbling."

Blinking, he searched the big room—the empty crib and the one bed. "Where are your friends?"

"Gone. They must've started their day."

He frowned. "Before eight? Are you testing me? You didn't have to make up people."

If I let him think Enna and Noah were lies, was that better than telling him the truth? And he definitely wouldn't want to hear I sent my family away from his. It was safer.

"Cecilia, if you say they are out, I believe you. We can wait for them, or maybe we head out on our own." He turned his face to my hip and the heat of his breath scorched the thin wool of my gown straight to my thigh.

This was bad. Felton slipped beneath my coat and put his hot cheek to my leg.

"My lord, I no longer wish to go. Your cousin, your whole family will be there. You have enough family."

He half smiled. "You don't want to see Tramel anymore?"

"I'll remember him in his strength, the picture of kindness. I'm tired. I need to sleep. Then I need to look for my next commission."

His eyes became saucers, wide, even a little panicked. "But what of our bargain? You're to go with me, then I finalize a legal separation."

"It's almost been a year. I've survived this in-between state.

Sooner or later, you will grow tired of hanging on. You'll annul this marriage to go to your next adventure, the next person to enjoy your bed. I need no bargain."

He sat up and stared. His hands were deliberate, respectful, but caressing my knee. "You're the only one I want."

It was hard to think with palms on me and his fingers guiding me to all the memories, our memories, the ones that were good.

His blue-black gaze burned, intense like an eclipse when the moon was draped in shadows, like in 1810.

He took my hand and towed me to him. "I know what it is you want."

"Felton—"

"It's no joke. I know this time." His hands about my waist slid me closer. Another minute, I'd be on his lap.

"My lord, I'm tired. You need to get on the road and go back to Tramel and tell him you tried."

"I'll help you get what you desire if you come with me." He eased to my side, his lips on my ear. "Revenge."

I pressed against his coat. "Felton?"

"You want to kill Jeremiah Gladstone. I'll help you do it."

"You've a concussion of the skull? Or maybe it's me. I'm asleep and this is a dream."

"You need to dream of me again, Cilia. You know I can do this. I can be an instrument of your desire. I'll take you to Warwick. I'll teach you how to kill and get away without consequences."

"How can you do that, Felton?" I scrambled to my feet. "Don't be ridiculous."

His breathing was labored when he rose, but he came toward me and towed me into his embrace. "I've been in service to the Secretary of War and the Colonies. I am, or was, Lord Liverpool's man to gather intelligence to advance His Majesty's interests around the world."

Stretching, I fingered his skull again, looking for bumps. "You've been hit too hard on the head."

"You have to believe me."

"Felton, I didn't hit my head. This is fantastical."

"Cilia, just listen. Think of how we met. How I happened to have a residence in Jamaica. My ease of getting on a military frigate to return us to London."

Shaking my head like it would fall off. "No."

"I kept going on missions. I resigned in December, right before you left. I was in the dark, when I could've used the Department of War and the Colonies' resources to find you. I'm telling you the truth." He put his hands to my chin. "I can give you what you want, and make sure you're not at risk."

All I had to do was go with Felton, then the man who destroyed my sister's life would pay. Noah would truly be safe. It should be an easy thing to avenge Helena. Gladstone killed my sister. He needed to die.

But would Felton actually train me how to do it?

He closed his eyes for a moment. "I've been a political assassin when it was necessary. I can help you do this. Ready for our new bargain, Cilia? This is the adventure you always wanted."

Before I talked myself out of it, I brought his hands to my heart. "Yes, make me a killer."

Helena's murderer would die. With his help, I could do it.

Felton embraced me like I'd drift away, and maybe I would. I'd put my soul once again on the path to killing Gladstone.

Felton—Pack the Wife, the Cheese, and the Guns

Cecilia was sound asleep on the carriage seat by the time Watson had driven to his Town residence. There was a chill in the air and Felton put his greatcoat on top of her.

She curled into it and he wished it was his arms.

"I'll be right back, Cilia. You stay here."

Only a soft snore answered. He was tempted to see if she really slept or only pretended, like he had on the floor of her flat.

The Widow's Grace was a bunch of amateurs. The vase thing only works once at best, and not with cheap pottery. The first had knocked him flat. It blurred everything, until he saw Lady Ashbrook and the Duchess of Repington leave.

He should be warmed that the sisters were reunited, but this was his chance to reconcile with Cecilia. Had he heard a baby before Lady Ashbrook dropped the second vase?

Tucking his coat about her, he smoothed it along her abdomen. Had she borne his child?

Anger at Gladstone boiled. The man was somehow responsible for Helena's death. How? Why? Gladstone had to be a smuggler to get to Demerara during the blockades? But how had Helena become his target?

Felton kissed her brow. "Won't be long. Then I'll fix everything."

He bounced from the carriage and stormed inside to pack a few things.

This felt a little like old times, running to meet Johnson on the docks of Portsmouth, then they'd be off on Liverpool's latest mission.

Watson followed behind. "So, you and Lady Gantry . . . is the gang back together?"

"No, she's on loan. Can you pack up a few shirts, stockings, and my case of weapons?"

His dark bronze cheeks drained of their rich color. He looked ashy and in need of lotion. "You're joking. Surely, you and the missus aren't getting along that poorly? Widowhood or suicide is not necessary. Just let her leave."

"The weapons are not to do harm to my wife or myself."

His man nodded. "But they are to do harm to someone."

"Just get them, Watson."

He went up to the attic and in a few minutes returned with the special case. Watson met him in his bedchamber and laid it on the bed.

Felton ran his hand along the leather box made of the smoothest finish. He never took an assignment without his lucky portmanteau. The night Johnson died, these guns were back at their hideout. Breaking into the government building was supposed to be easy, not an ambush.

His man packed his bag with shirts and waistcoats. "Is this a Department of War and the Colonies assignment to do along the way to Warwick?"

"I left that service, remember. They cut me off from everything. When I needed help finding Lady Gantry, they offered none. No, I'm not returning to them."

"Then why the lucky guns? Is this to impress the woman? She no like guns like that. She like torches and that gold blade."

"Watson." Felton cleaned his teeth, then stepped into his

closet for a new shirt. "She left because I accused her of having an affair."

"You're not going to kill the man you suspect. The duke is dying. You needn't speed your ascension."

"Please, just help me pack."

"Yes, sir."

Felton splashed water on his face and cleaned the cut at his temple. "Amateurs. No, I'm not killing my father. I'd have done that ages ago, the minute he taught me to shoot. You know I've been tempted."

"Temptation can be seductive. Leave the weapons. Romance the girl. Say goodbye to Tramel."

He threaded sleeve buttons through his cuff. "I've a new mission. I have to train Lady Gantry to be an operative—sort of like I trained a young man in Grenada—while I'm trying to talk her out of killing my cousin Gladstone."

Watson's lips drew to a dot. "And if you cannot convince her to pursue peace?"

"Then I have to let her go through with it."

Watson's mouth dropped open, but he hurried and closed up the portmanteaus. "I will load these right away."

"I wouldn't consider it, but I think it might be deserved. I'll find out."

His man nodded and started to the door. "May I suggest you go down to the kitchen and see what treats you can take for the trip? A hardy cheese and a good crusty loaf always brought a smile to the marchioness. See if the cook has a spare pan to toast your bread in, on the side of the road. No need to kill on an empty stomach."

"You may be sarcastic, but I think it an excellent suggestion. The drive to Warwick is long. I'll make Lady Gantry comfortable."

Felton went to the first drawer in his chest and picked up the fine sketchbook and charcoals he'd purchased for Cecilia's birthday. Underneath was the half-done painting of him as a Roman soldier. He was this fool. He should be eaten by the jaguar.

"Taking the painting, Lord Gantry? I can put it next to Port Royal."

"You were right about that last mission, Watson. I made one arrest but didn't find the traitor. The trail to the man responsible for getting Johnson killed was too cold. I should've stayed. Should've let that one mission go and fought for what I had here."

"At least you know what you have, sir. That's the type of intelligence a spymaster needs when running a successful operation."

He put the painting back in the drawer. "I joined the Department of War and the Colonies to maintain the king's peace. Now I must teach my wife to kill. Is this the progress you talk of?"

"She's an artist and the action sort, my lord. Not the killing type. Distract her. Do for her, like you're always doing for others. You gathered her coffee and sweets last night. How did that go?"

Cecilia had smiled at him, the first one that held no tension, merely the ease that made him feel loved. "It went well, but it doesn't compare to trying to retrieve her sister from Demerara. The duke is hard to best."

"Sir, you'll have almost ten days alone on the road with the marchioness. I've never seen you more happy than when you took her to Warwick. Remember the fields, the places that she'd love to stop but you had no time."

"Our first journey was a fun trip." They were never out of each other's company. He'd had a month to get her acclimated to Warwick before Lord Liverpool started making demands.

"Well, now you can have a trip to remember."

"I promised her adventure when we married. Setting off to kill my cousin definitely isn't boring. If we manage to succeed without swinging from the gallows, we'll have a tale for the grandchildren."

Watson nodded. "You haven't lost yet. I believe in you."

Someone needed to. Felton was adrift. "Check on Lady Gantry, make sure she hasn't flown away again. She should be sound asleep in the carriage."

His man nodded and headed out.

Portable treats like a hearty cheese would delight Lady Gantry. Felton went to the kitchen to see what might loosen her tongue and tell him how his cousin was responsible for Helena's death.

CHAPTER 42

CECILIA—LIKE OLD TIMES

I offered a yawn and then curled again into the strong arms that held me. The heat radiating from this man was wondrous. Loved dreaming of my big bed in Demerara with the windows open during the rainy season. A fresh breeze filtered inside, and I bundled under the bedclothes. It was beautiful and warm. I missed . . .

What?

Springing up, I saw Felton's face, his cheesy grin. Then I realized I had curled against his chest while I slept, and he let me.

"Afternoon, Lady Gantry." He tied back his hair, then he buttoned his shirt. "You're a heavy sleeper, but your fingernails against my skin, they do bring a sweet torment."

Watching as he closed up his shirt, I realized it was his bare chest against my cheek.

"I don't remember you being such a heavy sleeper. Changes."

A shiver coursed through me. Not exactly one of pleasure. More of pure prickling embarrassment. "Why are your shirt and waistcoat undone? What happened?"

His grin burst like the vase, shooting spurts of laughter. "With my coat and that blanket, you generate a lot of heat. I needed to cool off a bit before you pounced again. Who again is the jaguar?"

Felton's chest was solid and smooth with finger-worthy definition, not a hair, no pox or scars like the mottling upon his arms and legs. In addition to his heat, it was one of the best things to lie in bed and touch his heart. He was an iron, a bed warmer, a firepit. Pure flame.

When he was with me.

When my heart was fully his.

When some missive from Lord Liverpool didn't take him away. He could've been killed, slain in some field, or on an island far away, and I might never have known.

Scooting farther away, I shook my head. "I couldn't have unbuttoned all of that."

"If you insist. That's our secret. You like secrets."

"Stop grinning."

That only made him show more teeth.

With my hands covering my face, I turned to the window. Outside were trees. No city buildings—townhomes and theatres and mews. No more cobbled streets. "How long have we been driving?"

"About three hours. We're out of London. We'll stop soon to rest the horses."

Three hours. I'd been lying against Felton that long.

"Cecilia, you look a little flushed."

I drew my arms over my head. I didn't want to hear his voice, and the smug insinuation that we'd found one another again.

"You must be hungry. You haven't eaten since early morning." He picked up a basket from the floor. "Let's see what Cook has procured for us."

Digging into the contents, he pulled out a pile of blackberries. Placing one of the purplish morsels to his lips, he gulped it. "Oh, very sweet, a little tart."

He slid halfway to me and held out the fruit.

It looked good and my mouth watered.

"They are very good, Cecilia. Too good."

He took back the offering and bit the berry. Purple, almost indigo juice painted his lower lip. He did it again, and then lifted another one to me. "Don't miss the pleasure. Neither this blackberry, nor I, bite."

That wasn't true. Not the way he used to like my earlobes.

"Cecilia, you must keep up your strength."

He put the largest one I'd ever seen into the curve of my palm. Didn't roll it in my hand, couldn't think of the texture of fine drupelets, just the juice—the promise of the sweetness. I popped it on my tongue like it was a last supper. It exploded and the seeds, the hull, danced in my mouth. It was a sea of deliciousness.

That look on Felton's face wasn't unreadable. That contented thing he did with his smile—not a smirk, not a grin, but something in between that meant he was happy and plotting. "You like?" he asked.

"Cook does gather the best."

"She does. You missed strawberry season. The berries were so good. Here's another."

We did this, one berry at a time, each of us drawing closer until we were again side by side. When I peeked over his shoulder, he snapped the basket closed. "Lady Gantry, are you trying to ruin my surprises?"

"I do like surprises."

He lifted one of my favorites, Stilton cheese. "And there's bread."

"And marmalade from the quinces?"

"Of course, what kind of fool do you take me for?"

The crust of the roll snapped as he broke it into small manageable bites. That warm, buttery, yeasty scent filled the carriage. He put on it a small cut of the cheese, and a generous dollop of the jam. "Here. A celebration for your completed masterpiece. I love witnessing you finishing a painting."

His voice sounded merry, but his telltale gaze held a sadness. Perhaps there should be sadness in mine too, for I withheld that piece of me from him. I purposely hid it.

One finger stroked my chin and lifted it. "I'm glad to see it now. I don't think I would have appreciated it fully, not before."

"I suppose you were distracted by more important things for the Department of War and the Colonies." I put my empty hand on his for the briefest moment. "Thank you for this feast."

Then I sank my teeth into the bread and cheese and the miracle of marmalade. Ecstasy.

"My pleasure. I have always adored how your eyes sparkle when you're sated with treats. I love it." His countenance changed, far from the joyful man passing berries, offering jam.

"What's the matter, my lord? Did something happen whilst I was asleep?"

He wiped his hands on a napkin. "Nothing out of the usual. Just missed this. Miss us."

Stretching, he returned the basket to the floor, then twirled a napkin in his hand. "You have marmalade on your mouth."

"Where?"

"There." Felton leaned over and I thought he'd use the cloth to wipe it up, like I did Noah. But he licked at the marmalade, then kissed me.

It was shocking, his mouth on mine. The growing pressure. The growling of my jaguarete when my fingers touched his neck.

I couldn't understand why he'd want me, after everything. Then I didn't care, just that he kept at it.

Memories pressed and that intangible feeling that we should be like this, made me open to him, more deeply than I had at the King's Theatre.

His fingers slipped past my coat to the lace fichu of my sky-blue carriage gown. His hands became more insistent, molding me to his chest, scooping me onto his lap.

This was his way; with every food-filled seduction of the past, he left me helpless, helpless and panting and wanting.

Then he left.

I should stop him—his hands, these wayward feelings, but the words never formed on my tongue.

Felton caressed me to let him back into my heart and my bed. Food and this gentle, stirring passion always made me feel treasured, even loved.

But he didn't love me, not like I needed. It was far too easy for him to leave me.

And I couldn't love him anymore, for I had left him and done the worst.

He caught my hand before I punched the roof to signal the carriage to stop. "What's the matter? The Stilton?"

"The Felton."

"Cilia, what?"

Didn't have any words to say aloud that I was a fool.

Chapter 43

Felton—Off to Kill the Cousin

In the carriage, Cecilia looked stunned. Her hands within Felton's were ice blocks, but he kept them. If he had his druthers, he'd never let go. He kissed one and blew on the other. "Cold, my little blueberry?"

She didn't respond and stared at the door as if she'd run.

Felton couldn't allow it. So he drew her back and put her hands to his chest, bundling them into his coat. "Your hands are chilled."

"Always cold, Felton, and you need to stop trying to sway me."

Ignoring the failure of his obvious tactics, he decided to focus on warming her up, rubbing her palms as he used to rub the soles of her feet. Slow and steady along the curves of each digit made her sigh.

"Tsk. How are you going to target Gladstone if you have to sit outside for hours?"

"You will truly teach me?"

He nodded. "I've left you so many times for missions. I think this is quite a fun husband-wife activity."

"Pity the thing that bonds is killing."

He shrugged. "It's how we met. You saved my life. Perhaps cloak-and-dagger is a coupling activity."

Felton stretched to offer her a blanket, and she jumped.

"Cecilia Lance, what is it? I've never brought a hand to you. Why act like I have?"

She pulled her arms tighter about her. "Bad dreams. That's all."

He thought of witnesses who'd survived Aponte's rebellion in Cuba, witnesses who'd gone through trauma. Getting the British planters out of harm's way, before the four-hundred-man freedom force began their fight, was hard. Yet, Felton was left changed by the Spanish forces' brutal reprisals on colonists or anyone who supported José Antonio Aponte movement to end enslavement. He was lucky to get his team out alive.

"Felton. You went away. That's usually me."

"Sorry, Cecilia." He hung his head. "I can't believe I'm joking about teaching you to kill."

Tentatively, she reached for him, putting her palm atop his wrist. "When I teach Agatha and Amelia art, I do it step by step. Explain each piece. Is there a method?"

He sat back, easing from her touch. "To kill, it can't be emotional."

"That makes no sense." She pulled the blanket up against her chest. "Why else would you kill someone?"

"If you feel too much, you make mistakes." He pulled the slipping blanket back to her shoulder. "First, I'll teach you how to be in the room with Gladstone and ignore him, so he'll not see you coming for him."

"The fool didn't see me at the King's Theatre and he's not dead."

"Was that why you were there?"

"Was that why you, who don't like the theatre, were there—to stop me?"

"Liverpool. I was going to beseech him again for his help, to see if you were in Demerara. Had I known you were there to kill Gladstone, I would've stopped you. Too many witnesses."

Squinting at him, she looked stunned. Perhaps she was musing that he indeed would teach her to kill. Stretching his arms to the seat back, he said, "Why don't you rest a little more? I need to think about your training."

She tucked her feet up onto the seat, carefully taking her boots off. Cecilia had the smallest feet.

To change the subject or divert his thoughts, Felton placed her cold toes onto his lap. With his thumbs, he began a small massage to her soles.

Cecilia cuddled into the blanket and kept his jacket close. "Your missions truly were missions."

He shrugged. "I never lied to you."

"And you kept putting yourself at risk. What of Agatha and Amelia, even Lady Jane? How would they manage without you?"

"Tramel would provide. Then there was you."

"That's a job for family. I'm not that."

"Why do you feel like that? You're family. And your feet don't perspire. They must be very cold."

"They are ice, but I'm not family." Snuggling against the seat, she propped her neck onto her folded hands. "No, I was a dowry and adventure. Not much of that with you leaving all the time."

"It was in service to my country. I made a difference. British interests around the world depend upon men like me doing what must be done."

"That's honorable, Felton," she said with a yawn. "I never said you weren't that, but you have no concept of what it is for a woman to depend upon a man who's always leaving. I wonder if that's what made Helena desperate."

She moaned a little when he pressed on the ball of her little foot.

"Cilia, my job for the Department of War and the Colonies is done. I'm here. You can depend on me. We can build a home."

"How? I wasn't in charge at *your* house in London. I had more autonomy in Warwick."

"London was our house. It was to be ours away from Tramel,

and truthfully it kept me closer to Whitehall to serve Liverpool, but we could find another place."

She shrugged. "London was Jane's more than it ever was mine. The Department of War and the Colonies. No wonder the girls were so scared when you left. Did they know?"

"No. Only Tramel knew. Tramel and Watson."

"Should've told Jane. She thought you had a mistress."

How could he prove that he'd been faithful, that he dreamed of Cecilia and only Cecilia? "I've spoken to Jane. She knows my disapproval. I'll make her apologize."

Cecilia spun and put back on her boots. "There's no need for that. It doesn't matter."

"Some things matter. You left us for almost a year. I'm asking forgiveness and offering it with no conditions. Your dear friend Tramel would never forgive such betrayal."

Her gaze went to the floor, probably to the picnic basket. "Don't forgive me. Hold it against me. You're about to become the duke. I suppose you could use the practice in his ways."

"You mean practice in being vile?"

"Practice in having passion about something. He's not a perfect man, but he does the things he believes in. He protects those he loves."

"He loves you, not me. I think that's the difference."

"Tramel has said he wishes things were different in regard to you."

"He'd have killed me in the womb so that my mother might've lived."

Sitting up, she put a hand to her mouth. Then she reached for him and drew his head to hers. "You've never said that, Felton. I'm sorry. That's a horrible thing."

"It's not something I wish to say. Childbirth is a risky thing. It's why I'm a widower. I would've loved to have known my mother."

"Anything can go awry." Her voice held tears. "Is it worth the risk? I think a woman who tries to have a baby is brave."

Her voice sounded sorrowful and her eyes had become glossy.

Pity was not what he wanted, merely for his wife to understand him. "Why do you understand Tramel and not me?"

"We talk. He understands what's important to me. That'll always mean so much."

"If you knew what my sister and I have lived through, with constant shipping us off to aunts, boarding schools with instructors of questionable temperaments, or caught in the latest wars of wives two, then three, you'd not give him such grace."

"But I'm not privy to those stories. You and your sister never share these Lance family tales. You two are such good siblings. I'm a foreigner. Those were her words every time I wanted to help."

"Well, you're from Demerara."

"You know what I mean."

"Honestly, I do, Cecilia, but you never came to me with these concerns."

"When you arrived, I let the girls have you. They need their father most."

There was truth in her words. He felt himself frowning and couldn't stop. "You should've told me. It might've helped me change before I lost you."

"Felton, we lost each other. We married on a whim. I don't want you to make a series of incremental changes to appease me. And if you no longer want to help me kill Gladstone, just say so. I'll go with you to Tramel and then we let each other go."

Her voice was clear, with the Dutch-island twang he loved, but her words still meant they were done.

But it had to be a lie.

How could they be done when they still kissed like newlyweds? Their passion was still there.

"Cecilia, this has been your first lesson. You have to release all your angst, every complaint. You must be numb. Then you'll be ready to kill."

"Numb to it? No passion, Felton?"

"Yes. See, you've told me there is no hope of our reconciliation, and I appear calm, as though the prospect doesn't crush my soul. As though I don't hunger to strip you bare . . . of your doubts . . . and love you here and now and for all time."

Her eyes, chocolaty polished agate, grew wide.

"I told you. Nothing but truth from me to you." Marveling at how red her face had become, he folded his arms. "How did you plan to assassinate my cousin? That night at the King's Theatre, did you have a weapon? I don't remember feeling a gun on your person."

Whipping her knife from her pocket, Cecilia brandished it like it was a sword. "With this. My father gave it to me."

"This pretty thing that I held, modeling your Roman soldier." He fingered the cut near his temple. "Where's the torch? Bang Gladstone over the head with it. You'd have more luck."

She flipped the blade and put it by his nose. "Don't laugh. This could be deadly, Felton."

"Please lower the weapon, my dear. You might cut the air."

"You don't take me seriously. You never took my concerns seriously."

He caught her wrist and made the knife fall to the floor. Then he towed her to him. "Everything about us was serious, and this is your second lesson. Never underestimate a soul, a friend, an enemy, or lover." She wriggled within his hold, but his grip was solid. "You have to be passionless. Emotion makes you react, makes you miss the signs of aggression. That's how you die."

"How . . ." Her jaw tensed. "How many people have you killed?"

Letting go, he tugged at his sleeve, then he bent and scooped up the knife. "Enough, but no one who didn't deserve it."

Her eyes were large. Her heart beat fast and loud. He saw it, heard it pounding beneath her coat. "You're truly going to help me."

"I intend to help you do what you must."

She frowned, her soft lips thinning. "That means you're going to try to talk me out if it."

"I'll advise. I'll train you. If you kill, you'll do it right."

"You pompous fool. You think it just a whim. Just like you assumed my art was."

"That's your fault—the whim part, not the pomposity. All you showed me was the soldier and jaguar. You kept your art from me. You have secrets too, ones only Tramel or the girls are privy to, not me. Why is that, Cilia?"

"They were around, Felton. You only came for a visit, a laugh, and a shared bed."

"It was quite a bed."

She closed her eyes, then opened them with shiny tears. "I don't want to be a joke. Tramel took me seriously. He'd kill for me if he could. I should've let him. Then all would be done. We could both move forward."

"Why did you stop the duke? With his connections, he'd get out of any inquest. I doubt he'd serve any length of a sentence with all the secrets and influence he possesses."

"Didn't think it well for Tramel to kill your cousin on your patio."

The day she left.

The blood on his cousin's collar. It was Tramel who struck at Gladstone, not Cecilia.

"Gladstone was horrible, disrespectful. But it's been ten months. Why can't you move forward?"

"If someone killed Jane, would you laugh it away? At least you could visit her grave to tell her you forgave her killer."

"Certainly not. I'd seek justice in the courts."

"That's what you're afforded on English shores—justice. Not for me. Me and my family don't matter here. I only have a memory of my sister dying in May to take with me."

Links to the mystery—of all the things she said, and didn't—came together. "Are you trying to tell me you want to murder my cousin because he murdered Helena?"

"Jeremiah Gladstone killed my sister. He needs to die."

Before he could stop her again, she knocked on the ceiling, signaling Watson to stop. As soon as the carriage slowed, she popped out and started running.

"Cecilia. Come back. It can be dangerous in unknown woods."

Without a second thought, Felton reached in the compartment under the seat, whipped out his case and pulled his pistol, then jumped down and gave chase. He wasn't letting his wife out of his sight, and he needed to know how his cousin, who'd been in the country since December, was responsible for Helena's May death.

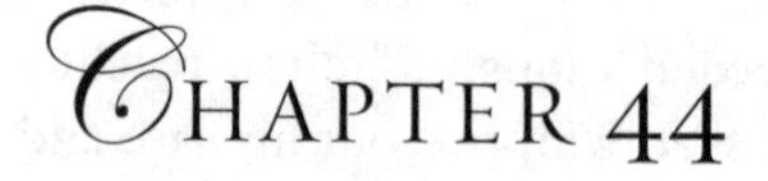

Chapter 44

Cecilia—The Heady Howling Woods

Red and gold maple trees waved at me, beckoning. The land was green and rocky, but I had to get away and let the cold air chill the heat, the hate in my thoughts.

"Lady Gantry, stop." That was Felton's voice, loud, giving orders as if to troops. He'd decided to give chase this time. That was new.

I lifted a finger to the wind and went in that direction.

"Cecilia Lance, the terrain can be dangerous."

Head down, with my hands pinned to my chest, I kept moving.

"Cecilia Charity Thomas Lance." His tone sharpened, like my papa's.

It was silly to run like a child in the woods, but it felt freeing and safer than being in his carriage and letting a little lust lull us into thinking all was well.

"No more running, Cecilia."

The breeze cooled my face, but I stopped chasing it.

My boots dug into a pile of leaves. Then I stood with eyes closed, imagining the blur of scenery when I ran—the golds and the red, the emerald of an evergreen pine. I'd save this moment for a canvas.

With his hands lighting to my shoulder, Felton caught me. "You have failed this lesson."

"Wouldn't be the first. My tutors could tell you stories."

"Cecilia, I don't think you have what it takes to be an assassin. You haven't the discipline for it. You should abandon course and let Gladstone live."

"Failed your test? What are you talking about?"

"The carriage. That was an example of how you're not ready."

I rotated to see if my befuddlement would affect him. "So, because I'm not allowing you liberties, you don't think I can seek revenge." I kicked leaves at him. "I'm not going to be seduced by you. That wasn't part of our bargain."

"A side benefit perhaps, but it was all a test."

"Being sweet, helping with my art, keeping me warm, feeding me, that's how you always did it, twisting me up, pulling me back to the moments I needed and wanted you. We don't go back to the way things were because you now have time to love me."

He pulled his hands behind his back. "You're feeling, not observing. An assassin needs to feel nothing and observe everything. You must be numb to everything. That's how you get to your target."

I pulled at the collar of my redingote. "So, I'm your target?"

"Yes."

His arms slipped to my waist and he spun me until my back was too him. "You tremble in my arms. That's feelings. What you haven't observed is where the carriage is, where Watson or the footman stand. Have they unhitched the horses? Or if I have a weapon in my hand."

"You don't have—"

His arm lifted, and a straight as anything, small pistol was in his palm. It was ready to fire.

A rumble of laughter tumbled. The breath of it swept along my neck. "I'm listening."

"Cecilia, I've studied you. I know how to get to you emotionally and physically. I do use it to distract you. Look at how flustered you are. You can't be like this. Your target can say or do something that will cause you to react."

Dropping my head back against his chest, I heard his heart raging. "You're just as excited. Why is it that I fail?"

He looped my arm about his forearm. Mine shook a little, his never quivered.

"Because I can still shoot and kill, no matter what's going on. Getting emotional means you die."

I turned in his arms and looked at his face. A flush of our passion still stained his cheeks.

"Tell me now what Gladstone will say to make you angry."

"Felton?"

"Tell me what he said last December that put you in my father's arms."

There was no running this time. Not from the warm arms that held me, or the gun I longed to use to smite Gladstone between the eyes.

He fired the gun. He loaded and fired it again. The noise ripped through me.

The wind whipped my face. My salty tears tangled in the curls falling from my chignon.

I could barely see, but I could bear no more.

The red leaves of the oaks, the gold of the alders went away.

Everything became purple. Purple jacaranda.

The smell of the fallen flowers—no more the honey of blooms like a wedding day, but the humid stench of horses' leavings and death.

I had to be away. I ran from everything, driving deeper into the trees.

The images of Helena and the dray, the noises of guns, all the evil of that night returned to my ears.

My shaking, I couldn't stop.

The rebels' shouts, crying for freedom.

The smugglers' guns blasting.

Helena's screams.

Mine.

I dropped to my knees. The crackle of red leaves deafened. The wind crossed my body, sending a bone-aching shiver.

Nothing stopped moving, not till I was caught.

Chapter 45

Felton—Putting Pieces Together

Felton had never shot a gun near a woman, but in these deep woods, the unfamiliar terrain, one had to be prepared.

Yet, here he crouched with Cecilia in one arm and smoke wafting from his favorite blunderbuss pistol in the other.

He pulled her closer. "Cecilia?"

She trembled against him.

"Cecilia, did you fall? Are you hurt?"

She didn't respond, but her thumb trailed scars on the back of his hand and the cocked handle of the gun that was ready to engage.

Her silence unnerved Felton's battlefield-hardened soul.

Setting the gun to his side, he tugged her onto his lap. Felton would be her blanket, her anchor, everything to draw her back from whatever dark place she'd sunken into.

"Talk to me, Cilia. Tell me what Gladstone did?"

"He followed me out on the patio." Tears sprouted and pooled at her chin. "He said Helena's name, like a curse. That it was her fault he didn't get her dowry."

"What dowry? He'd have to marry—"

"Helena was sweet and trusting. She'd give you the best mat

or mattress to sleep on, the first chance to pick from a bundle of new linens. She was afraid of woods like these, unless I held her hand. We'd tease each other that a jaguarete would come if we let go."

"I'm so sorry."

"Hush. Let me get through this." Clinging to his arm, she tucked his fingers under her coat sleeve. "When Jeremiah Gladstone returned to Demerara, he targeted her."

"Returned?"

"He was one of the suitors my father wanted me to meet, that night we met."

Gladstone was at the ball in Stabroek? He tried to reimagine the ballroom, the dim light of the candles. All he saw was Cecilia, and how he had to act gallant and in command when his insides were ripping. His friend Johnson had been shot moments before, and died from those wounds.

"Gladstone made Helena think she was in love. She says they wed. Then he sold her off to a manager at the Elizabeth Ann Plantation."

"He did what? No. That can't be possible."

"Use up a colored girl, hide their vows, then sell a free woman, a daughter of the deceased Wilhelm Thomas—Gladstone had no right, no honor."

"You went to Demerara. You found her at the Elizabeth Ann Plantation?"

"Sick, broken, preg . . . perspiring with fever. In the middle of a rebellion, I helped her escape, but it was too late. She stopped breathing in my arms before morn. That's why he must die."

Felton jammed his gun into his pocket and held Cecilia more tightly.

"Under the jacaranda trees. They were in bloom. Her favorite color, mine too. And then she was gone. What type of life is that? Suffering for love."

"Cilia—"

"Had Gladstone just left her and not feared word would get

back to Aunty Nelly or Lady Jane about his brown wife, my sister, my baby sister, would be alive. He had to rid himself of her forever."

Unemotional.

Logical.

Unhinged.

That's who Felton was at this moment. Right on the precipice of killing his cousin himself. Why would Gladstone do this? What fear did he have of their union being discovered? And why taunt Cecilia over his underhanded dealings?

Felton's plan to dissuade her of murder didn't seem right anymore. His cousin Jeremiah Gladstone was a rotten soul. How could one be redeemed from this?

And how would Felton be made worthy of Cecilia again? His missions and then the 1812 war had kept Helena from joining them. Under his wife's watchful eyes in London, Helena would be alive, navigating her way through English society.

"The duke made it possible for you to get to her?"

"Don't ask me how. I cannot betray him. Please don't ask me."

With his hands in her hair, he guided her teary face to his chest. "Then let it all out, all your fury. I deserve to suffer for this."

"I'm tired of crying. And, Felton, every time I think I can move on, it comes back."

His neglect, his duty to Liverpool allowed this to happen. He and his family weren't worthy of her. Only Tramel had honored Cecilia. Only he had helped.

For all the trouble his family had caused, he should beg her forgiveness. A better man would let Cecilia go, after the Warwick business was completed.

Felton wasn't a better man.

He was his father's son.

Like Tramel, Felton didn't care that she was a star and he was formed of dust. He wanted her and would have her. He merely needed to figure out how to have it all—forgiveness and her body and soul.

"My lord, my ears have settled. I'm better now. Let me go."

No.

Never.

Not again.

"There's, ummmm, something in the distance."

She gripped his chest tight and ducked her head to his shoulder. "What? Where?"

That lovely neck was exposed from her purple collar.

He threaded his fingers into her coat, deep along her back. "Don't move."

Heaven. She did as he asked. "What is it?"

"Something. Animal?"

"I did this. I entrapped us again. We didn't need a door."

Angling his face closer to hers. "Doors for us are good. Just be still."

When her brows knitted in the way she did with her eyes sparkling, he could no longer resist.

Felton lowered his head and brushed his lip against hers. "Don't move at all."

The first kiss was light. Tickling soft. With his nose smooth against her creamy cheek, he waited for her to yield. His fingers kneaded her back and worked their way down her sensitive hips.

When she gasped, he kissed her more deeply. She returned his kiss and molded against his chest.

They were back. It had to be. He laid her on the ground and unbuttoned more of her coat. "I want all of you, Cilia. Always."

Her brown eyes widened like she'd awakened from a dream. "No." She sat up. Then scrambled to her feet. "No."

"Cecilia. I'm yours. And you're still mine. Being with you is natural and right. Goodness, I miss us. I need you."

She touched her reddened lips. "No."

"Are you telling me you don't still love me? You taste like you do."

"Don't do that again. We have—"

"Don't what, Cilia? Pretend I don't love you?" He leapt up and neared. "I can't get you out of my head." He tapped his temple. "When I was away on missions, you were right here. I had to come home to you. You're in every dream, sharing my bed each night. All this time apart, nothing has changed."

"We can't go back. Too much has happened. This is not why I agreed to come."

"Maybe I've finally become your jaguar. I saw the opportunity to pounce, to claim your heart."

"Then I need to be away from you again. I should walk back to London."

"Cecilia, we're hours from Town." He lifted his hand. "I'll behave, but as I told you, I will be honest. You need to know that I'm ready to begin again."

"I can't begin again when there's no end to my nightmare. Gladstone . . . I can't do this."

The stubborn woman turned from him, as if she could traipse back to London and started walking away.

Where's a jaguar when you need one?

Felton chased. "Let's go. We should head back and continue on our route to Warwick."

"No. You're determined to confuse me or use my fears to draw me back. This marriage is over."

"Is it? Or is that what you wish to tell yourself." He sped ahead and planted in her path. "You do still feel everything as I do."

"I don't. And I think we should stop this. You can't be impartial and let me seek revenge. Send me back to London."

"Cecilia, I'm a professional. If you don't have patience to deal with me, how will you be able to manage the anger you feel when Gladstone's in view? You're caught. The situation is too sticky with all the emotions you'll have to master."

"Seems I'm mastering them better than you. I'm not begging to be with you."

He wanted to say *not yet*. She was weak for him, their kiss told him he still had a chance if he could prove himself worthy. “You’ll never be invisible, not to me. Not with all the passion in your heart.”

“Not to Tramel either.” Her low voice said the truth he never wanted to hear. He’d not only lost her, but her heart had strayed.

He lifted her chin.

Guilt shadowed and darkened her eyes.

She started to run and go deeper into the woods, a vision of purple leaping into the golden leaves of autumn.

But Felton was frozen. He knew Tramel loved Cecilia, but he never thought that . . . she . . .

Watson approached. “The miss has gone rogue again. We need to keep moving, sir. This isn’t the place for a squabble. The coaching inns fill up fast.”

“Very well.”

Invisible.

All the feelings he had to swallow, the anguish at losing her love—Tramel had won.

He spun and charged Cecilia. “You heard Watson. We have to go. We both need a proper night’s sleep in decent beds. Then we start over.”

She ignored Felton and kept going.

“Enough of this.” He came behind Cecilia, hauled her up in the air. “A spy must stay on schedule.”

Felton slung her over his shoulder.

Cecilia was mad, but he’d achieved what he needed. He knew all the facts. Gladstone was evil, and the woman he loved had fallen for the duke.

CHAPTER 46

CECILIA—WALK AROUND THE INN

Under the intrusive eye of Mr. Watson, I walked around the coaching inn three times. It wasn't hard. The place was small. There was still good light in the day. It would be a shame to quit traveling today.

This wasn't working.

Felton remained quiet for what felt like hours, then he told me more of his life as a spy. The man pretended that I hadn't told him of my heart's troubles.

Uneasy as I was, I was assured he'd given up. A man couldn't forgive his wife's heart going astray. Still, I said nothing of Noah. Felton deserved to know of his nephew, the boy who'd be his heir since he had no living son and his first cousin, Gladstone did. But what good would it do if Gladstone didn't pay?

If I kept my mouth shut, Noah would be safe. If I had kept it closed in the woods, the duke and marquess, father and his son, might repair their bond before the good man died.

Slapping the fence in front of me, I startled a pig and what looked like a baby calf. The beasts seemed happy in the pen, munching out of a trough, grazing on the grass. Sort of hoped they weren't about to be slaughtered.

"Lady Gantry," Watson said as he approached from the left.

His dark mantle was crisp, with a few open buttons. "Lord Gantry wishes you to stay closer to the inn."

Blinking and stretching, I realized I'd walked quite far. I was another ten feet from thick woods. More rust-colored alders were before me, but the clean scent of emerald pines wiggled in the wind. "I'm not going to run again."

"Ya sure about that, ma'am? Well, at least give Lord Gantry the courtesy of knowing ya left."

"Watson, what's that supposed to mean?"

"He didn't know you'd left in December, not until wee hours later. Never seen him quite so disturbed. He thought you weren't speaking to him and locked yourself in ya studio."

"The closet with the window? It was locked? I told him goodbye. That wasn't good enough?"

He tipped his hat. "Just thought you should know. He'd chase ya every time. He cares deeply."

I covered my mouth for a second. I thought he had other things to do or was being respectful of my privacy like always. "Watson, do you know who gave him that idea?"

"Not sure, ma'am. But he suffered frostbite on his hands that night, walking the streets looking for you during the snowfall. If he'd found ya, he'd have tossed you over his shoulder then too. Come on back with me, Lady Gantry."

Felton's man-of-all-work had always been a fair arbiter. I nodded, tugged at my coat collar, and walked back with him.

We passed the pen again and that cute calf grazing. Didn't see a mama cow anywhere.

It had been less than a half a day. How was Noah? Did he miss me? Did he notice I was gone? Or had he just come to assume I was off painting?

The notions of what a baby understood or felt were beyond me, but it didn't remove the guilt wallowing in my gut.

No more thinking.

No more guilt today.

"Ma'am, you stopped again. Do you want the master to get you a baby cow? He'll do it."

A chuckle rose to my lips. "No, I don't need a cow, but their pen is bigger than a closet. Do they do that here? Make a pen so big for one?"

The man stopped and sighed. "A big pen is good for one. Better for two."

"Not everyone feels that way."

"Lord Gantry is not a beast. He has survived much, and he gives much. If he has decided that it's better for two, not much I can say. Maybe you should use your fancy education and tell him clearly what you want. Paint him a picture, if words fail."

I wasn't sure that I wanted to talk with him just yet. Didn't know what to say other than sorry, sorry I wasn't careful with my heart.

"Where's the next coaching inn we will stop at? Where will we spend the night?"

"New Town, near the Royal Military College."

"Thank you, Watson. I'll take the stagecoach and meet you and Lord Gantry there."

He shook his head. "No, ma'am. Let me get his lordship to convince ya."

"No, Watson. I'm Lady Gantry, and I've made my decision. You can inform him of my decision. He'll know what I'm doing when he sees me. It's for the best."

The man frowned then bowed. "As you wish, ma'am."

He turned on his heel and went toward the carriage, while I breathed the sweet pine, in and out, in and out. I'd had enough talk and tactics today. Felton would understand or not. This was my decision.

Chapter 47

Felton—A Scheme or Two Might Do

With his temper finally cooled and his picnic basket refilled for the next portion of their trip, he hoped the new treats would brighten her sour mood.

The guilt she bore over Helena was heartbreaking, but Tramel was now in her affections.

Was it the duke she kissed when their lips met in the carriage and again in the woods?

Tramel had confused her, taken advantage of Cecilia's trusting soul. That's what he wanted to believe. He had to.

He paced and wrung his hands. Felton had to believe in the truth of their touch. She wouldn't curl to his chest to sleep, or kiss him in the fields, if she felt nothing.

When he walked out of the inn, Felton determined that he would be patient. What they had wasn't gone. It needed to be reborn.

What to do with Gladstone? That fateful night in Stabroek, he was there. Did he have designs on Cecilia? Why hadn't he said something if he was at the ball?

Why had he not said anything since?

The fool had a lot of explaining to do. Felton could only hope that some mistake was made, but his gut said no. The fool was guilty. Cecilia couldn't be wrong about what he'd done to her sister.

The fellow he'd practically grown up with, learned to shoot with in the woods of Warwick with the duke, was dastardly. How could Jeremiah Gladstone have changed that much?

Was there another way to pay for enslaving Helena, other than death?

Watson sped toward him. Panic spread across his features, his wide upturned nose and broad lips poked into a disapproving frown. "Lady Gantry's going rogue again, sir."

Felton started running to their carriage, but she wasn't there. "Watson, where is she?"

"She has her portmanteau and wants to catch a coach to the next stop at New Town, near the Royal Military College."

Pushing past Watson, he saw Cecilia, purple coat flaring, standing in line with people readying to board the crowded transport.

"Sir, go put your foot down! This is ridiculous. A marquess's wife does not ride on the stage when she's traveling with her husband, who has a perfectly good coach available."

"What do you suggest, Watson? Toss her over my shoulder again? You see how effective the Neanderthal approach has gone. Instead of begrudgingly sharing my carriage, she's actively fleeing it."

His man shook his head. "I'd say we're losing this war. When do we cut our losses?"

Felton had tried to do things according to his training, by the Repington's instructions—all to no avail. He leaned against the carriage. "What would Tramel do?"

The man wouldn't let the woman he loved or the women he married leave him, until he wanted them gone. Yet, he allowed Cecilia to leave when it was obvious he'd rather she stay. Why? Was she determined to leave all Lance men?

"Lady Gantry has left me twice. This will make thrice. Seems I'm not listening again. In country, I'd leave and prepare a report for Liverpool."

His man's eyes narrowed, and he offered an awful scowl. "Paperwork? That's your response? Truly, sir. Now I see Tramel's troubles."

Not another person taking his father's side. "Out with your suggestion, Mr. Watson."

"Be Tramel. He'd toss her over his shoulder if he was heading to bed. During the day, he'd shred enough of her pride to make her see his way was right."

"That's not who I am, Watson."

"Who are you, sir? A retiring spy? The errand-running art lover? Or a man on a mission?"

That was a good question. When his father passed, Felton would have a new title and inherit the powerful legacy of a man who always claimed what he wanted.

"You are to be the duke, sir. Any woman would kill to be your wife."

Cecilia wanted a killing alright, but that was part of the problem.

With a defeated shrug, he turned to walk away, but Watson barreled in front of him. "The old duke would make someone who crossed him feel the weight of the decision. Lady Gantry should rue the inconvenience of not traveling in the protection of your coach."

"Finally, you've said something useful. Go into the inn. Hire every woman you can, to take the stage to the next destination with our marchioness. Let's make her feel the joy of a crowd. Lady Gantry is like me. She'll detest that."

A slow smile crossed his man's face. "Not what I was talking about, but better than nothing."

He tossed Watson his purse. "Give them passage back too. But choose fair-minded people."

"Fair-minded, sir?"

"Traveling alone into the country can make tongues less civil.

I don't want my wife terrorized or suffering offense. Let her be crowded, but with no loss of her peace."

"Very good, Lord Gantry. Not what your father would insist upon, but better than stewing."

Watson had missed his calling. He'd have been one of Tramel's top henchmen.

Yet, if becoming more like the duke meant returning Cecilia to Felton's arms, the gambit was worth it.

CHAPTER 48

CECILIA—ALONE IN A CROWD

Waiting to board the coach was not terrible. I'd traveled a great deal by myself, so the prospects weren't scary. Yet my throat tightened watching Felton glaring at me.

Across from me, ten feet away, he leaned against a barrel. With folded arms, he frowned. His shoulders, even beneath his great-coat, looked tense enough to pop.

He mopped at his brow, then turned as he looked toward the rear of the line.

This was new, to see emotions on his face.

With his jaw stiff and the same bow-legged gait he had in Stabroek, he came to me. My breath caught. I thought I'd escaped his arguments or his attempts at persuasion.

"Lady Gantry, you seem very set in this course."

"I am, sir. No need to toss me with abandon."

He sighed and looked over my head. "I apologize for man-handling you. I was at my wit's end, but I besiege you to reconsider. I'll behave. I have plenty of room and another basket of treats to share."

"Felton, you're glorious with gifts, but we don't know how to be. We are either too affectionate or—"

"Or you're running and I'm chasing, my Lady Gantry."

"I won't be that much longer."

"You are for now, Cilia." His lips had flattened, then curled up. "This will give me time to plan the next pieces of your training."

"Plan? You're still going to help me?"

He took my hand, his warm palm cutting through my chill. "Yes, I've been thinking about it. Justice is deserved. When we're calm and rational and not given to running, we can work through the steps."

This was a new tack for him to take. The professional sound didn't match his eyes. Had they always been this clear, declaring his feelings?

Maybe the glass of the lantern containing his soul had chipped.

I lowered my chin. "You're right. When my emotions are easier, I won't be given to run. I look forward to—"

"Dinner this evening in New Town. My carriage will get there a little faster than the coach." He looked over my head. "Well, my man is signaling that we are done. Your fare is paid." Felton had my hand and led me to the coach's entry.

A woman with a big sack knocked past us. She wasn't rude, just busy. All my comings and goings in the city had taught me the difference.

Transport especially near the ports, made people more tolerant of differences. The stares went away completely by Portsmouth and London. I had no need to hide or costume myself as I had in Covent Garden to keep people away.

"You're sure about this, Cilia? It looks very crowded. And we haven't discussed how to tell the children where you've been and why you're still not coming home."

Home was a strange word, and now that I had Patience and Enna and Noah, I had my own.

"Make it all my fault. That way they hate me and not you, their father. I'm not required to be a relation to them."

"You're a relation to them. And everyone wants to know a famous artist. I'm sure that's what you will be. The painting of me and Tramel is superb."

I should've known he'd see that one at Warwick. "It's not finished. I couldn't picture how . . ."

"It will come to you. You paint what's not there, remember?" He leaned in close. "The heart wants what it wants."

When he put my hand to his breast and I felt the fast thud, I was sure my cheeks became fire.

Turning away, I rubbed my temples. We were separating. I wouldn't succumb to the attraction between us anymore.

"Well, Lady Gantry, I'll see you for dinner. I'll secure rooms as well."

"Thank you, my lord."

"We'll have to see how much this slows us down. There won't be time to drive past Stonehenge."

"My lord, you never want to stop when we go to Warwick."

"It's the closest ancient artifact in England. It sort of inspires me of Rome because of the massive stonework. Since I never took you, here on our last trip together, we should attempt to stretch our legs—"

"Stop, Felton. I don't want to be tempted. I believe we will have more charity for one another if we forgo remembering what we had."

His gaze burned and it became fire to my lungs. He wasn't thinking of separating. "We had something. I feel it's worth fighting for. I've fought for so many things, for the betterment of England. I'm fighting for what I want."

He looked down, then peered toward the people standing ahead of me. "But it takes two for an argument. One for a grudge. Tramel has taught me the distinction." Felton clasped my portmanteau. "I'll take this. The driver said the coach was very crowded. I'd rather you come with me. I will let you be. And you will be able to rest or draw. Whatever you want."

I took it from him. Didn't want to depend on him or anyone else. If Noah and Enna were to continue to depend upon me, I had to be strong. "I'll be fine."

"Are you sure? It will be crowded and noisy."

Noisy? Was it wise to put myself in a situation that put my peace at risk?

I was about to protest when I saw an older woman, her daughter, and a calf, the calf from the pen, precede me into the coach.

He slipped the portmanteau from my fingers, bowed, and left for his carriage.

If I wasn't so stubborn, I'd change my mind and ask if I could go with him, but I'd rather sit with livestock than chance another moment weighing what Felton and I had and why it was gone.

I was wrong.

Two hours with a calf chewing my handkerchief, while pressed between the breasts of two burly matrons, was horrid. Trying not to breathe the stench of people who thought bathing was bad for one's health convinced me that I wasn't too proud to beg.

Help.

Moooooo.

Then the noises ripped at me. Snippets of this conversation, then that one, hurt my ears. Booming voices inside the coach, more voices dumping through the roof like a waterfall.

Drowning, fending off a cute cow attack, I didn't know how to calm.

She was cute, with light brown eyes like Helena's. Big ears like Noah's but with splotchy white patches on her tawny coat, she shouldn't be a monster. Or smell bad like one, not with such pink lips. Maybe I'll call her Jacaranda, but that would mean she'd always end up smelling bad.

Mooooo.

Then *moomoo*. That would be how I'd tell the tale of the handkerchief killer.

Fidgeting, I received an elbow to my ribs and a "Sorry."

Pinned, I could neither walk nor run away. I was losing this fight for control.

Nothing to sketch.

Nothing to draw my mind to peace.

No one to tell me all would be well.

Rocking on my seat, I shivered and shut my eyes tightly.

Praying to think myself safe.

Praying to find a placid sea.

Let me be on the cliffs of Ballard, held in strength, even if I stand alone. Lord, give me that moment.

The buxom women began to quiet, nodding in slumber.

Noises ramped up, then subsided.

That spinning sense inside me slowed.

Felton.

If I survived being smothered by the scents, I'd apologize immediately. In this instance, he did know best.

We were civilized enough to ride in silence.

Moo.

The calf seized the rest of the snowy cloth and chewed it. She looked as if she wanted to eat my coat. The way she pressed at my side, I think she would.

My only hope was that Felton wouldn't gloat too badly when I met him at dinner.

Moo.

No, I wasn't too proud to beg after all.

Chapter 49

Cecilia—Dinner for Two

Horrible.

I climbed out of the carriage. My limbs shook, not from fear but from being cramped by my companions. A runaway wife, public transport, and Moomoo didn't make a proper mix.

The sun had set but the small coaching inn's entry was lit with torches. People came in and out, heading to their carriages or the barn. I hadn't the energy to cross the threshold.

Had to catch my breath and let my ears stop ringing. Yet, I couldn't settle.

One close of my eyes exposed nothing—no landscapes, no faces. Blank and black, that was better than seeing the faces I shouldn't, or remembering Helena no longer hearing my chatter.

Wrapping my arms about me, I almost wished Felton had waited at the entry. That he'd ease my shakes. I'd tell him he was right about the carriage.

My hesitation grew. My fingers became damp even in the chill of the air. I wished I smelled tea roses, but the lathered horses were too close. I had the scent of a pasture in my clothes, none of the sweet clover or the fresh honeyed smell of jacarandas before they fell. This was definitely after.

When I stuck my hands in my pocket, my fingers went through

the holes Moomoo made. I loved this coat. Felton bought it for my first snow in England. Agatha and Amelia, we all flopped in the white ice, the creamy snow, to make what they called an angel. I was wet and cold, and Felton fished me out.

One thing was certain, another day with Moomoo on public transport and my purple velvet coat would be beyond repair.

Yet, that was also my problem. Like stage scaffolding, not knowing what to repair and what to let alone.

More noise. More crowds. I ran inside to escape.

Conversations, loud and boisterous, were everywhere, but my ears perked to a baby's coo.

A mother with her babe sat at a table. The birdlike peep sounded like Noah, how he greeted me early in the morning when I returned from a commission.

My heart whimpered.

I'd hug the murderous Moomoo if the calf made sounds like that boy . . . my boy.

Noah was with Patience, and I knew my sister would be loving to him. He probably didn't miss me.

Knowing he was well cared for, that should keep me cheered, but I had to fan my eyes.

Helena would be happy that her sisters were together again. Even with all the doubts I had about me and mothering, I knew I didn't want to lose Noah or the bond we shared.

I'd promised to raise my nephew, but Patience had a house and a loving husband. Well, I sort of had those too, but I chose to abandon them.

Felton's London residence wouldn't be lonely if I had Enna and my boy.

Watson approached. His mantle was unbuttoned. His shoulders sagged. He looked very tired. "Ma'am. Lord Gantry wishes you to dine with him in the private room upstairs."

"Private?" I loved the sound of that, but I smelled like the baby cow.

All the noises around me boomed in a slowed dance. *Boom*—banging pots. *Boom*—crying and shrieking. *Boom*—mooing. *Boom boom*—voices talking. Talk. Talk. Talk.

Grasping his arm, I leaned into him. "Where's Lord Gantry?"

"Ma'am, it will be alright. He's up the stairs on the left. Have a pleasant meal while I finish arrangements for the lodgings. We slowed our carriage to follow the stage. His lordship wanted to be assured that it wouldn't tip over and fall by the wayside." He offered one of those it-will-be-better smiles with a little serves-you-right-stubborn-woman tossed in, then pointed again to the steps, bowed, and went outside.

To sit in quiet, without a cow eating my coat, over a nice dinner with a respectful man sounded like heaven.

The stairs creaked as I took them by twos. After a quick knock, I let myself inside.

The scent of seasoned beefsteak with garlic filled the air. My mouth pooled with drool.

Brows lifting, Felton waved me to a seat. "I hope you haven't come to tell me you're opposed to eating together too? I thought we agreed on dinner." He waved his fork with a cut of the juicy beef. "That would be a shame."

Oh, the scent of the thick brown gravy had my stomach dancing, but my ears rejoiced at the calm. One could barely hear the crowd below. "A truce can be had if you can forgive me for smelling like a barn."

Nose wriggling, he came to me and pulled out the chair. "Your perfume is special tonight. Not the smell of lavender or tea roses. And goodness, your poor coat, the color . . . what were those purple flowers?"

"Jacaranda. It sort of smells like it now, thanks to my cow."

"You own a cow? Another secret venture."

Shoving my hands through the holes, I wriggled my fingers. "Payment for a new coat."

"Enterprising." He slid the ruined velvet from my shoulders. "This is a shame. I remember—"

My fingers went to his lips. "Can we sit and not say a word for a few? My ears ring from the chatter."

With a kiss to my thumb, he folded my coat, crisp on the seams like he did all his clothes, and laid it over a chair.

His hair was loose and flipped to the side as he tilted his head. The next I knew, he'd embraced me and gentled my back.

Tired, I didn't resist and collapsed against him. His fingers where at the base of my neck, pressing and easing the tense muscles.

To be honest, if he laid me out on this table and kept me warm and away from noise and Moomoo, I'd be his.

"Cecilia, are you alright?"

"Mmm." My arms wound about his waist and I held him so tight I couldn't see the light, just his onyx waistcoat.

"You need to rest and eat."

With his palms stroking and claiming everything, Felton helped me sit and returned to rubbing my shoulders and that spot on my neck prone to aches.

"It's not fair. You being sweet, with all these wonderful smells, and I'm *eau de cow*."

He put a finger to my lips, then worked his thumbs along my temples. Then the beautiful pressure was gone. He'd stepped behind me and pushed my chair to the table. When he sat down, his face seemed concerned and maybe guilty. "I'm taking advantage of you. That's surely wrong."

The way I was so adamant about not being near him, he must think I didn't want his touch. He couldn't be more wrong.

Felton returned to his seat far away, but not before filling my plate with a cut of the beefsteak and a hearty roasted potato.

The man was faithful, offering no talking, but he bowed his head as if to offer me a wordless blessing for the meal.

Seizing my fork and knife, I started to dive in, but then I thought of Moomoo. Yes, she was awful, and she ate my handkerchief and my coat, but this could be her mother or cousin.

And now she was mine, part of my new family.

"I know you asked for no words, Lady Gantry, but you seem in agony."

The lump in my throat was hard to swallow, but it went down when I sipped at my water.

"You know that was the problem, us not talking, Cecilia."

"We communicated in other ways. I think that's what you said."

With a sad sort of curl to his lips, he sat back and lifted his goblet. "I miss every way we said or showed affection, you know that."

If I closed my eyes, I'd remember too. Instead, I looked down at my traitorous plate.

"Is the beefsteak not to your liking? I thought it your favorite." He lifted a silver dome. "What about some cod?"

Grilled with onions and wild greens, it seemed perfect and it wasn't related to Moomoo. "The fish, Felton. Yes, the fish, please."

Switching plates, he offered me a feast of fluffy white cod, a dip of greens, and a tangy brown sauce.

Felton scooted closer. "You do look tired. Should I feed you?"

And so it begins.

"No, my lord. But you're right. We should've stayed at the last inn. I will so enjoy sleeping, sound sleeping, like near-death sleep tonight."

His grin held a tinge more of the guilt I saw before, but I didn't care so much. His countenance was not guarded. It was open to me.

"My lord, it isn't like you have to feel guilty for riding in comfort when the coach was my choice."

He forked a piece of the savory fish into my mouth. "If you say so, Lady Gantry."

I tasted a piece of the tender flesh of the cod. Salty, buttery—it all tasted so good.

He carved into the beef. The juices ran. Dark and rich, the gravy puddled on the lip he licked.

The way he ate, savoring every last bite, enjoying every morsel like it was his last.

Understanding what he'd done for the Department of War and the Colonies made me feel his joy for the present so much better.

"You're yawning, Lady Gantry. I think you're going to oversleep and miss the stagecoach. It leaves at nine."

Mouth so full, all I could do was nod, nod and fork in more fish. "It has been a long day," I said when my mouth was clear, "but if I miss it I will . . . I will try not to miss it, but I'll catch the next coach."

He waved his fork and the roasted garlic wafted. If I had a small piece, would Moomoo know?

"Cecilia, I'm not leaving this inn unless I'm sure you're on the coach. But you could ride with me. Plenty of room."

Room sounded nice, and Moomoo was no respecter of personal space or redingotes. "May I answer in the morning?"

A wicked smile appeared on his lips. "Yes. Are you sure you don't want this final piece?" He waved an inch-cut chunk on his fork. "Beefsteak is your favorite. I know you, Cecilia."

Though the cod was good, my flesh was weak. Sorry, Moomoo. I opened my mouth and Felton stretched and put the beef to my tongue. Taking my time, I chewed heaven. "Thank you. Don't tell my cow."

"I won't, my dear. Our secret."

"Felton, thank you for the meal, but I'm so tired. The sooner I sleep, the better company I will be."

He smiled and finished his drink. "Do you still hog the sheets? I found that an unusual thing when we wed, but the first thing I missed."

It was the only way to stay warm in English winters. Felton was fire. I missed that too. "My lord, you'll not have to fight for blankets once you end this marriage."

"It was a battle worth winning."

A frown overtook his face. He poured more claret.

"Felton?"

"We're adults. I ceded to you that we will end our marriage. But I give no grounds on desiring you."

My fork hit hard on my plate. The look in his eyes mirrored the one he had when I finally let him stop posing, put down the torch and knife, and come to me.

"I miss you. Miss your body like a treasure map. You were made for me to behold, to caress and discover."

My mind was too tired to run from these memories. I should ask if we could snuggle first, get a few hours of sleep before my corsair pirate hung the Jolly Roger flag and claimed his territory.

"Watson said he was making arrangements. I wish he'd hurry."

"He should be, Cilia." He downed his glass and poured another. "What shall we tell the girls?"

"They know I'm coming?"

"They haven't lost hope that I'd find you. They still think I can fix anything."

"Felton, you were confident that I'd come with you?"

"You're loyal to Tramel. The bond you two have formed is very strong. I knew Tramel would get his last wish."

"His last wish would be for you two to reconcile."

"A little hard to do that when we battle for the same thing. Only one man can win."

Everything shone in Felton's face—hate, love, frustration.

"Is it assured that he'll die? No chance of recovery?" My voice sounded small, but it needed to hide when I was the cause of Felton's pain.

"The palsy seems very bad this time." His saddened gaze went beyond me, probably to those wishes of things being different that seemed out of reach.

This time I lifted from my seat. My arms reached for him before I could change my mind. He always had my heart when he unveiled himself.

He swallowed hard as he stood, taking me with him. "You do smell like cow."

His laugh sounded forced, but he held on to me. "My offer to share my carriage still remains. I hear a pig may join you on the next leg. Pigs make terrible traveling companions."

"Then I'll ride with you so my craving for roast boar will not be challenged."

His chuckles echoed through me. I stepped away when the door opened.

Watson had returned. His face looked cross. "Sir, they only have one room."

Felton's bemused smile struck at my chest. "One bed?" I said. "My lord, truly? This is our pattern. You feed me, talk nice, and we just pick back up. I was hooked this time. I trusted you."

Felton picked up his coat and moved to the door. "Where is this room?"

"The last one, top of the stairs."

"Good. Have them ready a hot bath. Nothing communal for me. I don't share well."

"Yes, sir."

The door closed.

Arms crossing, he turned to me. "If I intended to do a trick, I'd own up to it, like making the coach as crowded as possible. I own my mistakes. Goodnight, Cecilia, I'll see you in the morning."

"Felton, where are you going?"

"To bed."

"But there's only one bed."

"Yes, my lady, one bed. Mine. You're resourceful. You'll figure something out since it is impossible for a man and woman to be in the same place and it be platonic, even fatherly."

"Felton . . ." The accusation was still there, just softer than last December. That moment I could honestly say I adored my father-in-law and that nothing untoward had occurred.

That moment.

Couldn't quite say that now. The look in Felton's eyes said he knew it too, even whispered he understood why.

He grabbed the doorknob. "Goodnight, Cilia. You know where to find me. I'll never run out on you."

"No, you'll announce you're leaving because of Liverpool or some reason that's important to you. And you'll never once acknowledge that I might have needed you to stay. I wanted your encouragement for more than a month."

His gaze flickered. "It seems that we should've talked more. Good night." He dipped his head and left.

More tired than ever, I put my face on the table. I was weighed down by the stones in my chest. I was guilty of thinking of Tramel too much and that for a long time he was the measure of a hero.

I couldn't explain that, even though I was tempted. I hadn't broken any vow. But why say all this only for Felton to think that meant I was still his?

My stubborn heart was mine and mine alone.

Nonetheless, it took everything in me to leave Felton before. I didn't think I'd have that kind of strength again.

FELTON—COZY ROOM FOR ONE

The room seemed small to Felton, but elegant with a hammered copper tub laid in front of the hearth. Steam rose from the water. Everything would feel better after a hot bath. Everything would be better if Cecilia had come.

He paced back and forth, telling his gut that Watson would be able to get her another room and that maybe she'd cede to the small bit of wisdom that being under his protection was best.

Stubborn woman.

The knock at the door ramped up his pulse. He smoothed his grin. It took a lot for Cecilia to admit she was wrong, and he could do that too. Felton stalked to the door and flung it open.

No wife stood in the doorway, just Watson.

All the air in Felton's lungs leached out in a frustrated sigh. "Yes."

"Sorry, sir. I checked again. All the rooms are rented. There's truly no room at the inn."

"Not your fault, Watson."

He flicked dust from the braiding of his jacket. "Lady Gantry remains downstairs in the dining room. She won't be able to stay there long. I can let her stay in the carriage or she'll have to be in the barn with the others."

"Well, she might prefer that, sleeping with the calf she now owns. Good job on that."

"Just lucky, my lord, that a woman was transporting the beast. That was none of my doing."

Felton picked up his greatcoat. "Lady Gantry is always cold. Might as well make sure she's warm and safe tonight."

"You're going to sleep in the barn?"

Chuckling, he slipped on his coat. "I've slept in worst places."

"But this room, Lord Gantry, it shouldn't go to waste."

"No, it shouldn't. You stay, Watson. You had too long a night last night awaiting me at the theatre. Sleep well. Just have the room ready for Lady Gantry to refresh herself at eight in the morning."

The man looked as if he was about to jump onto the bed but held still. "You sure, sir?"

Felton looked at the cozy room. The lovely fire in the hearth, the warm bath that would've been fine for friends or a reuniting husband and wife. "You sleep well tonight. I have a calf and an estranged wife to attend."

He headed down the stairs toward his dining room. Looking over the railing he saw the crowded tables being emptied. If this were Grenada or Jamaica, he'd have a remote hut or an out-of-the-way house ready and available.

Head shaking, he went into the private dining room. Cecilia was facedown near her plate. Well, plates. She did finish the beefsteak. "Why are you so stubborn?"

She startled. "Felton?"

"Looks like they are out of rooms for me too. May I escort you to the stables? Let me meet your cow."

"Moomoo?"

"Yes, Moomoo Lance, as Amelia would say."

Her eyes shifted and pure pleasure crossed her face. Her lips curled into the easiest smile he'd seen since they stepped onto the boat leaving Demerara.

"If I'd known a cow was what it took to give you joy, you would've had one by now."

Her lips bloomed into a grin, and she laughed, gentle and soulful like a brass bell.

"You're sleep deprived." Suddenly, he didn't feel so stupid for giving up his bed. "Come along, my dear. We may have to negotiate haystacks."

When she stood, he wrapped her up in her abused purple redingote. His blueberry was in need of a new one.

Arm in arm, they made it out of the inn and onto the path heading to the barn.

"Normally, I would sleep for a day after a big commission."

He stopped. Under the starlit sky, he found nothing better to do than pause and look at how everything reflected in her eyes.

"How many commissions have you done since returning from Demerara?"

"Four, counting the King's Theatre and Drury Lane."

"Busy busy. So, this little trip is like a good getaway."

Their gazes teased, then she broke away, looking up like she could capture a falling star.

Impossible to catch herself.

It was his job now to support her and help her reach for whatever she wanted. That was a new mission he could grasp if she would accept him.

"My lord, never seen so many lights in a night sky."

"There were many the night we met. Remember, Cecilia?"

"Can't quite forget. It was the warmest I've been in forever. You could see Cepheus in the sky. Tonight, I see Orion."

"You saved me that night. I will always be grateful."

She stopped in front of him. "Guess you sort of saved me. I could've been wed to Gladstone. I could've been Helena." She bit her lip. "I would rather have suffered than my little sister."

He rubbed her arms and pulled her closer. "No thinking of him tonight. Let us save that for tomorrow's mission planning."

"Do you ever think about becoming the duke, the new Tramel?"

"Haven't thought of much but you."

She stroked his arm. "Felton, I didn't want you angry."

"Do I want my father to die? No. Do I want to be around him? No. Do I want to lose you to him? Never."

Cecilia jerked away and headed in the opposite direction.

"Stop running. Please."

With her back to him, she did, planting her slippers into the gravel. "I'm not running. I'm walking. I like to walk."

He paced to her and caught her hand. "Cecilia, you've been gone a long time. Much of that time was at Warwick. I don't want Tramel to come between us anymore, but I don't know how he won't."

Her head dropped forward, then she spun to him.

"I spent three months at Warwick. Tramel was wonderful, so caring. When you and the girls didn't come for Christmas, the duke and I spent the season together. It was magical, the food, the walks along the grounds, the cliffs of Ballard. The way the fog skims the water and flows to the top is pure magic. He had fireworks explode, sparkling over the house. I painted and walked every day until I left for Demerara."

It was an answer, but it didn't match the sadness in her eyes. "I didn't break my vows, but as my art found freedom, I loved you a little less each day."

"And you began to love Tramel a little more."

Her head buried against his chest. "Yes. It's why I didn't go back to him after Demerara. I couldn't risk a deeper attachment."

Her suppressed accent was full and lush. "I never, we never . . . but he took your place in my dreams. It was very confusing to have these feelings for you and Tramel."

If he completed a thorough investigation, he'd have to ask who she loved more. But a fool prone to jealousy didn't need more ammunition. "Your returning to London saved us, the possibility of us remaining friends?"

"It saved me. I couldn't risk losing any more of my heart. I had hoped you'd have given up on me, so I'd never have to tell you how much my heart changed because I was careless."

"Cilia, I was careless. Tramel will always be Tramel, but it was I who caused the alienation of your affections. Accusing you of infidelity broke your trust and left you vulnerable to a man like the duke, who's lived a life collecting art and women."

"Tell me you forgive me, Felton. I never meant . . ."

"I studied your paintings and how you dated them on the back. I saw the progressive sadness in the images. I'd already lost you when I left on my last mission. The final image—the stark winter—is heartbreaking."

Smoothing her shoulders, he wanted to go back in time and fix everything. "The ones at Warwick grow bright and get warmer, until you—I suspect you confirmed your sister's fate."

He put his fingers to her temples. "I know I still have a piece of your heart. Your art says that too. That's why you couldn't finish the canvas of father and son."

"I'm ashamed. Did I love him all along? Is that why you accused me of being unfaithful in December?"

"No. No, Cilia. That was pure jealousy, as a result of something Gladstone said, and my seeing you in Tramel's arms."

She took his hands into hers, kissed them, then left him and dashed a little ahead.

"Everything is now disclosed, Felton. We can part as friends. You have your family and I have . . . haven't damaged things between us."

He strode to her and put his arms about her. "That is what you said. But if Tramel is the reason for you wanting to end us—"

"I think we're talked out tonight. Let's enter the barn and I can show you my calf, the infamous Moomoo Lance. Hopefully, she will be more reserved in regard to your greatcoat. I'm sure the two of you will be fast friends."

He didn't move and kept his embrace strong, staying in her orbit like Orion or Cepheus. Something fixed, unmoving, that was what a shooting star needed to ground her. "I have your painting of Port Royal. It's so different from your landscapes. I don't understand its meaning."

"It's after our wedding. Everything is perfect. This gamble two strangers took seemed so wonderful. You were this funny stranger who seemed larger than life. Adventure and excitement seemed to be our destiny. I fell instantly in love and you took a shine to me and my dowry."

"You, Cilia. Always you."

"Well, our honeymoon adventure was happy and fun and dream worthy, like Port Royal. Neither one of us saw the shadows in the offing. Like the inhabitants of that harbor city in Jamaica, no one knew it would be destroyed."

He kissed the crown of her head. "That's utterly depressing. My friend Lady Ashbrook paints fruit. You might need to try that. Or maybe less coffee. Anything to keep your art from triumphantly calling for doom."

She laughed and relaxed against him.

It was a shame how they let circumstances and people destroy them. Yet this easy way of standing beneath the stars had to mean there was still light for them.

"You have feelings for me. When you close your eyes, I want to be the one you see. You've never left my dreams. Never have you strayed from my heart."

"You still want me, Felton? After what I've said?"

Words wouldn't do. Not that he had the right ones. These months apart, he'd been searching his heart for why he couldn't move forward.

The answer was always Cecilia.

A slow spin turned her from the barn's doors to him. Felton bent and kissed her brow. Then the tip of her round nose. "I'm patient. All my training in intelligence tells me how this will end for us. I'll win your love all over again."

When she looked up, he dipped his head and sought her plump lip, the upper one. He tasted and suckled the tenderness until she opened for him. Like a key fitting the workings of a lock, he surged forward and took her mouth wholly, angling their faces until all was aligned.

With one arm slipping under her choice bottom, he lifted her high.

She wrapped her hands about his shoulders. "Felton, put me down. I've gained a bit. You could hurt—"

"You're still perfect. Still soft and curvy, a ripe blueberry. And we've a barn threshold to cross. Us and doorways. I want to get this right."

"Put me down, Felton."

"Your Roman soldier could be made compliant with a kiss. It's a sacrifice to allow more kisses as I haven't a toga or torch."

"You did feed me beefsteak. That should make up for no cheese."

It took forever and a minute, before she uttered, "Yes, compliant."

Then she sought Felton, leaning into him, and claimed his kiss and all he offered.

Chapter 51

Cecilia—Barn Fire

In the loft of the barn, I looked over the side at Moomoo. Felton had secured her and gotten her a nice bale of hay for her comfort. I crouched down low on the bed of straw we'd amassed. "My lord, do you think she's comfortable?"

He stooped, dimming the carriage lantern. "Cows can stand and sleep, but I suspect your Moomoo will settle and lie down when everything is quiet."

"She likes quiet too."

I kept my eyes on the cow and the chatter below. The barn had people camped on blankets or in horse pens. Felton bribed a couple to have this spot. I was happy for the privacy, but unsure of things, especially with Felton and I kissing outside of the barn.

The man hadn't lost his skill at leaving me breathless, still delicious, still something to crave.

"Cecilia, your calf is not going anywhere, but I will try to get her bathed before we start on the next leg of our journey." He waved at me. "Off with the coat, Lady Gantry. I'm not bedding a cow."

"But I'm already chilly."

"I have standards, ma'am. And from what I recall, I can keep you quite toasty."

Sitting up, I plucked button by button. Shivering, I touched the seams together and handed it to him.

Felton took it and laid it over a bale, something downwind of where we would sleep. He turned like a soldier, snappy and sharp, wrenched off his coat, and draped the heavy chocolate wool atop me.

"Thank you." My voice was small, for I had so many questions, particularly when his onyx waistcoat fell to the side.

Then he started unbuttoning his wrinkled cuffs. The look in his eyes was a bit of a dare. I should remind him of the people below, but Felton was somewhat unleashed, definitely not sheltering behind a lantern.

Off came his cravat, leaving him in a white shirt and buff breeches, but a fireball rarely slept like that.

If I closed my eyes, my imagination would remind me of every detail—the smoothness of his chest, the rough scars covering his arms. I could paint my Roman soldier with or without his toga.

But my eyes were open.

Button after button came undone. That white shirt fluttered as he pulled it over his head, snapped it and folded it, then laid it to the side.

His hands were on his waistband.

"What if you— What if we need to leave quickly to help Moomoo?"

His laughter fell as he trimmed the wick, putting the lantern to its lowest setting. I could see his outline but not much else.

Felton dropped beside me, fluffed straw for a pillow, and wrenched off his boots. His small pistol went to the side. "Freezing, Cecilia? I do remember you're always a little chilled."

"Always." I peeked at him between my lashes and missed him adjusting the blankets.

The next thing, the best thing, was lying against him. No sense of cold could douse the heat radiating from his skin. No amount of darkness could contain the fire in his eyes when he leaned over me. "Comfortable and cow-free, Lady Gantry?"

It took a second to form the simplest reply. "Yes."

Were we doing this pattern again? Or was this something new?

Shifting away, Felton lay beside me inches away, not touching me, not sharing all his heat. "I'm here with no demands or promises, but I would have no problem with you moving closer, Lady Gantry."

A leap of faith, that's what it was to slide to him, but I'd pressed my luck enough, telling him the truth of my conflicted heart.

"Stubborn." He scooted to me, making the distance disappear. Like a magnet, my cheek burrowed against his bare shoulder, which was smooth like silk.

His hand went to my thigh, high by my hip. Caressing me, cupping and touching as he dragged off my boots and placed my stocking feet on his shin. "There. I know those little digits will turn to ice blocks if left unattended. Ten months couldn't have changed that."

"It can change a lot." Especially with Enna knowing how to make proper cakes.

"Nothing but fine improvements." His fingers stroked my side, my abdomen, the space between my bosoms. "Fine like a wine, and you're still freezing. Let me warm you up."

I stopped fretting about what he thought of me being a little thicker, a little fluffier here or there. I was beautiful and would never be one of the thin maidens Lady Jane strived to be.

Nonetheless, it was nice hearing him say it.

He pulled me tighter against him. "You have a pretty cow."

"Excuse me."

"The calf." He draped his arm over my hip. "I don't think I've seen one with so many spots on its face. Wonder what her parents looked like."

"I hope we didn't eat them."

Our chuckles blended and soon Felton's wondrous heat scorched my cold limbs like a coal stove. I put my hand to his bare arm, right atop the scars at his elbow.

"Guess you truly like jaguars."

"Did you know that the jaguarete spots are little rosettes that add to his beauty? They help him blend with nature and have empathy for his surroundings."

"Beauty and empathy, aye? Never thought of things in such a manner."

"You need an artist's eye, my lord."

He put a long kiss at the base of my neck, his teeth slightly raking the skin at my hairline. "No, just need an artist. Tomorrow this is how things will go. I'll have Moomoo bathed and boarded in my carriage. You'll refresh yourself in the room that Watson is currently enjoying. Then we leave together. We need to make up enough time to get to Stonehenge."

"Stonehenge?"

"You always wanted to go."

"That sounds lovely."

"It is, but this is training, Cecilia. We need to plan out your mission. I haven't forgotten our bargain. Gladstone killed Helena—"

"He needs to die." The refrain came to my lips automatically, and in my head I could paint the scene of his dropping to the ground.

"I don't know how to rehabilitate someone who could do such evil. If you want to be the one to bring justice, I'll not stop you."

"No one is better able to help me complete this mission without being caught than one of the spies from the Department of War and the Colonies."

"I won't allow you to ruin the rest of your life trying to make a man pay." His words sounded rich like sweet marmalade.

"Does the same go for sons with grudges against fathers?"

"Cilia."

"Tramel never did anything untoward, and deep down he respects you."

Felton turned, taking his heat with him. Then I wondered if

all his talk of forgiveness outside the barn, before we crossed the threshold, was just talk.

Before I could ask, he again pivoted to me and rested his cheek upon mine. "There's an obligation between fathers and sons. Sometimes it is strained, but it's always there."

Always with fathers and sons? Even the ones they'd never known? I wanted clarity, but I didn't want to make him uneasy when I had a great need to warm my toes on his thigh.

I relaxed against him again, enjoying the smoothness of his chest. My hands may have had a mind of their own, again touching my personal lantern.

His heat needed to burn up the niggling concern that Noah, Gladstone's son, would one day ask about his father, the man I had to kill.

CHAPTER 52

FELTON—A GOOD ROMAN SOLDIER

Three more days of steady travel allowed Watson to make good time. It also gave Felton the luxury to instruct Cecilia on the art of war.

It was odd telling these secrets to a woman, but she seemed pleased and grasped concepts more quickly than some of Liverpool's recruits.

"Cecilia, you're sitting very pretty in your pale yellow carriage gown, but you're regrettably quiet, too quiet."

She hid a little more beneath her cream shawl—another muted color. "You have declared my redingote quite dead. Bad Moomoo."

The calf didn't seem to pay her any attention. Watson made sure the beast was well fed and cleaned at each stop. That seemed to tame its ravenous tendencies.

"I shall have to have another one made for you. Purple again, or something else bright and bold. Except for your coat, I noticed you dress in soft colors."

"Lady Jane was right that bright colors and figure-hugging gowns do attract attention. I didn't need attention in Covent Garden, particularly the hours I worked."

He glanced at this glorious creature who couldn't hide her loveliness in anything. Their platonic-not-platonic sharing of rooms and beds these past days made him realize he liked her with color and without—well, the anticipation of without.

Bare toes were all she'd worked up to, and that was after a great deal of convincing and kissing. Kissed her socks off.

"What are you laughing at, my lord?"

Sitting back upon the seat, he couldn't grin at her. "Thinking of darning socks. Such a necessary task."

She offered a shrug and began her sketching again.

It was good to see her drawing, even if it was the Ballard Cliffs and fog. Was she happy or merely content that they were getting along?

Was he winning, or would Tramel always be larger-than-life? He craned his head onto the seatback. The duke should be glad that he was putting that other foot in the grave. Felton was helping to plot his cousin's murder. It wouldn't be hard to eliminate the duke too.

"What if I can't do it, Felton?"

"Do what, Cecilia?" *Please say 'go through with separation.' No separation. Be with me. Now!*

He ran a hand through a lock of his hair that loosed from his onyx ribbon. "What is it you think you can't do?"

"What if I look at Gladstone and can't fire the gun?"

"Then he'll kill you and be justified."

She deflated in the seat.

He moved beside her, took his pistol from his pocket, and set it into her hand. "That is why we are going over the planning, step by step. You'll know if you can do it, well before you ever confront Gladstone."

Wrapping their fingers about the handle, he wanted her to be comfortable with the power, but her hand shook. He set the pistol to the side. "You don't have to go through with this at all."

"What, Felton?"

"Maybe you need to focus on the future. Not the past. When I broach the subject of us, you devour bread. If butter and rolls were aphrodisiacs, I wouldn't have a problem."

"What are you saying, my lord?"

Anytime she became so formal, it was her way of hiding. He sighed and kissed her hand. "Nothing. Nothing more than we're almost to our next training."

The carriage headed up Amesbury Road. Dark green pastures lay on each side. These fields were massive, endless.

"What do you see when you look out the window?"

She stretched over Moomoo, who seemed content with Watson's bucket of hay, and peered out the glass. "Wonderful meadows, so very green. Autumn has not turned it all brown. It's escaped."

"That's a pretty dismal way to think of meadows. What about the natural course of things? Of time making things grow and change."

She offered him a blank look, and he realized subtlety wasn't his strong suit, at least not with his wife.

When they crossed onto Shrewton Road, he gave up glancing at her fine neck, the fichu shawl that covered the lush swells of heaven. Maybe it was he who needed training to understand her. She was cautious and restrained. That wasn't Cilia. That's what these months away . . . what he'd done.

More training was at hand for him to restore a star's light. "Look, the ancient stones are finally in view."

The carriage slowed, then stopped. They'd arrived at the closest place he knew that she'd love. Green pastures and ancient monuments. Stonehenge.

"Ready for adventure, Lady Gantry?"

Cecilia tore away from the window and wrapped her arms about his shoulders. "You were serious this time. You meant to do it."

Felton forced a smile to cover what would be a guilty frown. He didn't realize how his broken promises had affected her.

She looked confused. "But are we making good time? I know we must get to Warwick."

"Tramel will hang on, gripping every gust of breath just to see you."

Her lips flattened and she pulled away.

And he hated, hated that he was still jealous of a dying man.

To be the bigger man, to act as a liberal champion, all rubbish. "I burn with jealousy. It can't be helped."

She leaned against him, gripping the revers of his indigo coat. "Nice to know you care."

"Our walk to the barn didn't convince you? The kisses in bed, left you in doubt?"

Her eyes narrowed. "We haven't kissed in bed."

"Oh. Those were my dreams."

With a shake of her head, she folded her arms. "We've always been good with passion, Felton. That wasn't our problem."

"I think you need to be sure. Practice makes perfect."

A laugh fell from her lips, ones he hadn't touched in three days. The darn Repington was right about restraint.

Moomoo stood up, lolling as though the calf readied to be walked like a pup.

She released Felton and offered her attention to the cuter beast.

He put his small gun into his pocket. "Watson will attend her. You and I have practice, practice with weapons."

He picked up a picnic basket and put it on her lap. Then he took up his gun case from the compartment under the seat. With it in one arm, he popped down and raised his free hand back into the carriage. "Come, Lady Gantry."

Basket at her side, she clasped his fingers and joined him.

"Watson, come back for us in the morning. Take care of my lady's calf too."

His man's eyes went wide but he nodded. "Of course. I was born for such work."

The carriage slowly moved forward, then disappeared down the long road.

"My lord, you told him tomorrow. We're going to be out here all night?"

"You need training. And since you have a penchant for ancient monuments, I thought you could be inspired as we commit to your plan of revenge." He started walking toward the raised stones, but Cecilia was still on the side of the road.

"Now is not the time to dawdle. Come along, my dear."

The indecision shadowing her eyes was palpable, but he waited.

Soon, she dipped her chin and started moving.

"Look at Stonehenge, Cecilia. These tall blue stones are older than England. Older than Rome and your beloved Roman Colosseum."

Down the cleared dirt path that had long ditches on either side, he led her past the outer ring of raised rocks to the inner one. "Twenty-four-feet-high at some points, this is an incredible feat to be made by man."

"What men? All men, or enslaved?"

"I'd like to think the free had a hand in this, but I don't know. No one knows. It's just here. The Roman Diodorus called it a temple. I want to believe it was religious people who used this place for lively ceremonies full of food and dance."

Cecilia was quiet but she floated about the stones, touching some, drawing back from others like they might fall. He stood still, watching her go round and round and round.

Her steps in her short boots were like she heard music. It had been a long time since he'd seen her move so freely.

Setting down his gun portmanteau, he decided to join her. After taking the basket from her, he grasped her hand. Her fingers wove with his, and they circled. Then they danced. She spun in his arms until they made several laps about the ancient monument.

The day was getting away. There was so much more to do, but how could he stop her when this madness and rhythm made her so happy?

They took three more turns but then, with both arms about her waist, he made her slow and pointed to the opening between the largest alignment of stones. "See the henge, Cilia? That's a grand doorway."

"Doorway, my lord?"

"Yes, an entry that aligns to the midsummer sunrise and in midwinter, the solstice. I hear that it's quite impressive, seeing the heavens, the stars and sun, align."

Cupping her eyes, she stared straight ahead. Her breaths were fast and ragged. "This is majestic."

"Hundreds, if not thousands, of years old. I'd like to think it was built before man learned to line his pockets by trafficking others. It's here, resilient and strong. I'm glad it still stands just as it is."

"My sister would say that an Obeah spirit could visit here."

Remembering the Widow's Grace intervention at her residence, he felt emboldened. "You mean Patience Jordan, now Patience Strathmore, the new duchess of Repington?"

Her gaze searched and picked at his as if he had intentionally withheld the name.

"When I visited Repington, I didn't know how the paths would entwine. I only met the Widow Jordan in February. She looked like you, but I saw your face everywhere."

Cecilia turned away, back toward the largest henge. "It does look like a setting sun or rising moon could slip through."

He stooped to his case and began opening the locks. "Perhaps we can all dine together when this is all over, and you've escaped undetected. Repington is my dearest living friend."

Was she paying attention?

She didn't look at him. The large henge still claimed her, and her hands moved in and out as if to catalog the width and height of each piece of stone. "You said living. What about dead?"

"That would be Johnson. I visit his son every so often. He died the night you saved me."

With her eyes closing, she crossed her arms. "That could've been you every mission. The girls—"

"I've been lucky. I'll never take a moment for granted." Felton flipped open his case. His faithful blunderbusses shined. "You boys haven't seen action in almost a year."

Cecilia peered over his shoulder. Her breath tickled his neck. "What are those?"

"Peacekeepers. These flintlocks have been made for my particular use. They came in handy with the various assignments."

She fingered the smooth handle of his favorite, Old Brown. "How many times have you shot these?"

He picked up Brown and slipped his hand along the well-oiled barrel. "Enough."

She nodded and turned away. Did she sense how close he'd come to life and death?

"Cecilia, this place may have been built for religion, for healing, maybe even honoring the dead. Men . . . and women built something that outlived them. What my cousin has done is reprehensible. The consequences for us, our family, will outlive him. Are you sure that you want to be the instrument to bring permanent justice?"

She stared as if the henge would guide her.

Shuddering, clasping tightly to her shawl, she nodded. "Show me what to do."

Taking Brown, he stood next to her. "This is a blunderbuss. It's small enough to fit in a reticule. It's small but will shoot a distance. One could easily dispatch and be rid of the weapon, but with such craftsmanship that would be regrettable."

Linking her hand about the shaft, he steadied her. "Don't disrespect the size. Like you, it is tiny and potent."

"I suppose size doesn't matter."

"No, it does. Unlike the pistol in my pocket, Brown will do the job better at a distance. The more lethal, the faster death comes." He pulled her close, wedging her to his ribs, then he raised their arms and pointed to the henge, the doorway-like opening between two of the largest stones. "We practice until you can shoot straight."

"Shoot at the henge? Doorways are us."

"Well, Cilia, neither of us is going to leave when a weapon is drawn." He wrapped his free arm about her. "Ready? Let's practice."

"Practice killing, don't you mean?"

Her nerves churned. Felton knew the noise would disturb her, but there was no other way. "Killing is either a success or failure. Trying to strike a man twice your size with a knife is too dangerous. One hit from the bullet packet of this gun will either kill Gladstone or infection will set in to claim his soul."

"He has no soul, Felton. He couldn't have one and do what he did." Her heart beat strongly and threaded through and around him. Fear and respect of the weapon was what she needed, but they had to fire the gun.

He leaned near her ear. "Curl your finger about the trigger."

"Yes, my lord." Her shaking hand did so.

With his index finger over hers, he fired the gun and absorbed the kickback.

The smoke fluttered and surrounded them.

Cecilia was quiet, not moving, staying as stiff as a board against him.

"We keep at it, until you feel comfortable. When you fire the trigger there is no going back."

She nodded and he loaded the gun again.

The sun had lowered a little. That was good because the bright shine of the light finally spared Felton's eyes. They'd practiced shooting his blunderbuss through the biggest henge in Stonehenge. Except for her heavy breaths, Cecilia could be a statue.

"Let's do it again, Lady Gantry."

"Felton. We've shot twenty times. My ears are ringing. Is that not enough?"

He put his hand on her shoulder. "We have to see that you can handle this. Otherwise, I will suggest you abandon your revenge."

"I'm just tired, my lord. And hungry."

"Oh, I have treats, but let's do more practice."

Her stomach gurgled, and he dipped his hand to her abdomen. The pressure moved his hand and he thought back to his first wife and how their son moved in the earliest days.

Another mission had taken him away, so he'd missed much of her excitement. He'd returned for her lying-in, but Felton would never know if things would've been different if he'd been with Elizabeth every day.

"My lord, now you've gone quiet."

"You must be hungry. I feel it." His voice dropped away. His thoughts weren't on his lost son but the bare crib back at Covent Garden. Lady Ashbrook said the artist was with child. Was she right about Cecilia, the woman who painted Point Royal? Had she finally become pregnant in December?

Had the worst come again?

Cecilia had prepared for a life without him—her own place, a small crib. Though he thought he'd heard a baby cry, there was not one in sight.

Had she gone through the pain of loss alone, not even allowing Tramel to be of comfort?

"Felton, your eyes are watery. Are you well? The smoke from the gun."

"What, Cecilia?"

"You're holding me too tight."

Was he? He shifted but held on. "I've been given assignments to protect England and her colonies. Strangers across the seas, I did more for them than my own household, my family. I didn't protect you or Elizabeth."

"Your first wife, Felton? You never speak of her."

"My life fell apart when Elizabeth died." His voice was low and pained and he could barely catch his breath. "I don't think she knew how great she was, how wonderful she was to keep our household, the girls, safe and happy whilst I was away."

Cecilia turned in his embrace and wiped away tears that stung his eyes. "Talk to me."

"I wasn't enough for her or I didn't give her enough, because my missions were so important. She was a good woman, a good friend. She deserved better."

Blinking, Felton couldn't quite see. He set Old Brown down. "I didn't learn anything about marriage or friendship or miracles, did I? Because I did the same to you."

He held Cilia tightly, but he finally accepted how his leaving and not explaining his work or his loyalties had hurt her.

It caused another empty crib.

Tramel wasn't the reason she didn't want to return. It was Felton's neglect and the sorrow of loss, loss he surely caused.

"It's me, Cilia. I ruined us and our future. It's my fault."

"We both did poorly, Felton."

His wet cheeks stung in the breeze. He kissed her brow, then said, "I'll not battle anymore. Cecilia, I'll keep my word to you and let you be free."

After ten months of fighting for what he wanted, for what he thought in his bones was best, he did what was right for Cecilia.

He let go.

CECILIA—A SPY'S SURRENDER

The wind scattered the sharp burnt scent around us. The noise of our practice kept echoing in my ear.

Boom.

Boom.

Boom.

The noise needed to die.

But I couldn't focus on me. Felton needed me.

The man looked lost, lost like a boy in the woods who couldn't find his footing.

I moved to him. "I don't know what's happened, but I'm here. Do you need to walk about the stones? Walking settles me."

Putting more distance between us, he juggled his handkerchief from his pocket and mopped his face. "I've taken a lot of risks in my life, but you, you are, were, the best one. I wish I'd done a better job of showing you how much I care."

This was goodbye. He stood near. We were alone in a field, but somehow he'd left me. "Felton, I don't understand."

He didn't answer. Instead, he stooped and put his blunderbuss into its case. "Perhaps we should try the larger gun. We need something that will feel natural in your hands. Something you can depend upon when your nerves start to pound. You shook too much for Brown."

Felton felt something. Some loss that made him run. I knew him, he'd broken free of the thick glass of the lantern and kept going. I needed him to stop so that I could hang on to him and keep him safe.

I sat beside my husband as he cleaned the second blunderbuss and wrapped my arms about his shoulders.

"Cilia." He put the gun down and patted my fingers. "I'm fine. I'm choked up from the smoke."

"You're not fine. Don't flee from me, Felton. Tell me what you're thinking, be open with me."

"That if I hadn't gone away for Lord Liverpool, we might have had a child. We were so good, then I went on that last mission. I didn't trust us then. There's no hope for us now. I don't know how you'll ever trust me."

His blue-black eyes were rimmed with red. His pain came to me, like it hadn't before. I felt it ripping into my chest, tearing down the wall I'd erected to protect my heart.

"No. No escaping us." On my knees, I leaned into him and advanced my hold to his neck.

"What are you doing, Cecilia?"

"I think it best you don't ask too many questions, my lord. Just surrender. Isn't a spy taught how to do that when he's caught?"

His eyes held all of the sun, red and orange in the wet sea of black. "Surrender, one of Liverpool's best? Not sure—"

I kissed him quiet and pushed us flat onto grass that had heady clover. "You're formerly Liverpool's. I think that means you're fully mine."

He folded me into his jacket. "Just like that, a simple enough plan? Seduce me?"

"Yes."

Felton lifted his head to mine and took my mouth. His hands slipped under my shawl. He reached for me and my fingers curled into his hair. It was unleashed, wild, splaying about us.

Then we became free—free of his coat and shirt, free of my shawl and a few buttons of my carriage dress. My fingers traced the cut of his chest, then I kissed and connected the red rosette scars on his shoulder.

If he looked into my eyes, Felton should see they never frightened me. They let me know he was a survivor and was tough. He'd get us through any storm.

"After my father's death and my sister Patience's disappearance, I feared you dying, of you being taken away. It made me so full of nerves. To learn it could have truly happened because of your service . . ."

He fingered my nose. "I'm done with that. I'm not leaving you. Does this mean you're no longer done with us, because I will be if you say—"

I didn't let him finish. Kisses of surrender needed no explanation. They needed fire.

When his mouth overtook mine and he touched me again, filling his hands with all my curves, I knew he understood. No one was quitting us.

My pulse ramped up. I panted his name. He was here, tasting so sweet. The hunger of his fingertips rivaled mine. I sought his solid back, his trim legs.

Clasping both my hands, Felton perched on an elbow. "Wait. Wait. We're in a field. Stonehenge. Is this what you want?"

"I want you, my lord. Do you want me too, without a toga or treats?"

He angled my chin and helped himself to lips that needed his, lips that were hungry and pliant. "Yes. You win everything. You're everything."

The winning was for us. He reached for me, dividing my corset and chemise. I wanted to close my eyes, but we'd missed so much being apart. Instead, I waited and hoped, begged a little for him to make me his.

His mouth sought my throat. The soft skin of my bosom he teased. I saw no one in my imagination but Felton. He would be there when I closed my eyes.

My mind had been his for days.

It was time for my body to win.

In the middle of this place of ancient doors, we'd walked inside and returned to our best. I waited for him to disrobe and caress me, waited for him to open my love like a jacaranda bloom. We would be beautiful, better than before.

Because I was hungry, and I knew he'd fill me.

The colors of the sunset shone around us, streaking the sky.

Me and my husband tore away fabric and slid past our fears. With an endless embrace, we rebuilt our marriage bed. I trusted the love we had and wrapped myself in him.

Couldn't miss this moment, no mind wandering, not when my Roman soldier, my jaguarete had come home.

Maybe this time, neither of us would leave our love again.

CHAPTER 54

FELTON—THE ROAD TO DAMASCUS

Her calf, Moomoo, didn't smell so bad now that Watson gave it a proper bath each day. Over the past three days, the beast was practically domesticated, lolling, wanting its ear scratched.

Felton could concur with the contentment. Cilia's affection for him had returned. They shared everything—a room, a bath, and a bed made for crowding, and cold toes to be rested on his shin.

The miracle of Stonehenge brought them together when he'd given up.

His wife sketched, concentrating on her charcoals. They'd be at Warwick within the hour. All could change again.

The duke might've already passed. Felton could be Tramel, the title he'd inherit. Cilia would be his duchess.

He tapped Repington's note that had arrived at the coaching inn last night. His dearest friend reported that Her Grace had custody of her sister's babe and that this boy had Felton's eyes.

The duke's hints weren't subtle.

A son.

A male child who would be Lord Gantry. How does one bring that up to the wife he'd just reclaimed?

Wife, I know that we've repaired our trust, but tell me of the son you're keeping from me.

No, that wouldn't go over well.

Cilia would tell him in time. She should know he'd understand. The Widow's Grace business had taught him how easily children were taken from their mothers, especially foreign-born women.

He'd not dwell on this, not when they shared a bed, an embrace every night.

Still, not a word about their son?

To be fair, being starved of her affection for almost a year, he had no need of talking.

But to be across from him now, with her guard cow, as she drew, the woman could say something.

The fact that the boy was healthy and alive had to be enough. There was still time to love him and watch him grow.

Was he smiling too much? He drummed the seat in triumph. He had a son.

"Whatever have you read, my lord? It has you grinning."

"Yes, my friend sends me news of winning."

"Odd. And his wins make you happy?"

"Yes." He tried to keep his expression blank, but his lips were in rebellion. They had a beautiful babe. Did he have her hair, her beautiful toes?

Felton stared at his wife, wondering how beautiful she'd looked, heavy with his babe. What food did she crave? He'd have hunted all over London for her. Did her feet need a massage?

Reaching down, he picked up one of her legs and undid the lacings to her boot.

"What are you doing?"

"Nothing much." He whipped off her boot and pressed his thumbs into the sole of her foot. "There. How is that?"

She closed up her sketchbook and put her head to the seat back.

Did she miss their child? "Cilia, we need to talk."

Purring, she nodded. "Your touch, my lord."

"Maybe there's another way we could punish my cousin that

doesn't require you to kill. You're a creator, a creator of art and life."

She looked as if she wanted to sit up, but the lull of the massage kept her slouched on the seat. "You're trying too hard, Felton. Not that I will complain. Your fingers are a treat."

"You're not a trained spy, or a retired one. Despite my tutelage, I think you'll fail."

Cecilia jerked away. "I can load a blunderbuss. That's what you taught me."

"That's not enough, Cilia. Gladstone's been trained to shoot since he was a boy. The duke taught us both. My cousin served a bit in the military. I don't think you should try. We have so much to live for, us together."

She folded her arms like she was cold. "What is it that you want me to do, Felton? Forgive Gladstone?"

"No. We can hate him forever."

"I can, but maybe your love is again lacking. You won't love me if I have blood on my hands?"

"Do you love me? I have blood on mine. I killed the enemy. I engaged in battles for my king, and people died. How can I hold you to a standard I cannot keep?"

"Felton, I want him dead. He should pay for everything."

He lifted from his seat and knelt before her. "We are united. We have accepted who the other person is. I value you, all of you."

"And I you, Felton."

He sat beside her. "This's why we must let him live. So we can be truly free."

Tears ran down Cecilia's face. He wiped them with his thumb. "Nothing will dissolve us, and when you're ready, you will bring your friends. All of us, we can be one big family."

"Us, Felton?"

It was like lightning flashed in his head. "Us. That's what you wanted. That's what you'd said before. I just didn't understand. Yes, Cilia, us."

"Even if one of us is a baby? You once told me how you love that your children were older."

He pulled her to him and held her so tightly. "I said that because you felt pressured to be with child. I know you struggled with thinking about motherhood every month, with the maid's checking for your courses. Rest assured, I want this baby."

She flopped against him. Moomoo lolled as Cecilia cried.

Her tears wet through his shirt. She didn't have to make the disclosure now. Cecilia said *us* would include the baby.

He kissed her and held her close.

Felton had to get his wife through the next week without being upset enough to walk away. Then the *us* they'd just reformed would last. Keeping Gladstone out of her sight was his main priority. Cilia would never survive being made into a murderer.

CHAPTER 55

CECILIA—ARRIVING AT WARWICK

Never before had I thought my cow had a murderous stare. She sort of did, though, as we stood on Warwick's drive. Mr. Watson put a rope leash on her and began towing her away.

Moo.

"Sir, that's not too tight?"

"Lady Gantry, she'll be fine. I'll make sure she plays nice with the other animals."

Felton put his hands about my middle. Did the man think he'd already filled this womb? Well, we'd been very friendly these past few days. Lots of practice.

He held out his arm for me while he cradled my Port Royal painting. "Shall we, my dear?"

"My lord, I hope we have not arrived too late. Tramel will enjoy this one."

Felton put a palm to my cheek. "Things get crazed and confusing in grief. We'll get through this together. No separating, no running."

"Then let's say goodbye to Tramel together."

"Yes, Cilia. I need you for that."

"And I need you to keep us safe." I put my knife into his pocket. "See, I won't stab at Gladstone again."

"My father took your knife and cut him. He told me."

I grabbed his coat, scrunching up the fabric that had my weapon. "But I wanted it done. Tramel saved me that day. He saved us by not letting me go through with it. Yet, now I have to look at Gladstone and know what he's done."

He scooped me up, pressed me close. His heat warming everything in me. "I won't let him or anyone near you. We'll stay in the studio."

Setting my boots down, he put my hand in his and we walked into Warwick.

This place, the walls, the gilded trim, these were the first things to notice. The servants in silver appeared. Then the quiet hit. Warwick was always quiet.

"Felton . . . you've returned. You've both returned." That high-pitched voice belonged to Lady Jane. She fluttered down the stairs in a coconut-white gown. Her frown was longer than her train.

"I'm glad you're back, brother. I'm surprised. Nice to see you—"

"Don't trouble yourself. My lord, let's go to Tramel." I wasn't in the mood for her lukewarm words. I took my painting from Felton and headed to the stairs.

His beautiful daughters ran out from a parlor. Little cherubs in India print, blue and emerald gowns, jumped up and down. This noise I missed.

Amelia clapped and leapt at me. "Mrs. Cecilia!! Papa, you brought her home."

Agatha started to come forward, but then she stopped. "He said he would. We never doubted our father."

I understood the girl's hurt and wanted to bundle her into my arms. "Sorry," I choked out, but words changed nothing. I walked out on Felton; that meant I'd left them too.

Setting the painting to the floor, I reached for this girl. "I had some things to do, but I've returned."

"For how long?" Lady Jane clicked her teeth, but I didn't care about her, and she wasn't going to make me feel worse.

Stoic Agatha took one step and I dashed the rest, then scooped her up. "Sorry. So sorry."

When her arms tightened about my neck, I stooped and grabbed a better hold. This felt like what my husband said in the carriage, *us*. The hold was us.

"I came back for us, Agatha. Us."

With Amelia climbing on his back, Felton helped me stand. "How is Tramel, Jane?"

"Weak. But he's asking for her. Some visitor or gift will be here tomorrow for Lady Gantry."

Felton put down Amelia, and then snatched up Agatha and kissed her brow. "Girls, continue to mind your aunt. Come on, my lady, let's see Tramel together."

He clasped my hand and kissed it.

That made his sister's eyes glaze with a kiln's fire. Part of me didn't blame her. I know how protective I'd always been about my siblings.

But Felton wove my fingers with his. He wasn't letting me wallow. We walked up the stairs, sharing each tread.

He leaned over the rail. "Have that painting brought to Tramel once we greet him. In ten minutes."

Felton retook my arm, and we walked to the end of the hall into duke's chambers.

The room was hot, feverishly so. My powerful friend was bundled into his bed, buried in burgundy blankets. He looked gray and weak, when before Tramel was always color.

All my thoughts went to Helena, and how pale she turned before she slept forever.

"Wake up, my lord. Your artist has returned."

His eyes opened. His ringed hand extended.

I flew to it. "What are you doing in this bed? A man like you has too much life to sleep all day."

"You think so, my dear?" His chuckle sounded dry and without strength.

"I know so, Your Grace." I kissed and held his palm.

Felton stayed a few feet away, poking at the fireplace.

"So, you did it, son? You brought her to me."

My husband jabbed at a log. "Glad you stuck it out until I returned. Lady Gantry was most anxious to see you."

Half a smirk claimed Tramel's face. "Had to. I have a surprise for you, my dearest Cecilia."

The duke eased back into his pillows. "Gantry, you're showing a certain fortitude, winning against the odds. Maybe you're more like me than you'll admit. Singularly focused on the object of your love. That's good."

Tramel coughed. It didn't sound so awful, but that might be my hope.

Father and son looked civil, but that could change in a moment. "You need to save your energy. And I need no surprise, Lord Tramel. You've already been very generous."

Felton turned his back to the bed. "Yes, most generous."

"Tomorrow, my surprise shall be here. I shall live to see it."

The thoughtful man probably had some new type of brush or canvas for me, but I couldn't be concerned about this. "You must recover, my lord. I shall hear of nothing less."

"But I had my men search—"

"Yes, your network of smugglers, Tramel. Do you know how much trouble you could—"

My glance at Felton silenced him. He knew that it was only his father's methods that brought me peace about my sister.

"Sorry," he said. His countenance wasn't stone. It had more emotion than I'd ever seen, a mash of reddened, flushed cheeks and a tight frown. He was conflicted. Felton may have forgiven me, but not Tramel.

Chapter 56

Cecilia—The Portrait

A knock on the duke's bedchamber door startled me, but I was already full of nerves witnessing the tension betwixt father and son.

"We have a surprise for you," I said. "You'll love it."

I rose from the chair. My pale rose carriage gown belled about me as I hurried and retrieved the painting from the servant.

Felton went the opposite direction toward the balcony doors. The disquieted look settling on his countenance broke me up inside. He wasn't hiding his emotions, but the way his lips flattened wrenched my heart.

Trembling, with the painting in my fingers, I waited for his approval. "Felton?"

He nodded, then went out on the balcony.

"Here you go, Your Grace. Port Royal."

Tramel took the painting and sat it on his chest. Then he arose, as though the art gave him strength. "Phenomenal, my dear," he said. "You're amazing. I can see the destruction coming. Can't you see it too, Felton?"

My husband came back inside. The look that passed between them made my blood chill. "I see everything this time, old man. I'm no longer a fool."

"Good. A fool can't lose a treasure twice. And a father can finally say sorry for all the bad. I'm glad you won, son. I'm glad you two are united. You'll need to be when *all* the family has gathered."

Lady Jane came in. "Papa, you should rest. Felton, you and Lady Gantry should retire and freshen up before the guests arrive. Traveling always makes one smell like a cow."

My laughter fell before I could stop myself.

Felton's too.

"Yes," Lady Jane sneered. "Your dresses Father purchased are in your closet if you need something else to wear."

Then Felton lifted me from the chair. "My wife is tired. I think we'll retire and then breakfast with you in the morning, Tramel."

"Tomorrow will be a big day, Lady Gantry. I found it for you. I won't miss it. My surprise has come a long way, from Demerara."

Helena's stone marker? Could that be what his men were bringing back?

"Rest, Your Grace." I clasped Felton's hand and went into the hall.

"So, he's told you," Jane said in huff.

"Told us what, sister?"

"That I have accepted Gladstone's offer of marriage."

I looked up at my sister-in-law. I hadn't thought of how much I'd come to despise her, not until this moment. But even with all my reasons, I'd not wish Gladstone upon her.

"I think it a mistake, Lady Jane. Excuse me."

Felton wouldn't release my hand. "You'll go nowhere. We are talking to my sister, giving her sage advice about not marrying the fiend."

"Just to my studio, my lord." I tried to pull free, but he'd not budge an inch.

His sister glared at me with a haughty, stinging gaze. "The studio shouldn't be here."

"It's here because Tramel lives. It's his house, not yours, Lady Jane. You'd never go against his wishes."

Felton nodded. "The duke didn't sanction an engagement. I know he wouldn't, Jane."

"No, Father has not agreed, but I thought you would. Any day you'll be Tramel."

"Never, Jane. Gladstone is worse than a toad, very undeserving of you."

Watching the two exchange words, I had to slip away. Finally, Felton let me flee and I entered my sanctuary down the hall. My paintings lining the walls gave me comfort, except my unfinished work of father and son.

I slid the heavy thing to lean on my gilded easel. "Time to finish. I saw what it should be."

Commotion sounded in the hall. Then Jane's cries.

My hand slipped to my mouth. I had my own gripes against her, but they were siblings about to lose their father. There should be common ground.

Somber-faced, Felton slipped into the room.

"Sorry, my lord."

"No. No. None of that."

Looking away, I concentrated on my canvas. "I always loved painting here."

"We never did finish my other portrait." Felton stood behind me with his hand about my waist then dropping to my stomach. "Toga, no toga?"

I turned, ready to chastise him for being so glib, but his face had no smile. The baggage of me and Gladstone had come between him and his sister. I hated that. "You can tell her what Gladstone has done if that will save her. She—"

"She's accepted a man who has proven himself unworthy. I'll not be silent on that. Or anything else that needs to be said. I've done that too long."

"I suppose it's better than running away."

He dropped his head on mine. "I want my family whole. I fear time has come too late for Tramel and me to reconcile. I don't want to be like him in that regard, him or my grandfather."

I put my arms behind me to hold him in place. "You're not either. You'll not be distant and regretful to Agatha and Amelia. Now that you've withdrawn from service, everything will be better."

"I won't be like him to my son. I won't be distant or smothering. You can count on that."

"That is nice, but let's go down and dine with the daughters you do have. Though we've enjoyed each other's company, there's no guarantee."

He spun me and set his gaze to me. "The babe who will join us is my son. I know all of it."

There was no laughter in his eyes. He was serious. "The spymaster has something wrong." I balled my fists and stepped away. "Was that why you've been so determined to fix us? You think I bore your son? It's not our love but an heir that has placed my heart in jeopardy again."

"No. You and I are meant to be. My love shall never diminish, and you shouldn't test it."

The doors barged opened. Jane sauntered inside. "Papa said that the decision is up to you, Felton. I can have a husband or be a derided spinster."

"No, Jane. No."

She grabbed his arm. "Felton, be a part of the shooting party in the morn. Let Gladstone talk with you. Let him convince you, not her."

Felton shook his head.

"It's this woman who left you. She may control you, but she can't have control over my life too."

"But that's what you want, Lady Jane, to control everything—here, the house in London. My leaving. Felton said that my studio was locked that night. He thought me there, but you and I had words before I stormed out. You knew when I left."

Felton's face burned red. "Jane, she could've died in the snowfall. How could you?"

She put a hand to her hip, wrinkling her gown that was meant to make her look young and innocent, not the bitter harpy she'd become. "Didn't think it would snow so badly."

Felton stormed to the doors and opened one. "Out, Jane. Can't look at you now."

She started to the door. "Gladstone is my way to have my own. I should be happy that you, brother, went to Demerara and snatched up your wealthy bride. You beat him already, be satisfied with that."

"Jane, you almost deserve the whoremonger." Felton wrenched off his black tailcoat. "He's a cad. You're better than this."

"This is her influence."

I put on my painting smock, which was folded, seams together, as I had left it on the snack table. "Perhaps it is. Gladstone hurt my family. For his crimes, he needs to die. And you, as awful as you are, Lady Jane, you deserve better. You just want him because you're scared and he's settling scores." Pivoting, I caught Felton's gaze. "He's not done."

"Brother, wake up. She's defaming my betrothed. There's no depths to which she will not sink."

"Jane, remove yourself. This is Lady Gantry's studio. I'm her gatekeeper."

She threw up her hands and slunk away, down the hall.

Felton slammed the door. It banged. He pounded it then locked it.

More harsh sounds.

I should've thrown my hands over my ears, but I finally knew how to finish this portrait.

He went to my adjoining bedroom and returned with sheets.

"What are you doing, Felton?"

His boots flew off, followed by his waistcoat. Then his shirt sailed over my head. "I'm going for the toga. I know I was on the verge of saying something stupid. The least I must do is pay for that, and Jane."

Bare chested, arms displaying all the scars of his childhood, my jaguarete stood in front of me. "I received a report that the artist who sold the Port Royal painting was with child. I know you're housing a beautiful baby boy with the Duke and Duchess of Repington. His Grace says the boy's handsome like me."

"Noah is not yours."

Felton blinked a few times. I knew it wrong to tell him so little of the truth, but I couldn't risk the secret of Noah's parentage when doubt had crept into my heart.

Ten, nine, eight. I counted and waited to see what would rise, Felton's jealousy or his faith in me.

Three, two, one. I searched his face, his shiny blue-black eyes, to see the flame behind the lantern. Was love snuffed or had it broken free from the glass?

CHAPTER 57

FELTON—A FOOL FOR LOVE

It was a universal truth that a fool doesn't deserve a loyal wife and a loyal wife doesn't need a fool. In his circumstance, he'd decided to be fortunate and a fool and keep his wife.

Felton couldn't respond as he stood draped in a sheet, bared and scarred in front of Cecilia. The evening sun had set, lowering the dark curtains of night.

She had that look in her eyes, where she waited for an argument, or evidence to have no faith in Felton. He didn't want to respond to those doubts, just her love.

Draping the cloth over his ruddy shoulder, he looked down at his bare, scarred feet. "Should you sketch me here or should I go to the window for better lighting? I don't want you to miss my best attributes."

"Do you not care what I said? Noah is not your son."

Tears were in her eyes. Her lips trembled like that day she left him.

His father had cut Gladstone and had meant to kill him.

For a moment he'd returned to that December day. Gladstone's disheveled clothes. Tramel wanting to kill him. Gladstone not saying a word about that attack.

Perhaps there was a greater secret that forced his cousin's hand.

Not Felton's son. But had the Lance family eyes.

Had Tramel been acting as a protector and saved Cecilia from Gladstone?

Or almost saved her. Had his cousin done the worst to Cilia?

Was rape not an excuse to want a man dead?

Wouldn't that brutality transform a dove of peace into a warrior hunting like an eagle?

Everything made sense now.

Why wouldn't a woman run if her husband accused her of infidelity when she'd been used most cruelly? Why would she return to her doubting husband if she were to have the brute's babe?

It was hard to breathe.

Then he didn't want to. Swallowing his own hypocrisy made his mouth bitter.

He forced a smile and held up her knife. "It matters not." His voice was low and dry like Tramel's.

Then he wanted to be his father, the man who lived like the devil and still had everything. Almost everything, but not Cecilia.

Felton moved to her and set the torch onto the table. "I'll welcome this boy. He's now a part of us."

Her creamy, perfect brow perspired, very different from her always freezing ways.

With a dip of his head, he kissed her forehead. Then he turned to the window and loosed his hair. "Will you begin with my jaguar painting?"

"There's no anger in you?"

"I'm a volcanic cone, burning and breaking inside. That man down the hall is full of bitterness. The only reason he's not dying alone is because of you, and all the relatives angling for something in his will. I can't be angry at things that cannot be changed. I'd rather accept my part in all this. My negligence has made everything possible."

She was still, standing as if she posed for him. He marched forward and took up her hand, fluffing the art brush between her fingers. "I've lived what felt like an eternity without you. It was hell. I'm not journeying back when heaven is within my grasp."

"Your mama didn't birth a fool."

Hand in hand, like he'd guided her with the flintlock, she whipped the brush over the scars on his shoulder. Up and down, side to side, he let her union their fingers to move the brushes from pox rosette to rosette. "I'm open to you. All of you. Be open to me. Accept my struggles and flaws."

"Felton." Her face was a river. "I need to confess all."

"No more confessions. None tonight. That's the work of spies. Tonight, we are the work of a lover and his artist."

Like a man facing his mortality or even the breaking of his sanity, he swept her up into his arms. Spinning her fast, he dipped her, his little dumpling. "No more cross-purposes. Just us, the collective us."

"Felton, I love you, but—"

He kissed her silent and let the magic of their touch take over. He needed her tonight. He couldn't think of revenge and love at the same time.

The softness of her bosom had to block out the notions of his cousin, Jane, Tramel, his own jealous nature—all the things that made Cecilia run. The best revenge would be to have a restored life and committed wife.

Easing her onto the chaise, he divested her of her gown and wrapped his makeshift toga about their love.

One touch of her smooth hand on his rough shoulder cooled like lotion, producing a deep shudder in his bones. Her curly braids unraveled from their chignon as their kisses grew. He wove his fingers into the tight spirals, and she did the same to his locks.

Making love to her, his beautiful wife—this was the only freedom he'd truly known. Never, ever would he give her up.

"Wrap yourself, Cilia, about me. Hold on. Don't think of me without you, ever."

Burning with desire and revenge, he gave himself over to the perfect fit of her love.

The taste of honey that was her lips.

The movements of two entwined forever—this was perfect love.

They made it to the bed this time. It was more comfortable than the chaise, with enough room so that when they finally slept, she could be at his side with her toes on his shin.

"I love you, Cecilia. I will make your dreams come true. I promise this time. Us, we will be forever."

"You already have, by believing in us. I love—"

Felton kissed her again along her sensitive neck, which made her purr. "So, who is the jaguar?"

"I think we both are. And we know how to hunt—me for art, you for Lord Liverpool or a nation's peace, and then come home."

"Now I hunt for the family."

"Us, Felton. You'll love Noah."

"I already do because you love him." That was how good she was to love a child created in such circumstances. "Cilia, you're so . . . wonderful."

He wouldn't say *strong*, even though she was. A survivor can be weak and vulnerable and in need of another's strength even if they live through the worst.

"Felton, you're too far away. Don't let your thoughts take you from me."

His mind had drifted to his next assignment and sending word to Watson to have Brown ready as well as his flintlock rifle.

She'd gripped his hair and towed his chin to hers. He loved this face, but his mind mapped the terrain of Warrick's woods and how easy it would be to divide a hunting party.

"My wish is for us to be happy. Felton, I want that for us."

With her fingers circling his scars, drawing him closer, he

growled. The fury at her pain and how she'd carried on would make Felton insane. Instead, he gave himself over to the maddening hunger for her bosom, the feel of her. This fever of loving her more than anything would never die.

But this was tonight.

In the morn, Gladstone would pay for his crimes. A retired spy could perform one last mission and not get caught. Hunting accidents happened all the time.

Like the hurricane approaching Port Royal to destroy the city, he'd bring Cilia justice in one bullet.

Two if needed.

For Jeremiah Gladstone had not only killed Helena, he'd abused Cecilia. For these crimes he would die.

CHAPTER 58

CECILIA—MIRACLE MORNING

I woke up spent and alone, basking in the quiet that only Warwick offered. In the bedchamber attached to my studio, I stretched in sheets that were warm. The pillow, Felton's pillow, smelled of his pine soap.

He couldn't have been gone very long. Was he always such an early riser?

Of course, I wasn't that great a judge of time, since I didn't quite know when sleep finally came.

Felton said he'd love Noah.

He didn't know that the boy was his cousin through Gladstone. I should've told him and would, as soon as he came back. Felton would never let the boy have anything to do with the awful man. He'd keep my secret.

Dragging my blanket, I got up to dress. I needed to find Lady Jane and see if we could repair things. Felton loved his sister. If he was willing to accept my family with no questions, then I should do the same for his.

That was what I told myself, yet I steadied my nerves and prepared for a battle.

* * *

Down the stairs I floated. Warwick was a buzz of gentle noises. Servants in silver going about their duties—dusting, sweeping, sauntering about the stairs on some important task.

Agatha and Amelia ran through the hall below.

Singing. A maid offered a hymn of thanksgiving.

No.

That was me. Singing to myself like I used to do when I comforted myself as I walked. Like a butterfly, I fluttered my shawl over my simple moss-green gown. It was more color than I'd worn in months. I didn't mind being seen by the Lance family because I had mine, with Felton and the girls and Enna and Noah and my sister.

In the hall, the plinking keys of the pianoforte raged. Was it Mozart—a drunk one?

Popping into the main parlor, I saw Lady Jane at the pianoforte. She looked anguished tapping out the tune. At least this time it sounded from her heart.

Soft, then slow, and every meter in between, she kept hitting the instrument. When I could take the haphazard tune no longer, I clapped. "Well done. Much improved."

She lifted a tearstained face to me. "I don't need your pity."

"Well, that's good. I have none to offer."

Lady Jane stretched her fingers and began a new song, something soft and airy. "I didn't want you hurt. I just wanted you gone. I thought Felton didn't care for you."

"You weren't the only one."

With a nod, I turned, readying to go. There wasn't much else to say, especially if she was determined to ruin her life marrying Gladstone. "Have a good morning, Lady Jane."

"I love my brother very much."

Stopping at the doorway, I clasped the trim, the beautiful gilded trim that wrapped the walls like ribbons on hems. "I know you do. He can love me and still love you. He sees you. You don't have to marry a monster to have attention."

Her hands banged the keys. Then her fists. "Felton told me. I can't believe it. But I do believe him."

"Yes, he betrayed his last wife, my sister."

"What? No, that Papa cut him for attacking you."

I leaped to the pianoforte. "What?"

"Yes, Felton told me. He told me everything this morning. And the duke agreed to every fact."

"Jane, are you lying?"

"That's what he said. It's you who are lying. Trying to cover some bastard's baby you had. Why do you want them all—Felton, my father, and now Gladstone?"

Wrapping my shawl tightly about my arm, I wanted to strangle her. "Where's Lord Gantry?"

"He left a note."

Ripping it from her fingers, I snapped the note instead of her chicken neck.

I popped the wax seal.

> *Dearest Cecilia,*
> *Debts will be paid by noon.*
> *F.*

Another terse note, but very Felton. He wasn't poetry and stars. He was steady and prone to take action. Thinking Gladstone had hurt me pushed him over the edge.

And Tramel, who knew the truth, let Felton stew in a dangerous lie. He wanted his son to kill for me.

"Jane, do you know where your brother has gone?"

"Shooting with the men."

Shooting. The memory of the noise of the practice shots at Stonehenge trembled through me. Felton would do it and not get caught.

I left the parlor. I had to get to Watson. Someone needed to take me to my husband before it was too late.

Horses sounded outside. Was it done? Had Felton killed Gladstone for the wrong reason? If what Lady Jane said about the fiend assaulting me got out, my husband would be the prime suspect.

"Excellent." A deep voice bellowed down.

"Tramel?"

The duke was dressed in his typical elegant manner, jade waistcoat, beech-colored breeches and ebony tailcoat that held a shine. He was still pale, but he seemed to have strength. "Had to see your face when my surprise comes."

Surprises? Felton killing Gladstone then being taken away for murder?

"No, Tramel. No more gifts. I only want my husband. His love and safety are all that matters."

He clutched the rail. His balance seemed shaky. "Some gifts are not returnable."

I ran past Tramel and went to the studio. Felton's gun case was open. He'd taken the larger one but Old Brown, the blunderbuss, was there. I scooped it up along with bullet packets and wrapped it in my shawl.

Tramel caught my arm as I tried to run back down the stairs. "You can't go out there. What's set in motion—"

"I have to try. I can't let things happen this way."

He pulled me against him while I cried, but it didn't feel the same. And I saw in his face the manipulative influence Felton had always warned me about.

"Did you think that killing Gladstone would make me turn to you? And what if Felton is rusty? What if he is hurt?"

My gaze sought the truth, but the openness I believed I'd always seen was masked. I ran from this man.

The grand doors of Warwick started to tremble. The trim, the fretwork, the gold, shook. I wanted my husband to come back through this wooden henge, alive, not under any suspicion but as much in love with me as I was with him.

* * *

"The surprise is here." Tramel's baritone lost power. "It is for you."

My eyes almost closed but I had to hope it was Felton.

The scuffle of slippers.

My lungs quit completely.

In the doorway was my sister, my precious sister.

Helena entered Warwick. Walking stick in hand, she stood in the hall, alive, maybe even whole.

Charging her, I almost dropped the gun, but I hugged her until I felt her heart beating hard against mine. "You were dead. You weren't breathing. Quamina, he was to bury you."

"I might've died but then I was renewed. Quamina and his wife tended to me until the duke's smugglers returned."

Clapping came from above.

Then from behind me.

Tramel leaned on his cane. "I sent them back to Demerara to find the location of her gravestone, but they found her instead. I arranged for them to bring Helena Gladstone to you."

I put my hand to Tramel's cheek. "There's more good in you than not."

His blue-black gaze, tired, loving, and perhaps unrepentant, stared through me. If he looked at my heart, he would see it was as it always should've been—his son's.

"You've always thought so, Lady Gantry. Now it is time for me to prove it. The men go shooting miles from here. Let's take the carriage."

Holding my sister, we followed behind. In the carriage I'd explain how my husband was about to kill hers.

Chapter 59

Felton—Mission of Love

Like he'd done on every assignment, Felton made an assessment of the surroundings. His uncles and a few of Tramel's friends had gone ahead, farther into the emerald woods.

He and Jeremiah Gladstone stayed behind. Like always, they'd let the older men get farther ahead.

"So, Gantry, Lady Jane says the errant wife has returned."

"Not errant, more errand-finishing. She had a few things to accomplish before she could spare a moment. Now she's done."

"A few things? She was gone almost a year. Sounds like she has you convinced."

Felton stopped and took his favorite flintlock and pointed up in the trees. "You know how long travel to the colonies can take. She had urgent business to tend to in Demerara."

"Is that what she said? The blockades, sir. How could the little lady get through? She's lying. But if the wench is half as good as the curves and the plump backside suggests, I'd take her back for a while."

Felton's finger was on the trigger of his longer flintlock. A shot through the man's heart would alert the party ahead. Just another minute and there'd be more than enough distance to blow the man's mouth off his head and they'd think someone shot a covey.

"Gantry, you look angry. You believe she went to Demerara, on the other side of the world?"

"She got there the same way as anyone who is determined to go and doesn't mind breaking a few embargoes. She went via the smuggling routes."

Gladstone stopped laughing. "It's very costly to secure those networks if you can't ask favors. You know who her contact is?"

The man thought him a fool. He'd not admit to Tramel's involvement. Yet, Gladstone had to know of the smuggling routes. That would have been the only way for him to have traveled there to seduce and ruin Helena.

"So, you're just going to take her back, just like that? Haven't you been searching? Liverpool told me you had."

Gladstone talked with Liverpool? Felton looked through the sight of the gun. Falling over the nearby cliffs would mangle the body, even one filled with lead pellets.

"I've had to disappear time and time again. Should I truly be picky when she chooses to go on business, especially when we both know why she had to go?"

He pointed his gun at his cousin. Time was up.

"Gantry, what are you doing?"

"Taking care of a little business. Move."

Gladstone put his hands up. "You're joking. You'd kill me? Your own cousin."

"Maybe you should confess and beg for mercy. Maybe I will grant it. But how can I, when I know how you injured me—"

"I didn't know Liverpool would send you on that assignment. I told my contact on the Demeraran council that spies would be sent that night to the government building. I didn't know it would be you. Didn't think he'd set up an ambush. Sorry about your man Johnson."

"What?"

"I saw his body the next day. Head severed. Body riddled with bullets. I didn't know, but it proved to the council I was loyal."

Felton didn't lower the gun, even as shock overtook him.

Gladstone didn't confess to attacking Cecilia, but to getting Felton's partner killed.

Jeremiah Gladstone was the informant that Felton had been looking for in 1811.

"You're a double agent? Gladstone, do you know how many people died because of your leaks? The council has been heavy-handed in its reprisals. And Johnson has a little boy who will never see his father because he came along to make sure I got back safely."

Gladstone backed up. His rifle was slung on his back. If he reached for any part of it, Felton would blow a hole through him.

"All this time I thought my cousin was merely sowing his seed in the Caribbean. You're a traitor to England."

"When I saw you in that ballroom in Stabroek, I knew my dealings had been discovered, but then you acted like a libertine lord and won the hand of the daughter of one of the wealthiest men in Demerara. I was spared because you chose to act the fool."

"The fool?" Felton raised his weapon and shot him in the arm. Then quickly reloaded. "Gladstone, you will die today. I have license from the Crown on behalf of Johnson. But I will kill you for what you did to Cecilia and then do something to your body for Helena."

Gladstone was on the ground, wrenching off his cravat to staunch the bleeding. "Cecilia? What did she say?"

"That you hurt her."

"That's a lie. I never touched her. I'm going to bleed out, cousin."

"You may prefer to bleed out than your head being blown clean off."

"I swear on my father's life that I didn't touch Lady Gantry. I only tried to humiliate her. She never once looked my way. Just had eyes for you and Tramel."

He shot at him again. He missed on purpose so that a few of the fine pellets would pepper the man's coat sleeve.

"She's made you crazy because of what I did to her sister. I never touched Lady Gantry."

A chime went off in Felton's head. The gonging of truth. He eased his finger from the trigger. "Admit to your crime and tell me why."

He dropped his head. "Mr. Thomas died before paying the dowry. The uncles would give no money. I was married with no money for it. Then she was with child. What was I to do with that?"

"Gladstone, you used her up and sold her."

"I'm a blackguard, but I couldn't bring an island woman and babe with no money to show for the trouble. No brown children would be accepted as a Gladstone."

Felton realized what Cecilia had meant. Gladstone was Noah's father, but Cecilia wasn't the boy's mother, Helena was.

"You shot me. You're going to forgive me. We are blood, Gantry. My cousin. No one has to know."

"But I know. Cecilia does. Liverpool will know." Felton raised his gun.

Gladstone backed up to the cliff.

The sounds of the waves below could lull a soul to sleep, but not one set for revenge. Putting his finger again on the trigger, he aimed the flintlock. "You were trying to marry my sister. What misery would you've caused her?"

"That one might've been a misery to me, but I still need a dowry." His cousin fell to his knees. "I want forgiveness. You can't do any worse than the torture to my soul. Helena was the most trusting woman, so kind. And I betrayed her in every way. Turn me in to the Department of War and the Colonies or kill me now."

Gladstone was untrustworthy and a traitor. Felton should finish him off, but his aim was never good being this emotional. He'd have one more shot before the hunting party returned and Gladstone could confess to being hunted.

Along the winding road that followed the cliffs, a carriage rushed toward them.

Reluctantly, he'd waited too long, Felton again lowered his gun.

"You may have gotten a reprieve. The Department of War and the Colonies will deal with you."

The carriage door opened, and Cecilia bounced out and ran toward Felton. "Don't have to kill him for me. He's not guilty of rape. Not of me."

"Stay back, Cecilia. Head away. My cousin and I are with a shooting party."

"He's gone mad, Lady Gantry. Servant, he's trying to kill me." He looked up but the footman didn't move. With all the things Tramel had done, they were trained not to admit to anything.

Cecilia pressed forward and locked her arms about Felton's waist. "Don't do this for me."

Felton patted her arms. "I won't have to. He'll be dealt with as a traitor and executed by Lord Liverpool himself."

Gladstone got up, wrenched the gun from behind his back. "I'll kill you, Gantry, or the wife if you don't order a horse set free. I have one shot. You know I'll get one of you."

"No, you won't." Felton raised his weapon. "You're a hunted man. You'll never have rest."

The fiend ran to the footman, who'd begun to untie the horse.

The carriage door opened. A young, thin woman in a ghostly gray shawl popped out. "Yes, Jeremiah. You'll never have rest."

As if he'd seen a specter, the man backed away. "Helena? You're alive? They said you died in a rebellion."

She said nothing but paced toward him.

There was something in her hand. Oh, Lord, she had Old Brown, Felton's blunderbuss.

"Helena, stop. He's going to be taken in."

"It's Mrs. Gladstone, Lord Gantry." His sister-in-law's hand shook. "He's a thief. I'm dealing with the rotten horse thief. He needs to cower and be terrorized. Beg for your life, like I did."

Gladstone backed up to the cliff again. His heels dangled close to the edge. He could've shot Helena, but he shook too badly. "Helena, I'm sorry. Let me explain."

She held the gun out straight.

She squeezed the trigger.

The shot sounded and whizzed at Gladstone.

The smoke cleared.

The sand gave way.

Gladstone clutched his chest and fell backward.

The impact of his body hitting the rocks was like an explosion.

Cecilia and Felton ran to Helena. His wife dragged her sister away from the edge and he took the gun.

The door to the carriage opened. "Gantry!" Tramel sat inside propping the door with his cane. "Gantry, get the ladies into the carriage."

His father, who seemed to have made a full recovery, waved them forward.

"Tramel, Father, take the ladies back to Warwick and let's make this all disappear." He gave him his discharged rifle. "Make this disappear before the inquest."

Cecilia intercepted the gun. "It's warm, Felton."

"Yes. That's what happens when it's used. Have I taught you nothing?"

The duke held out his hand for Helena. The woman looked like an empty shell.

Felton kissed Cecilia's cheek. "Take care of our family, you and Tramel back at Warwick."

Cecilia didn't get in the carriage. She reached for his neck. "Felton, I don't want to leave you. We don't do well separated."

"Only for a moment." He scooped her up and put her into the carriage. "Go to Warwick. Nowhere else. Once I'm done, I'm heading straight to your arms."

Cilia clasped his hand, kissed the red marks on the back of his wrist. Then let go.

The door closed and soon the carriage headed up the path. They wouldn't be seen by his uncles.

Felton had to force a frown and feign grief for a terrible man who deserved to die. With his hand wrapped on the cold barrel of Old Brown, he needed to understand where the final shot had come from.

It didn't come from Helena's gun.

That mystery would be solved later, once he survived an inquest for a man falling off the cliffs of Ballard with multiple gunshot wounds.

Shouldn't be too hard. This was Tramel's Isle of Purbeck, after all.

Chapter 60

Cecilia and Felton—The Thing About Jaguars

Warwick was awash in noises. Crying. Servants' heels clomping. Moving of things and trunks. Mourners coming in and out. Tramel might be good at secrets but not all the uncles and aunts who'd come to pay respects to the duke were.

Closing my studio door did little to keep it out. The sorrow leaked into my safe place.

Yet, I wouldn't feel like all was well, not until Felton returned to us.

Quiet.

Lady Jane had at last stopped wailing. Maybe she did love Gladstone. Or maybe she liked the attention that she garnered as if she were his widow.

It mattered not. I felt for her. Despite everything, she was a woman seeking her place in the world. Someday she'd know that she didn't have to fight other women to be afforded hers.

"Stop pacing, Chari."

Those were the first words Helena had uttered since I brought her to my studio.

"I'm glad Gladstone is dead."

"Well, you pulled the trigger."

"The gun didn't feel like it shot, but I'm glad he's gone."

Old Brown didn't kick back, not the way Felton had shown me, but the bullet that struck Gladstone's chest, the noise of his fall—none of it was muffled by the sea.

"I don't want Lord Gantry troubled. Chari, I certainly don't want you to be blamed for what I've done. I should go down and give myself to the authorities."

Her face, bronzed and tired, lowered. "I wanted him to fear me."

She moved off my chaise and sat with her legs folded on the floor and fingered the painting of us three sisters, her and Patience and me under a canopy of jacarandas.

"You know those flowers stink when they *laten vallen*, drop. People slip and fall on them too."

"Yes, Helena, but these are still thriving, like us sisters."

As commotion raged outside, my room grew quiet again. The youngest of the Thomas girls was alive. We would all survive and continue to blossom.

Setting the painting aside, she looked up at me. "He's dead." Her voice was low and changed. The sweetest girl in the world had learned to hate.

That had to be the saddest testament, how a heart that had been willing to love was trampled by a man and a system and a government.

"My prayer for you is to heal, Helena. You're here. You'll be restored."

My words bore a confident air, but I didn't know how this would end. We weren't spies, not even retired ones. We were foreign women seeking justice on these shores.

Footsteps sounded outside. The trim around the door vibrated but the door never opened. I still didn't know if Felton was safe.

I freed my arms from twisting in my shawl. "Say something, sister. I need to know that you're well."

"I am, Chari, just a little hard to breathe sometimes. So many others are trapped. They have no recourse. Demerara is still a colony of free, enslaved, and slavers."

Sitting beside her, I put my arms about her and held her shaking limbs. "We'll find ways to help from here. My husband and father-in-law have connections. We'll aid the cause of abolition. I can definitely paint images to evoke emotion."

Helena hadn't asked the obvious, about her son, Noah. Other than a few tears of gratitude that he was alive and well, she didn't say much. Maybe she couldn't. Maybe a mind or a body could only take so much.

Helena linked her hands with mine. "I've lived for six months thinking you all gone. Thinking I'd never see any of you. It will take a bit of adjusting, having a future, having a living family, not merely ghosts in my head."

"You've time. And you can be new. We'll invent new dreams. My father-in-law will make sure your rights are recognized. You and Noah will be fine. I sent word to Patience. Enna, Quamina's sister, and your son will be sent here. As soon as things die down, we'll visit Patience."

Helena gripped my hand. "Our son, Chari. Your son. I have no means to do anything. I'm not enough for him."

She cried in my arms. I knew that feeling, and I had more support and means than many. "You shall be wonderful. Our Noah will be wonderful."

"It all sounds nice, Chari. But I've learned to wait for each day to come."

That had to be the worst part, the waiting. And though time heals all wounds, it does nothing about memories.

Her arms wrapped about my neck. She felt so small. "Seems you made up your mind about keeping that husband of yours."

Looking at the door, waiting for it to move and a free Felton to rush inside, I rocked my baby sister but spared her my fears. Felton could be charged for murder—something he didn't do, something he attempted for me but for the wrong reasons.

In the main drawing room of Warwick, the local magistrate stood by the roaring fireplace and continued to ask questions.

He was particularly incensed about the multiple gunshot wounds to Gladstone—the one Felton had put to the man's arm and the mysterious one to his chest.

The gun Helena held had misfired. She didn't kill Gladstone. It was a pleasure to give the magistrate Old Brown.

The only person who had a clear shot was the man everyone least suspected, the man everyone thought dying.

Tramel.

Felton schooled his face from years of practice to hide his suspicions. With a shot of brandy, he feigned adequate remorse for his duplicitous cousin's death.

"So, you shot at a covey, Lord Gantry. Do you admit to shooting Gladstone?"

"I admit to nothing of the sort, except hunting with my party and having trouble with my gun. You saw it, the lodged bullet packet. It didn't shoot at all."

The man nodded. "The fall and the rocks below would've brought death instantly. There was no need for the wound to the chest and arm."

His father sat in a chair, tapping his cane. "Please, gentlemen, let's hurry this. Warwick is in chaos. There's family to comfort. My sister, Nelly—Gladstone's mother—will be here soon. I have to tell her about her youngest."

The magistrate wiped at his spectacles, thick glass pieces.

A younger man, one of his runners, came in. "We've checked all the weapons. All shots accounted for. The bullets must have been from the shooting party. It's an accident. Gladstone was well-liked by all."

The magistrate nodded. "Perhaps Jeremiah Gladstone was in the wrong place at the wrong time. He lost his balance and fell. It was meant for him to die."

Tramel rose up, slow like a phoenix. "My household must grieve. The loss of my nephew is tragic. Magistrate, make everyone leave us."

"Yes, Your Grace," the man said. Like before, like always, the local law enforcement bowed and scraped and left Warwick.

When all was quiet, Felton approached his father. He lent an arm for support. "Decided you had enough dying? Shall you now have a complete recovery?"

"Both of us couldn't be abled-bodied and good shots." He started to smile and lost his balance a little.

Felton steadied him. "Did you plan this? Were we all part of a game?"

"Family needs to be able to bring family to heal. Justice has been served."

"Was Gladstone part of your network of special friends near Demerara?"

"No, but I suspect some of my friends may dance with different horrid partners. No one I personally supported would aid smugglers who'd shoot at British ships. Or warn entities that could get my son killed."

Tramel knew about Gladstone's betrayal, but never said a word.

He let the duke lean upon him as they made it up the stairs. "Glad you're not dying, this time."

"I let her go, you know. Cecilia truly loves you. And your faithfulness to her proved you worthy in my eyes. I let her go," he repeated. "Keep your lady this time."

This was something upon which a son and father could agree.

Helena finally went to sleep in a nearby guest room. Amelia let her borrow Miss Ellie. The doll brought my sister comfort. The way the little one smiled, it brought her cheer too.

Now, the daughters and I stood behind easels in my studio, just as we used to do when I first arrived as Felton's new wife.

"Mrs. Cecilia," Amelia said, "why are we drawing fruit? I like when we imagine things."

The glorious bowl of dimpled oranges sat on a silver plate on a mahogany stand.

"Your father thought it would be a safe endeavor to master fruit. I thought it would be good to give it a try. We have plenty of time to return to our landscapes."

Amelia smiled her carefree smile, the beautiful blond sprite in her Saxon-blue gown, and tried again to stipple the outline of an orange. Her little fingers still hadn't quite mastered angling the brush and offering the canvas the right pressure.

Agatha pinched up her nose, her countenance reddening. "Will it remain this noisy? I can't concentrate."

Lady Jane had taken to the pianoforte again. Many of the notes seemed right and on tempo. She held court for the mourners coming to pay respects.

Noise had always been a delicate balance for me to manage. My gaze upon Felton's oldest sought signs of difficulty like mine when things were loud.

I saw none but her typical impatience.

"Agatha, I'm sure Warwick will return to normal in a few days."

"No," she said, huffing and using a cloth to smear a glop of paint she'd put near her perfect bowl. "I don't much like normal, Lady Gantry. That always means one of my parents will be away. I'd rather things stay as they are, a house full of noise with you and Papa here."

Kneeling beside her, I took the child into my arms. "I'm here. This time I promise not to leave. This time we stay, and we don't leave, any of us."

The girls swarmed like jaguars who'd stalked their prey, piling on top of me.

But I held them, like I'd caught distant stars.

The doors behind us opened.

Footfalls.

I kept my eyes shut until I felt strong arms embracing me, all of us.

"It's done," Felton said. "The magistrate is satisfied. No charges."

If I closed my eyes, then the image stitched to my lids would be—all of us. My imagination would add my sisters, each alive and well, my friends—Tramel and Enna, and our little boy, Noah, whose future was safe, today.

In the bedchamber adjacent to my studio, I lay on my husband's chest. Two candles flickered on either side of the bed.

Not a stitch of cloth separated us, not even a toga.

I could see his face and chest and more.

No more hiding.

It was wonderful that both of us were open and free—or mostly free.

I had a final confession. I pushed up my fingers, skimming his muscles, running my hands along his ribs. "I must tell you the truth."

His hot fingers worked their way into my loose hair. "No, no more words tonight."

Taking the crisp linen sheet with me, I sat up. "I have to confess."

"You don't have to say more, Cilia."

"I do, Felton. I tested you and that was wrong. I should've told you straightaway that Noah is Helena and Gladstone's son. I helped bring him into the world and I thought my sister died from the birthing fever."

"Well, you tend to get things wrong when it comes to fevers." He kissed my knuckles.

Drawing my knees up, I clung to them. "I was never pregnant. Lady Ashbrook must've seen one of my disguises to keep men from bothering me in the marketplace."

"You owe me no . . . no explanation."

Clasping his shoulder, I traced his scars and prepared to bare mine. "The last time you were away, I thought I might be with child, but I was wrong. And I wasn't unhappy."

He sat up and began massaging my foot. "I told you, you didn't have to say anything."

Slipping back against the pillows, I nodded and enjoyed his firm hands. "I need to. For three weeks I was terrified. So frightened. Didn't know if I could be a good mother. Or how I'd survive your household . . . the London house—"

Leaning over me, he kissed me, silencing my regrets, but this had to be said. I put my palm to his lips. "Felton, then I wasn't with child, and I was relieved. I didn't know if I was enough. Still don't know, but Noah, he's making me think I am. And I can be a mother to him and still have my art and us."

Brushing a curl from my ear, his smile returned, then he burned brighter. "Well, I'm here now. I've done the baby duty in increments. You and I can be calm, think things through, plan each day as a family, and act as loving parents. We can do everything together, you and I, us. We are enough."

"Wouldn't be much us if you had been hung for killing Gladstone. It was Helena who shot him."

"Well, your master spy survived. Our fiend is gone."

"But what he's done lives on. My sister's a shell. She wants me, us, to raise Noah."

Felton shifted and started thumbing the sole of my foot. "Since I was sent on a mission to dispatch Noah's father, it seems only right."

"F-e-l-l-l-l-ton." I purred his name, my accent heavy when he tickled my arch.

His grin was wicked. "Gladstone had a price on his head. All those who do evil or take advantage of evil systems, they will get their due. Liverpool has been informed."

"The Department of War and the Colonies? Will they take you away?"

"No. Especially since Tramel has had his strength return."

My eyes felt like they'd pop, but he tucked me into his arms, holding me like he thought I'd run. There was no running from my confusion or how I now saw things clearly.

"The man is full of surprises, my lord."

"And gifted with truth. I saw myself in him and my mistakes.

I'll have to get to know my father all over again. I actually want to, now that our biggest disagreement is settled." He slipped again to my side and to that spot on my neck that brought silver shivers. "Completely done. Cold, my little blueberry? I'll take care of that."

He drew the bedclothes about us and warmed me with his fevered skin. "We'll stay here at Warwick, this place you love. And I can show you how to properly load the blunderbuss. Helena's gun didn't fire."

"Then whose did?"

"Seems the duke was determined to give you what you wanted if I failed."

"Tramel shot him? I should tell Helena."

Felton held me in place. "Tomorrow. Let's let the master spy's plan work. Our staying here will be good. The girls can't keep a pet cow in Mayfair. Well, not easily."

Turning to his countenance, I saw the openness of his love shimmering in his eyes. "I love you, David Felton Lance, my Lord Gantry. Everything in my heart is yours."

"We're together. Our family is whole. Two solitary jaguars have found a home. You do know what jaguars do when they finally settle down?"

"No."

"I'll show you." When he took my lips and began the quiet workings of love, his hands sculpting me, shifting me, guiding me, I figured this was the next part of Felton's great plan to keep me safe and warm.

EPILOGUE

October 15, 1815

My sisters and I walked by the great cliffs. Helena can go to them now. I'd like to think that she can just hear the water lapping below, nothing more.

Felton was right. Learning that she hadn't actually shot Gladstone was healing.

It was I who cataloged the sounds of that day—the guns, the scream, the slam against rocks. Couldn't forget it. These feelings would come out in some painting. I found fruit bowls unsatisfying.

Patience and Jemina and Enna whirled and danced in the breeze. Our eldest sister grinned and looked so beautiful in a poppy pink gown. "His Grace is in love with our little girl."

Jemina shook her head. She was the only one to wear a bonnet, a pouf of creamy feathers, one I thought the wind would whip away. "Did you fret, Patience? I've never in my life seen a man so taken by babies."

"I did. I thought he wanted a son, but he's convinced that his daughter can plan war strategies as fine as Lionel will one day."

I wanted to say that Felton could train them too, but that didn't seem right for babies.

Helena frowned and crossed her arms in her light gray gown as the wind fluttered her hem. She sat on a blanket, watching the sea, scribbling in a book that Patience bought her.

Noah was fully mine now. She wanted to forget everything about Demerara and Gladstone. We both rather liked to think he looked like Felton. He was my husband's heir, so it was fine by me.

"Mary and Lord Ashbrook love riding horses along the cliffs. My daughter is so smiley here. Neither one has noticed I'm not riding," Jemina said.

"Lord Ashbrook will find out soon enough." Patience laughed and offered her dearest friend a bit of cracker to settle her stomach.

Jemina curled onto our picnic blanket. "Thank you again for the invitation."

I clasped her hand, and she embraced me in my new jacaranda-purple redingote. Felton had it made special for our anniversary. It wasn't going anywhere near Moomoo. The naughty cow was a favorite of Agatha and Amelia's, but they never wore bright colors around her. One can never be too careful with a guard cow.

Patience stretched. "This is refreshing, a moment alone, just us women, but we should return before chaos happens. Well, with Lady Shrewsbury coming tonight, it just might."

Enna sat by our picnic basket and cut pieces of cheese. "I see why you love the Lord Gantry. I would too for this rich food."

The basket was from Tramel. He had more of the delicious French cheese and bread in the basket. He was a dear to me, as always. He and Felton often came into my studio to watch me paint, but only my husband modeled for me. "Lord Gantry is trying to get us blackberries. He can source the best blackberries you've ever tasted."

Jemina drooled. "His berries are the best. Your mother-in-law is teasing of some pie. Wouldn't it be grand if Tramel and Lady Strathmore—"

"No!" Patience and I said the same time. My sister looked at me and we knew if the duke had a fourth wife, she would be nothing like her loud mother-in-law.

"As dear as the woman has become, I don't think there will be a match." Patience stepped close, her voice lowering to a whisper. "The duke still looks at you with love in his eyes. It has not diminished in a year."

I shrugged. "I think it a Lance trait to love for a long time, but he knows where my heart resides. Perhaps when your Widow's Grace women arrive, one of them will catch his eye."

"They are a handful—Lady Shrewsbury too. Chari, your teaching them art will give them a skill. If they can become independent, they won't need to marry again."

Patience's words were for Helena. I hoped my sister took it to heart, but watching her smile and breathe easier and easier, I knew the shadows would lift. Her new day, her second season would come soon.

Spinning the ring his father gave him—containing a large ruby stone—about his finger, Felton sat back in his chair and planned his next chess move.

The drawing room was warm, and the food was plentiful.

Tramel was in his corner, feigning reading. His glances were to the chessboard. He anticipated Felton's win against the Duke of Repington.

Repington said, "Do take your time. My son may only awaken from his nap in an hour or so."

"But that beautiful little girl, Lady Eliza Strathmore, sleeps pretty well. Your Grace, it is good that your wife is so beautiful and the babe takes after her. Ashbrook, when do you think you'll add to your brood?"

Lord Ashbrook sat across from Tramel, actually reading. The documents looked like wills and such. No matter how the man tried, he simply couldn't extricate himself from Widow's Grace business. "I think we'll take our time building memories. Watching you two with napkins and such gives me no need to rush."

A maid came into the room. “All the babes and children are accounted for. Mary Thackery, Amelia and Agatha Lance are in the kitchen watching the cook following Lord Ashbrook’s ambrosia recipe. Seems Lady Strathmore’s gooseberry pie made the countess nauseous and crave the earl’s mash.”

She curtsied and left. Ashbrook looked puzzled, then concerned, then he grinned.

Tramel stood and stoked the coals in the fireplace. “My, my, Warwick is domesticated and teeming with women. Perhaps it is good I remain a bachelor.”

Felton wondered if his father had been this funny all along. He wished Jane could be here enjoying these friends, but she chose to travel more with Aunt Nelly.

It was her choice, and as sad as it was that his love for Cecilia came between him and his sister, his wife was his treasure. He’d cede no more room to anyone who’d cause enmity to grow. Only love would bloom at Warwick, now and forever.

Cecilia and her sister-friends were returning. They were in view of the window. His blueberry was so beautiful in the sunshine, smiling, coming home to him.

Felton moved his bishop to B5 and placed Repington’s king in check.

His friend’s eyes bulged.

“Cannon, Papa.” Lionel stood and pointed at the pieces.

“No, son. That’s not how we win, not this battle.”

It wasn’t. It was accepting and loving and risking through every storm, forgiving flaws and scars, and even journeying across rocky seas.

A few minutes later, Cilia came to him with Noah in her arms. The boy went to his lap easily. “Noah, you want to watch your papa win?”

The cutest blue-black eyes beamed up at him.

Felton clutched Cecilia’s hand. Their shared smile warmed a fire in his soul. Trusting the heart of the one you love was worth every sacrifice.

Acknowledgments

Thank you to my Heavenly Father, everything I possess or accomplish is by Your grace.

Esi Sogah, thank you for loving this heartwarming series. You've made each story better, even the road trip.

To my sister agent, Sarah Younger, I'm grateful your guidance and support.

To those who inspire my pen: Beverly, Brenda, Farrah, Sarah, Julia, Kristan, Alyssa, Maya, Lenora, Sophia, Joanna, Grace, Laurie Alice, Julie, Cathy, Katharine, Carrie, Christina, Georgette, Jane, Linda, Margie, Liz, Lasheera, Alexis, and Ann—thank you.

To those who inspire my soul: Bishop Dale and Dr. Nina, Reverend Courtney, Piper, Eileen, Rhonda, Angela, Michelle, and Pat—thank you.

And to my family: Frank, Ellen, Sandra, David, Kala, and Emma: love you all so much.

Hey, Mama. I think you'd enjoy this one with ambrosia.
Love you always.

Recipes

Ashbrook's Heavenly Ambrosia

Daniel's favorite ambrosia (from *An Earl, the Girl, and a Toddler*) is revisited here. It is a blend of the Islands and South London.

Ingredients

- 4 cups of fresh cherries, pitted, halved, rinsed, drained (can substitute defrosted frozen cherries or 16-ounce jar of maraschino cherries, rinsed and sliced in half)
- 1 15-ounce can crushed pineapple, drained
- 4 medium oranges, peeled and sectioned with each wedge cut into thirds or 1 15-ounce can mandarin orange segments, drained
- 1 15-ounce can diced mangos, drained
- 1 15-ounce can fruit cocktail, drained
- 1 cup sweetened toasted coconut
- ½ cup toasted and cooled pecans, chopped
- ½ cup vanilla Greek yogurt (or ½ cup of sour cream)
- ½ cup whipped topping

Mix all the ingredients in a bowl. Cover the bowl with a lid or plastic wrap, then refrigerate for at least 4 hours.

Felton's Fabulous Chocolate Sauce

Make this sauce, dip over berries, and you'll understand why Cecilia kept forgiving Felton.

Ingredients

1 cup Demerara sugar
½ cup granulated sugar
⅓ cup water
¼ cup light corn syrup
1⅓ cups heavy cream
4 ounces milk chocolate (chopped finely)
3 ounces dark chocolate (chopped finely)
3 teaspoons vanilla extract
⅓ teaspoon kosher salt

In a saucepan, combine all the sugar and water. Get as much dissolved as possible, then add the corn syrup. Place on a medium flame. Stir and swirl so nothing burns. Burned makes for bad eats. This can take up to 10 minutes. You're looking for the mixture to turn golden brown. When you get to this stage, remove from heat and add the heavy cream. It will hiss at you and even bubble. This lets you know you're close. Next, dump in the chopped chocolate and stir until all is smooth. Whisk in the vanilla and the salt. Do a final vigorous whisking. Let it cool. You now have delicious chocolate sauce.

Author's Notes

I hope you enjoyed Cecilia and Felton's love story and the antics of the Widow's Grace. I went a little *Princess Bride* on this one to soften the themes of vengeance. The Gladstone family is a typical family who had holdings in the West Indies during the periods of colonization and made their fortune using enslaved labor. Even worse, they denied knowledge of the harsh conditions that made their fortune. When slavery was abolished in 1830, the Gladstones falsely recruited workers from India and treated them as badly as they did the enslaved. So, my happy warriors went off to kill the grand wizard, so to speak.

Cecilia is written as a woman who is on the spectrum, a level one. Noise is her trigger. She is able to self-calm by walking and with her art. Autism was not a diagnosed condition during the Regency, but was probably noted as being otherworldly or having vapors or palsy.

This tale covers many themes, showcasing a sliver of the diversity of the Regency and the power structure afforded women. It is my hope that on the road trip of life you're able to stop and enjoy the simple pleasures.

There is nothing better than to enjoy food and drink and to find satisfaction in work, for these pleasures are from the hand of God. (Ecclesiastes 2:24).

Visit my website, VanessaRiley.com, to gain more insight.

Mulattoes and Blackamoors During the Regency

Mulattoes and Blackamoors numbered between ten thousand and twenty thousand in London and throughout England during the time of Jane Austen. Wealthy British with children born to native West Indies women brought them to London for schooling. Many forget that Jane Austen was a contemporary fiction writer. In her novel *Sanditon*, she writes of Miss Lambe, a mulatto, the wealthiest woman in the book. Her wealth made her desirable to the ton.

Mulatto and Blackamoor children were often told to "pass," to achieve elevated positions within Society. Wealthy plantation owners with mixed-race children, or wealthy mulattoes like Dorothy Kirwan Thomas from the island of Demerara, often sent their children abroad for education and for them to marry in England.

Island and African Gods During the Regency

The various influences in the Caribbean allowed for many beliefs to flourish. Erzulie-Dantor is the goddess of women and sometimes referred to as the vengeful protector of women. Agassou is the guardian spirit. Erzulie Ge-Rouge is the red-eyed goddess of revenge. The Obeah is a system of belief in healing and justice originating in West Africa and the Caribbean.

Many people from the West Indies of African descent were often converted to Catholicism because it was the faith of their planters and missionaries.

Potts's Artificial Limb

With England being in so many wars, the number of wounded veterans increased. Medical technology advanced to create artificial limbs. In 1816, James Potts crafted an artificial limb for the Marquess of Anglesey whose leg had been amputated after he fought alongside Lord Wellesley during the Battle of Waterloo (June 1815). The limb created was comfortable to wear and carved to be lifelike in appearance. By being made hollow, it was lighter than earlier models and possessed an articulating knee with ankle and toe joints to make walking easier and appear more natural. Catgut was added to simulate quiet tendons, so the clicking and clanging of earlier models was no more. The new artificial leg was called the Anglesey leg.

The Peninsular War

The Peninsular War, May 2, 1808–April 17, 1814, was a series of military campaigns between Napoleon's empire, Spain, Britain, Ireland, and Portugal for control of the Iberian Peninsula during the Napoleonic Wars. Napoleon was not fully contained until Waterloo in 1815.

Wowski was a character in the comic opera *Inkle and Yarico*, written by George Colman in 1787. It was one of the plays most frequently acted in the latter part of the eighteenth century.

Quamina was a carpenter who worked on the "Success" and "Ann" plantations in Demerara. He and his mother were sold into slavery when he was a child. He is surnamed Gladstone. He later became a principal in the great Demerara slave rebellion of 1823.

King's Theatre was established in 1705 mainly for opera. Handel and Haydn have performed here.

Drury Lane Theatre is a West End theatre in Covent Garden, London. The building faces Catherine Street (or Brydges Street, as it was known) and dates to 1663. It is one of the oldest theatres in London still in use.

Lamb and Flag is a public house at Rose Street in Covent Garden built in 1772. An upstairs room used to host bare-knuckle prizefights.

Smallpox is a contagious disease that has existed as early as the fourth century. The healing process usually left scars. Smallpox killed three out of ten who contracted it.